Thomas from the Sea

MIRA GIBSON

ISBN: 979-8-9901812-1-2

*For anyone who has ever stared at the sea
and realized the sea was staring back.*

DEATH ROW INMATE 439

Kowalski, Arthur

On April 22, 1973, Kimberly Swan tucked her eleven-year-old daughter, Crystal, into bed at around 10 pm and went downstairs for a glass of seltzer in the kitchen. She was wearing a white nightgown and was stabbed to death from behind. According to the autopsy report, Kimberly was approximately three months pregnant, sustained over twenty stab-wounds to her lungs, kidneys, and heart, and never saw her attacker. Her daughter, Crystal, woke to the sounds of screaming, raced downstairs, and saw her mother's former boyfriend, Arthur Kowalski, fleeing the scene. According to the young girl, Kowalski had tried to force his way into their Easter celebration earlier that day and had not taken it well when Kimberly had insisted that he leave. Kowalski had threatened his former girlfriend at that time, promising to stab her in the back as viciously as she had to him.

The killing of Kimberly Swan was tried as a capital murder case due to the fact that the crime involved the following aggravating factors:

- *The victim was pregnant.*
- *The murder was premeditated and the result of substantial planning. Such planning was to the commission of the murder itself and not simply as to the commission or attempted commission of any underlying felony.*

Kowalski was found guilty after conviction by a court of law and has therefore been sentenced to be executed by lethal injection at the James T. Vaughn Correctional Center in Smyrna, DE.

Execution to commence: July 20, 1986

THE STRIPPER

I USED TO BE CUTE as a button. The little girl with wispy, blonde hair held down with sparkling barrettes. A dress to match. I had giant, trusting eyes and loved to smile and twirl.

I hadn't the wherewithal to see that the world around me was bleak, impoverished, all mobile homes and chained dogs. Overcast skies. Cigarette butts and leaking roofs.

I had this glitter inside me. I pranced because of it. Friends of my mother called me "doll" while they counted cash at the drop-down kitchen table of our tiny RV. One lady fanned a dollar in my face, just tickled by me. Another one clapped her hands, delighted. My singing and dancing and the comedy routines I liked to perform never failed to get their attention—I was the snappiest six-year-old this side of the Mason-Dixon line, for sure.

"Run along now, Mommy has business to tend to with the girls."

When I got a bit older, an uneasy feeling started to creep in. I grew suspicious of my mother's friends, the neighbors, the chains that were supposed to hold those dogs. I was less trusting, less willing to smile. I still clipped my hair with barrettes but they laid on my head crooked and wouldn't do their job. Wisps of blonde fell in my eyes. I outgrew my princess dresses, and I was suddenly expected to wear thrift store clothes.

Saggy-bottomed overalls. Boxy tee shirts with pit stains no amount of bleach could get out. Clunky shoes and weird underwear with elastic waistbands so dry I heard crackling when I stretched them.

The dirt under my fingernails seemed permanent.

It was as though the uneasy feeling I was living with had taken over, seeping out from my knotted stomach only to consume me entirely, outfits and all, without my being aware of it until it was too late.

I was smart enough to connect where it was coming from—the apprehension.

My apprehension was coming from the money. And I was also smart enough to connect where the money was coming from—all that cash.

The money was coming from behind the beaded curtain of my mother's bedroom in that dismal RV. The things she was doing back there. The types she was doing it with. The mysterious darkness of it all was the reason my anxiety soon reached a fever-pitch.

That feeling never left me. The sinking spleen feeling. The 'something's wrong' feeling. The waxy ears, itchy heart, can't-sit-still feeling.

I could sense that Mom's secrets were of the devil.

That dark feeling was with me when, at nine-years-old, I caught her once, a tangle of flesh and sweat and pink parts beneath a man I didn't know.

The dark feeling was with me when, at ten-years-old, I loved my mother fiercely for taking a job as a clerk at the local grocery store. She promised me things were going to be different now, better.

But the dark feeling was still with me when, at eleven-years-old, I watched my mother welcome Arthur Kowalski into the rowhome that we'd only just been awarded four months prior thanks to Kent County and the State of Delaware accepting our welfare application.

And the dark feeling was *still* with me—that cloying, thick-as-smoke dread that kept me wild-eyed and breathless—when, six months later, life as I'd come to know it was forever changed.

The night I found my mother murdered in our brand-new kitchen.

After that, the feeling of dark unease was replaced by quiet rage.

What followed were court appointments, social workers, child psychologists, orphanages, foster homes—so many foster homes—and foster parents who wanted checks more than they wanted me. Foster siblings who spat and bit and hit. Others that tried to touch me in inappropriate places.

As a little girl, I used to be the sweetest child in the whole wide world, an innocent beacon of light some might have said.

I didn't know what I was now—the adult I had become—but it was safe to say I wasn't a saint.

I blamed my mother for that. I also missed her fiercely.

I was furious at her.

I was never going to be like her.

Or so I thought.

❄

MY BIKINI TOP was tiny and new. Glittery. Slick. An aquamarine color that I hoped was flattering. The G-string I had fished out from the bottom of my locker, however, was not. Faded black and ugly, it was tattered enough that keeping my butt in a chair and my legs crossed was my only option. I didn't feel like getting into an argument with Jimbo about it.

Jimbo liked to argue.

He also liked to conduct these pep-talks in the ladies' dressing room like he was a football coach motivating his team on Superbowl Sunday.

"Ladies, ladies! My mermaids! Listen up, girls!"

Mermaids was a strip club. We were strippers. Exotic dancers if you felt like being generous about it. All five of us on the schedule tonight—Amber, Destiny, Miracle, Original Jewel, and myself of course—had packed into the dressing room at Jimbo's non-negotiable request.

He clapped and hollered, but was met with very little respect.

"Can I have your attention? Please!"

Me and the girls glared at him but we were sultry about it. Sitting amidst leopard print furniture, vanity mirrors, and a fog of hairspray and perfume so thick I could taste it on my tongue, we regarded our boss with a cool mix of revulsion and curiosity.

Jimbo—by profound contrast to our collective curves—was all muscles and chest hair; pinky rings and Hawaiian prints. He had a mustache, a mortgage, and way too much enthusiasm for a strip club like ours, which was located in the-middle-of-nowhere Delaware—even though I liked to say that we weren't too far from the beach.

"We're still getting pushback from the county," he informed us. Grumbling from the girls followed. "They don't want us in business? Well, I know the laws and I know our rights! We're going to keep fighting!"

Fighting didn't accurately describe what the exotic dancers of Mermaids had been doing for the past few months. Yes, our tips had been cut in half as a direct result of community pressure to close the club. Residents had gotten local law enforcement to make Mermaids a very uncomfortable place for our customers. But while we weren't fighting at the level of city hall or anything, we *had* been complaining consistently every night as we straightened our cash earnings before heading home.

The good people of Woodland Beach wanted Jimbo to shut the club down, but he always said that boobs were in his blood. He came from a long line of titty-bar owners. He would die before he would cave.

We had all been struggling. Amber hadn't been able to get caught up with her electric bills. She smelled like candles now, and I was starting to wonder when she might accidentally burn her apartment down. Destiny's dark roots had come in and she wasn't going to be able to afford to pay Cherry to touch them up. And Cherry, who wasn't scheduled to dance tonight, had been a ball of stress because, unlike the rest of us, her bread and butter was all wrapped up in doing our hair, nails, and waxes. Cherry wasn't the best stripper. But her beauty services were topnotch and we all took care of her because of it.

I, myself, had barely been scraping by. I had a few loyal customers who were keeping me afloat, though. Not all of the girls were so lucky.

Jimbo yelled over our noisy griping, "Here's what we're going to do! Discounts!"

"No!" objected Miracle who sprang to her feet as we all chimed in, outraged. "You can't cut our pay!"

"Instead of ten-dollar lap dances, we're going to charge two dollars!" he went on.

Someone tried to throw a stiletto heel at Jimbo's face, but he just batted it away and kept going.

"Private rooms will be ten instead of fifteen!"

"I'm not going to do ten-dollar private rooms!" Original Jewel informed him. "Not for five songs! I won't make any money!"

"The club hardly gets any customers!" complained Amber, who was the best at math. "If I'm stuck in a private room for twenty minutes and only walk out of there with ten dollars, I would have to do, like, fifty private rooms to make ends meet!"

Jimbo doubted that and told her, "Your multiplication is funky."

Destiny sling-shot her thong at Jimbo's face, but it didn't have the same effect as the heel that was thrown earlier. Then another stiletto struck his forehead from out of nowhere thanks to Miracle's aim. He paused long enough to stop horrifying all of us with the new discounted rates. He seemed a twinge irritated. Definitely distracted.

The girls were seething, closing in on him.

"Do you want *some* money? Or *no* money?" he challenged. "Because if we close down, there will be no money for any of you. We're going to have to pull together if we want to get through this!"

Amber was the first to pick up a chair, but by that point I had heard—and seen—enough.

It was a tight squeeze getting out of the dressing room. After I teetered down a short, dark hallway, I stepped through a velvet curtain, coming into the club itself where the air was acrid with all kinds of delightful smells. Stale beer, cigarettes, cleaning solution, and the faintest tinge of cologne... I felt sticky and I hadn't even gotten on stage yet.

Lit with bluish lights was how Jimbo kept the place. Dim enough to conceal the stains and tears on the lounge benches, along with the imperfections of the girls' figures.

I was what you might call a Tuesday afternoon stripper, as in, schedule her when the club is dead. Didn't exactly have the body for this kind of work. I was all lines and sharp angles, too much height and not enough meat. As if the chronic anxiety inside me had literally increased my metabolism. Needless to say, I looked better in the dark. But as Jimbo liked to remind me, men have a taste for all types. Variety was, after all, the spice of life.

Only the stages were brightly lit. The silver poles gleamed. Jimbo had decorated with the mermaid theme in mind and I couldn't glance up at the big, dumb-looking mermaid mural on the wall without thinking of Cherry playing crass word games—*Seamen! Jimbo, we should call the place Mermaids and Semen! Get it? Semen???*

Cherry was stupid like that, but she did a great job on my nails.

There were a few customers nursing beers at the bar, but the club was otherwise quiet, which made sense considering the hour and the political climate. It was maybe 9 pm. Definitely not nine-thirty or ten, but I didn't really know. A wristwatch wouldn't have gone with my G-string and bikini top.

Robert wasn't here.

The only way I could make discounts work was if Robert kept coming in and coming in *regularly*.

I slid up to the long bar counter, coming in-between two dusty looking customers.

Chest out, back arched, I smiled at the first one, then at the second, while Bruce Springsteen's rugged singing voice lent some mood through the speakers. Neither customer seemed particularly impressed with me so I rolled my eyes and asked Timbo if he would make me a double-vodka on the rocks.

Timbo looked like a malnourished version of his cousin, Jimbo. His neck was scrawny and his legs were emaciated. Even his mustache looked hungry. He also usually looked wet for reasons I had never been able to figure out.

Timbo doubled-up as the barkeep and bouncer most nights if he wasn't hiding in a private room with Miracle, one of us veteran girls. He was also in charge of the music we danced to. He had been favoring The Boss all spring.

Just as Timbo slid my drink over, New Jewel spilled into the club. She scanned the near-empty floor, looking out of sorts.

She shouldn't have come in tonight, not when Original Jewel was on the schedule.

For the past month, there had been a battle of the Jewels, but if you asked me, Jimbo should've never hired New Jewel in the first place, not when the club had been suffering and Original Jewel had already been fighting to keep her weight down. If I had been running things, I would've told New Jewel that she would have to pick a different stage name since the club already had a Jewel. But that wasn't how Jimbo's inflamed mind worked.

"Hey," I called out to her before she could rush into the dressing room and cause some real trouble. "You picked the wrong night to show up unannounced. Original Jewel is here."

"Did you hear about Cherry?" She wasn't so much talking as murmuring words through her lips. "She's dead."

"Cherry's dead?"

She had my full attention. I forgot my drink. Forgot that I was 99% naked. Forgot that if Original Jewel caught New Jewel at Mermaids, she would make good on her threat to tear the imposter's hair out—I had been serving as the primary peacemaker since the battle of the Jewels had begun.

She shook her head emphatically, stunned as she was at the news herself. "She was killed."

Timbo leaned in. The customers were interested, too. I was in shock.

New Jewel eased away from the bar and breathed, "I have to tell the girls."

As she turned on her heel, stomped through the club, and disappeared down the curtained hallway, the uneasiness that lived in the pit of my stomach turned to acid.

From inside the dressing room, I heard Original Jewel, muffled but furious, "The hell is she doing here?"

"No one likes you, New Jewel!" another one balked at the intrusion.

If the girls were throwing their heels at her in there, I was a million miles away.

I didn't hear New Jewel's low, sober response and whatever transpired in the dressing room next was so upsetting that Jimbo and the girls did not come out for a very long time.

THERE WAS VIRTUALLY no information about Cherry, or at least none that New Jewel had been able to relay beyond the fact that Cherry had been found murdered on the shore of Woodland Beach.

We didn't know how she was killed, when she was killed, or why she was killed.

All we knew was that one of us was dead, and I doubted the case was burning a hole in some homicide detective's desk right now. Maybe it was my distrusting nature. Maybe it was the cramp of pessimism I had come to regard as my actual soul. But I really didn't think the same cops who'd been intimidating our customers away from Mermaids since April were going to stop at nothing to solve this one.

I kept my opinion to myself, though.

Jimbo had already warned us not to be 'even more of a downer' tonight... all things considered. This, of course, was during his second pep-talk to us, the one he had called to order after New Jewel had given us the horrifying news and left.

Jimbo had also warned us not to go and get ourselves killed like Cherry. It reflected poorly on the club, he pointed out. Was bad for business.

Pearls of wisdom... A real sage, our Jimbo.

It was getting late. Now there were customers seated across the lounge benches, along the bar, throughout the tabled areas. Girls in G-strings oozed around them. Flirted. Pushed themselves up against one loner then the next, trying and failing and trying again to sell dances.

"No thanks, honey, just here for a drink."

"Can't tonight, sweetheart, but I like what you did up there."

"Maybe in a bit, baby. Gave my last dollar to the girl who was on stage. Need to break this fiver first."

Timbo's voice suddenly blared through the PA system, "Crystal, to the stage."

I scanned the club for Robert, one of my regulars. I wouldn't have to spend the next fifteen minutes wrapped around a pole if I was already with a customer. Company policy. But he wasn't here yet.

"Crystal—"

"Alright!" I barked. He didn't have to use the microphone. I was standing right next to him. I thwacked his arm and a little feedback screamed through the speakers. "Get me a double-vodka. The lights are hot."

He knew what to do so I pushed away from the end of the bar counter where I had been perched and on the lookout for the one man in Delaware who had a thing for skinny chicks—Robert.

I had only done two lap dances so far. I had made a whopping four dollars plus a tip in the shape of a quarter that I had already lost. Well, actually, I think it *escaped*, bouncing on the dark floor and rolling away as if it wanted nothing to do with me.

Frankly, I wasn't too fond of myself either these days.

I made my way onto the long, T-shaped stage just as Timbo cued up another Bruce Springsteen song.

The music hit. The lights shifted. Someone whistled from the darkness. I grasped hold of the center stage pole and did my thing.

I sparkled. I twirled.

The busted clasp of one of my high heels was giving me problems but I smiled anyway and kept dancing. Exotic dancers wore stilettos that had a platform shape, provided five inches lift, and came with an ankle strap that was supposed to keep you from breaking your neck. One of my ankle straps had gotten badly stretched out during my last shift. It was tricky to dance in.

Nevertheless, I smiled. I sipped the vodka-on-ice once Timbo set the glass on the edge of the stage for me.

The panic and rage and fever-pitch anxiety—my silent hatred that felt like it was perpetually splitting my mind in two—was joined by a strangely carefree feeling.

It wasn't joy. It certainly wasn't elation, and it definitely wasn't childlike.

But it was as close to the real me as I was ever going to get.

The real me who, at six-years-old, used to entertain my mother and her friends, blissfully unaware of what I was destined to one day turn into.

This.

I didn't want to think about kid-Crystal. It would only lead to flashes of my mother. But the harder I tried not to, the worse my attention was mentally funneled towards Cherry.

It was surreal.

Unbelievable.

Could New Jewel have been mistaken? Misinformed? What did any of us know about New Jewel anyway? She was probably on pot...

Cherry couldn't have been killed. She was the endearingly plump red-head who giggled at the drop of a hat.

She couldn't be dead. I still had her Revlon Pink Passion #505 lipstick. She had been nagging me to give it back. I still had to get my nails done. She was still supposed to come over to my place this weekend to give me a manicure, have a drink, talk trash about Jimbo, and cackle to high heaven with me as we swapped Mermaids gossip.

This couldn't be real, because no one would ever murder Cherry. They just wouldn't.

They couldn't...

...because she didn't deserve it.

I wasn't going to let myself be the stripper who got emotional on stage. My eyes stung and my nose felt runny, but I continued to dance, and when my set was finally over, I crawled around the stage and collected the tips that had been tossed at me.

Seven dollars, and not all of it cash.

It was the nickels that made me the angriest. Nickels, dimes, *pennies*.

As I slid off the stage and tucked myself into a dark corner, Miracle stomping her hefty way up into the bright lights to take my place, I eyed my earnings and finally let the tears fall.

I was quiet about it. I kept my head down. I wasn't obnoxious and no one saw me.

I cried for Cherry and for my mother and for myself.

And when I lifted my head, there was Robert.

He was looking at me from the other side of the club.

He lifted his big hand and shot me a grin, his dark eyes twinkling, and for a moment I was tricked into thinking that everything was going to be okay.

BETWEEN THE CIGARETTE smoke and the occasional cloud burst from the fog machine, the room was cloaked in a dreamy haze. Destiny was dancing on stage, while the other girls gyrated over customers. Miracle leaned across the bar to whisper in Timbo's ear. Jimbo moved about, collecting empty bottles and glasses in a bin to keep the place tidy. And I was on my fourth lap dance with Robert. He had been coughing up two-bucks every third song without having to be asked. My money-bag was filling up nicely with bills.

We got a fair amount of truckers here at Mermaids—men passing through—and they all had the same bleary look about them. College-aged boys liked to stop in, as well. They tended to be thin and loud and deeply nervous, jittery underneath all their bravado. And then there were the locals. Some worked at the chicken plants and smelled like poultry. Others operated machinery or managed the assembly line at the soda factory. Those guys had a dim-witted look about them, but they tipped well and knew how to keep their hands to themselves. And then there were the husbands and dads. I could spot them a mile away because they dressed well, made a beeline for the girl they wanted, and went straight into one of the private rooms as if they were fleeing the scene of a crime.

Robert was nothing like any of those people. He didn't fit into a category. He wasn't a trucker, a factory worker, or a husband. He didn't exercise bravado or have a dim-witted look about him. He didn't dress particularly well, though I liked how he looked. I especially liked how he carried himself.

He had been coming to Mermaids for the past year or so and had been requesting me specifically for the last six months. He was a man of few words, which was fine. Most men who came here didn't come to chat, but with Robert I had been able to pick up a few things, figure out a detail or two, piece together the type of man he was.

He had never been married. No ring on his finger. He didn't have any kids that I was aware of, though he had let it slip once or twice that his nephew was around. I hadn't learned much else about the nephew. Didn't know his age or whether or not he lived with Robert. I knew that Robert had been born and raised in Delaware. He was in his mid-forties. Handsome. Tall. Unemotional. He had a rugged, grounded vibe to him. Nothing intimidated him. He wasn't one to flinch. He was the kind of man whose shadow I would like to curl up in. When I was around Robert, I didn't have to keep my guard up. He had never tried to take advantage of me.

During lap dances, I generally tried to keep conversation to a minimum, but if I wanted to sell Robert on the idea of getting a private room, I was going to have to say *something*. Two-dollar dances weren't going to cut it.

He was awfully relaxed on the bench where I had been swaying and dancing over him.

"Hey," I cooed softly in his ear. "We could go somewhere more private…"

Mirrored lights from the disco ball shimmied across his face.

Playing coy wasn't my strong suit so I bluntly suggested, "We could get a private room."

He pulled another two bucks out of the breast pocket of his blue-collar button-down and tucked the bills in my G-string, buying himself another three songs.

I tried not to let my smile falter. "It's much cooler in the private rooms…"

"I don't mind the heat…" he responded densely.

"I'm feeling a little *too* warm."

He sized me up. "If you're uncomfortable, I guess we better move into a private room."

I had him.

On my feet, I took him by the hand and tried not to wobble in my bad heel as I began leading him through the club.

"How tall are you?" he asked, noticing that I was eye level.

"Six-feet in heels," I told him as I let his hand go.

At the far corner of the club, opposite the velvet curtain that led to the ladies' dressing room, was another velvet curtain that connected to another dimly lit hallway, which was where the private rooms were located. Three on the left side, three on the right, each room had a purple, velvet curtain instead of a door. That way Jimbo could barge in at any moment and destroy a girl's chance of getting a good tip.

The PA system was hooked up back there as well, but the speaker volume was kept low so that us girls could provide our customers with better conversations if they wanted. When I first started stripping here, I was surprised to discover that many men opted for the private rooms simply because they wanted to talk. Or rather, they wanted a beautiful topless woman to sympathize while they vented about their hard, boring lives.

As we walked quietly down the hallway, we passed two occupied rooms on the right where I guessed Amber and Original Jewel were working.

I pulled back the last curtain on the left, inviting Robert into a little, private room. He stepped forward, filling the doorway, the décor having given him brief pause. A puffy, red, vinyl bench was against the wall. A round, tall table stood in one corner. I set my money-bag on the table, having closed the curtain. There were mosaic tiles on the walls with scenes of lighthouses, mermaids, and stormy seas, which momentarily stole Robert's attention.

"Have a seat," I said as I fanned my neck, cooling off in the crisp AC. "It's ten dollars."

"Not fifteen?"

"Special summer rate."

After handing me fifteen-cash anyway, he finally sat on the red, vinyl bench, glanced around the mosaicked room, and commented, "I like this song."

It was another Bruce Springsteen tune. Robert was sweet. I, on the other hand, tried hard not to roll my eyes as I made a mental note to have a talk with Timbo later about his playlist.

Nearing him, I began slowly swaying to the very quiet music, resuming the lap dance, my blonde hair spilling this way and that over my shoulders.

The glimmer behind Robert's eyes could not have prepared me for what he asked next.

"Are you going to the execution on the twentieth?"

Taken aback, it took me a second to jumpstart my brain. "I don't think I want to see that."

He nodded. "But you haven't decided?"

"You're going to be there?"

"I have to," he said, his voice deep, his expression neutral. From out of nowhere, he locked eyes with me and held my gaze as if we had known each other our entire lives. It was intimate, yet felt normal for some reason. "It's my job. The execution won't be in the gallows this time. Kowalski opted for the new method. Lethal injection."

My stomach twisted.

"Supposed to be more humane, easier to watch. They built a viewing gallery and everything—"

"Is that why you came here tonight? To ask me if I'm going to Kowalski's execution?"

He backed off, grew quiet. "No."

"Good."I softened and tried not to bristle.

But as I eased into the swaying rhythm of the song that was playing through the speakers, I couldn't shake the question.

Was I planning on driving out to the Vaughn Correctional Center to watch my mother's murderer be killed?

I had been putting off thinking about it, though every time Robert walked into Mermaids I was indirectly reminded.

Of the skimpy handful of things I knew about Robert, the fact that he worked over at the prison was one of them. It hadn't blown me away. I wouldn't necessarily have pegged him as a correctional officer per se, but when I had found out, it made sense. What *had* blown me away was hearing that he not only worked the Death Row block, but that he knew Arthur Kowalski. Kowalski was one of the inmates. Scheduled to die. Nearly fourteen years after he had stabbed my mother to death.

I had always suspected that this connection was the real reason that Robert started seeing me at the club regularly.

Yes, he claimed to be into skinny women. He liked when strippers had an oddly endearing praying mantis look about them, which meant that he had struck the jackpot with me. But the day he figured out that I wasn't only stripper-Crystal, but also the child who had been orphaned the day Kowalski had stabbed Kimberly Swan to death, Robert from then on looked at me differently.

I was the girl from the papers; the heart-rending subject of all those news stories about a brutal murder in a small, seaside town in Delaware. And Robert, in a way, was governing the man who had ruined my life.

I had begun to look at him differently, too. He wasn't just a wallet to me anymore. I wouldn't go so far as to say he had turned into a hero in my eyes, but finding out that he could rough Kowalski up, beat him down, and generally use him as a punching bag if I asked him to definitely changed how I saw him. Not that I had ever asked or even suggested to Robert that I wanted him to make Kowalski suffer. I just liked knowing I had the option. Robert had put it out there. I could take him up on it at any time.

I honestly didn't know if I felt the need to watch Arthur Kowalski be put to death.

Maybe it would make me feel better. Maybe the scorching rage in my chest would burn out and the flames in my stomach would cool down if I saw him die before my very eyes.

Or maybe I would feel nothing. Maybe witnessing him being killed would do nothing and fix nothing and leave me with as much as Kowalski had given me in the first place, which was nothing.

I had been suspicious of Arthur from the start. At eleven-years-old, I might have been gangly and snaggle-toothed, but I had wised up a lot. I wasn't the airy-fairy girl I used to be. I had known on a gut-intuition level that people like my mother were not going to make it on the nice side of town if they welcomed people like Arthur into their homes.

And my mother had given the guy a key.

Arthur had told us he was an oil meter reader and sometimes-mechanic. That was how they met. He came by one day to pretend to read the meter. Dressed in a khakis uniform that had his surname on the lapel, he showed up and conducted his so-called business around the side of the rowhouse that the State had just awarded to us. My mother had been an excellent candidate for welfare because she had a daughter and didn't have a drug problem.

Arthur had taken notice of the oil stains on the pavement beneath my mother's car. When he then took notice of my mother—those big, blonde curls, her huge blue eyes, her curves, Mom had an effect on men—he introduced himself right away, offered to tighten her oil caps, take a look under the hood for other issues, that sort of thing.

She had let him, completely unaware that he was full of it, while I looked on with folded arms and a cross attitude. That man hadn't wanted to fix her car. He had wanted to get into our house and my mother had let him not four months later. She had never realized that Arthur hadn't been working for the oil company and in terms of training and certificates, he had no business looking under the hood of anyone's car. He was a conman who had wanted to ride on my mother's welfare coattails.

It was sad.

And now that I was an adult looking back, it seemed even sadder.

He hadn't been all bad, though. He had wanted to be my father. He had wanted family vacations and Christmas holidays with us. He'd wanted a picture-perfect life, and my mother did, too, just not with him.

Then one morning, Easter Sunday, he handed me a present. A fairy princess dress just like the ones I used to wear when Mom and I had lived in the trailer park. Arthur had seen pictures, had seen the smile on my six-year-old face.

He wanted me to put it on—the fairy princess dress—and for me to run around our narrow backyard in search of Easter eggs, and he wanted my mother to laugh and clap and take photos with the brand-new camera he had gotten her.

But my mother had been able to smell the stolen goods from a mile away. She didn't let me put the dress on. She shoved the camera back at Arthur as soon as she had unwrapped it. She had told him that was it, the last straw. He had to go.

That very night, he came back, used the key she had given him months prior to sneak inside, and he killed her.

Whenever I thought about Arthur—and I tried very hard not to—a complicated mix of highly disturbing emotions came over me. The deepest sadness. A sharp, jagged edge of pity. Rage. An overwhelming compulsion to punch a wall or shatter a windshield or turn my anger inward and drink myself into the ground.

If I saw him leave this world—if I watched—would those ugly, hot, bone-splitting feelings disappear once and for all?

All I needed to hear from Robert was, *yes*; all I needed to hear from him was that I would never feel raw and rageful again so long as I showed up at Kowalski's execution. But that wasn't what he was telling me. It wasn't something he *could* tell me, because he didn't know. No one did.

I had worked up a bit of a sweat dancing for him in the private room. My skin felt slick and there was enough built-up tension between us that I sensed if I didn't step away from him, something might happen. Something I wouldn't be able to control.

So, I sat beside him on the red vinyl bench, crossed my legs, and lifted my hair off my damp neck.

Robert wasted no time counting out another fifteen dollars.

If he kept this up, buying more and more of my time, I just might be able to fall asleep tonight without my heart in my throat. It would take pressure off of feeling the need to hustle during the rest of my shifts this week. Robert was the best.

He motioned to tuck the cash under the side of my G-string, but I caught his hand before he could touch me and took the cash.

He let out a defeated sigh. "That's my favorite part of all this."

"I'm really not supposed to allow any form of touching," I reminded him.

It wasn't so much that I minded Robert's occasional touch. He was always respectful and had never tried to cross a line. But rules were rules, and I couldn't afford to get in trouble with Jimbo if he barged in.

Jimbo had the hearing of a German shepherd, and unfortunately, he was known to barge into the private rooms to make sure the girls were safe.

Knowing that Robert was loosely connected to local law enforcement, I asked him, "Did you hear about Cherry?"

"Who?"

"Cherry was one of the dancers here. Red hair? Curvy?"

It dawned on him who I was talking about, but not enough for him to comment.

"She was found on the beach. Someone killed her," I told him as I fanned the back of my neck some more. "You didn't hear about that?"

"No, I did. Yeah, the girl on the beach. Amanda Dover, I think her name is."

"Right," I agreed, a little embarrassed. I thought Cherry was her real name. Apparently, it was only a stage name? I used my real name at the club… As I tried to wrap my mind around the fact that Cherry's real name was Amanda Dover, I asked him, "So, you heard about Cherry? I mean, Amanda Dover? Did you hear about the murder through the prison?"

"On the radio," he said, drinking in the sight of me on the bench beside him. "They think it happened very early this morning, maybe around four or five."

"Did they say how she was killed?"

"They're not releasing that information."

"She was on the schedule last night," I mentioned, thinking out loud. "But she would've left at two with everyone else."

"Were you working last night?"

"No." I shook my head, bit down on my shiny, red fingernail, and waited to see if my brain would produce a helpful revelation.

It didn't.

"You look worried," he said.

"I'm fine."

"Are you going to make it home okay?" he asked me, and it loosely dawned on me that Cherry could've been targeted…

…because she was a stripper.

"I hope so," I said, alarmed. "You don't think a *customer* killed her, do you?"

He frowned, "I have no idea. Want me to see to it that you get home? I could follow you."

Follow me?

Suddenly paranoid—was this how Cherry had gotten herself into trouble? Had a customer offered to see her home only to lure her out to the beach where he murdered her on the shore? Had *Robert?*

"No, no thanks. I'll be fine."

I popped up, wobbled briefly on my bad heel, and began swaying to the music that was playing softly through the speakers as Robert watched from below, and when the time was up once again, he opened his wallet, but it was empty.

"Looks like you cleaned me out, Crystal."

I felt a grin coming on, but I concealed it as I turned on my heel to get my money-bag.

Then I faced him again, but the ankle strap on my *other* heel snapped. Thrown off balance, I spilled sideways. Robert jumped up and caught me before I could fall, scooping me into his surprisingly strong arms.

He held me.

He didn't want to let me go. I could feel it.

It was nice. But then it quickly began to feel too intimate.

Maybe even dangerous.

"Hey-ho!" hollered Jimbo as he poked his head through the curtain, ambushing us. He looked at me then at Robert then at me again, assessing our embrace. "Hey, come on now, guys! Leave a little room for the Holy Ghost!"

Jimbo was kidding…

…sort of.

THE MISSIONARY

I ENTERED THE CHURCH vestibule, having followed the faint sounds of moaning, and found my father on the floor. He was lying in front of the commercial drip coffee maker that had recently been donated to our church, Lighthouse Ministries.

Though he was a helpless heap, my mother stepped over him, determined to make coffee in time for the morning women's bible study she ran.

"Asa!" As soon as he saw me come in from the rectory, he reached for me, spreading his pudgy fingers. "Your mother won't help me up!"

"Quit your bellyaching!" she told him as she poured water into the back of the massive machine and dumped ground Folgers into its tremendous basket filter. "You haven't been on the floor longer than Jesus was on the cross!"

She crinkled her nose, looking for the Brew button on the coffeemaker. "If I tried to help you up, then we would both be on the floor!"

I stooped, hooked my arms around my father, and began heaving and hoisting, but Joseph Asbury was a rotund man, and as fit as I was, I couldn't easily get all three-hundred pounds of him off the ground.

He howled in pain.

As I strained, trying and failing to pull him up, I asked, "What happened, Dad?"

"Gracie keeps the coffee in the cabinet beneath the new coffeemaker." He sucked air through his teeth, tortured. "All I did was bend down to get it for her."

"I didn't ask you to do that!" my mother snapped.

"I was trying to be of service!"

"Now look at him," she muttered, rolling her eyes at me. "A real martyr."

Letting out a long, low, grunting sound, I used all my might and successfully hoisted him to his feet.

"Next time, wait for me," I offered, out of breath.

My dad gave his lower back a little stretch, investigating the damage.

"Do you think you slipped a disc?" I asked.

"No, no, I'm fine," he decided. "Nothing a prayer can't cure."

"Praise God," I said while my mother remained doubtfully quiet.

I silently sided with my mother. Joseph had been praying for nearly thirty years and in all that time, his aches and pains had only gotten worse thanks to his weight.

"Step aside, make room!" she snapped, shooing us away from the coffeemaker as she flitted about, busying herself with setting out paper cups, plastic lids, sugar, and individual-sized creamers. Towering stacks of napkins. *Doilies.* "The ladies will be here any minute!"

"Lay hands on me, Son," Dad asked me as we settled near a long table in the vestibule where stacks of pamphlets and fliers about the Methodist faith sat, along with an array of free calendars.

The smell of Mother's brewing coffee filled the air.

"Heal me with the Holy Spirit," he said.

I placed my hands on his tremendous shoulders and did what I could, praying in hushed tones that only the two of us could hear, while Mom puttered around the vestibule, fussing that there might not be enough bibles if Mary-Catherine brought those coworkers of hers that she had been mentioning… *oh dear…*

She was a spindly woman—my mother—but she wasn't flimsy. She had a backbone. Conviction. She had intimate knowledge of True North, and she assessed everything and everyone around her in terms of it. That was her litmus. Sin was acidic. Prayer was alkaline. Get with the program.

As a thirty-three-year-old man who liked to think he wasn't living under a rock, I tried to convince my mother to be tolerant and compassionate towards people who were different from us. She had chuckled at that.

"Sugar?" I offered my father when we returned to the coffeemaker.

My mother shot me a warning look, but I doubted that adding sugar to Dad's coffee this morning was really going to worsen his weight problem.

"Four, no five scoops, please," he told me so I heaped as much into a paper cup and poured coffee over it. "Leave a good inch or two for creamer."

Mother frowned.

Once I had splashed a tsunami-sized helping of creamer in and handed him his coffee, he asked, "How's the air down there? Not too damp? We have that second dehumidifier…"

I had been living in the rectory of the church, which was located in the basement. Lighthouse Ministries had a long history in Woodland Beach, and the building itself with its tall, white steeple and idyllic architecture replete with a sanctuary and fellowship hall had existed almost as long as the town itself. Dad could barely keep up with the renovations that were needed. The place was on the brink of falling apart. And no matter how many construction and plumbing materials were donated by our modest congregation, it seemed the repairs were never ending.

"The rectory is cool as a cucumber," I said, focusing on the positive when unfortunately, I felt like I was breathing mold spores every time I was down there.

"How's the Kids for Christ program getting on?"

"Very well, Dad, thank you for asking," I replied as I fixed my own coffee with cream and sugar. I had been serving as Lighthouse Ministries' new youth pastor, among my other responsibilities at the church, which spoke to the academic degree I had earned over a decade ago. I was finally putting it to use. "I like teenagers."

"No hovering!" my mother hissed at us, as church ladies began filtering into the vestibule, bringing the sunshine and the scent of cloying perfume with them. "Step aside! Let Ms. Bethany get some coffee! You're crowding the area, and oh, look! For goodness' sake, you've made a mess of the doilies!"

❄

TWO HOURS AND ONE pot of coffee later, which I had made, the Thursday morning women's bible study members shuffled out from the sanctuary and made their way through the vestibule, while a group of men who had come for the next bible study knocked and jostled each other at the coffeemaker.

I looked on, unsure if I should call some order to the situation or let them duke it out on their own. Dad wasn't alarmed by their behavior, so I chose to model his demeanor.

I smiled at the ladies as they left the church. Wished them a blessed day. Only occasionally did I flick my attention towards the cluster of noisy men.

Mom's bible study was serving grandmothers, widows, and mild-mannered types who were in the twilight years of their lives.

The men's bible study that Dad ran, by marked contrast, was filled with adulterers, first-time offenders who had narrowly escaped jail, and some AA spill-over from the YMCA across town. They were feral, ill-mannered, ill-tempered, and not entirely literate, though their ages ranged widely.

Eager to supply themselves with the right amount of caffeine to make it through an hour and a half bible study of the Book of Hosea, the men shuffled away from the coffeemaker one by one, double-fisting steaming cups in both hands, their bibles tucked under their arms, their brows furrowed, and mouths pressed, looking like soldiers heading off to battle.

As a Christian pastor, my father was respected, and he didn't have to beat people over the head with his faith. He wasn't a hammer like my mother, ever ready to slam down against the first nail she saw. He got *through* to people. He was a soft touch, you might say, and when it came to converting sinners, he had a quality that men trusted. They listened. They were easily won over. Dad changed lives. He had *the gift*.

I hoped that, somewhere deep down, I had the same gift, too.

As my mother held the exit door open and wished her parishioners a blessed day—*God bless! Have a wonderful day, God bless! Have a blessed day! God bless!*—a few ladies lingered.

Bethany, Suzanne, and Mary-Catherine, and others were whispering:

"…that poor dead woman…"

"…killed on the beach…"

"We should hold a prayer circle…"

My mother looked a bit irritated by them. "We *have* prayed," she reminded them. "The Lord requires our patience now."

My ears pricked up, curious, but then my father appeared in front of me, wide as the side of a barn.

"You're doing good work, Son. We'll miss you today," he said as he thumped his bible against his meaty palm. "Yours is an insightful voice to have in the room. These guys value you."

"Thanks," I responded in all sincerity.

As he waddled out of the vestibule, making his way to the fellowship hall where his bible study gathered, I checked my wrist watch. I needed to get moving if I was going to keep my tight schedule, but their gossiping sucked me in.

"I heard on the news," Suzanne said urgently as if she was answering Mary-Catherine. "They said, 'Amanda Dover.' It was her."

"I'm telling you," insisted Bethany in an edgy tone as if the others weren't getting it. "I saw a photograph of Amanda Dover. They showed it on Channel 7 at five-am this morning, and *I am telling you* there is no doubt in my mind that it's the same woman—"

They buttoned their lips, having caught me eavesdropping.

My mother glared at me and snapped, "What are you doing? You're going to be late for the prison!"

THE JAMES T. VAUGHN Correctional Center was located just outside of Smyrna, about a twenty-minute drive from Woodland Beach where I had left my mother and the church ladies of Lighthouse Ministries to puzzle over the mysterious lack of details surrounding Amanda Dover's murder.

Just about every radio station was broadcasting the news. The twenty-seven-year old redhead who had aspirations of becoming a courtroom stenographer had been discovered dead on the shore of Woodland Beach the morning of Monday July 8th. There was speculation of a high-risk lifestyle on some of the FM stations, but I couldn't stomach it. I turned the dial until I found my favorite Christian station and concentrated on the drive.

When I reached the prison, I was met with the usual red tape. Presented my ID. Spelled my name for the guard. Reached the first checkpoint then the second. One steel door buzzed open then the next. The correctional officers all knew my name by now, but they pretended not to. Didn't so much look *at* me as *through* me.

I knew I wasn't liked or wanted, but I wasn't there for anyone but the inmates sitting on Death Row.

That particular block was deep inside the prison compound. No matter how many times I came here, my heart rate always kicked up badly as soon as I entered the cell block. I became overly alert. Jittery. I startled easily at the sounds of jail cell doors slamming and the deafening blare of the general alarm system going off, though the latter rarely happened.

I could smell fear in the air—despair—when I reached the long corridor that hid all of the Death Row inmates behind steel doors.

There was a heaviness here. The silence wasn't peaceful but rather doomed. It weighed down on me as I neared the locked door of Arthur Kowalski's cell. My bible in one hand. A small sitting stool in my other hand that the guards always left for me just outside of the corridor.

I placed the stool down on the laminated floor in front of Arthur's door and sat on it. Facing the door's little slot that was ordinarily used to pass trays of food to the inmate, I said:

"Arthur? It's Pastor Asa Asbury from Lighthouse Ministries."

Arthur was scheduled to die in less than two weeks and he had not yet taken the Lord into his heart. I didn't condone what he had done to earn himself the death penalty, but I also strongly believed that no one deserved an eternity in hell.

I had been coming to see him for the past month or so, but the conversations had been consistently one-sided. Ministering to the inmates on Death Row sometimes felt like spitting in the wind.

"I would like to pray for you, Arthur," I told him when he didn't respond.

I could hear him breathing as I prayed fervently, asking God to save his soul. I knew Arthur was crouched in a ball, seated on the other side of the door that separated us. Sometimes I could see his shadow through the slot.

For the first time ever, he spoke. "I don't need saving."

I perked up. Froze a touch, I was so excited.

"Everyone needs saving," I told him.

"I've made peace with what I've done and where I'm going."

I peered through the slot, and there he was, sitting in profile on the floor like I had thought, his knees to his chin, lanky arms holding his legs together, his gaze downcast.

He looked hollow and despondent. A fragile vessel that had been filled with all the wrong ingredients. Living behind bars had aged him beyond his years. Living without hope might have already killed him.

I wanted to give him hope.

"Arthur, Christ was sentenced to death as punishment for his perceived crimes, just like you."

I let that hang as tension rose between us.

Palpable, volatile tension.

"He was executed, too."

"Yeah," Arthur agreed. "But he didn't deserve to die. I do."

THE EXECUTIONER

THE SO-CALLED EXPERT didn't strike me as terribly competent. My boss, Cromwell had flown the guy in from Missouri on the prison's dime. The expert, named Digby, had come highly recommended as the best man to train me to administer lethal injection, but I was skeptical.

"Robert is our most experienced executioner," Cromwell boasted about me.

It was a bit smug for my taste. I wasn't exactly proud of my long track record, not to mention that *hanging* convicted criminals wasn't rocket science.

Digby nodded to acknowledge Cromwell's statement, but he was distracted. The gurney straps weren't cooperating.

"Linoleum flooring. Adjacent viewing gallery. Black curtain to hide the executioner," said Cromwell, pointing out every aspect of the death chamber for the expert's benefit while I looked on with folded arms, peering over Digby's shoulder, disturbed but watchful.

"The machine is behind the black curtain?" Digby asked, politely participating in Cromwell's tour.

"Indeed," Cromwell confirmed.

Capital punishment over in Missouri had upgraded to lethal injection, considering the new method more humane than hanging or the electric chair, and since Delaware wanted to keep with the times, Warden Cromwell had seen to it that the Vaughn Correctional Center build a new facility to accommodate all the State mandated death sentences it planned on carrying out.

As far as Cromwell was concerned, there was no one better to train me than Senior CO Silas Digby, who had already performed half a dozen executions in his home state of Missouri.

I wouldn't exactly call the guy *seasoned*. Granted, Digby was *old*. White hair, light eyes, a southern drawl that made him sound like he was liquored up and without a care in the world—he made taking the lives of criminals seem as refreshing as a tall glass of water on a hot summer's day. Silas Digby had to have been at least sixty-five years old. Why the man had chosen to put down society's worst rather than retire was beyond me.

For all his years working in corrections, however, he didn't seem especially experienced when it came to navigating his way around our death chamber. Or perhaps I should say, he didn't appear to be familiar with the equipment. He had been bumbling beneath our brand-new gurney for what was starting to feel like an unusually long amount of time.

He clearly had no idea how the thing worked and seemed genuinely confused about the IV situation, or lack thereof, until Warden Cromwell mentioned that the techs had yet to install it.

Though *training* only loosely characterized the service that Digby was providing, I watched the man carefully as he jerked and rattled the levers on the underside of the sterile, green gurney.

There came a scraping sound then a clanking thud, and the gurney obeyed Digby at long last.

Together we lifted it so that the flatbed was vertical and facing the glass windows of the viewing gallery.

"Once the inmate is strapped in," Digby explained, referencing the brown, leather straps that were hanging loosely, "you'll prop him up, you see? This will give him a chance to face the gallery and speak his last words. The chamber will be mic'd."

He pointed to the ceiling where the techs had yet to string microphones.

"The inmate may say a few words. He may not. Then you lower the hood onto him."

Cromwell frowned. We were also waiting for the State-issued black hood to arrive. Bureaucrats. Nothing ever got underway on time.

"Y'all are familiar with the femoral artery, right?"

Cromwell and I exchanged a worrisome look, touching eyes with one another. Obviously neither of us had any idea what in the good God damn our expert was talking about.

Femoral artery?

As Digby began to both pantomime and verbalize how to effectively penetrate the inmate's femoral artery despite the fact that he had neither a syringe needle nor a dummy nor a diagram nor the vocabulary of a doctor, I had to ask myself if this so-called innovative method of capital punishment was, for all intents and purposes, a sick joke. Cruel and unusual punishment. The pet-project of some mad scientist that was going to make my professional life a living hell.

"Don't worry too badly about it, boys," Digby said when it dawned on all three of us that his game of charades wasn't even remotely helpful. "You can't mess this stuff up. They're supposed to die. They'll die," he told us assuredly. "One way or another, the chemicals will hit and they'll die."

I didn't like the sound of that.

I didn't trust it.

But then again, Arthur Kowalski had asked for this. Twice over, if you asked me. He had asked for this when he'd stabbed Kimberly Swan over two dozen times, attacking her with no sense of morality, proceeding in full knowledge that she was pregnant. And he had asked for this—*literally*—months ago, when he had been given a choice concerning the method of his execution. It was either this or the gallows. Kowalski hadn't opted to be hanged.

So here we were.

"The machine," Digby went on as he tugged the black curtain aside, exposing the executioner's alcove, "is electronic. All you have to do is push the buttons, but you have to push them in the right order."

Again, Cromwell and I glanced at one another.

"First, you push *these* buttons," he explained, using a knotty finger to indicate the yellow-lit buttons on the top that were paired.

I knew how to kill an inmate, and I knew how it made me feel to do it. When I had applied for a job as a correctional officer twenty years ago, I was fresh out of high school. I had been young, naïve, and idealistic. I hadn't known that six years later, I would suddenly find myself a caregiver to my sister's son without warning. I had heard about the pay for being a CO. It was good enough. I didn't think another two thoughts about it.

I had no idea that I had become the go-to CO whenever an inmate was scheduled to be executed.

It had made me sick—that first execution. But I had sucked it up. I had kept a stiff upper lip. I did my job, hanging a man I knew nothing about. When that man had pissed his pants, gurgling and sputtering for air that wouldn't come as he hanged, dying a slow death with a rope around his neck, I had urinated in my uniform slacks, too. Not much, but enough to know that I'd just been broken.

The next morning, I had prayed to God in heaven that this prison would never ask me to do that again.

But it did.

And I did.

Hanging after hanging after hanging. The only reason I got better at it was because I got used to it, and the only reason for that, that I could figure, was because with every man I watched hang to death, part of me died as well.

If lethal injection was supposed to somehow be better for the inmates as well as myself, I wasn't seeing it. Not the way Digby explained it. The machine was supposed to help dispel guilt, but it wasn't fooling me. As far as I was concerned, just because two COs pushed identical buttons at the same time and just because neither would ever really know which of them had administered the fatal shots, didn't mean that neither CO would feel guilty. Experience told me that there was no way to suspend the guilt that came with killing a man.

"I'll be the other man," Warden Cromwell volunteered, as if that made him noble. He locked eyes with me, pressed his mouth into a hard line. "I'll push the buttons with you, Robert. You and me."

"Sure," I agreed.

"You'll need at least four others on hand," Digby informed us, "in case the inmate tries to fight you tooth and nail."

As Digby went on to verbalize the actual protocol, articulating but not demonstrating how first pancuronium bromide would be used to cause the inmate's muscle paralysis and respiratory arrest—*You have to hit the saline flush buttons in-between every injection, you have to!*—Crystal Swan bubbled up in my mind.

I had a soft spot for her. I shouldn't have felt that way, but I did. Ever since I had found out who she was, I couldn't stop myself from seeing her as the eleven-year-old girl who had heard her mother screaming bloody murder. I couldn't stop myself from looking at her as though she was the little girl who the police had found covered in blood, holding her mother's lifeless body in that kitchen after Kowalski had fled—countless newspaper articles had been written about it. At the time, I had barely graduated from high school but I had kept myself apprised. To me, Crystal would always be the blue-eyed baby who showed the world why society needed the death penalty. You couldn't have looked at those eyes without wanting to kill Arthur Kowalski for what he'd done. What if he had also stabbed young Crystal to death that night? Capital punishment was invented for cases like this.

If Kowalski was fated to suffer and suffer horrendously in this very room on the 20th because I had absolutely no goddamned clue about what I was doing, then so be it.

Digby could explain this procedure as poorly as he wanted to. I didn't care. I didn't need to execute every step perfectly. Not for Arthur Kowalski.

Let the man writhe.

"Then you administer the potassium chloride to stop the heart," Digby went on, indicating the identical buttons that Cromwell and I would have to push next on execution day. "After that and another shot of saline—very important to always press the saline buttons, gentlemen!—then it's just the final set here, these two buttons. The sodium thiopental, which induces unconsciousness. One final saline wash to finish. Then you get your stethoscope here," he told us, pantomiming because, along with everything else, we didn't have that either. "And use it to make sure that the heart has stopped."

Digby asked us if we had any questions. I only had one.

How in God's name was this more humane than hanging?

I tried to never use the Lord's name as a swear word, but I was willing to make an exception after that tutorial.

After cursing under my breath, I said, "All the bells and whistles… It's still going to take, what, *three minutes* to put the inmate down? A bullet to the head takes a whopping three *seconds*. Hanging, which is what we've been doing, rounds out to a minute and a half, tops."

"With lethal injection, the inmate doesn't feel a thing."

"I doubt that."

Warden Cromwell stepped between us and narrowed his eyes on me. "If you can't perform your duties, Robert, speak now or forever hold your peace."

We stared at one another.

In the end, I said nothing, but it wasn't because I was holding my peace.

If anything, I was holding my tongue.

❄

I LEFT THE SHINY death chamber, making my way through the darkened interior of Cell Block D, otherwise known as Death Row. I had worked at the prison long enough to earn myself an office. It was located just outside of the long corridor that contained our twelve death row cells, four of which held inmates.

In addition to Arthur Kowalski, Death Row also contained Clifford Oppal, a longshoreman who had raped to death seven boys; Samuel "Dirty Sammy" Braun, a pimp who was convicted of not only murdering but also eating three prostitutes—his crimes were so horrendous that Delaware didn't allow 99% of the details to hit the news. Pig farmer Gary Olson was also on Death Row. Olson had been the only known member of a larger criminal ring who had solely taken the fall for heinous acts I couldn't bring myself to think about without a stiff drink and a soft woman; and also William "Willy" Prinkerton…

Over the years on Death Row, Prinkerton had been reduced to a bag of lamenting bones, rattling day in and day out to the tune of whatever harmonica riff he happened to be playing. If you asked me, he seemed hauntingly innocent.

But Prinkerton was black and when he was arrested for the abduction and murder of a little white girl, a conviction had swiftly followed.

The State's case had alleged that Prinkerton had abducted the girl—a blue-eyed blonde type that was sweeter than apple pie—only to maim and disfigure her as some kind of twisted offering to Lucifer.

Someone had done it. The body had turned up. But in terms of the State proving that Prinkerton had been responsible, in my opinion, the evidence hadn't been there.

I wasn't pleased that Cromwell had, over the course of twenty years give-or-take, turned me into Vaughn's sole executioner, but a job at the prison was better than anything else around Delaware.

On my best days, I found ways not to think about it. I cranked up the doo-whop. I poured myself a drink. I swung into Mermaids, feeling loose and generous.

But on my worst days, when there wasn't enough alcohol in the world to shut my brain down; when I couldn't seem to get the music loud enough and all the strippers in the world weren't cutting it, I was faced with the dark reality of it all…

…and it made me desperate. Desperate to find a way to justify—truly justify, not only to society at large, but also to God Almighty himself—what I was doing.

I had been taking the lives of men in exchange for money.

It suddenly occurred to me that I would do well to get my ass back to church.

I still donated to Lighthouse Ministries. Seth had been going there for a bunch of youth programs…

Damn, I really wasn't sure if any of the pastors would be willing to touch this—the fact that I was some kind of murderer—with a ten-foot pole…

Plus, it wasn't like my role as an executioner was public information among the churchgoers, either. I hadn't been straight-forward about it with anyone when I had been attending the Sunday services. The congregation knew I worked as a correctional officer and that was all I wanted them to know. Frankly, I was lucky Seth hadn't spilled the beans about me. I had been trusting him less and less with the secret, but as far as I knew, no one at Lighthouse Ministries had learned about what I really did for a living.

My office sat directly outside of Death Row. The death row corridor was walled off with a locked steel door, but my windows across from that door were large enough to see the COs' station and the corridors that led to the other cell blocks.

As I neared my office, another CO, Lyle McKay, who had never been asked to execute an inmate in his life, sidled up to me, getting ready to complain about Pastor Asbury.

"Religious freedoms," I reminded him before McKay could say a word. I knew exactly what his irritation was.

Asbury had been seated outside of Kowalski's cell, ministering to him for the past hour, and McKay didn't like it.

CO McKay was young, self-righteous, and angry, not a great combination in my book. He wasn't a churchgoer, but that didn't mean he liked the idea of spending an eternity in heaven with murderers thanks to the likes of Asa Asbury and his constant prayers.

"It's so easy to show up here, overlook what these people have done, and act like you're the big shot who's righteous enough to forgive them," he hissed, having pulled his toothpick out of his mouth for a second, disgusted at the whole situation.

I told my CO, "You're on the right side of this thing," because he needed to hear it. "Don't let Asbury get under your skin. Thanks to you, the bad guys stay behind bars. That's what Delaware wants. Some preacher man isn't going to change that."

He snorted, agreeing with me. "I say, let them burn in hell."

Burn in hell? McKay might get his wish.

There were less than twelve days until Kowalski's execution and no actual way for me to practice hitting a human femoral artery with a needle...

I had absolutely no goddamn idea what in the world I was doing.

Kowalski was going to be my guinea pig...which would be its own form of hell.

…I didn't want to think about it.

There was a blaring buzz. Pastor Asa had hit the button on the Death Row side of the steel door, asking to be let out.

CO Lyle McKay pushed the correlating button on our side of the door and it unlocked with a thud.

Asbury pushed out, emerging from Death Row with a stool in his hand. He kept his light eyes on the floor.

McKay loudly announced, "Speaking of the devil."

Asbury flicked a nervous smile our way and set the stool on the floor approximately where he had found it. He wasn't an idiot. He had to have known none of the COs liked him.

I didn't share the sentiment. I knew Asa and his parents, Joseph and Grace from church, not that I had been in ages.

"Speaking of the devil? Ha, ha, ha. You were talking about me? Anything I should know?"

McKay smirked, bit down on his toothpick. "Nothing bad, Pastor. Just that Robert and I were talking and we think you might be wasting your time on some of the inmates."

"Ah, well," he said with a mild-mannered shrug. "Every soul is precious in the eyes of God."

McKay snorted. "See, that's where you're mistaken. Not all of them have souls."

My CO was getting antagonistic so I changed the subject. "How's he holding up?" The fact of the matter was that, as the executioner, it was extremely important for me to know Kowalski's mental state.

A little thrown that I would care, he said, "He's accepted that he's going to die."

"He's not going to fight us tooth and nail?" I asked and CO McKay chortled beside me.

"I doubt it," said Pastor Asa. "He knows what he did and what he deserves because of it. I'll be there at the execution, in the gallery. He knows I'll be praying for him. I believe he's ready for the end."

I didn't believe that any man could ever be ready for the end, but I decided to take what he was saying at face value as he rounded the corridor and started down through the block, making his way to the exit with a small, leather-bound copy of the bible in hand.

CO McKay and I watched him go.

"That guy gives me the creeps," said McKay, as he tapped his holstered baton, something about him itching to assault the preacher-man, even now.

"Don't you worry about Asbury. You let him do what he's here to do, and don't pay him no mind. Because if you do, if you think about it too much, you're going to get yourself into serious trouble."

McKay didn't seem to appreciate the warning, but I didn't care. I knew what I was talking about and I knew that I was right.

Let he who has never sinned cast the first stone…

❄

IN MY OFFICE with the door closed and the blinds drawn, I turned on my FM radio which I kept set to a 50s doo-wop station. I didn't have to blast it.

55

Just needed a little white noise to help me concentrate. I began organizing the particulars of the 24-hour death watch, as The Five Satins sang *In the Still of the Night.*

Taking Digby's advice, I selected four other correctional officers to assist in Kowalski's execution. One of them, I decided, would be Lyle McKay. The others I chose were equally dispassionate towards Kowalski's sentence. Strong men who wouldn't be afraid to use their baton if the inmate put up a mean fight. Protocol being what it was, they would also be out of the death chamber before Cromwell and I started pushing buttons.

After double checking each COs schedule to be certain that including him wouldn't put him into overtime pay—the executions at Vaughn took place between the hours of 12:01 am and 3:00 am depending, so, using rotating shifts, all the COs would have to report to the prison twenty-four hours prior and be available on and off thereafter—I opened the Kowalski file that I had been keeping on my desk.

I would have to update it with the names of the correctional officers I had assigned.

I rolled a fresh sheet of paper into my typewriter, aligned the margins properly, and thwacked a heading across the top.

But before I could get the first name down, the open inmate file beside me caught my eye.

Every Death Row inmate file had an inmate summary that sat on top. The summary included the inmate's prison-issued number—Kowalski's was No. 439—along with a summary of the crime for which he was sentenced, the judges' ruling at the time of trial if the case had gone to trial, and the date on which the inmate's execution was to commence.

My predecessor had typed Kowalski's—his imprisonment was slightly before my time—but I must have read it a thousand times over the years. I could recite it by heart.

It wasn't there.

Where could I have put it?

Ordinarily, I was meticulous, but over the past few weeks my office had become disordered. I looked through the other Death Row inmate files, thinking I could've misplaced it there. I rummaged through my filing folders, through the CO schedules, the lap drawer of my desk, even the bottom cabinet where I kept a bottle of whiskey and a dusty copy of an old Gideon's bible that at one time I had actually thought could recalibrate my soul with its very presence.

Documents were not supposed to leave the prison and I sincerely hoped I hadn't left it at home. Would I have taken the report home with me? Given how little whiskey was left in that bottle, I had to allow at least a little room for the possibility.

A CO wouldn't have taken it. No one was itching to get into my office, and I kept it locked.

I tore my desk apart, hunting for the damn thing with growing agitation. I tossed just about every file in the metal filing cabinets that lined the room, refusing to believe it wasn't here. But no matter where I looked, I couldn't find Kowalski's inmate file.

Seth.

My nephew didn't just cross my mind, he slammed through it. If I had brought the report home, if I had absentmindedly left it there, and Seth happened upon it…

Of course, he would happen upon it. I ran my hand down my face, furious with myself. Seth liked to snoop. He knew who the inmates on death row were and it wasn't because I had ever told him. He was a nosy, precocious thirteen-year-old, obsessed with violence and gore…

…and he had also become a very good liar.

SETH LIVED WITH ME in a seaside cottage that had belonged to the Nash family for generations. Our quiet corner of Woodland Beach. My mother, rest her soul, had been the one to pour personality into the modest house. She had used a breezy blue color to paint the front and back doors, the shutters, and the flower beds that sat outside every window. Other than that, the siding was made of simple wooden clapboards, weathered from sun and sand.

Though it was two stories with a porch out back with views of the Delaware Bay—on a clear day, you could see New Jersey across the water—the place had never felt big enough for a family. There was barely enough room for Seth and me.

I should've been doing a much better job of maintaining the property. It was starting to look more than a bit rundown. But there were no leaks and when something serious needed fixing, I tended to it myself or hired a professional who could.

I arrived home as dusk gathered across the wide sky and immediately began tearing through the house in search of the missing Kowalski report.

It wasn't in the kitchen tucked among the bills and junk mail that lived on top of the Formica table. It wasn't in the den where stacks of outdated magazines had been piled up on the low, wooden coffee table. Nor was it anywhere in my threadbare bedroom.

As I searched and searched, I passed by the open doorway of Seth's bedroom again and again, feeling far more agitated than I should. It was his music. I was about to reach a boiling point and the loud, incessant thumps of the heavy metal song he was playing on his boombox were about to push me over the edge.

He was stretched out on his bed, thumbing through what I guessed was the New Testament. How AC / DC went with the teachings of Christ, I couldn't even begin to imagine.

"Turn that racket down!"

He hopped up, lowered the music, and stood at attention.

A skinny, doe-eyed boy, Seth had come into a recent growth spurt. He had always looked unbelievably like his mother. Fair-faced and gentle. I had been a lousy disciplinarian over the years because of it. But more and more, he seemed to be growing to resemble his father. I had never known who his father was, and my late sister, Abby, had taken that information to her grave.

As those paternal features had emerged, however, I found myself treating him roughly. I barked instead of talking. Ordered instead of asking. And had taken to moving throughout the house without acknowledging his presence.

Seth had also been stumbling into mischief as of late and I didn't think it was blindly. No matter how many church programs I enrolled him in, he still had way too much time on his hands, especially now that it was summer. And he was a loner at heart, often on the beach or skulking around town. I sometimes got calls from the local police about his behavior because, according to them, the loitering bordered on misdemeanor.

"Have you seen my paperwork?"

"Paperwork?" he asked as his cheeks flushed. "What kind of paperwork?"

"An inmate report. It's a one-pager."

I already knew he had taken it. Guilt was written all over his pink face.

"Give it here, Seth!" I barked, highly irritated.

His shoulders slumped, defeated, and his cheeks went from rosy to pale. Opening his bible, he pulled a tightly folded square of paper out of the back, unfolded it, and handed it over to me. It was badly creased.

"Can I go?"

"To the execution?"

"Yeah."

"Under absolutely no circumstances," I warned him. What in the hell was he thinking? I would never allow him to attend an execution.

"Why not?" he complained.

"It's no place for a boy."

"I'm thirteen," he reminded me. "How can you tell me I can't go, when it's what you do for a living?"

"I just told you why," I snapped, trying to smooth the deep creases out of the report.

As I made my way through the house into the kitchen, he kept at my heels. "You're going to kill him, right? It'll be you who throws the switch?"

"There's no switch."

"But he isn't going to hang. It says so right there in the report. Lethal injection. He killed that woman. It's going to be Old Testament justice, and I want to see it. That guy deserves to die."

"Enough," I grumbled, trying to make sense of what I might be able to throw together for dinner. We had SpaghettiOs but my sister wouldn't like me feeding her son canned food three nights in a row.

"More people should be put down for their sins," he went on.

"I mean it, now. That's enough." He had me unnerved. "All the time you spend in Sunday School and you have the gall to say that?"

He shrugged, committed to his opinion.

"What would Pastor Joe think of you? Or Youth Pastor Asa?"

Seth screwed his face up and stared at the floor.

"SpaghettiOs or ramen noodles?" I said, presenting the options I had found in the cupboard.

He didn't care so I chose for him and got the cooking underway.

Seth was the product of a one-night stand as far as I had been able to figure. There was a chance that Abby had been involved in an affair, but she had never told me about it. Either way, she had shown up in Woodland Beach after having lived over in New Jersey for a number of years. She hadn't looked pregnant when she had returned, but she was. Moved back into this old cottage by the sea that we had grown up in. Six months later, she died giving birth to Seth.

I had never lied to Seth about his mother. I could've told him I was his father and made up a pleasant-sounding story. I didn't do that. As soon as he was able to talk, I had educated him about what had happened to his mom. Maybe I shouldn't have. There was a hole in his heart, knowing that his real dad was somewhere out there; knowing that his real dad didn't have a clue that Seth existed. From the very start, it had warped him.

Since I didn't have answers, I didn't entertain his many questions. But dismissing the subject hurt him, too.

We ate in silence at the round, Formica table in the kitchen. The air felt thick between us. I had been spending too many nights and too much money over at Mermaids, but I was already doing the math on when I might be able to go back. I had a fairly solid system of sneaking off once I was sure Seth had fallen asleep.

"They still don't know who murdered that woman," he said, striking up a dark conversation out of nowhere.

"It's only been a few days," I reminded him. "The police will figure it out."

"I heard she was a hooker."

"Watch your mouth," I snapped. Sometimes when Seth opened up, I caught a glimmer of perversion that had to have come from his biological father. I didn't like it. "You shouldn't talk about a victim like that."

"But if she was—"

"If she was, what?" I challenged, glaring at him from across the tiny table.

"Some people think she deserved it," he answered. His tone was small, but his conviction was larger than life.

I didn't have the energy to combat him so I moved to the fridge and cracked open a second beer.

"I watched the cops, you know," he went on, fascinated. "They set up a yellow line so that no one could come down from the road, but they didn't block off the other side, so I walked right over from the house—"

I stared at him, appalled. "You did what, now?"

A grin unlike anything I had ever seen on the face of another human being came over him and he got an eerie, faraway look in his eyes.

"I saw the body. It was so cool."

THE BOY

DURING THE SUMMER of 1986, nothing was more exciting to me than the murder of Amanda Dover.

Back then, Barsky had the biggest morning show on the radio. Ogletown putt-putt dominated all of the mini-golf spots. You could drink booze on Dewey Beach not that I ever had—*wink, wink*—and the Brandywine Raceway attracted gamblers from all over who liked to bet on the ponies.

The Galaxy Arcade was the place to be if you were a thirteen-year-old boy like me. I had the highest score on Frogger, and fiercely defended my title position, shoving quarter after quarter into the game whenever someone else's winning initials bumped mine down.

You could watch movies at the drive-in, gorge yourself at the DelMarVa Chicken Festival, and get lost in the Christina Mall.

That was how I used to spend my summers as a boy growing up in Woodland Beach. Eating salt water taffy, feeding seagulls, and splashing along the shore was a typical day for me, if I wasn't hanging out around the bandshell, listening to music, and watching girls stroll by in their bathing suits and short-shorts.

But all that paled in comparison to Dead Amanda Dover.

I didn't tell anyone, but I had been the first to discover the body.

Having snuck out of the house at dawn with my boogie board, I had seen a heap—loose limbs and bright, auburn hair. I had veered away from the water to investigate, assuming at first that some lady had tied one too many on and passed out on the beach.

She had been soaking wet, grains of sand embedded in her hair and caked on her legs. Red high heels on her feet, her skimpy dress clung to all her curves like shrink wrap.

It had taken me a moment to realize she was dead.

Her eyes had been milky and open, surprised. Mouth slack, her lipstick smeared sideways across her cheek. Her expression had looked confused, as if she knew she was supposed to be alive but didn't understand why she wasn't.

I could've stared at her for hours, but when I heard sirens wailing, I sprinted off, scared that the cops were on their way.

I hadn't stopped running until I reached the house. I had flown in through the backdoor, certain not to wake Uncle Robert, and threw myself into bed. Heart pounding. Exhilarated. I had lain, wide awake that night, pondering what I had seen.

I couldn't entirely pinpoint why I was so fascinated. I wondered who had killed her and how she had gotten out onto the desolate stretch of sand behind my uncle's house. I tried to imagine her final thoughts, what it must have felt like to be murdered.

Had she felt relieved? If during her life Amanda Dover had ever felt the things I did—I had been walking around with an ocean's worth of regret in my chest—then dying might have come as a welcomed relief.

It was weird to admit, but I was carrying around a ton of regret. I never told Uncle Robert about it, mainly because I wouldn't know where to begin. My whole life, I had constantly felt like there was a dark storm brewing inside me.

I had killed my own mother, and I regretted it.

Supposedly, it hadn't been my fault. She had died during childbirth, but I still felt responsible.

I also regretted that I didn't know who my father was. I regretted that Uncle Robert couldn't tell me. Technically, he didn't have even the slightest clue, but I resented him for it anyway.

What, if anything, had the dead woman regretted?

Did she think she was better off now?

Where was she?

Was she in heaven or was she in hell?

I didn't know the answers to any of the questions that had been whipping through my mind ever since I saw the body on the beach.

All I knew was that for the first time in my life, I would be able to take a break from obsessing about who my father might be. Dead Amanda Dover was just too interesting.

Other kids also found Dead Amanda Dover fascinating, though not for the same reasons I did. As soon as I got into the fellowship hall at Lighthouse Ministries for Youth Group, all of the kids were whispering about it. This was the day after Uncle Robert had yelled at me for stealing his inmate report on Kowalski, not that it made a lick of sense for him to have gotten so angry about it. He knew I liked to steal.

Dead Amanda Dover. Kind of had a ring to it.

"I have juicy gossip," Sally announced. "It's about Dead Amanda Dover."

Everyone's eyes went white all around.

Sally was an alarmingly tall fourteen-year-old who thwacked boys whenever she was close enough. I thought that was what she was angling to do when she advanced on me, but instead she pulled me in close, using a hush-hush manner so Pastor Asa wouldn't overhear. She waited for the other kids to gather around. The boys were hesitant, familiar with Sally's brutality, but the girls promptly obeyed their ringleader. They all had banana clips in their crimped hair and adhered to Sally's every order, though it irked Pastor Gracie.

"She was a recent convert," Sally told us.

"Here, at our church?!" exclaimed Judith, a mousy girl whose parents worked over at the chicken plant. Judith had warned us about poultry. Said if we knew what happened over at the plant, we would never take another bite.

"Shh!" hissed Sally, paranoid all over again that the pastors would catch us. "Yes," she whispered. "Right here at Lighthouse Ministries."

"But I heard she was a stripper," one of the boys said, wholeheartedly confused.

"I heard *hooker*," I quietly corrected him.

Sally scowled at us then went on, "She was one of us. A *Christian*, which means we're all going to have to watch our backs."

"You think the killer will come after us?"

"That depends," she said. "We can't sin, that's all I know. If we sin, we're as good as dead."

"The killer is killing *sinners*?" another girl asked fearfully, terrified right down to her puffy socks and high-top sneakers.

"That's *exactly* what I think."

"Better stop dressing like a floozy," Walter teased, and all the boys chuckled while all the girls folded their arms, deeply offended that anyone would think of their fashion style as risqué. "What? Oh, come on! It was a joke!"

Sally was so insulted by the comment that she couldn't keep her voice down. "You better pray for Dead Amanda Dover, that's all I have to say! And pray that you don't wind up just like her!"

"Whoa! Whoa!" said Pastor Gracie, breaking us up. "What's this I hear?"

We all cowered. No one dared look up from the floor, knowing that whoever did first would get crucified.

"I sincerely hope you aren't making fun of that poor woman," she scolded as her son, Pastor Asa, frowned at us from the sidelines. "What happened on the beach is not a matter for children to discuss."

"But," Sally boldly objected, "wasn't she a member here? My mother told me her name was Cherry. She'd met her at one of the bible studies—"

"Your *mother* told you that?" interjected Pastor Asa, nearing the group.

He looked beside himself. Pastor Gracie looked furious as she confirmed Sally's suspicions.

"Yes," Pastor Gracie told us, "the woman who was found on the beach, Amanda Dover, had been coming to our church. We knew her as Cherry, and beyond that, all we knew was that she was interested in becoming a Christian. Well, being *interested* is not enough. You have to commit yourself to Christ. You have to repent. You have to turn away from your sinful lifestyle. But oftentimes the devil doesn't want to let you go. I'm very sorry to report that Satan lured Cherry back into her sinful life. And look what happened to her."

Sally and Judith touched eyes, sympathetic to Cherry's error, and Walter and Cole leaned against one another, offering each other guarded, boyish support. We all felt bad for Cherry, or rather Dead Amanda Dover.

Pastor Asa posed the question, "How can we learn from this?"

Sally was the first to promise, "I vow to never become a hooker," and all of the girls nodded in emphatic agreement.

Pastor Gracie wasn't impressed. "I suggest," she stated as she lorded over all of us, "that you pray to our Savior to keep your hearts pure. The world is a very dangerous, very filthy place. We are not of the world, do you understand? We are of Christ, and we mustn't deceive ourselves into thinking we can lead sinful lives and come out unscathed."

In response, we all said, "Yes, Pastor Gracie."

She led us into a prayer circle. I held Judith and Cole's hands. And then Pastor Asa distributed the bibles and we sat around one of the large, round tables in the fellowship hall. I had come prepared, having done my bible study homework, but I didn't feel like participating in any of the discussions.

An hour later, there was a thirty-minute break. Pastor Gracie set out juice and cookies for us, and after snacking, we played kickball in the yard behind the church.

Well, the girls didn't so much *play* as *squeal* and get upset whenever one of the boys messed up their fantastic hairdo.

By the end of the game, my team lost but I didn't care.

Whenever I was at the church, whether it was for Sunday School, church service, or one of the youth programs that Uncle Robert forced me to go to so that I wouldn't get into trouble around town, I always ended up feeling very low.

It was as though just being there ate at me. It was hard to explain. This was supposed to be a happy, loving place, but I never felt either of those things when I was there. The pastors that led the congregation didn't seem especially happy or loving, either.

It didn't make sense.

WHEN WE WERE excused, I biked home. The warm wind on my face brought me back to life, but I couldn't shake the sadness or the sea-sized regret in my heart. Church had magnified it and the only system I had for quieting the storm was to throw my swimming trunks on, grab my boogie board, and head out to the beach.

The body of Dead Amanda Dover had long since been carried away. The yellow police tape had been taken down. There wasn't an officer in sight, but I could still smell death in the air.

No one was around.

The news of a murdered woman on Woodland Beach must have been disturbing enough to cause the residents to steer clear. No one wanted to sunbathe and swim along this particular stretch of the Delaware Bay where a stripper had been killed.

I wedged my boogie board in the sand vertically, sat down on my towel, and began taking off my tee shirt.

I was glad to be alone. The only times I felt lonely was when I was supposed to play with kids my own age or converse with adults who asked me questions about myself that they didn't really want the answers to, which described pretty much every interaction I had at the church.

Gazing out at the sea, I couldn't tell where the water ended and the sky began.

It was hot, and I was looking forward to taking a dip, but when I stood, something out in the water gave me pause.

I stared in disbelief.

Didn't believe my own eyes.

Way out in the distance, it looked like a man was standing *on* the water.

For a moment, I thought my eyes were playing tricks on me. There was a bit of a haze. The man out there couldn't be *standing on* the water.

Could he?

I had to squint and strain to make sense of what I was seeing. But sure enough, I saw a man standing on the water. I could see his legs and his *feet*.

I didn't blink. Staring at him, I sized him up.

He was tall and lean, shirtless in swimming trunks, an adult man, but not anyone I could recall seeing before.

I walked towards the shore and tried to get a better look at him.

As I did, he must have seen me, too, and been just as curious, because he started heading straight towards me.

At least, I think he saw me. Why else would he be heading for the shore where I was standing?

He was walking on water…

It couldn't be…

But it was.

He was actually walking *on* the water!

As soon as he reached the sand, he looked at me and smiled.

"Hello," he said brightly. "I'm Thomas."

THE STRIPPER

I HAD ALWAYS FELT there was something magical about the sea. The way the summer sun sparkled over rippling waters, the hypnotic sounds of lapping waves, the shimmering sand—Woodland Beach had a tranquil quality even when the wide stretch of sand was crowded with sunbathers and huge, colored umbrellas, kids throwing frisbees and joggers exercising along the shore.

I couldn't bring myself to go out there, not after what had happened to Cherry. I had heard the place had turned into a ghost town. I understood why. No one could stomach the thought of enjoying that particular beach. It was now known as the location where a young woman had been killed, and for most people, the idea of treading on an open grave was unthinkable.

News reports were everywhere. I couldn't walk into a convenience store without seeing Cherry's face on the TV behind the counter, or turn on the radio in my car without hearing a broadcaster repeating the same vague information—the approximate time of death, the location of the attack, and how tragic it was that a woman who had her whole life ahead of her had been murdered.

I wanted to change the channel in the laundromat, but it wouldn't have helped. Cherry's story was being reported on every station. There was nowhere you could turn without hearing about it—the same repeating facts, the lack of updates, and how the police had no idea who had done it—so I challenged myself not to glance up at any of the three TVs and focused instead on separating my whites and delicates from my colored clothes.

Cherry had left the club at 2 am. Three hours later, someone had taken her life on the beach. I had spent days puzzling over what could've happened. Part of me wished I had been on the schedule that night. Would I have seen something? Would a suspicious character have caught my eye? Or would it have been me who had been discovered dead on Woodland Beach instead?

Police had arrived early in the morning just after dawn. The news reports had been repeating that detail and how the body had still been warm. But no one was saying who had tipped off the police. Someone must have found Cherry dead on the beach and called it in. How else would local law enforcement have known to drive out there, sirens blaring? But who had tipped them off? The media couldn't give a name because local law enforcement wasn't willing to release the 9-1-1 call.

I realized I had gotten sucked into watching the latest broadcast—news reporter, Missy Chance, was reporting *LIVE!* from Woodland Beach—when the dryer I had been waiting on stopped spinning.

I pulled my hot clothes out in one gigantic wad, heaved the heap onto a nearby plastic counter, and folded every article carefully, trying to be as discreet as possible about my racy G-strings, leopard print push-up bras, fishnets, and other telltale signs that I worked as an adult entertainer. Some of the people in this laundromat had prying eyes.

It wasn't like I was ashamed of what I did for a living, but I didn't exactly want to be a walking billboard for exotic dancing either.

When I went out around town, I dressed sensibly for my age and the weather. Today I was wearing a pink tee shirt, the neckline of which I had cut so I wouldn't feel strangled, a denim skirt that was only too short because I was too tall, and a pair of high heel sandals. I had fashioned my hair into a side ponytail, which I'd tied with a big, fake-flower scrunchie for a little flare.

The bangle bracelets I had thrown on jingled and jangled as I wrestled my humongous laundry bag into the backseat of my car, a rusty old thing that I had decided I would drive until the wheels fell off. It guzzled gas and needed an oil change, but it was reliable.

At the grocery store, I collected the usual items in my shopping basket as Muzak softly played. People were talking about Amanda Dover in hushed tones. PTA mothers clumped around the oranges to swap tidbits they had heard. Fathers commented on the mysterious murder to one another in front of the deli section while their soccer sons shoved each other. It seemed every aisle was billowing with rumors and gossip.

I wanted to scream at each and every one of them—*Who cares that she took her clothes off for money! She didn't deserve what she got!*—but I couldn't defend Cherry without revealing that I was like her. A stripper who worked at a club that the entire town was trying to shut down.

Not everyone blamed Cherry as if she had been asking for it. I overheard a group of college-aged girls dignifying Amanda Dover's profession. They made feminist arguments to one another like a priest preaching to his own choir. As far as they were concerned, a woman had a right to do as she pleased with her own body, including make money as a stripper to pay for stenography school!

This was the first I was hearing about stenography school, but Cherry had obviously been keeping a lot from me. Her real name, for example, and whatever secret wildness within her personality that had somehow contributed to her murder.

After the post office, the liquor store, and the bank where I made a nice cash deposit thanks to Robert, I arrived home.

I lived in an apartment building on the Smyrna side of Woodland Beach. It was a walk-up and since I was on the third floor, it took me several sweaty trips to get my laundry and groceries inside.

Once I had, there was just enough time to hang my clothes, clean every square inch of the place, and eat a little something before I had to start getting ready for the club.

I found the lipstick Cherry had lent me. It was hiding in the medicine cabinet behind a box of false eyelashes. Holding it in my hand, I sat on the toilet lid and a terrible feeling slammed into me.

A thick film of sweat broke out across my skin. Overwhelming remorse took hold. Too many women in my life had been killed.

I wanted to kill the killer. I wanted to find out who had murdered Cherry and kill him myself. I wanted to exact a kind of sick revenge on him even if doing so wouldn't bring her back.

"I'M NOT *ORIGINAL* Jewel! I was here first! That means I'm *Jewel!* Just *Jewel!*"

"You don't have to fly off the handle!" Destiny yelled, hotly defending herself. She was standing beside Amber in the ladies' dressing room of the club. Amber was clearly on her side. "I wasn't even talking to you!"

"But I'm right here! You think I can't hear you?" Original Jewel snapped as she planted her fists on her hips and got in Destiny's exotic face.

Miracle slipped in-between them so that they couldn't claw each other's curls out. As she urged them apart, Original Jewel looked about ready to clobber Destiny. An Amazonian obstacle meant nothing to her.

"You two need to calm down!" Miracle insisted. "We're all on edge! Let's not turn on each other when the real issue is that there is no damn money in this club!"

"The real issue is that you guys have been calling me *Original* Jewel behind my back!"

"The real issue," I reminded them, "is that Cherry, a girl we knew and loved, was murdered!"

The air turned heavy. The nasty tension that had risen between the girls was quickly replaced with quiet shame. Original Jewel paced away and Amber tended to her, while Destiny adjusted her G-string to hide the tears that were welling up in her eyes.

Amber touched eyes with me and said darkly, "Cherry was running her own game."

"What?" I breathed.

She didn't respond, only flicked her eyes away.

In horrendous timing—as was often the case with Jimbo—he barged into the room, clapped his huge hands together, and, ignoring the mood among the girls, announced, "I've got some, let's say, *tricky* news—"

Tricky news?

I groaned. Amber buried her face in her hands and made a similar sound. Destiny was already unclasping her stiletto, readying to chuck her heel at him. Miracle glared at Jimbo. And Original Jewel yelled on behalf of all of us:

"What does that mean?"

"We have a new *challenge*…" he informed us.

No degree of a positive spin could persuade us into remaining levelheaded.

"Just remember I went to battle for you," he preemptively reminded us. "But, unfortunately, the county has revoked our liquor license."

A beat of horrific confusion lapsed.

Then it hit us like a fist to the gut and we all shouted, "What?!"

Mermaids was no longer legally allowed to serve alcohol? Who the hell was going to watch me twirl around a pole now? This was not the kind of place anyone wanted to be while stone-cold sober, myself included.

The girls flew off the handle, shredding Jimbo with insults and accusations like a pack of feral cats:

"We're done for!"

"This is your fault, Jimbo!"

"Were you even using a *lawyer*?"

"Never trust a man with a mustache and a Hawaiian shirt!"

Jimbo desperately tried to highlight the silver linings with as much optimism as he could muster:

"We have options! Timbo just put in a nice, big order of O'Doul's non-alcoholic beer! It's the finest! And we all know that the customers come to see all you beautiful mermaids on stage! You're the main event! No one's going to care about the booze!"

"Screw you, Jimbo!"

I thought I was going to be sick. There was no way I would be able to make my rent, pay my bills, keep my life going if the customers couldn't order a stiff drink. As soon as word got out that Mermaids wasn't serving, who would come here?

The girls closed in, ready to clobber Jimbo, but he extricated himself from the dressing room, hollering encouragements that no one was buying as he went:

"We're going to have a great night! Lots of money out there! You girls are the best!"

When we finally pulled ourselves together and got out on the floor, it was obvious that no one was going to have a great night. Mermaids didn't have a single customer. Clearly, word had already spread about the fact that the club could no longer serve alcohol.

The club was empty except for the five of us agitated strippers gliding between vacant tables like hungry sharks. No Robert to save the day. Jimbo tried to push Evian water on us, and Timbo played so much Bruce Springsteen as the night wore on that by eleven o'clock I lashed out at him, yanked the electrical cord out of the wall, and used my Evian water bottle to clock him right in the mouth.

But then, at a little after 1:00 am, the situation went from dismal to dangerous when a group of long-haul truckers stopped in. They obviously hadn't heard about our liquor license, maybe because they had been on the road since Nevada...

They might as well have been chum in the water.

We swarmed the truckers. Even Amber, who was on stage and supposed to stay there for the rest of her set, jumped down and literally *ran* over to claim one of the men.

I counted a total of four truckers, which wasn't enough for us. It was like a game of musical chairs except with too many strippers and not enough men to sit on.

Miracle snagged the largest of them, yanking him away from the frenzy. Destiny grabbed a man by both wrists and slapped his palms against her boobs—it was a major no-no, but what was Jimbo going to do about it? As I inserted myself in front of one of the truckers, I caught limited sight of Amber pulling another man into a private room. Girl did not waste time.

These guys didn't have a chance to think, much less try to order a non-alcoholic beer. Maybe this whole no-liquor-license thing wouldn't be so bad, or so I thought...

From out of nowhere, Original Jewel shoved me and I flew sideways, stumbling into one of the tables. The sticky table broke my fall and also my dignity. When I looked up, furious, Original Jewel had full-on stolen my customer. She was already walking him across the club to one of the long benches to get her lap dance on.

Timbo helped me up and offered me a bottle of Evian water, but I told him to shove it.

"It's vodka," he whispered as he shot me a sympathetic smile. "I poured the water out and filled it with Smirnoff."

"God bless you."

I guzzled down more than I should have and it went straight to my head.

"This situation is impossible, Timbo," I complained. "I haven't made a dime."

"Get aggressive. Get in there. As soon as Amber comes out of the private room, grab her guy," he suggested, but it would be far easier said than done. "Truckers like to go from girl to girl when they come in from the road. Just keep on your toes."

"Right," I agreed, but only because agreeing was easier than expressing what I really thought, which was that the situation was brutal.

If I didn't make money, my entire life could go into ruins, but thanks to the vodka I was starting to feel more buzzed than scared.

"You know what pisses me off?"

"What?" he asked, distracted. He had one eye on Miracle.

"Cherry's murder didn't bring business here to a screeching halt. Losing our liquor license did. How messed up is that?"

"Hmm."

Timbo hadn't even heard me. His favorite stripper, Miracle, was taking her boobs out. The trucker she was dancing for grinned at her tremendous, chocolatey curves from where he was sitting on one of the long benches.

Clearly, desperation amongst the girls was at an all-time high, but Jimbo didn't stop the rule-breaking madness. If we didn't work, we wouldn't be able to pay him the house fee at the end of the night. He made his money off the sweat of our labor. Hard times called for hard decisions, and sometimes the hardest decision of all was to look the other way.

"Never mind," I grumbled as I limped off with my Evian bottle full of vodka in hand.

I felt raw and frustrated. Upset about Cherry. Furious about my financial prospects. Part of me was mad that Robert hadn't come tonight. But I knew that putting all of my eggs in the Robert basket as I had been doing for months had been very stupid.

Jimbo had the audacity to tell me to "smile" as I tried to get past him. I was heading towards the private rooms like Timbo had suggested to catch Amber's customer on his way out, assuming she wouldn't devour his wallet first. I would've told Jimbo he could stick his smile where the sun didn't shine, but I didn't want him to catch a whiff of my vodka breath. Didn't feel like getting into trouble so I flashed him a great, big, sarcastic, thousand watt, I-hate-my-life smile.

He grabbed my arm, reeling me back.

"I don't like the attitude," he warned me.

"I don't like the situation."

"Look," he said. "For tonight only, I'm not going to ask you for the house fee. Now, that has to stay between you and me, Crystal."

"Yes, of course," I told him, brightening. Jimbo never wanted to be the bad guy. "Thanks, I appreciate it."

He nodded. In moments like this, he reminded me of Tom Selleck from Magnum, P.I.—trustworthy, masculine, *likable*.

"I know Cherry's death has hit you the hardest," he said. Jimbo knew about my mom.

He also knew Cherry and I had spent a lot of time together outside of the club. But he couldn't have known that her murder had hit me harder than the other girls. Not even I had known that... until now. As he added a few more kind words about Cherry, commenting on the friendship I'd had with her, I realized how deeply disturbed her death had made me feel. The world really wasn't a safe place. There was nowhere I could go, nowhere I could hide, bad things would find me.

"But Cherry had her own life, a secret life," he went on. "I told her that man was no good for her—"

"Wait, what are you talking about?" I interrupted. "What man?"

"Her boyfriend."

Cherry didn't have a boyfriend.

"She was seeing someone?" I questioned.

"Yeah, what's-his-name," he said as if that summed it up.

"*What's-his-name?* What *is* his name?"

"I don't know."

Unbelievable.

"Have you been drinking?" he asked when I had left my mouth gaping a moment too long.

"Timbo gave me vodka!" I admitted, throwing his cousin under the bus.

"Crystal—"

"Are you telling me Cherry was seeing someone who was *no good?*" I asked, sticking to the only point that mattered. "Do you think the guy could've killed her?"

NEARLY A WEEK passed. We hardly got any customers at the club. Robert hadn't shown. And as hard as Jimbo wracked his brain, he couldn't remember the name of Cherry's so-called boyfriend.

Destiny ended up getting a part-time job as a receptionist at a nail salon, but was already complaining that with Cherry gone, most of her salon income was going towards getting her own nails done. Miracle had a similar idea to make ends meet, but she only lasted two days at the Cotton Candy Factory on the promenade. Said she wasn't built to serve entitled, snot-nosed kids. But rumor had it that she had actually backhanded her teenage coworker, not because he touched her rear-end, but because he hadn't cashed her for it. *You could take the stripper out of the club, but you couldn't take the club out of the stripper…* or however the expression went.

The news on Cherry had petered out. There wasn't much updated information to relay to the public so her story faded into the background, other news reports about petty theft and pickpockets taking her place. People started going to the beach again, but not because they wanted to sunbathe at the scene of a recent crime. Temperatures had climbed to the upper 90s. Cooling off by jumping in the Delaware Bay was the only option for residents who didn't have the best AC. Not for me, though. Woodland Beach still gave me the creeps.

It had been nagging at me all week—what Jimbo had mentioned about Cherry having a boyfriend and a secret life.

Amber had *also* alluded to Cherry *running her own game*…

I was curious to find out about this alleged boyfriend. What was his name? What was the real nature of his relationship with Cherry? Could he have had something to do with her murder?

I didn't know why I hadn't thought of it before, but I decided to drive over to Cherry's apartment, which wasn't far from my own.

It was the middle of July. She had paid rent through the 31st. I had every reason to hope that the landlord hadn't put all of her stuff out on the street.

There could be clues tucked among her belongings, evidence of her secret life and the secret, as-of-yet-unidentified boyfriend. Maybe he was also a Mermaids customer… That would be neat and tidy of him.

I sensed I was onto something, but when I arrived at Cherry's building, I found her apartment door open and an older couple—*her parents?*—were inside. I wasn't going to be able to rummage through her things, not with Mr. and Mrs. Dover putting everything Cherry had owned into boxes.

"For the toss pile?" Mr. Dover asked his wife.

He looked pale and weak, like he hadn't eaten in days, but was dressed in a cheerful sweater and long, khaki slacks despite the heat. An accountant, perhaps, one that tried to act hip in the hopes of being liked by his employees.

He was holding up a glossy calendar for Mrs. Dover's opinion.

She took the calendar and ran her fingertips over her daughter's big, loopy cursive. Cherry had filled in the days of the calendar with her busy schedule of stripping at the club and providing beauty services to the girls. My name was written all over the calendar.

A mile-long stare came over Mrs. Dover, her huge, soulful eyes misting.

"For the toss pile," she finally decided, but she wasn't quite ready to let go of the calendar.

They were broken—the Dovers.

I would've never guessed that Cherry had nice parents like the people I was spying through the open doorway. What had she been doing in a strip club?

I gave the doorframe a little knock, getting their attention.

"Hi, I'm sorry to bother you. I'm Crystal Swan. I'm a friend of your daughter's." First, I double-checked, "You're Mr. and Mrs. Dover, right?"

Cherry's mother looked me up and down, as Mr. Dover told me, "Yes, we are. Can I help you?"

Mrs. Dover went from staring at me to glaring. I felt suddenly self-conscious as I entered the little, bohemian apartment. Mrs. Dover was dressed conservatively and there I was, wearing a tube top, cropped shorts, six inches worth of bangles on my left wrist, and purple sunglasses on top of my head.

I knew exactly what people like her thought of me.

"It's hot out there," I commented as if that would explain why I was showing so much skin. "Especially at the beach."

They soured at my mention of the place where their daughter had been killed.

"Not that I've gone out there since… well, since…" I stammered, meaning to apologize or at least backtrack. This was going badly already. "I'm here because I was hoping to have a look at her things. See if there are any—"

"You want to look through her *things*?" Mrs. Dover balked. "I haven't even buried my daughter yet and you're here to see what's in it for you? What do you want? Her nail polish collection? Her wigs?"

"Cora, please," Mr. Dover pleaded in a kind tone, begging his wife not to explode.

"Or would you like her high heels?!" she yelled, her eyes sharp with tears, her voice turning shrill. She grabbed a pair of sparkling, purple stiletto heels that screamed 'sex worker'. "Or perhaps you're here to get your grubby hands on some of my late daughter's fishnet stockings or panties or—"

"Cora!" her husband barked.

"Outrageous," Mrs. Dover grumbled beneath her breath. Shaking her head, she walked into Cherry's bedroom to get away from me.

I tried to assure Mr. Dover, "I'm not here because I want anything—"

"You're contradicting yourself," he pointed out.

I was getting flustered. "I mean, I do want something. I want to find out what happened, and I didn't expect to find anyone here, but I'm glad to meet you both. I think the police could be doing more."

"That makes two of us," Mr. Dover allowed.

I didn't want to linger and invade the Dovers' privacy worse than I already had, but I felt compelled to ask, "Did Cherry have a boyfriend? I think the police should question him—"

"Did *who* have a boyfriend?" Mrs. Dover blurted out, horrified, as she charged back into the room.

Oh, God.

"*What* did you just call my daughter?" she yelled.

"I'm so sorry," I said, stammering even worse than before.

"Did you just refer to her as *Cherry?*" she challenged me so confrontationally that I began shuffling backwards to make my escape. "My daughter had a name and her name was Amanda Dover. You might have known her as a *stripper*," she sneered, spitting the word out as if it was poison, "but she was a person. A beautiful, sweet, and kind child who grew into an even more beautiful, sweeter, and kinder woman."

"I agree," I promised. "I loved your daughter. She was my friend—"

"Amanda stumbled!" Mrs. Dover went on, shouting over me yet trying not to break down. Determined to speak her mind, she insisted, "We all stumble! I've stumbled! Amanda was trying so hard to get back on track! She was going to church and to school! She was taking our calls again! But it was *you* and people like *you* who wouldn't let her go! *You're* the reason she's dead!"

Wailing with emotions, Mrs. Dover nearly collapsed, but Mr. Dover pulled her close.

"Go!" he ordered, as he protected his sobbing wife from me. "Get out of here and don't come back!"

LATER THAT NIGHT, as I drove past the front of Mermaids, heading to work, I noticed a police cruiser idling out front. The cruiser's lights weren't flashing, but they didn't have to be. Something was up.

After parking behind the club, I walked around to the front entrance, lugging my stripper bag with me. All the girls had one—a giant bag bursting at the seams with heels, hairspray, makeup, baby wipes, baby powder, perfume, nail polish, at least three different bra-and-panty combos, and liquor now that the club wasn't legally allowed to serve.

Two police officers were seated in the cruiser, which meant that they weren't inside interviewing the girls about Cherry or investigating who might've killed our friend.

As I approached the front door, Jimbo flew out onto the sidewalk as if he had been waiting for me to arrive.

"Come inside quickly," he said as he ushered me into the anteroom where Timbo was counting and organizing bills into large stacks behind the counter. As if we would actually have customers who would want to break large bills in order to generously tip the girls.

Once I was safely behind the glass door, Jimbo darted back outside, threw his balled fist in the air, and cursed at the police. "You can tell the Kent County Commissioner that I know how to play hardball! I know the laws and I know my rights! The residents of Woodland Beach don't want boobs in their backyard? By the time I'm through, Woodland Beach won't know what the hell hit it! You tell the Commissioner *that*!"

The police officer behind the wheel used the cruiser's bullhorn to say, "I'll be sure to get the message to him." His partner chuckled in the passenger's seat.

"Sons of bitches," Jimbo muttered as he returned and crossed through the anteroom.

I followed him into the club. "What was that all about?"

"Bastards are going to sit out there. Question our customers. Try to bleed us dry," he complained.

I got the distinct impression the cops weren't out there to find Cherry's killer.

Having crossed the length of the club's hazy blue floor, I breezed behind the velvet curtain and joined the girls in the ladies' dressing room, threw on a bikini top made of two plastic, turquoise seashells, a magenta-pink G-string, and fishnet thigh highs. I needed to make some serious money tonight.

As I jerry-rigged the busted clasps of my stiletto heels, I realized that Original Jewel wasn't here yet, which meant she was late, which meant that Jimbo was probably going to rip her a new one.

"Hey," I said to Miracle as I sidled her. She was standing in front of one of the vanity mirrors where I needed to load hairspray onto my Farrah Fawcett wings. "Have you seen Original Jewel?"

"You are *not* calling her that," she scolded me with sass and an *oh-hell-no* look on her face, as she rubbed shimmering body lotion onto her long, thick thighs. "After the fit she threw at Destiny, referring to *Original* Jewel as anything but *Jewel* is going to get you in serious trouble. I can't always break up fights around here, you know."

I rolled my eyes. "She isn't here."

"Doesn't surprise me," Amber chimed in. "After the lousy money we've all been making, why would any of us show up?"

"I bet you anything she's a Foster's having a cocktail or two," said Destiny. "That's where I would be on a Saturday night."

"Anyone got the hard stuff?" Miracle asked, but the other girls weren't willing to share their alcohol with her. "What?"

"As if Timbo doesn't give you whatever you want to drink," Amber said with a knowing smile. "He still keeps vodka behind the bar for *emergencies*."

The emergencies she was alluding to, when they happened, had occurred when one of the girls was flipping out because the tips were so bad.

"Timbo ain't here now, is he?" Miracle pointed out as Destiny inched in and gave her a nudge with her elbow.

"Have my tequila, but don't drink it all," Destiny warned.

As the girls got loose with Destiny's tequila, I put on my false eyelashes, sprayed my neck with a spritz of perfume, and fought the sudden urge to punch a wall.

It turned into a slow night, but the club wasn't completely empty. Jimbo was still running those promotional discounts that were financially killing us. All the girls except for me were breaking one rule after another with men on the floor and in the private rooms. They thought it was the only way to make money, and this was happening while the cops were sitting in their parked, idling, and highly visible cruiser right outside the club.

Jimbo marched up to me and demanded, "Where the hell is Jewel?" He looked furious.

"*Original* Jewel?"

"Who else?"

"New Jewel?" I guessed.

"Right," he said absently before shaking the thought of New Jewel out of his head. "Original Jewel hasn't shown up."

"Still?"

"I'm going to fire that girl," he decided. "Maybe I can get New Jewel in here to take her place for the rest of the night..."

"For what?" I asked, looking around the dismal club.

There were hardly enough customers to justify four dancers. Five would be too much. But I didn't get the chance to make a case in favor of letting New Jewel be, wherever she was tonight. Jimbo was already making a beeline for his office.

Not twenty minutes later, I was giving a kid a lap dance. He had told me he was a college freshman, but I honestly wondered if he had even graduated high school yet, which certainly begged the question of what the cops were even doing outside. They couldn't be questioning customers and checking IDs if kids were getting in. Were they even pretending to investigate Cherry's homicide?

Then Robert walked into the club.

I felt like I hadn't seen him in ages, but it had only been a little over a week. I caught his eye and he grinned at me as he neared the long bar counter where Timbo was in the habit of cracking open O'Doul's and apologizing to customers once they figured out what they were drinking.

"This isn't beer."

"It is."

"Tastes funny."

"Lots of people like it."

"Hey…is this…?"

"Sir, I'm so sorry—"

"…*non*-alcoholic?"

"We're in-between liquor licenses at the moment—"

"You charged me *four* dollars for *this*?"

Timbo's deadpan response: "No refunds or exchanges."

Robert didn't order a drink when Timbo greeted him. He shot me a nod instead, and I felt a warm rush of excitement swell in my chest.

I climbed off the kid.

"Hey, where are you going?"

"Song's over."

"No, it's not!" he objected, unable to leave the bench and chase after me because of what was happening in his pants.

Miracle swayed up to Robert, as I crossed the floor, but he didn't take his eyes off me. He waved her off and did the same to Destiny when she breezed by, trying to entice him.

"Hey stranger, haven't seen you in a while," I said, happy to see him. "Want a lap dance?"

"How about ten?" he grinned.

"How about a private room?" I countered.

He narrowed his eyes at me, realized we were negotiating, and liked it. He looked down the length of me. Drank in the sight of my skimpy, seashell top. "How about two-rounds?"

My eyebrows shot up to my hairline. "In a private room?"

"Yeah, you think you can get your boss not to barge in?"

"I haven't been able to get my boss to do anything that's good for business," I teased.

"I heard about the beer… And the police seem persistent."

"And yet, here you are," I said as I took his large hand between both of mine, turned on my very high heels, and led him through the dimly lit club while The Human League's hit song *Don't You Want Me* blared through the club.

As we made our way to the private rooms, Robert glanced at my top and said, "I like this."

"My seashell bikini?"

"Did you make it yourself?"

Cherry had helped me… but I didn't let myself go there. As I pulled the velvet curtain aside for him, I said, "Yup," and hoped he would leave it at that.

The private rooms were quiet except for the sound of music softly playing through the PA system. We went into the first room on the left. Robert sat on the red, vinyl bench, opened his wallet, and thumbed through his cash. This time he wasn't distracted by his surroundings, the mosaicked mermaids, lighthouses, and seascapes on the walls.

I practically drooled when he produced a fifty dollar bill.

He didn't hand it over, but rather asked, "How much for us to stay in here until closing?"

I felt my eyebrows shoot up to my hairline for the second time that night. I didn't have to do the math to know I would make a very decent amount of money if Robert wanted to pay for a private room to be with me until closing.

"Is that too much work for you?" he asked when I was so speechless, I hadn't responded. "The execution is coming up."

My stomach tightened. I didn't want to think about Kowalski.

"It's going to be me who kills him," Robert told me.

"*You're* going to execute Kowalski?" I asked, stunned.

I knew that Robert worked at the prison and oversaw Death Row specifically, but I didn't know that he was an executioner.

He suddenly looked gaunt and worried.

In an instant, I felt immensely sympathetic. I couldn't imagine the emotional burden of having to carry out something like that. I saw Robert with new eyes at that moment. He was vulnerable. There were cracks in his foundation—very deep cracks—and I understood why he wouldn't want to be alone tonight. Kowalski's execution was only a day away. Robert must have felt like he was winding up tighter and tighter with every passing hour.

"I'm going to push the buttons," he said, "and kill him."

I felt drawn to him. He was going to kill the man who had killed my mother. He was going to murder the man who had ruined my life.

He locked eyes with me. "I want to be with you tonight until the club closes."

My heart was pounding so hard, I could feel it in my throat.

I wanted to be with him, too. I loved the idea, but I didn't think I would get away with being in a private room with Robert for hours on end. Jimbo would suspect hanky-panky. Plus, after the house fee, Jimbo took a percentage of our earnings…

"Never mind," he said when I hadn't responded. "You probably have other customers—"

"No, I definitely want to dance for you," I blurted out. "I'm just worried my boss will have a problem with it if I'm in here too long."

"No big deal," he said, handing me fifty to massively overpay for a half-hour. "It's just that I practically emptied my bank account with you in mind."

I didn't want to mess this up. I plopped down beside him and hoped that what I was about to say wouldn't sound deplorable. But I had to try. I didn't want to get in trouble at the club, or worse, have to fork over a cut of my pay to Jimbo.

Whispering, I wondered out loud, "What if we met somewhere?"

Robert searched my face, trying to figure out if I was proposing what he thought I was proposing.

"What are you proposing?"

I shrugged suggestively. "I could meet you somewhere…for the rest of the night?" I let that hang and watched his handsome face light up. "But," I went on in an even more discreet tone, "we should do a few dances in here. Then you can have a non-alcoholic beer at the bar while I tell Jimbo I don't feel well… We'll leave separately, but—"

"Sounds like a plan."

For three songs, I danced for him in the private room then we left. He found the bar, and I found Jimbo, feigned stomach cramps, mentioned my period and the flu and lingering grief about Cherry.

Jimbo said, "You had me at *menstruation*," and he excused me from finishing my shift once I had paid the house fee along with Jimbo's cut.

I winked at Robert. Amber was hanging all over him. He knew to stay for a minute while I left first.

When I did, walking out into the hot, humid night, I felt thrilled. I also felt like the police officers sitting in the parked cruiser would be able to smell what I was up to. Did I look suspicious? Could they tell that one of my customers was going to follow me out? Did they know that I was about to commit a crime?

I kept my head low and my eyes down as I walked briskly around to the back of the club. I jumped in my sedan and waited for Robert to leave next, drive his car back here, and lead the way to his seaside cottage.

Robert's only instructions were to remain very, very quiet once I got into the house. Robert's nephew lived with him and he didn't want either of us to wake the boy up.

I had never done anything so dangerous in my entire life.

I should've been thinking about Cherry. I should've been paranoid, on guard, and downright hypervigilant about my safety. I should've been terrified of winding up like her.

But instead, I was pretty sure that I was going to trade hanky-panky for money with a strange man at a location I knew nothing about.

THE MISSIONARY

THE 24-HOUR death watch was in full swing.

I had gotten clearance from prison officials to sit with Arthur from 11:00 pm to 11:55 pm. As was customary at Vaughn, the execution would commence at 12:01 am. Arthur would only have to navigate his own emotions for six minutes without me, but we didn't have to think about that yet.

The clock inside of his cell read 11:38 pm.

There was time. Not much, but enough to hope that Arthur would make the choice to ask the Lord to save his soul. I was having trouble fathoming why he had been adamantly refusing the possibility of salvation since day one.

Warden Cromwell had generously permitted me to enter Arthur's cell. This was my first execution—Lighthouse Ministries' association with the prison was a very new endeavor—and I had never been inside one of the death row prison cells before.

The cement walls had been painted a depressed shade of green. The linoleum floors were a sad combination of blue and gray. There was one tiny window, but it was so high up the wall, it practically reached the ceiling. The narrow cell had been stripped bare. Even the bedding had been removed.

Arthur was seated on a steel bench. His wrists and ankles were shackled, but he was holding a box that contained his belongings.

He clutched the box protectively, and for a moment I wondered if perhaps he thought he would be able to take it with him into the afterlife.

I had gotten to know Arthur over the past few weeks. He wasn't the killer he had once been. If anything, Arthur was exhausted. His life had amounted to a series of disappointments. I had learned he had struggled as a boy. He wasn't able to talk until he had turned six years old. His father had beaten him regularly for no reason and had told Arthur he was worthless.

Every time I had tried to explain to Arthur the importance of forgiveness, he had snorted in disgust. I could tell he blamed his father. When I had once suggested to Arthur that his father might have loved him, Arthur still refused to consider forgiving him.

The best thing that had ever happened to Arthur—to my understanding—was Kimberly Swan…

…and he had killed her.

During all our meetings, Arthur had never been able to make sense of that; of why he had taken her life.

I surmised that the reason Arthur was reluctant to ask Christ to save him was because Arthur felt that he deserved to go to hell for what he had done to the love of his life. In a sense, he refused to be saved because he thought that it would be unfair to Kimberly and her daughter, Crystal. Why should he be allowed to go to the same place Kimberly went, which was heaven?

I understood his logic, but I agreed with the Apostle Paul. No man should choose to perish when the free gift of salvation was available for all.

I was determined to help Arthur see the light.

For his own sake, I was prepared to fight him, if that's what it would take to save him.

I was willing to sit here and argue with him and minister my heart out until the bitter end.

Doing so wouldn't *only* be for his sake. It was for *my* sake, too. I didn't want to fail. I didn't want to fail the mission I had been assigned. I didn't want to have to face my parents and explain that after weeks ministering to Arthur, he had gone to the death chamber never having taken Christ into his heart. I didn't want to have to admit to my parents that I couldn't convince Arthur of the value of being saved by Christ.

The cell door had been kept open. Every minute, one of the guards strolled by slowly and peeked at us. There was an entire team of COs assigned to Arthur's 24-hour death watch. Included in the team were correctional officers Robert Nash and Lyle McKay, as well as Warden Cromwell. Other COs were present, but I didn't know their names.

CO McKay made me nervous in general, but the way he was glaring at me now set my teeth on edge. He looked like he was fantasizing about throttling me with his bare hands. Unlike McKay, CO Robert Nash was a man I both knew and liked.

Though Robert hadn't attended a Sunday service at Lighthouse Ministries since I had been in college, he had remained a member of our congregation. His monthly donations had never stopped and were much appreciated, though Mom always said that she would rather see Robert's face in church than see his checks come in the mail. His nephew, Seth, attended several of the youth programs I ran at Lighthouse Ministries, and I probably thought I knew Robert a lot better than I really did simply because I was familiar with his nephew.

Seth was one of the kids I had to keep my eye on.

At the moment, I was keeping my eye on Robert, as well. Now that I was at the prison preparing Arthur to meet the Lord, it gradually dawned on me why Robert hadn't come to church in nearly a decade.

If he played an integral role executing inmates at Vaughn, that would explain a thing or two…

Robert slowly strolled by the open cell door just as I reiterated to Arthur, "Christ came for the sinners. I don't like your excuses, Arthur, and I don't accept them. Forgiveness is waiting for you. You just have to ask for it, and it will be given."

"Forgiveness?" Arthur balked. "The only person whose forgiveness matters is Kimberly. I wish Crystal would forgive me for what I did to her mother… But I wouldn't dare expect either of them to forgive me—"

"Ten minutes, Kowalski," CO Robert Nash informed us from where he stood, filling the doorway.

I let out a rocky breath and nodded at him.

Arthur and I were boiling in a horrendous pressure cooker.

As Robert moved away from the doorway, I returned my attention to Arthur. I was this-close to begging him to ask Christ to save him. *Begging.* I scrambled for the right things to say that might win him over to the Christian faith before it was too late.

"You mentioned you would like Crystal's forgiveness?"

"I was making a point," he allowed. "I was saying that the only people whose forgiveness matters are the ones whose lives I destroyed. It's too late for Kimberly to forgive me. And I don't see why Crystal would."

"Arthur, it sounds to me like you need to forgive yourself."

"I don't need anything," he said as he held his box of belongings even tighter.

"Would you like me to do something with your belongings after you're gone?" I asked him.

He loosened his grip, glanced into the box, then returned his gaze to me. He looked bewildered, as if it hadn't occurred to him that he wouldn't have his belongings much longer.

Dumbfounded, Arthur couldn't seem to produce any words. A mental fog came over him, and his eyes wouldn't focus. He was becoming vacant. Drifting further and further away.

Absently, he found a photograph in the box. The corners were bent. There was dusty, looped masking tape on the back of the photo where it had clung to the wall of his cell for years.

"If possible," he said as he offered the photo to me, "would you return this photo to Crystal Swan?"

"Return it?"

"She mailed it to me, along with a letter, about seven years ago. It was the nicest thing anyone's ever done to me."

"She sent this to you?" I asked as I studied the photo.

In it were Kimberly Swan, Arthur, and a young Crystal. She looked about eleven years old. Snaggle-toothed and gangly, yet there was a glimmer of mischief behind her huge, blue eyes. All three of them were smiling in front of a Christmas tree. Arthur wore a big, ugly reindeer sweater and looked elated. Kimberly looked like she could've won Miss Delaware 1972, she was so dolled up. A real beauty queen.

"Arthur, that was very kind of her."

"She was a good girl. A smart kid," he said, his voice cracking with emotion. "I wanted to adopt her," he added, squeezing the words out as he finally broke down. "I wasn't perfect, Pastor, far from it. I wanted to have a family. That's all. A family."

He was weeping now. I moved to the bench, placed my hand on his shoulder, and prayed, as Arthur sucked air through his teeth, desperately trying to pull himself together.

"I killed her," he stuttered out. He sucked in another jagged gasp of air and blurted out, "I killed her because she wouldn't let us be a family."

As he curled up, his head in his hands, his shoulders quaking, sobbing out all the pain and remorse and regret and self-hatred, I felt like a phony. I didn't know what to say. Everything that came to mind—Ephesians 6 and 1 Corinthians 20 and even Lamentations 21, *Restore us to yourself, Lord, that we may return, renew our days as of old*—all seemed trite and unfitting.

All I could think to say was, "You're repenting, and that's good."

"Kowalski, it's time," Robert announced as he entered the cell with CO McKay and two others I didn't recognize.

As the guards filed in and surrounded Arthur, I was pushed to the very back of the small holding cell.

"Pastor!" Arthur pleaded as they jerked him to his feet, his box spilling to the floor. Arthur turned to rubber as the COs tried to wrangle him into the corridor. He turned limp, letting his weight go heavy. He wasn't going to cooperate.

"Come on, Kowalski, we practiced this," Robert reminded him. "You know the drill."

"Pastor Asa!" he cried out again as the guards dragged him farther down the corridor.

"I'll pray for you, Arthur! I'll be out in the gallery!" I assured him as I followed into the corridor just in time to see Robert and CO McKay pulling Arthur through a steel door that led into the death chamber. "Ask Christ for forgiveness!"

As the guards dragged him out of view and the steel door shut behind them, Arthur began yelling at the top of his lungs like a howling dog, "Save me, Lord! Forgive me, Lord! I want to go with you, Lord! Please!"

It was music to my ears.

Mission accomplished.

I smiled to myself.

I couldn't wait to tell my parents.

THE STRIPPER

I HAD NEVER BEEN truly able to figure out how I felt towards Arthur. Not really. He brought to mind too many conflicting emotions. If I tried to write a list of every emotion, the ink in my pen would run dry before I could get all of them down on paper. I had attempted it once. Some idiot therapist had encouraged me. She thought journaling about Arthur Kowalski would help me make sense of my feelings. It was an infuriating, heartbreaking exercise that had left me feeling wounded and exposed. I was fourteen at the time, and after the failed exercise, I spent future therapy sessions with my arms crossed and my mouth shut, fully convinced the woman wasn't qualified to help me.

On the one hand, Arthur Kowalski was at the heart of some of my best childhood memories. But on the other hand, he had single-handedly derailed my chances of having a normal life…

Among the sweetest memories was the time I had once walked home from school when I was almost twelve years old. It had been the day before Thanksgiving. I had slipped inside the row home I shared with my mother to find Arthur bopping around the kitchen. The apron he wore was covered in flour. There were oven mitts on his hands. Our small radio was blasting a catchy, Frank Sinatra holiday song. It made sense that Arthur had been over-the-top excited about Thanksgiving. He loved holidays and wanted life to be picture perfect like it was in the movies. Arthur lived in his head. He had big dreams. His mind was in the clouds most days. But I had been like that, too. Back then, I had thought my aspirations were attainable. I was a kid. Arthur, as an adult, should've known better.

"Want to help me make cornbread just like the Indians?"

"Okay!" I had said, beaming a great, big smile from ear to ear.

I hadn't known what I was getting myself into when I agreed. I just liked how festive he had made our rowhome. Arthur had decorated the kitchen with construction paper turkeys, and in the living room, he had draped tinsel over the mantle, windowsills, and banister, getting a jump on Christmas.

That was the whole memory. Baking cornbread with Arthur and the joy I had felt because of it. He had shown me how to mix the ingredients. I hadn't cared that he'd used a box recipe or that the cornbread didn't taste very good when all was said and done. I had never had cornbread and all the fixings on Thanksgiving.

When Mom had come home a few hours later from her shift at the grocery store, she started dancing around the kitchen with Arthur. By then, we had moved on to making apple pie, which was a much more complicated process.

I had never forgotten that magical moment, which never would've happened without Arthur. I had loved him that day. How in the world could I ever reconcile the love I had once felt for him when I also had a ball of hatred in my heart with his name on it? Arthur had been responsible for one of the most incredible memories of my childhood! Hollywood should've made a movie about the Thanksgiving we had celebrated that year, which had been joyful because of Arthur!

But he ended up murdering my mother.

I had been suffering from a form of cognitive dissonance for the last fifteen years, as if I was two different people on the inside. The bright side of myself loved Arthur Kowalski. That side of me was the one who always put on her makeup with her mother in mind, who didn't care that she took her clothes off for a living. But the other side of myself was dark, angry, and constantly itching for a fight.

My dark side had convinced me to drive out to the prison for Arthur Kowalski's execution. My dark side was starting to frighten me. And I thought the darkness inside me might go away if I did what it wanted me to do, which was watch my mother's killer be put to death by lethal injection.

I had never been to the prison before. This was my first time entering the compound and my first time sitting in a viewing gallery outside of a death chamber. At the moment, I couldn't see the actual death chamber on the other side of the window. The blinds had been drawn.

I was surprised the execution was scheduled so late at night.

I had been at a complete loss in terms of figuring out what would be appropriate to wear to something like this. I must have lost my mind getting ready earlier, because I had thrown on a red cocktail dress, my faux fur coat, and four-inch heels. I probably looked as ridiculous as I felt.

But no one else had come.

I was the only person in the gallery.

There was no one there to sneak sideways glances at me and judge what they saw.

Then the door in the back opened, and as I glanced over my shoulder, I touched eyes with the clean-cut looking man who was entering. He was carrying a cardboard box. The mild sweater and tidy slacks he wore told me that he wasn't a correctional officer or a prison official.

I guessed he was in his thirties and pleased with himself. He seemed interested in me, but not for the reasons I was used to.

He didn't look me up and down, per se, as he neared the second row where I had parked myself. He wasn't checking me out, but he was curious about me and didn't take his eyes off me even though I had faced forward again.

"Excuse me," he said, as he edged into my row and angled over me with that cardboard box in his hands, giving me no choice but to acknowledge him. "I'm sorry to bother you, but are you Crystal Swan?"

I should've expected this. There were all kinds of weirdos floating around Delaware. Most of them came to the strip club. One of them had killed Cherry. Of course a kook would show up for Kowalski's execution. This guy probably had a scrapbook full of newspaper clippings about my mother's 1973 murder. He had that look about him—the kind of 'squeaky clean' that couldn't be trusted.

"Are you Crystal?" he pushed.

"What if I am?"

"I thought that was you," he said, a relieved smile coming over him. He welcomed himself to sit down right beside me. I was too close to the aisle for him to fit, but he didn't let that stop him. I scooted over, irritated, as he settled in with his cardboard box on his lap. "I'm so sorry for your loss."

"It was a long time ago," I said in a flat tone meant to suggest I wasn't interested in talking.

"Where are my manners?" he said with a strange, little chortle. "I haven't even introduced myself. I'm Pastor Asa Asbury from Lighthouse Ministries."

"Who cares?"

A tad offended, he politely explained, "I minister to the inmates on Death Row, not that they care. But my parents do. Pastors Joe and Grace Asbury?"

"I've never heard of them."

He wasn't here to get an eyeful of the train wreck that had become my life. He had come to the prison today as a religious zealot in support of Kowalski, which made him an entirely different kind of wacko.

I scooted even further down the metal bench, but he didn't get the hint. He thought I was making room for him. I wasn't.

He offered me his hand to shake, and I proceeded with a healthy degree of skepticism.

"It's so nice to meet you, Crystal. I've been meeting with Arthur for the last few weeks," he went on as if we were old high school friends getting reacquainted. "He's deeply remorseful for what he's done."

"Great," I murmured dryly without giving the pastor a shred of my attention.

The covered window wasn't much to look at, so I began rummaging through my purse in search of Cherry's lipstick, not that I needed to reapply.

"I would like you to know that he repented."

"Yeah, well, given that he's been locked up, I doubt it was hard for him to *stop* killing people. That *is* what *repent* means, right? To stop doing whatever garbage you've been up to?"

My sarcastic point flew right over his head. Instead of leaving me alone, he grinned at me as if he were impressed.

"Yes, that *is* what repent means."

"If you don't mind, I'd like to, you know, have some privacy."

The guy did not get it.

"Arthur was hoping to have your forgiveness."

"*Forgiveness?*" I blurted out, suddenly furious—Arthur had the audacity to want something from me after all he had taken away?

"Yes, he would like your forgiveness," he said in a thoughtful, measured voice that turned my stomach. "Arthur has been hurting for a very long time. Suffering. He'll never know one way or the other if you've found it in your heart to forgive him, but God will know. For your own sake, you should—"

"I'm going to stop you right there," I interrupted, offended beyond belief. Who in the hell did this sanctimonious jerk think he was? *Arthur* had been hurting for a very long time? *Arthur* had been suffering? And what had I been doing this whole time? Moon-walking through life, giddy and overjoyed? Hardly! "You are massively overstepping your bounds. You don't know me. You don't know my life. You don't get to lecture me about moral high ground."

"Forgive me," he said, but he might as well have told me to *calm down*. "I didn't mean to insult you. I meant only to comfort you."

"You know what, give me a call after Kowalski murders *your* mother."

Sliding down the row, I put five-feet of space between us, but it wasn't enough. Evidently, he wasn't done rubbing me the wrong way. He pushed closer and closer, until he was practically on top of me. Then he offered me the cardboard box he had been holding.

"Arthur wanted you to have this."

I didn't take it. "A box of junk? Gee."

As I stared straight ahead, determined to ignore him, he set the cardboard box at my feet, found a business card in his wallet, and placed the card inside the box.

Before he returned to his side of the bench, he had another unwanted invitation for me. "If you would ever like to talk about anything, you have my card. I don't mean to suggest that forgiveness is easy. It can take time. Years, in fact. But I want you to know that everyone at Lighthouse Ministries is here for you if you need us. Crystal?"

I glared at him.

"It's not just about forgiving Arthur," he went on. "God has already done that. Arthur will go straight from the gurney into the Lord's arms. He's been saved."

I snorted a laugh. This guy's entire belief system was on crack. *Saved*!

"By forgiving him," he explained, "you, yourself, can heal. And you, too, can be forgiven by Christ, just like Arthur was."

Was this jackass for real?

"I haven't done anything wrong," I lied, images of my long night with Robert surging to the forefront of my mind.

I didn't like how he was looking at me in response to that, but I kept going.

"I don't need to forgive and I don't need forgiveness," I asserted.

The rising confrontation between us ended when a terrible commotion kicked up from inside the death chamber.

THE EXECUTIONER

KOWALSKI DID NOT want to be strapped down.

It took all five of us to wrangle him onto the gurney. CO McKay and Warden Cromwell had captured his flailing arms, while the other two COs and myself had him by the legs, but he was still writhing and wriggling, slippery as a worm trying not to get skewered by a hook.

The sounds Kowalski was making—low, guttural, animalistic howls—were heart-rending.

"Work with us, Kowalski!" I ordered as I slammed his right leg down onto the gurney and whipped the nearest leather strap over his shin.

He used his other leg to kick CO Boone in the chest, but I caught his foot and the moment I slammed his leg down against the gurney, the other two COs came to my aid and we strapped him down, buckled him in, and gained control.

The gurney was T-shaped, so Warden Cromwell and CO McKay had a slightly easier time securing Kowalski's arms to the apparatus.

My brow had broken out in a hot sweat by the time we had him tightly buckled down.

Kowalski bucked and jerked, but he wasn't going anywhere.

I ran a handkerchief across my forehead, caught my breath, and shot Warden Cromwell a nod.

He moved to the viewing gallery window, the blinds of which had shielded whoever was out there from seeing what had just taken place.

There was a power console on the wall next to the covered window. Cromwell depressed one of the buttons, and the blinds opened electronically. A moment later, the spectators in the viewing gallery could see Kowalski strapped to the gurney in the death chamber.

Crystal.

She had come.

Crystal was seated relatively close to the front. Our eyes locked, but I felt thrown. Momentarily sickened. Why had I pushed her to come? Did I really want her to see me and a team of COs take Kowalski's life?

Shame climbed up my throat.

She looked uncomfortable. Maybe even nauseous. She appeared to be making a concerted effort not to grimace, and we hadn't even gotten started yet in the death chamber.

Pastor Asa Asbury was on the far side of Crystal's row. His hands were folded, his gaze downward. His lips were moving in prayer.

I neared Kowalski, whose wailing had turned into whimpering, and told him, "Just like we practiced."

The protocol I had learned from Senior CO Silas Digby called for the IV needle to be administered once the inmate had been strapped down.

I stepped behind the black curtain that concealed the executioner's alcove where the machine was located. Out of view, I put on a pair of latex gloves, pulled the plastic cap off an IV needle, and grabbed an alcohol-soaked cotton ball I had prepared earlier. After returning to Kowalski, I rubbed the sterilizing cotton ball across Kowalski's right, inner elbow.

"It'll all be over soon," I promised him. "I'm going to first get the IV in your artery. Then I'll prop you up so that you can address the gallery with your last words, okay? After that I'm going to put the black hood over your head and lower the gurney back down, just like we practiced this morning."

CO Lyle McKay joined the other COs who were standing next to Warden Cromwell at the side of the room.

Only me, Kowalski, and one needle were center stage…

God damn, my hands were trembling something fierce…

Kowalski began whimpering all over again, as I felt for a vein.

His femoral artery was hiding.

Quickly, I ducked behind the curtain again and found the tourniquet that Digby had advised me to use—*Christ, I'd almost forgotten it!*

When I returned, I wrapped Kowalski's arm as tightly as I could, waited a moment, and felt around his inner elbow until a thick vein emerged.

Letting out an unsteady breath, I punctured the needle through his skin, but his ropey vein slid sideways, evading me.

Kowalski winced.

"Sorry," I muttered.

I tried again, poking him, but his vein dodged the needle. The third time I pierced his skin, my angle was so bad that he shrieked.

I had read about how you could damage the arterial walls if you tried and failed to hit a vein too many times, so I gave up and moved to the other arm. Fixed the tourniquet on. Wiped alcohol over his inner elbow. Felt for a vein.

Cromwell was staring daggers at me. The man looked like he was about ready to rip me a new one for taking so long and for moving from arm to arm like an amateur.

I didn't allow myself to get distracted.

My hands were shaking worse than an alcoholic in withdrawal, as I kept trying and failing to puncture Kowalski's damn artery.

But after five tries on that arm with no luck, I gave up, found the lever beneath the gurney, and hoisted Kowalski up so that he could address the gallery with his last words.

"What the hell are you doing?" Cromwell hissed, keeping at my heels, as I slipped behind the black curtain, entering the executioner's alcove. I flipped on the overhead microphone so that attendees in the viewing gallery would be able to hear Kowalski's last words.

"I can't find his vein!" I complained, as I frantically flipped through the medical pamphlet that Digby had left us.

"For God's sake," Cromwell muttered through clenched teeth, seething. "This is a disaster!"

I was only vaguely aware of what Kowalski was saying. He was trying to personally address Crystal, but his sobbing was too loud.

"I'm not a doctor!" I whispered, annoyed that Cromwell would have the gall to blame me for this. "*You* want to try finding his femoral artery?"

"Unbelievable," he spat, pacing away.

"*I'm* unbelievable?" I challenged, using hushed, irate tones. "Lethal injection was *your* big idea! *You're* unbelievable!"

"You better pull it together and get out there!"

"*You* better pull it together and get out there!" I shot right back. "You can put the hood on him, too!"

Cromwell angled his finger in my face, and I could tell he was bursting at the seams to let me have it. But instead of exploding, he snatched the black hood off the death machine, turned on his heel, and marched out, giving me a moment to collect myself.

The last thing I wanted to do was botch Kowalski's execution.

But that was precisely what followed—a messy, inhumane, deplorable execution that would haunt me for the rest of my life.

When I returned with a fresh IV needle in hand, I tried and failed to puncture the femoral artery in Kowalski's original elbow, but I taped the syringe down, anyway. The needle was deep in his skin. It was hitting *something*, just not the artery.

There was nothing I could do. Hell, I could stab him all day and *still* not hit the right vein.

Kowalski was looking this way and that, blinded by the hood over his head, but sensing that something was very wrong. His panic was palpable.

I returned to the executioner's alcove, pulled the curtain aside, and stepped out of view.

Behind the curtain, I pushed the first set of buttons just as Digby had taught me, never minding that Cromwell had abandoned me.

Kowalski shrieked.

Oh, no!

The solution wasn't flowing into his artery, because I hadn't been able to find the damn thing, so instead, pancuronium bromide was pooling in his flesh and causing immense pain.

Quickly, I hit the second set of buttons, forgetting the damn saline flush that Digby had drilled into my brain was absolutely imperative to administer in-between.

Kowalski screamed bloody murder from the gurney, and for a second, I thought I heard Crystal gasping on the other side of the viewing gallery window.

Cromwell barked, "Turn off the microphones!"

Scrambling, I flipped the switch for what I believed were the microphones, but I wasn't able to think or see straight. I didn't know which switch I had flipped, but based on Cromwell's cursing, I knew I'd turned off the wrong thing. The lights?

Damnit!

I couldn't think straight with Kowalski howling like that!

I smacked the final set of buttons on the death machine, administering what should have been a fatal dose of potassium chloride, but Kowalski wasn't dying. The chemicals weren't flowing through his arteries and reaching his heart.

I emerged from the alcove and found Kowalski twisting in agony on the gurney and crying at the top of his lungs in the dark.

Cromwell shoved me aside, tore through the alcove, and the next thing I knew the lights were on and the overhead microphones were off—I could no longer hear Kowalski's howling cries reverberating through the speakers on the other side of the window. But Crystal and Pastor Asa were no less shocked by what was happening just because they suddenly couldn't hear Arthur.

Kowalski was racked with pain unlike anything I had ever seen.

Someone had to put him out of his misery.

"For God's sake, McKay! Close the blinds!" Cromwell barked.

CO McKay rushed to the power console and depressed the switch, causing the eggshell-white blinds to inch down and slowly cover the window.

Kowalski's suffering had gone on long enough.

I advanced on Kowalski, determined to put him out of his misery.

Warden Cromwell didn't have time to stop me. The other COs couldn't make logical sense of what they were witnessing until it was too late.

I took firm hold of Kowalski's black-hooded head...

"What are you doing?!"

...and in one swift, brutal motion, I snapped his neck.

DEATH ROW INMATE 513
Oppal, Clifford

On December 24, 1977, Clifford Oppal was discovered naked and rambling inside of Trains, Toys, and Hobbies, a popular toy store in Claymont, DE. Customers alerted the store clerks, and the manager called the police to have the offender removed. Several children witnessed Oppal's indecent exposure and later noted to police that the naked man had been humming Christmas carols and muttering boys' names as he tossed toys into his shopping basket. Danny, Timmy, Adam, and Travis were among the names that the witnesses could recall.

Mention of these names tipped investigators off to Oppal's potential involvement in a series of child abductions that took place between 1968 and 1976 across Delaware. A total of seven boys had gone missing. Their ages ranged from 7 to 9 years old. All were Caucasian and had brown hair, light eyes, and an active sports schedule. Their names were Daniel Weaver, Timothy Gravesend, Adam Wood, Travis Millhouse, Paul Taite, Owen Gibbs, and Lucas Lippman.

After obtaining a search warrant on December 29, 1977, local law enforcement entered Oppal's home and found a number of 57-gallon steel drums in the basement. The missing boys' bodies were inside seven of them, perfectly preserved with formaldehyde and other chemicals.

When questioned, Oppal confessed to kidnapping, sexually assaulting, and killing the boys, but he refused to tell police where he had gotten the formaldehyde and other preservative chemicals. Instead, Oppal told investigators: "Little boys shouldn't have to grow up."

The criminal offenses were tried as a capital murder case due to the fact that the crimes involved the following aggravating factors:

- *The murders were outrageously or wantonly vile, horrible or inhumane in that it involved torture, depravity of mind, use of an explosive device or poison or the defendant used such means on the victims prior to murdering them.*
- *The victims were children all 14 years of age or younger, and the murders were committed by an individual who is at least 4 years older than the victim.*
- *The murders were committed for the purpose of avoiding or preventing an arrest.*

Oppal was found guilty after conviction by a court of law and has therefore been sentenced to be executed by lethal injection at the James T. Vaughn Correctional Center in Smyrna, DE.

On July 21, 1986 Oppal changed his method of execution from lethal injection to hanging, formally asking the warden. Warden Cromwell approved the change on July 24, 1986.

Execution to commence: August 13, 1986

THE BOY

I NEVER WANTED to stop being a kid.

Uncle Robert seemed miserable all the time. Pastor Gracie was mean, and Pastor Joe was one cookie away from giving himself a fatal heart attack. Dead Amanda Dover was, well, *dead*. So was my mother and everyone else who had been buried in the church cemetery. To grow up was to die, as far as I was concerned. Not that I felt especially full of life at thirteen. I didn't particularly like the other kids my age, but then again, I wasn't a fan of adults, either. Wherever I went, I was closely watched. I didn't have that much freedom thanks to my rigorous Christian youth group schedule—Uncle Robert had enrolled me in literally *every* program—but I still managed to get into a decent amount of trouble around town when I was left to my own devices. I would never want to give that up. Summertime was precious.

But with each passing day, I sensed I was inching closer and closer to death.

My own? Or someone else's? I couldn't decide…

THE GALAXY ARCADE was teeming with kids. The place had energy. The games were noisy, ringing, buzzing, and whistling whenever someone scored. Boys joked around. Girls crowded the display counter where prizes—giant teddy bears, colored rabbits' foot keychains, and everything in-between—gleamed under glass. Older girls told their boyfriends exactly what prizes they wanted them to win.

I was in "the zone," playing Frogger. Kids kept knocking into me, it was so crowded, but I didn't blink. I had just come from church where Pastor Asa had lectured all of us about how short our time here on Earth was. We could go at any minute, he had explained, terrifying us. Where we went once we died, though, would depend on how we had lived our lives. Did we want to go to heaven or hell? he had asked, fully expecting an honest answer.

He had seemed rattled, like something had deeply disturbed him. Pastor Gracie had noticed, too, and dismissed Asa so that he could lie down in the rectory. She had taken over his class.

Whenever I was at church, it was easy to forget there was a whole world out there. Interestingly, whenever I left Lighthouse Ministries after Youth Group and discovered that someone had beat my high score on Frogger, I would forget all about Pastor Asa's weird teachings and get locked into "the zone."

I was a lean, mean, Frogger-playing machine.

News reporters might have stopped talking about Dead Amanda Dover, but the kids at Lighthouse Ministries hadn't. Sally and Judith had been bringing fresh tidbits to everyone's attention. The tidbits weren't necessarily *clues*, but they were enough to keep us interested whenever we were at the church.

Some members of the congregation had known the dead woman as *Cherry*. Apparently, she had an arrest record, but only for *misdemeanors*. Anyone could rack up misdemeanors, that was nothing special. But what *was* special, and downright riveting to all of us, was that—according to Sally's paternal aunt's hairdresser's brand-new daughter-in-law whose husband was a police officer down in Wilmington—no signs of sexual activity had been found on the victim.

Dead Amanda Dover, or Cherry, had not been sexually assaulted, and she also had not gotten down-and-consensually-dirty, either.

The plot was thickening.

We knew that Dead Amanda Dover was a stripper and probably a hooker, and yet she hadn't slept with her killer on the beach?

It completely shattered the motive that our congregation had come up with. Meaning, the parishioners could no longer *assume* that their newest member, Cherry, had been murdered *because of* her sinful lifestyle. Of course, they still *hoped* that was the reason Cherry had been killed. But I could tell, doubts had risen in their minds. It was groundbreaking, because it meant that no one at our church was safe. Anyone could be killed.

Though the bedrock of our church had been shaken, the residents of Woodland Beach had more or less resumed their usual summertime routines. The beach where the body had been found was once again as crowded as ever, so much so in fact that I stopped going.

I hadn't seen Thomas again, either. Not since the afternoon I had biked from Youth Group to the desolate beach. I had thought about him often, though—Thomas—but mostly because I couldn't figure out if he was real or not.

Perhaps he was a ghost, anchored to Woodland Beach.

Perhaps *he* was real, and *I* was a ghost…

Or perhaps, I was losing my mind…

…because I rarely interacted with kids my own age unless I was forced, and because I filled my head with AC / DC and Jethro Tull, much to my uncle's chagrin.

Was I losing my mind?

Maybe.

At the church, I had asked Pastor Gracie to double and triple check whether or not a modern-day Christian would be able to walk on water.

She had assured me that only Christ could walk on water, and though Christ had enabled Peter to walk out on the water, too, there was simply no way, in 1986, for a living, breathing human being to perform that kind of miracle.

Perhaps I would never see Thomas again…

Whether or not I would didn't matter.

At the moment, I was obsessed.

"WELL, IF IT ISN'T Seth," Sally announced to Judith, Walter, and Cole, as she flicked her puffy side-ponytail and shoved me away from the game of Frogger I was winning.

"Hey!"

She didn't so much smile as smirk down at me from her towering height. Sally could be as cruel as a Siamese cat, but unfortunately, most grown-ups thought she was sweeter than an angel.

As Judith, Walter, and Cole surrounded me, Sally said, "Funny running into you here."

She was up to something.

"Is this your spot, Seth?"

"Yeah, and Frogger's my game," I told her. "You just ruined my chances of winning back my high score."

"Awe, I ruined your chances, did I?" she mocked.

"What do you want, Sally?"

Sally and Judith exchanged a sly look. Walter and Cole grew a bit nervous, as if they might not be able to go through with whatever cruelty Sally had cooked up.

I could only guess what was coming. They had been ganging up on me all week. Just another reason why I never liked going to church anymore.

Suddenly vicious, Sally told me, "We all know that your dad killed Dead Amanda Dover!"

"What? No, he didn't!" I shot back, hoping I was right. I didn't know who my dad was, but I knew he didn't kill Dead Amanda Dover.

Following Sally's lead, all the girls closed in on me and began chanting, "What did your dad do to Dead Amanda Dover? What did your dad do to Dead Amanda Dover…"

As they repeated the creepy churchyard taunt over and over again, Sally cackled to high heaven. Then Walter and Cole joined in the harassment, singing along with Judith and the girls, "What did your dad do to Dead Amanda Dover? What did your dad do to Dead Amanda Dover?"

"Shut up!" I yelled. I needed to get out of there. I felt claustrophobic. I shoved Walter with all my might, but the boys had locked elbows, and I couldn't escape. "My dad didn't do anything! I don't even know where he is! He could be dead for all I know!"

My opinion didn't matter. Sally had dreamed up a whole story, and the kids were convinced. According to Sally's imagination, after my biological father had gotten my mother pregnant thirteen years ago, he slipped off into the night, and then had returned months later to murder my mother after she had given birth. None of it made any sense but in the twisted gutters of Sally's teenage mind, my real dad was a serial killer, and I was destined to become like him.

I was so mad, I could have strangled Sally with my bare hands!

"What did your dad do to Dead Amanda Dover?" they sang maliciously, over and over again, as I turned this way and that, trying to break free of their circle.

I shoved Walter, but used too much force. The tight cluster of us stumbled into the Frogger arcade game and the impact cracked the plastic siding.

"Shut up! Shut up!" I yelled, as the boys tangled around me.

I threw the meanest punch I could. My balled fist landed awkwardly against Cole's ear, and he screamed. The horrible circle broke. Everyone was shocked that I had punched Cole. He had asked for it! They all had!

Sally glared at me, appalled. Judith said something outrageous about me being as violent as my murdering father. But it was Walter who retaliated.

He grabbed me by the front of my tee shirt, cocked his huge fist back, and clocked me—hard—in the left eye, sending me flying sideways into another arcade game. Kids in the immediate area took notice and began hollering, "Fight, fight, fight!"

As soon as I scraped myself off the floor, Walter leapt on top of me and began pummeling me, throwing right and left hooks in rapid, unrelenting succession. He was too slippery for me to grasp hold of him. All I could do was cover my head with my hands and pray that my skull was hard enough to break his knuckles.

"Walter! Let's go!" Cole exclaimed, jerking him off of me so that he wouldn't get in trouble.

The arcade manager rushed over, but didn't make it in time to apprehend any of them. Sally, Judith, Walter, and Cole disappeared into the lively crowd, but I was too disoriented to get away.

"You again?" the manager complained. He grabbed the back of my shirt and jerked me to my feet. As he dragged me towards the front of the store like I was some kind of repeat offender—I sort of was, but still, this time it wasn't my fault—he yelled, "I told you if you caused any more trouble here, I would get the police involved!"

"It was the other kids! They beat me up!"

"Save it!" he barked as he tossed me out of the arcade. "Don't come back here again—"

"What?!"

"You're banned for life!"

"But I didn't do anything!" I protested.

"You're banned!"

"But—"

"Banned!"

MY CHEEKS BURNED and I felt like my heart was about to leap out of my chest, I was so pissed off as I stomped out of the arcade, coming into the blinding sunlight.

The injustice of it all!

I hopped on my bicycle and tore out of the strip mall, nearly running into an oncoming car. As soon as I veered around the car, a pedestrian was in my way, but I dodged him just in the nick of time.

I wobbled this way and that, but soon regained my balance, bared down on the handle bars, and pedaled as hard as I could.

Banned?!

I was seeing red.

Those kids were supposed to be my friends! They were supposed to be *Christians*. But they had singled me out, antagonized me, and on top of all that, they had just gotten me kicked out of the Galaxy Arcade *for life*.

It was perfect, just perfect! That was Lighthouse Ministries in a nutshell! The so-called friends I had made there were the types of kids who would punch the snot out of me and set me up to take the blame for damaging an arcade game.

The church kids were fake! The parishioners were fake, every last one of them! No wonder Uncle Robert never went there anymore. I shouldn't have to go, either. Walter should pray I don't set foot in the place…

I could feel my eye swelling up, as I rode my bicycle in a blind rage all the way to the beach. When I reached the dunes, having glided to the bike rack, I felt no less like exploding. I hopped off and wedged my bicycle among the others.

I was hot, too, blistering.

I ran across the scorching sand, shuffling between sunbathers. At the water's edge, I stripped out of my tee shirt, flung my tennis shoes off, and tried to shed the anger I felt, as well.

Stomping and splashing through the surf, I pushed through wave after wave then dove headfirst into the water.

Submerged in the sea, I was finally filled with a sense of calm. The water had killed the noise. Cooled me off. Saved me, or so I thought.

As soon as I floated up again and broke through the surface, all those aggressive emotions that I thought I had washed away in the ocean took hold of me all over again.

What if Sally was right? What if my biological dad *was* the killer? What if he was hiding in plain sight? What if he had been here this whole time, murdering women and crossing paths with me, both of us never knowing who the other one was?

What if my father was walking around with a Seth-shaped hole in his heart, feeling regret and rage just like I did, without knowing why? And what if it was that very regret and rage that had driven him to murder the stripper named Cherry?

What *had* my dad done to Dead Amanda Dover?!

Spitting salt-water out of my mouth, I swam—panicking—farther and farther until I was far beyond the breakers, way over my head.

I wanted to keep going and leave all of Delaware, including my dad and whatever horrors he had inflicted on Dead Amanda Dover in the distance behind me… God, could Sally and the rest of them be right?

From out of nowhere, Thomas emerged buoyantly beside me and answered the very question I had just thought in my head:

"I don't think so, do you?"

"AH!!!" He startled me so badly, I almost choked on a mouth full of seawater. "Thomas?"

"Hello, Seth."

Astonished, I stared at him in complete disbelief, as I treaded water in place, the deep blue sea bubbling up all around us.

"Where did you come from?" I tried to ask, but my vision started going dark.

"I think we should swim back to the shore before—"

But it was too late. The shock of encountering my imaginary friend was too much. My vision tunneled. I couldn't breathe. I lost all sense of myself and began to sink.

❄

WHEN I REGAINED consciousness on the shore, Thomas was gazing down at me, backlit with brilliant, afternoon sunlight. Strangely luminous, he looked like an angel. He also looked completely unconcerned that I had almost drowned to death.

My lungs burned then bile shot up my esophagus and I thought I might puke. I rolled onto my side just in time to cough salt water out.

Thomas gave me a few firm pats between my shoulder blades, helped me to sit upright, and once I seemed okay, he stared out at the sea.

"You should've let me drown!" I said, flying into a rant. "You should've let me die! Should've put me out of my misery! My stupid life has only gotten worse the older I get! I can't trust my friends. Everyone at church sucks. Why *wouldn't* my dad be the killer? That's the kind of luck I've been having! Uncle Robert is a killer! The State pays him to kill people and everything! Maybe I should be a killer, too? Maybe that's what life is all about! Kill or be killed!"

Thomas let me rant. He didn't interrupt me. Didn't tell me I was wrong or shut me down. He didn't scold me like Pastor Asa would have. Didn't tell me I ought to be ashamed of myself for how I was talking or lecture me like Pastor Gracie used to whenever I got out of control.

Instead, he listened, and when I had gotten every last twisted, violent, mind-splitting emotion out of my system, he placed his hand on my sandy shoulder.

Then something happened.

Something magical or supernatural or spiritual.

As soon as he placed his hand on me, I started feeling better.

Much better.

The sting of anger I had been feeling softened.

It felt like Thomas was taking the sharp edges of my pain away.

Or maybe he was *sharing* the pain so that I wouldn't have to carry the burden of how I felt all by myself.

I calmed down. Felt at peace. I wished we could sit on the beach and gaze at the sea forever.

Then, after a long moment, he asked, "What are you seeking?"

What was I seeking? Did he mean, what was I looking for, or what did I want to do next?

I didn't know. To maintain my high score on Frogger? To find my biological father? To walk into church without my stomach knotting up and my heart sinking down beneath my liver? To have one—*just one!*—friend that wouldn't stab me in the back?

"I would like to be your friend," he offered.

I stared up at him—*was he reading my mind?*

He smiled brightly as if to say, *yup!*

He suggested, "We could hit the ferris wheel, get salt water taffy, and catch the Def Leppard cover band at the gazebo?" listing my favorite activities.

"Definitely!" I agreed, as I jumped to my feet. "I just have to grab my shirt and shoes!"

THE EXECUTIONER

WARDEN CROMWELL started yelling before I could even shut the door.

"What in the name of sweet, baby Jesus were you thinking! Christ, Robert! You executed Kowalski with your goddamn bare hands like you were back in Vietnam! How in the holy hell do you expect me to explain what you did to the governor? This whole situation is beyond comprehension!"

I wasn't going to be able to talk my way out of this. What I had done—broken Kowalski's neck—was indefensible. But, quite frankly, so was lethal injection as a method of execution unless a medically trained professional was in the death chamber. What the hell did the State think was going to happen? I had never executed a medical procedure before! Digby had given me a crash course and his pamphlet hadn't cut it!

"Incompetent!" Cromwell muttered.

I took it on the chin, but remained on the opposite side of his office, my hand resting on the doorknob so I could make a fast escape if need be.

"Word has gotten around the prison, you know," he informed me from where he was seated on the business side of his desk. "All of death row is terrified of you. Oppal has refused lethal injection, did you know that?"

I did. I had revised Oppal's paperwork to include Oppal's request to be hanged in the gallows instead of being executed by lethal injection, so I knew that Cromwell had signed off on it.

Ordinarily, it was easy to forget that Cromwell wasn't a sizable man. He usually came across larger than life. The creases in his face and crow's feet around his eyes caused his expression to look severe, intimidating, almost formidable. But in moments like this, the warden appeared as petite as he truly was at barely five-six. He slumped in his chair, at a genuine loss for how he could possibly characterize the current fiasco so that the higher-ups wouldn't demand his resignation.

"Thank God the governor wasn't in the viewing gallery to see that disgraceful nightmare." He shook his head, disgusted with me, and added, "I don't see how this disaster is going to blow over."

"I couldn't find the femoral—"

"Artery?" he interjected, thoroughly sick of hearing the same excuse. "Doped-up street junkies who are mentally on the moon can find each other's God damned arteries, Robert, and they do it in the *dark*, so don't give me that crap!" Rubbing his hand down his face didn't relieve his frustration one bit. "The question is, what am I going to do with you? There are consequences. There have to be… not that the Vaughn protocol guidelines specifically address this sort of thing…"

I wasn't going to fight him. A suspension sounded good right about now. I had already been drinking myself into the ground since I had messed up astronomically. I couldn't bring myself to eat at the same table as Seth, and the idea of looking Crystal in the eye made me cower, which was why I hadn't stopped by Mermaids.

I hadn't seen her *at all*…

…and I wasn't sure if I ever would again, that was how mortified I was.

Cromwell cursed under his breath and muttered, "It's not like I can replace you…"

"CO McKay seems ready."

"CO McKay is barely out of diapers and he thinks with his pecker and reacts with his balls," he snapped, dismissing the suggestion. "I'm going to have to come up with something, run it up the chain of command, see what the higher-ups say. At least Oppal is set to hang. You've done enough of those that I'll trust you not to screw it up."

"Thank you, Sir," I said even though the last thing I wanted was to put another inmate to death twenty calendar days from now.

He dismissed me and began grumbling under his breath how this prison was going to be the death of him. Found a bottle of booze in his desk drawer and twisted off the cap.

I left him to drink in private. I could do the same in my own office, but first I had to walk through Death Row and pass the inmates' cells. The inmates might have been locked behind steel doors with nothing but a narrow slot to peek through, but Oppal, Prinkerton, and Olson would be able to recognize the sounds of my boots striking linoleum. They knew my gait. They were familiar with my stride, the swish of my uniform slacks.

They had heard what I had done to Kowalski.

Ever since the botched execution, whenever I passed through Death Row, the corridor fell into an eerie silence, as if I was the grim reaper himself coming to steal their souls.

Just as I expected, when I buzzed through the locked door and began walking down the corridor, Prinkerton stopped playing his bluesy harmonica tune. Former pig farmer, Gary Olson, didn't fall silent like the rest. Instead, he shouted nonsense like a madman about the State's conspiracy to torture inmates to death. According to the insanity he was spouting today, the governor had planted me at Vaughn to violate the inmates' human rights.

I was prepared to let him think what he wanted.

Pastor Asa, who was seated on his stool as usual, glanced up over his shoulder at me as I approached. The pastor was ministering to Oppal since he was the next inmate who would be put to death. Asa's bible was open and resting on his lap. His pointed finger was holding his place. He acknowledged me with a nod, but I could see fear behind his light eyes… and, if I wasn't mistaken, he seemed to regard me with a glimmer of reverence.

If that was the case, his reverence was misplaced. Badly.

I had no interest in attempting to wrap my head around that one. Pastor Asa had never seen a man put to death at Vaughn before. Kowalski had been his first execution. I guessed it had impressed him, or—and this was far more likely—Pastor Asa was chomping at the bit to save my soul. Thanks to what he had witnessed from the viewing gallery, Asa now had firsthand knowledge that I was just as violent and dangerous as the inmates on Death Row.

I was a sinner.

But I sincerely hoped he wasn't going to attempt to turn me into a saint…

I wasn't in the mood to talk so I kept walking, giving him only the smallest greeting, slightly waving my hand, before I broke eye contact and passed by him.

From behind the steel door separating them, Oppal asked, "Would you read a passage about how sweet little boys are, Pastor?"

I sensed more than saw Pastor Asa grimace. It was no secret what Oppal had done to earn himself a spot on Death Row. He had killed a number of little boys after doing the unthinkable to them. The pastor had his work cut out for him with Oppal if he wanted to put him on the path to salvation, that was for damn sure, and he knew it.

CO Lyle McKay buzzed himself into the corridor two seconds after Pastor Asa had resumed reading his scriptures out loud, "'Lord, *make me to know my end and what is the extent of my days; Let me know how transient I am'...*"

Walking briskly, CO McKay blew past me and got right in the pastor's face.

"I'm sick of hearing that crap! All this bible-thumping is a waste! Go push your religion somewhere else!" he spat, angling over the pastor with such intensity that I ended up pulling him away.

"Leave him be," I ordered as I pushed McKay back, having gotten between them.

The pastor was crouched defensively on his little stool, while steam shot out of CO McKay's ears.

"Let's have a talk," I barked.

As I moved McKay up the corridor, passed through the buzzing door, and neared my office, McKay complained, "It's been all day and night with that pastor. He's coddling the scum of the earth. I'm sick of hearing it."

"You don't have a say in the matter," I reminded him, "and you're going to get yourself into trouble if you get hostile like that again. I've already warned you about this—"

"I don't trust a man who volunteers to spend all of his time with murderers."

"And yet here you are," I pointed out. He hardly appreciated the comparison. Getting down to brass tacks, I changed the subject to what I really wanted to talk about. "Oppal put in a request to be hanged, and Cromwell approved it. I would like to start training you. I won't be here forever. Sooner or later, I'm going to have to pass the torch."

CO McKay gaped at me, alarmed, and blurted out, "I don't want your job. Kowalski's execution was a total disaster. No way in hell am I going to sign up for that."

I HAD SUCKED down six beers and there weren't enough SpaghettiOs in all of Woodland Beach, much less my kitchen, to sop up the puddle of alcohol that was sitting in my stomach. I had no intention of slowing down, either. Night had fallen and the only way I wasn't going to keep cracking beers open, one after the next, and chugging them down was if I passed out. In the murky haze of my loose thinking, it sounded like a plan.

I couldn't seem to get drunk, however, not in the way I was aiming for. I wanted that warm glow to wash over me, the kind that made me feel like everything was going to be okay. I used to be able to conjure the feeling after only a few drinks. Nowadays, no matter how hard I chased that feeling, it evaded me.

At least, I *thought* I wasn't drunk. I realized how inebriated I really was, though, when Seth barreled into the house, having been God knows where doing God knows what until nine o'clock at night.

I tried not to stagger as I got out of my recliner to have a look at him. His legs were caked with beach sand, his face was sun-kissed more than usual, and unless I was seeing things, I was pretty sure he had a black eye.

"Where have you been?" I barked so that I wouldn't slur.

"Around town with my new friend Thomas," he cheerfully reported.

"What happened to your eye?"

"Oh, this? It's nothing," he said, avoiding the question. I allowed it. The cops hadn't called. That was all that mattered at this point. "Something smells good. Did you make SpaghettiOs?" he asked as he wriggled his tennis shoes off and skipped into the kitchen.

I followed him and watched as he helped himself to a big bowl of pasta and rambled about some new friend named Thomas. Apparently, his friend Thomas knew everything there was to know about Woodland Beach, Delaware, salt water taffy, and the bible.

I stopped listening after that.

He had made a friend, which meant that he had actually *exceeded* my expectations…

I hadn't seen that one coming…

"Maybe this Thomas kid will keep you out of trouble," I said, which was my way of ending the conversation.

An hour later, I lumbered up the stairs, leaving my nephew with the television remote control. We had been watching Magnum P.I. but the plot was lost on me.

"Night, Uncle Robert!" he called out after me.

When I reached my bed, I passed out on top of the covers with my clothes on. But I woke up in the dead of night and couldn't get back to sleep. Kicking my boots off, undressing, and climbing properly into bed didn't help.

Tossing and turning, I flipped my pillow over again and again whenever I felt too hot, but it was no use.

Irritated, I jumped in the shower, thinking that the steaming water would relax me, but it had the opposite effect. I returned to my bedroom feeling downright invigorated.

The clock on the nightstand read 1:13 am.

Mermaids closed at two…

Crystal was on the schedule most Friday nights…

Making a snap decision, I threw on some clothes, made sure I had my wallet, and tiptoed out of the house so I wouldn't wake up Seth.

I hoped Crystal wouldn't hate me now that she had seen for herself what I was capable of—killing a man with my bare hands—but I also knew that if she did, I deserved it.

WHEN I WALKED into Mermaids, stepping out of the balmy night and into the shadowy anteroom of the strip club, the music was booming and I was sober.

One of the dancers was standing behind a little counter where the manager usually worked. She collected the cover charge from customers like myself. She had big hair and a bad attitude. Wearing only a red, string bikini and lipstick to match, she popped bubblegum and barely acknowledged me as she took the bills I was offering.

"Crystal dancing tonight?"

"Sure," she said dryly. She flicked her heavily made-up eyes at me and handed me five bucks change in the form of one-dollar bills. "Need me to break big bills?"

I told her I was fine for the time being and started for the club, as two dancers poured out through the velvet curtains, bypassing me. I had seen both of them here before. The Amazonian and the Asian. Their names might have been Miracle and Destiny, but I wasn't certain. For some reason, they gave me pause.

Miracle tried to hand the disgruntled stripper behind the counter a twenty. "Break this."

"Only customers can break bills with me. Company policy. Sorry."

"No one likes you, New Jewel," said the Asian, narrowing her eyes at the suspicious woman.

"I'm not *New* Jewel," she griped. "I'm *Jewel* and I'm not going to get into trouble with Jimbo for you."

Miracle corrected her, "Only *Original* Jewel is just *Jewel.*"

"Yeah, well, Original Jewel isn't here, is she?"

"Whose fault is that?" Destiny accused.

"Break the damn bill," Miracle demanded, but New Jewel folded her arms and held her head high in refusal.

Before they could get into a cat fight over it, I opened my wallet, counted out twenty ones as I neared them, and said, "I can make change for you."

All three of them melted. Smiled up at me with smoldering gazes. Oozed against me.

"How you doing tonight, sugar?"

"I like these strong arms, honey, do you work out?"

"You want a dance, baby?"

I plucked the twenty out of Miracle's hand and she took the bills I had offered.

"Where are you going, sexy?" Destiny called out after me, as I finally pulled the curtain aside and entered the club where a saxophone melody whirled through the air like smoke.

The long bar counter glowed. The T-shaped stage sparkled, poles catching the light. The stripper on stage was Crystal. Her skin gleamed with sweat as she twirled around one pole then the next, using the whole stage to dance, her blonde hair clinging to her cheeks and her shoulders as she moved. Her legs were long and toned. Watching her got me stirring.

As I eased deeper into the club, making my way to one of the tables near the stage so I could enjoy a closer view of her, I noticed the other dancers complaining.

"Where the hell is Original Jewel?"

"Please, girl, she probably knows she's as good as fired for not showing up *five* shifts in a row. Why would she come now?"

"I can't stand how smug New Jewel has been about this!"

"I know! Can you believe that she actually thinks we're going to start calling her *Jewel*?"

"Only *Original* Jewel is just *Jewel*," she agreed before all of them saw me sit down.

In an instant, the strippers enveloped me.

One slid onto my lap and the other wrapped her perfumed arms around me from behind and whispered in my ear:

"Hey, good-looking, you want a two-dollar lap dance?"

"Or we could go straight to a private room?" cooed the woman who had sat on me.

"Sorry, ladies, I already have my favorite," I told them, indicating Crystal who was twirling effortlessly on stage.

Frowning, they gave up, left me, and began making the rounds, soliciting one customer then the next throughout the club in the same aggressive manner.

I didn't *watch* Crystal.

I *marveled* at her.

She was beautifully acrobatic. When she spun around the pole, her stilettoed feet didn't touch the floor. She kept her toes pointed in those heels. Her movements were balletic, as she took flight and touched down, over and over again. Her dancing was classy and graceful. She had rhythm. She swayed her hips, at times closing her eyes and breathing deeply. She was enjoying herself up there. And she had my undivided attention.

The memory of spending the night with her came rushing back—the smell of her hair, the taste of her skin, the way she had felt.

I couldn't completely believe it had happened, but it had. My bedsheets still held her scent. Maybe that was why I hadn't been able to fall asleep…

Maybe that was why I was here… I wanted to be with her again.

But I also wasn't sure what to make of this.

Was she a working girl? A seasoned pro? She hadn't seemed like one that night. *I had* certainly never paid for a woman's overnight company before. The time we had spent in my bedroom had felt profoundly intimate, but that didn't mean she wasn't in the habit of servicing other men after hours...

Would I care if she was?

Yes, I would care—*a lot*—I decided as I watched her pirouette and fly gorgeously around her dancing partner, the twinkling pole.

As far as I had heard, the authorities still didn't know how Amanda Dover had gotten out on Woodland Beach that night. They hadn't pieced together her final hours. To my knowledge they had zero suspects and though they were aware that she had been stripping here at Mermaids under the stage name Cherry, they hadn't probed the club or properly investigated whether or not one of the customers had done it.

If Cherry had been secretly adding more to the menu than just lap dances, she could have attracted a real psycho. Any other dancers playing the same dangerous game would be risking their lives, too.

I felt suddenly protective towards Crystal, and worried. She shouldn't have propositioned me. She shouldn't proposition anyone! She shouldn't have come home with me. She shouldn't ever go home with anyone! What if she solicited the murderer? That kind of behavior could get her killed!

Had she learned nothing from Cherry?

Had she learned nothing from her own mother?

The song came to an end and I tossed ten bills on the stage to get her attention.

It worked.

As she kneeled down to pick up her cash, she locked eyes with me.

She didn't smile.

For a split second, I wondered if our connection had been broken now that Kowalski was dead.

Once she hopped down from the stage, I waited for her to tuck her bills into her money-bag.

The Asian called Destiny made her way to the pole, fiercely stomping in her stilettos to the beat of the song that was playing through the club.

I moved from the table, ready with cash in my hand, but Crystal was having a hard time looking at me.

A little out of breath. Slick with sweat and devastatingly beautiful. She touched eyes with me.

I wanted to hold her.

"How are you doing?" I asked, my voice weighed down. The full severity of everything that had happened to Kowalski surged to mind. I didn't want any dead air between us so when she said nothing, I explained, "It doesn't usually go like that. I shouldn't have pressured you to come. You probably weren't expecting to see something like that."

Finally, she held my gaze. The expression on her face told me that she couldn't figure out whether I was a man or a monster. "The club's going to close in a few minutes."

If she had meant to be dismissive, I wasn't about to let that stop me. I had driven to the club in the middle of the night for a reason.

"Come to my place again," I said discreetly.

I thought she was going to tell me to go to hell, but she surprised me.

"Same amount?"

I suppressed the grin that was coming over me and promised, "I'll take care of you."

THE STRIPPER

MY BEDROOM WAS stifling. The fan propped in the window was blowing in nothing but hot air. I was seated at my threadbare vanity. Counting cash and wearing a 50s-style, retro bathing suit and flip flops, I had high hopes of hitting the beach in a couple of hours.

It was two in the afternoon, ninety-eight degrees out, and the first day of August, and I had a long list of errands to get done which included making a deposit at the bank, investigating an address in Smyrna, and stopping by Original Jewel's place.

No one had seen Original Jewel at the club in over a week. It wasn't like her, but the girls and I had been keeping our fingers crossed that she was just being irresponsible. Mermaids had been dead all summer. None of us had been making money on stage or on the floor. Why wouldn't Original Jewel say *screw it* and never come back? It wasn't like she had signed a contract. She owed Jimbo nothing, though it would've been considerate of her to at least call Amber to let her know what was up. The two had been tight from the start and if any of us were harboring secret fears about Original Jewel's welfare, it was because Amber didn't have a line on her whereabouts.

I couldn't let myself worry too much about Original Jewel. Not when I was determined to find out who had killed Cherry.

Getting the address in Smyrna—a single clue— hadn't been easy.

The clue itself was the only thing keeping me going at this point.

The police had been doing absolutely nothing about Cherry.

A few days back, I had been foolish enough to stop by the precinct to ask if any of the cops knew who Cherry's boyfriend was. Did they know his name? Had they questioned the guy? But there had been so much red tape that I had quickly given up, suddenly paranoid that one of them might have a hunch I was a prostitute and try to arrest me.

I had established a routine with Robert and it wasn't exactly legal…

After the failed attempt at the police station, I talked to a number of Cherry's customers—not men who had bought lap dances but ladies around Woodland Beach who had paid Cherry to paint their nails. I had learned that Cherry did, in fact, have a boyfriend. His name was Lars. He was from Sweden and sang lead in a Queen cover band that often played at the gazebo on the weekends. I didn't like the sound of any of that, and when one of the bartenders at Foster's mentioned that Lars lived on Woodland Beach Road near the airport, my gut told me that paying him a visit could lead to solid information about who had taken Cherry's life. Part of me suspected Lars had killed her.

The exact address had been relatively easy to pinpoint since there weren't too many residents listed in the telephone book named "Lars" who lived on that particular side of the airport. When I had discovered Lars Svensson's address in the phone book, I had every reason to believe he was the no-good boyfriend that Jimbo had eluded to weeks prior.

Of course, I had no idea what I was going to do other than spec the area out, perhaps follow Lars if he was heading out, and look for clues… I was no detective, but I had obtained Lars' address, which meant that I had accomplished more than the Woodland Beach police. I had every reason to keep going.

It was something to focus on. It took my mind off the paranoia I had been feeling based on what I had been up to with Robert. Honestly, I loved our late-night rendezvous, but I didn't love that I had turned into my mother. I tried to tell myself that Robert was a good man, but the justification was thin, if not wishful thinking. I didn't know anything about Robert in the grand scheme of things.

What I had been doing with him was illegal, dirty, and dangerous.

Hell, I had seen Robert kill Kowalski with his bare hands. If anything, messing around with him was even *more* dangerous than whatever Cherry had done that had resulted in her murder.

From time to time, the possibility that Robert had killed her slammed into me.

I couldn't handle the thought, though, and I had been doing a soldierly job of not thinking about it. But the image of Robert breaking Arthur's neck crept in from time to time, which put into question what Robert might be capable of.

He had killed Arthur without thinking twice. Could he do the same to a woman?

After what I had seen at the prison, I wasn't so sure…

When Robert and I got together, I couldn't tell if I was sleeping with my hero—the man who had avenged my mother's murder—or with an animal who was capable of killing without discretion or emotion.

If I could just forget the good memories I had of Arthur and only remember how he had left my mother in a bloody heap on the kitchen floor, I might be able to believe that justice had been served, and move on.

But it was impossible.

I hadn't touched the cardboard box that Pastor Asa Asbury had given me at the prison. It contained Kowalski's belongings and had felt so light when I had finally picked it up. I hadn't been able to bring myself to throw it in a dumpster. After seeing Arthur put to death in the most unexpected way imaginable, I didn't have it in me to throw away his stuff.

At my vanity, I stopped counting my cash. I had organized the bills into piles of ones, fives, tens, and twenties. I leaned back and glanced at the cardboard box. It was sitting on top of my dresser. How could a man fit his whole life into such a small box?

The sight of it was too sad. There was no way I would be able to go through the contents without breaking down. I had hated Arthur at times. But I had also loved him deep down. To this day, loving Arthur felt like nursing a broken arm.

Years ago, I had written him a letter, and before mailing it, I had decided to enclose an old holiday photograph of the three of us—my mother, Arthur, and me. A happy memory.

My heart had been softer back when I was twenty-one. I had thought writing Arthur at the prison was a good idea. Well, back then I had been fearlessly optimistic about my future. I had decided one morning that the universe wasn't going to make all of my dreams come true if I harbored hatred in my heart for anyone, even my mother's killer.

Finding the emotional strength at twenty-one years old to forgive Arthur for what he had done to my mother had been a Herculean feat, but after wrestling with my conscience and crying, I had forced myself to put pen to paper and wrote him a letter.

But I hadn't been able to tell him that he was forgiven. I hadn't been able to get the words down. I had barely been able to write three sentences.

Looking back, maybe I hadn't really forgiven him. Maybe I had been drunk with delusions of grandeur, desperate to turn into the woman I'd always hoped to become, a normal, sensible, valuable person. I had devised a sort of quid-pro-quo to attain it. Forgive Arthur and reap the blessings that were supposed to follow. That was my logic. But my logic had been wrong.

The result of having mailed the letter with the Christmas photo had not been the dream come true I had expected, and that was the worst blow of all.

In the years that followed, things fell apart. I flunked out of community college. I lost the apartment I had been living in at the time. I had started sleeping in my car, and before winter hit, I became an exotic dancer at Mermaids.

Just thinking about how badly my life had been derailed made my stomach tighten and my teeth clench. I tore across my bedroom, grabbed the cardboard box off of the dresser, and charged through my apartment, determined to put it someplace out of sight where it wouldn't be able to remind me of things I couldn't stand.

The living room was no good. The kitchen was a joke. There was no room in the bathroom for it so I marched back into my bedroom and shoved it under the bed as far as it would go.

I had a little over five hundred dollars on my vanity.

If I was going to think about anything, it would be that.

AFTER MAKING MY deposit at the bank and swinging by Original Jewel's apartment, which turned out to be a waste of time—I pounded and pounded on the door but she wasn't home—I realized I was running late and wouldn't have time to hit the beach and also investigate the address near the airport before my shift at the club.

I would rather relax on the beach for a few hours than potentially get into a sticky situation with a Swedish man named Lars who had probably killed my friend. I would've decided differently if I wasn't due at Mermaids later tonight, but that wasn't the case.

The beach was gorgeous with clear blue skies and frothy waves rolling up the shore. The sun on my skin instantly put me in a good mood. It was crowded, but I navigated my way across the sand, walking carefully in-between sunbathers who were stretched out on towels. Kids were running about, playing games.

I found the perfect spot, spread my beach towel out, and sat down.

But as I got situated, removing my cut-off shorts and lathering sunscreen on my arms and legs, I started to feel mildly creeped out…

…like someone was watching me.

NIGHT HAD FALLEN, but the air was no less humid than it had been all afternoon.

The temperature was downright oppressive and I didn't expect to find any relief inside Mermaids. Jimbo had been too cheap to spring for a new air conditioning system. Said the girls looked better a little dewy. If you asked me, we closely resembled wet racoons, but Jimbo wasn't convinced. He argued that his mermaids had never looked sexier.

That was how we all knew he had been drinking…heavily…

…but then again, so had we, and five burnt pots weren't about to call the biggest kettle *black*.

Having parked my clunker behind the club, I walked to the front where Jimbo was dragging a humongous sandwich board out onto the sidewalk, an electrical cord trailing after it. The cord suddenly went taut, jerking Jimbo back. He didn't fight it, but rather set the sign down and flipped the switch.

The thing lit up like a perverted Christmas tree.

Neon pink flashing—*LIVE!*

Neon blue flashing—*NUDE!*

Neon green flashing—*GIRLS!*

What… the…hell?

Jimbo didn't stop to catch his breath even though he had overexerted himself. He shook his fist at the police cruiser that had been permanently parked in front of the club, and as two uniformed officers climbed out, staring in disbelief at the sign, he yelled:

"You think I'm going to stand for the county revoking my liquor license?! You know what I found out at the *law library* today? My girls can dance *fully nude* now! You know why? Because my club *isn't serving alcohol!* That's the *law*, you sons of bitches! You tell the Kent County commissioner he can take his liquor license and shove it up his ass! I'm back, baby! Back in business better than ever! I bet you the governor didn't count on *that!*"

Upping the ante, Jimbo flipped them the bird.

The cops weren't pleased.

But their horrified reaction was nothing compared to how the girls took the news.

"The club has gone full nude!" Jimbo enthusiastically informed us. "Company policy!"

"You think I'm going to take my G-string off and let those lousy tippers get an eyeful of my privates?!" said Miracle, flying into a hot rage once we had all gathered around Jimbo in the ladies' dressing room.

Even Timbo had squeezed in, alarmed.

"No one's getting a look between my legs!" Amber asserted.

Then New Jewel pushed forward and yelled, "I might be a stripper, but I have standards! I'm not taking my panties off, either!"

"Shut up, New Jewel!" Destiny snapped, "No one likes you!"

Jimbo had asked New Jewel to replace Original Jewel's shifts since, in his opinion, Original Jewel had effectively quit.

"But I'm on your side!" New Jewel insisted. "I'm one of you now!"

Destiny balked at that. "How do we know *you* aren't the reason Original Jewel has been a no-show? Huh?"

"My mermaids!" Jimbo hollered, getting our attention. "Original Jewel is out of the picture! New Jewel is here to stay! Call her *Jewel!* Now!" he sang, as he clapped his hands together, "I've decided to discontinue the discounts!"

Finally, news that was actually good.

"I've quadrupled all the prices!" he told us. "Full nude is reserved for the stage and the private rooms! Which means, drumroll please... The cost of the private rooms is now a hundred bucks, does that sound good?"

"A hundred bucks to be with a naked girl in a private room?" Miracle asked. "Jimbo, they're going to think we're hookers."

Jimbo was hardly fazed. "Timbo and I are doing a great deal of promotion!" he added, emphasizing the potential earnings on the horizon. "We are now the one-and-only *all nude* club in Delaware! No other strip clubs within one hundred miles are featuring completely nude dancers! Mermaids is going to attract gentlemen from all over! Pretty soon, there'll be more money in this club than any of you will know what to do with!"

I doubted that.

Shaking my head and reading the temperature in the room, I argued, "This is going to draw in some seriously twisted perverts."

"I don't like your negativity," Jimbo replied, a bit indignant for my taste.

Timbo wasn't sure who to side with, his cousin or the woman he had fallen in love with, who was now expected to flash her clam for clams.

"We have no idea who killed Cherry. It could've been a customer," I pointed out. "Now Original Jewel is missing in action. We've been in enough danger—"

"Hey!" he warned, pointing his finger in my face. "What happened to Cherry had nothing to do with this club—"

"You don't know that!"

"And Original Jewel," he went on, bulldozing straight over my objection, "is just trying to punish me for her financial losses. We've all taken a hit from the county. But did I roll over and take it? No! I hit back, and I hit them where it hurts! Now, you're all going to get up on that stage and take everything off except your high heels! That's how we win this fight!"

"Are you listening to yourself?" I yelled.

"Are *you* listening to me?" he shot back. "I just told you that you'll earn a hundred bucks in the private rooms. You think big tips won't follow? They will!"

"You will have *no idea* what goes on in the private rooms," I sneered, getting right up in his face as well.

"You think I won't?" he challenged.

I shook my head. "This isn't safe, Jimbo."

I needed a drink.

I tore around him, shoved my way through the girls then squeezed in-between Timbo and Miracle, and bolted out of the dressing room.

I wasn't quite put together. I had pulled a thong bikini bottom on, but hadn't changed out of my regular lace bra yet. It was black and the club was dark, lit with Jimbo's signature bluish lights. At least I had my stilettos on.

I knew where Timbo kept the emergency vodka so after blowing through the lounge, I rounded behind the long bar counter, opened a cabinet, and grabbed the damn bottle. I slugged down as much as I could.

Was I going to stay here and take *all* my clothes off? Did I have it in me to spin around a pole completely nude? Would I have the energy to manage the unwanted advances that were guaranteed to happen in the private rooms the second I got fully naked with a customer?

Was this the beginning of the end?

I drank more vodka then startled at the blaring sound of Timbo announcing my name through the

PA system—*Crystal to the stage. Crystal? To the stage, please.*

"I'm right here!" I glared at him.

He had snuck in at the opposite side of the long bar counter. The girls emerged from the dressing room and dispersed across the floor. Jimbo crossed the club and started chatting up a customer who had pulled his chair to the very edge of the stage, eager to watch the show.

Timbo returned the microphone to his mouth but I shot him a look that said I would kill him if he tried to rush me. He lowered the mic.

I drank more vodka. It burned, but helped. I gulped it down, wincing as it stung my throat.

As Jimbo cut through the club, making a beeline to the anteroom where customers were lining up to pay the cover, I returned the bottle to the cabinet, marched out from behind the bar, and climbed up onto the stage.

Two seconds later, I felt dirty and I hadn't even taken my outfit off yet.

The popular Madonna song that had been playing on low was replaced with a loud punch of music. *Addicted to Love* started booming through the speakers. That was my cue, but I was lost.

I couldn't see the customers in the lounge, the lights were so bright, which should have helped me suck it up and strip. But it didn't matter that I couldn't see the men out there. They could see me, and more of them were piling in from the anteroom.

I knew I wasn't going to be able to go fully nude.

A man in the front whistled and yelled, "Take it off, baby!" but I was already hopping down from the stage, already running towards the dressing room, already visually plotting how I was going to get out of Mermaids without Jimbo making a big stink about it.

In the ladies' dressing room, I flew into a blind panic, collecting my things. Once I had my giant stripper bag slung over my shoulder, I raced to the emergency exit door at the very back of the ladies' dressing room.

I knew the alarm would be triggered the moment I pushed the bar, but I couldn't face Jimbo in the front of the club. This was the only way.

I slammed into the exit door, triggering the alarm system, and spilled out into the sticky night, the deafening siren filling all of Woodland Beach.

Jimbo was not going to forgive me for this, but I didn't care.

Cherry was dead. My mother had been killed. Original Jewel was missing. I had become a prostitute with a man who was used to taking lives.

If I had stayed at Mermaids and gotten buck-naked up on stage, I knew it would've sealed my fate.

Running away, however, would change everything for the better…

…or so I hoped.

I didn't know it at the time, but the moment I had bailed on Mermaids that night, I started down a collision course that would ultimately cost me my life.

❋

THE ADDRESS IN Smyrna where I understood Lars Svensson lived was a lone beach house directly across from the airport, and about eighteen miles from the Delaware Bay where Cherry had been murdered. By the looks of it, I had to wonder if a past hurricane had dislodged the house from the nearby nautical mile and deposited it here. That's how badly out of place it looked smack dab in the industrial side of town.

I had driven here straight from the club, knowing that if I had gone home, I would have felt too disturbed to sleep.

In my car, I found a tank top and my cut-off shorts in my stripper bag, wriggled into both, then climbed out. An airplane took off overhead. I threw on my heeled sandals next and locked my sedan.

That's when I noticed the weathered couch in front of Lars' beach house. I realized there were shadowy figures lounging on the couch. People who had watched me emerge from my car.

When the overhead aircraft disappeared, I heard a Euro-pop song playing. The song was coming from a master blaster boombox near the men on the couch. There were five guys, total—maybe they lived with Lars at the beach house or maybe they were members of his band. Perhaps they were both. I saw more spiked dog collars and gelled mohawks than I would've liked.

One of them had to be Cherry's boyfriend.

As I approached them, it wasn't lost on me that I hadn't thought any of this through. It was late.

This wasn't a populated street. No one would hear me scream if they decided to attack me.

"Guys, look, we have company," said a mohawked Swede who was sitting on the arm of the couch. He wore zebra-print pants and a faded Tears for Fears tee-shirt. He had a thick accent and, I soon realized, a pit bull on a leash. The dog snarled at me, lifting up from its haunches.

"Hello," he said, greeting me in a way I didn't trust.

The one sitting closest to the boombox turned the volume down and that was when things got really scary.

"I'm looking for Lars Svensson," I said. "I'm a friend of Cherry's."

I glanced from one man to the next, hoping that Lars would identify himself.

He didn't.

One of them told me, "Lars is inside."

I might as well have hit a dead end, because I was not about to venture into that dark house.

"Could you ask him to come outside?"

"A friend of Cherry's, huh?" another one asked.

"You heard what happened to her?" his friend said.

"That's why you're here?" asked the first guy.

I hesitated, unsure if they were curious or offended.

"Yeah," I said.

"Lars is devastated," another one told me.

"So am I," I offered, thinking I could appeal to them.

"He's in the kitchen."

They weren't going to get him for me. If I wanted to talk to Lars, I would have to suck it up and go inside the house. I didn't want to.

"He won't bite."

"Do you know if the police talked to him?" I asked.

The mohawked man on the armrest loosened his grip on the leash he had been holding, and the pit bull lunged. My heart shot up my throat. It didn't matter that the dog was feet away or that the chain yanked him back.

He told me, "My dog doesn't like people who assume the boyfriend did it."

"I didn't assume—"

"Yes, you did," he said, reading me accurately.

"Have the police talked to *anyone*?" another one complained.

"No, they haven't," I answered, launching into rambling mode, I was so nervous. "The police should be talking to everyone, but they're not. I'm Cherry's friend and I didn't know she was seeing Lars. He might know more than anyone at this point, and I'm not saying that because I suspect him—"

"No one's stopping you from talking to him. The door is right there."

"Right," I said in a small voice.

It was time to push myself forward.

For a terrifying second, I envisioned all of them piling in behind me, trapping me in the house, and killing me, but I put one foot in front of the other and kept moving despite my fear.

I pulled the screen door open and entered the dimly lit beach house. The kitchen was to my immediate right, but I paused. There were even more people inside—punk rock chicks and shirtless guys with stars drawn in eyeliner across their cheeks, lounging about.

I realized there was only one man in the dingy kitchen where dishes were piling up in the sink. Cigarette smoke hung in the air.

The man looked languid. He was seated backwards on a chair with his forearms draped over a table that looked more like driftwood than furniture. His platinum hair was limp and hung down the side of his head, the other side of his head had been shaved. He looked like he was dressed for a show, but something told me his friends weren't going to be able to drag him anywhere.

"Lars?" I asked.

"Who wants to know?"

"I'm Crystal, a friend of Cherry's."

At the mention of his deceased girlfriend, he seemed to bristle.

Highly suspicious of me, he asked, "What do you want?"

"The cops haven't arrested anyone. They obviously don't know what they're doing," I explained. "I was working with Cherry at Mermaids and last week another dancer went missing."

He perked up at that. Pushed away from the table. Appraised me as if he might be able to work out my true motives if he sized me up long enough. *Maybe this woman wasn't here to accuse me.* I took his change in demeanor as an invitation and sat down across from him.

"Cherry was working the night she was killed. I wasn't," I went on. "Did you see her that night? There's a three-hour hole I'm trying to fill in."

He snorted out a strange sounding laugh. "You're not a cop."

"Were you with her?"

He slumped darkly and breathed, "No."

I waited.

"She broke up with me. Didn't have a reason for it." He let out another defeated laugh. "Something about church. I knew what she did for a living… at that club. She acted like I was the same kind of poison. You should talk to her parents."

"I tried. It didn't go well or last long." After a beat, I questioned, "You really didn't see her?"

"She dumped me."

"When?"

"Look, I didn't even know her name was Amanda Dover, alright? I don't know anything about her, and I don't know anything about what happened to her that night. It's like I fell in love with a mirage."

He stared at me. Screwed his face up.

"Three days before Cherry was killed," he told me. "That's when I saw Cherry last."

A faraway look filled his eyes.

"This past spring," he went on, "I met her for the first time at one of my shows. When I found out she was stripping, she warned me not to go to Mermaids and I didn't." He shrugged. "I never knew her. She was far wilder than I ever was. I could barely keep up."

"Wild, how?"

He shook his head, which led me to believe that he had never been able to comprehend Cherry.

"Wild like she had the devil inside of her."

I was suddenly filled with a very bad feeling…

…but only because I often sensed that the devil was living inside of me, too.

THE BOY

HAVING A FRIEND like Thomas was out of this world, and Thomas wasn't just my *friend*. He was my *best* friend.

He could read my mind, walk on water, and appear and disappear like magic.

Together, we palled around Woodland Beach and had all kinds of adventures. We fished at the pier, gorged ourselves on fried chicken, and lazed around the drive-in most nights, though we rarely agreed on what movie to watch. Thomas didn't like blood and gore so the horror films I was itching to see were put on hold in favor of us watching tamer flicks like *Ferris Bueller's Day Off* and *Pretty in Pink*. I was willing to allow it. Just because we were best friends didn't mean we had to agree on *everything*.

I introduced him to Motley Crue, Guns N' Roses, and Judas Priest, fitting my Walkman over his ears and insisting that the guitar riffs and heavy hooks of my favorite bands were evidence of the emerging musical genius of the early- to mid-80s. It was surprising to me that he hadn't heard of any of them, and it was even more surprising to me that he preferred hymnal songs and the sounds of the wind and ocean to anything I could find on a cassette tape, but that was Thomas for you. Quirky, cheerful, weirdly innocent, and wise.

He was so *wise*, and that wasn't a term I used lightly or often.

No matter what adventures we found ourselves in, Thomas had a knack for relating our experiences to the greater meaning of life. When we found a driver's license on the beach and went on a mission to find its owner, Thomas taught me the importance of treating others how I would like to be treated. When we found ourselves in a competition to see who could collect the most seashells, Thomas reminded me of the tenth commandment. And when I snuck back into the Galaxy Arcade to reclaim my high score on Frogger, Thomas appeared from out of nowhere and yanked me outside before the arcade manager could have me arrested.

There was no better friend in the world to have than Thomas from the sea!

And the thing of it was that Thomas really did know about *life*. He knew how to live life to the fullest and to live it with a sense of humor. He was always laughing. He also felt things deeply, but nothing rattled him. I intuitively sensed that he had seen it all. He knew pain, but he was so incredibly strong. He liked to say that God was everywhere and existed in all things, including other people, even mean people. This was how he weathered any storm. He believed a larger plan was always at work, and he trusted the Heavenly Father no matter what.

If Pastor Gracie hadn't told me otherwise, I would've been about 99% convinced that my new friend was the actual Son of God... But everyone at Lighthouse Ministries kept telling me that the second coming of Christ wasn't due for at least a hundred years, and his return would bring trials and tribulations, not salted pretzels and sunburns...

The kids at church were still teasing me about my biological father's presumed involvement with Dead Amanda Dover, but their taunting chants and sideways glares no longer cut me to the core. When I left Youth Group day after day, I wasn't bogged down with a sinking feeling or searing emotions, because I always had Thomas to look forward to. Like clockwork, we would meet at the beach and no matter what harassment I had undergone while playing kickball or studying the Gospel of Luke with Pastor Asa—who had been acting more and more odd if you asked me—the moment I saw Thomas smiling at me from the frothy water, I felt instantly uplifted.

The only downside, and it wasn't much of one, was that Pastor Gracie suspected my high spirits were the result of marijuana. She thought I was on pot. She didn't believe me when I told her I was excited about life and my new friend Thomas. She had never met him, but she didn't trust the relationship was headed in a healthy direction. Said grown men shouldn't befriend thirteen-year-old boys. She assumed there was something fishy about the whole thing.

From her stringent perspective, she also thought, because she knew my personal history and how my mom had died giving birth to me, that I had nothing to be cheerful about. In the judgmental back-alleys of her fast-working mind, something wasn't adding up quite right if I was in a good mood all the time. There was nothing I could do to convince her otherwise so I let her believe what she wanted. I even peed in a cup.

At the crack of dawn, the Sunday morning of August 7th, I sprang out of bed, delighted for the day ahead. Scratch that. *Delighted* didn't capture the feeling in my heart. I was positively *euphoric* because Thomas had agreed to meet me on the beach. There was nothing like boogie boarding at sunrise when the water was strong and the air felt crisp. But this time, Thomas had promised to bring his surfboards. Said I could use his six-footer. He was going to teach me to pop up and ride swells, something I had always wanted to do but couldn't because Uncle Robert wouldn't buy me a proper surfboard.

I was still expected at church later for children's Sunday School, which would be followed by the regular service at 10:00 am. My new friend had been a real stickler about me keeping up with my church commitments and attending the Sunday worship services at Lighthouse Ministries. I begged Thomas to come with me if he was so big on worshiping the Lord, but he only chuckled and told me he would always be there in spirit.

Think about what you're putting into *that place*, he had once told me. *Think about what everyone else is* getting *as a result of you being there. Your perspective is an important contribution.*

If he had even the slightest clue about Pastor Gracie's attitude towards me, I doubted he would've made such a claim, but I didn't fight him. If he was entitled to his opinion about the *Friday the 13th* franchise, and he *was*, then it would also be his prerogative if he wanted to give that woman the benefit of the doubt, or any of the churchgoers for that matter.

I found my swimming trunks in a tangled heap of sandy clothes on the floor, gave them a good shake, and threw them on, along with a fresh tee shirt, my flip flops, and a ballcap so that the rising sun wouldn't get in my eyes.

Having grabbed a beach towel, I eased my bedroom door open and listened out for signs of life. My uncle was snoring soundly on the other side of his door. Good.

I tiptoed out and walked slowly so that my flip-flops wouldn't smack against my heels.

When I got downstairs, however, all of my efforts to be quiet were ruined—

"Oh!" yelped a woman who was seated on the living room couch.

She clutched her chest and let out a laugh as if she had just survived a heart attack. "You scared the living daylights out of me!" she whispered.

She hadn't expected to encounter me, and I certainly hadn't expected to encounter her.

It looked like she was putting herself together with the aim of slipping out before my uncle got up.

I didn't recognize her face from around town. I had never seen her before—the huge blue eyes, the sadness behind them, her giant mane of blonde, cascading hair. She was wearing a slinky dress and wobbly high heels. I could guess who she was, though. Uncle Robert had gotten in the habit of sneaking out in the middle of the night and returning with a woman. He thought I didn't know.

I knew, and I despised her. She was the reason Uncle Robert had been breaking the seventh commandment.

"You must be Robert's nephew," she said, trying so hard to sound friendly when it was obvious that she was worried I had caught her. "I'm a friend of your uncle's."

I wasn't an idiot.

"You're a heathen," I said, correcting her as sharply as I could. I didn't like her and I didn't want her here. "You're going straight to hell."

The clumsy smile on her face faltered and she looked taken aback.

If I had hurt her feelings, it was her own damn fault.

I had to get out of there before I felt bad for her.

I darted out the door and as I made my urgent way around the outside of the house and down the beach, I forbade myself to feel anything but rage.

Rampaging across cold sand, I cursed her to hell, as sunlight dawned across the horizon in front of me. I couldn't even see how beautiful the morning was, I was so mad.

How dare she!

How dare she corrupt my uncle? Who did she think she was?

What gave her the right to seduce my uncle and ruin his chances of salvation? Uncle Robert had an uphill battle as it was, considering he killed people for a living! The last thing he needed was to get mixed up with the Harlot of Babylon!

"Is that really what you think she's doing?" asked Thomas, startling me. Whenever he suddenly appeared beside me like that, I jumped. I didn't think I would ever get used to it. "You think she's plotting your uncle's damnation?"

"Yes, I do!" I insisted, as I stomped around the shore, furious. I didn't know what to do with myself, I was so mad. "Uncle Robert forces me to go to church, but all the while he's gallivanting around town with a sinner! And don't tell me I should worry about the beam in my own eye before I try to pick the speck out of Uncle Robert's eye! That woman is way bigger than a speck! Plus, they think I have no idea what's going on! I'm not *retarded*!"

"Are you mad at Crystal or are you mad at your uncle?" he asked me, but I suspected he was trying to show off. So what, he magically knew the woman's name. Big deal. Thomas knew all kinds of things I couldn't fathom.

"I'm mad at *you*!" I told him, straight up.

"*Me?*"

"If you're going to stand there and defend her, then yes!" I asserted. "I'm mad at *you*!"

Thomas began to look sorry for me and I didn't appreciate it.

"She doesn't have parents, either, you know," he said.

"Oh, I see!" I said, throwing my hands into the air. "My mom and dad aren't around, and *her* mom and dad aren't around, so I guess we should make nice, share a bowl of granola, and sing Kum Ba-Yah together! Is that it? We have so much in common, we ought to be friends?!"

"Kum-Ba-Yah is my favorite song."

"Don't change the subject!"

He fell silent, which was his best weapon against me. Whenever he went quiet, I felt disarmed. Whatever rage I had been feeling completely defused, without fail, every time. Thomas had *ways* of beating me at my own games. Magical, mysterious, *mute* ways…

I was still fuming, but not at a full boil—my feelings were more like a bubbling simmer—when he said, "Come with me, I want to show you something."

"Unless you're going to show me how to ride a six-foot wave, I'm not interested."

"Just come with me," he nudged, and I couldn't refuse.

We walked along the shore as waves rolled in.

Then he cut up the sand, walking away from the water, and I followed. The dawning sun hadn't reached this side of the beach where the dunes rose up and beachgrass shimmied in the soft breeze.

He led me deeper and deeper into the beachgrass.

Then he stopped and parted the long, waving blades with his hands.

There, lying in the grassy dunes, was the body of a dead woman.

She reminded me of Dead Amanda Dover, who I had discovered three weeks earlier, mainly because, like Dover, this dead woman had the same surprised look on her face.

She was wearing a skimpy dress, similar to the one I had seen Dead Amanda Dover in.

As I studied her, a sickening mix of shock, disgust, and the rawest empathy I had ever felt burned through my chest.

Thomas placed his hand on my shoulder and said, "Crystal needs you, Seth. If you can't set your judgment aside and love her in the way I've taught you, she's going to end up like that."

It felt like an eternity had passed before the shock wore off.

When I glanced up, Thomas was gone, and I was left with another dead body on the beach.

This time, I ran to get the police.

"THIS IS MISSY Chance reporting LIVE from Woodland Beach! I'm standing on Woodland Beach where the body of another young woman was found at approximately 5:58 am this morning, just after dawn! Jewel Payson, known by her closest friends as 'Original Jewel,' had been working at the gentlemen's club, Mermaids! Though Kent and New Castle Counties have been actively working together to shut down the club, it remains in operation, and let me tell you, Andy—and for all of our viewers out there—this club NEEDS to close! Amanda Dover, the first woman who was discovered murdered right here on Woodland Beach, had ALSO been a dancer at Mermaids! Draw your own conclusions, folks! As far as I'm concerned, the connection is plain as day! Now, authorities have advised local residents not to be alarmed. According to police, only 'working girls' are a target and should curtail their at-risk behavior to prevent their own abduction slash murder. I have to say, it's starting to look like we have a serial killer in our midst!

Everyone should stay very alert if venturing down to Woodland Beach! I, for one, am not planning on spending any time along this particular stretch! Scary stuff, Andy! This is Missy Chance reporting LIVE from Woodland Beach! Back to the studio!"

THE LOCAL NEWS reporter, Missy Chance, kept distracting me from the cops' questions, and I was pretty sure I was standing in the background of her cameraman's shot.

Behind me, a yellow police line flapped in the breeze. Beyond the yellow line, the body of Dead Jewel Payson was covered with a sheet. Forensics had cleared the beachgrass and were combing the immediate vicinity for clues, but I could already tell, based on how the cops were looking at me, that I was the most promising piece of evidence they had.

"You said you came out here to surf, so where's your surfboard?" I was asked.

"My friend was supposed to bring two boards for us."

"You were meeting a friend out here?" the first cop asked me.

Before I could answer, the second cop said, "Did he show up?"

"Yes," I told them.

"A kid your age?" the first one assumed.

"No, he's probably thirty or so," I innocently explained. "He's the one who showed me where the body was."

The cops froze and glanced at one another in a way that made me nervous.

It was then that I realized my colossal error.

"Your adult-age, male friend led you up these dunes and showed you the body?" asked the first cop.

"Is he Caucasian? How tall would you say your friend is?"

"Son, can you tell us his name?"

THE MISSIONARY

"CONTINUE PLEASE, Cole, with Verse 36."

"Even though it starts in the middle of the sentence?"

"Walter just read the beginning of the sentence."

"Yeah, I just read the beginning of the sentence."

"'*...and they can no longer die*,'" Cole read out loud, enunciating each word carefully as he hogged the bible he was supposed to be sharing with Judith. "'*for they are like the angels. They are God's children, since they are children of the resurrection.*'"

"What is Luke referring to here when he mentions *children of the resurrection?*" I asked my Sunday School students.

We were gathered around one of the round tables in the fellowship hall. Morning light washed through the room. Judith pulled the bible away from Cole and poured over the gospels in search of an answer, while Sally twisted her crimped hair and Walter squirmed in his chair, stumped.

"The Lord conquered death?" guessed Judith, coming up for air briefly before diving back in.

"He did," I agreed.

"Does it mean that all of us have conquered death, too?" Cole wondered.

Sally rolled her eyes, let out a little huff.

"Sally, would you like to add something?" I asked her.

"We're still going to *die*," she informed her peers. "Everyone *dies*."

"But we'll be resurrected afterwards," Walter reminded her. "Just like our Lord and Savior."

"Will we?" she questioned as she eyed Walter, Cole, and then Judith, who was often disturbed by Sally's reasoning. "I heard that Dead Amanda Dover was saved right here at this very church, and look at what happened to her. She didn't rise up from the grave three days later."

Judith shrank in her seat and Cole went pale, trembling.

"When Luke speaks of us as children of God," I immediately began explaining, "and mentions our belief in the resurrection, he's reminding us of God's promise. Whoever believes in the Lord and in the resurrection of Christ will receive eternal life in heaven."

Sally wasn't satisfied. She was too smart for semantics. "Which means that *death* is still *literal*. People are still going to *die* just like Dead Amanda Dover and just like Dead Jewel Payson."

"Dead Jewel Payson wasn't a believer," Cathy-Anne, a mousy, underweight child whose father owned a dairy farm, added to the discussion, but she didn't seem sure of herself. "Was she?"

"Let's take a step back," I suggested. "Let's define *life* and *death*."

"Life is when you're alive," Sally answered like a know-it-all, "and *death* is when you wind up murdered on Woodland Beach."

Obviously, the topic of conversation had moved away from the Gospel of Luke, so I rushed through defining a few biblical terms before I lost total control of the class.

First, I posed a rhetorical question and supplied the answer. "What do we know about Adam and Eve? We know that they were immortal in the Garden of Eden *until* they disobeyed God by eating fruit from the tree of the knowledge of good and evil, right?"

I was met with a monotone response from all eight of them, "Yes, Pastor Asa."

"And what is disobeying God called?"

"Sin, Pastor Asa," they answered in concert.

"And what is the result of sin?" I asked, pushing the logic through. They knew this. We had been working on defining and recognizing sin all summer. "The result is *separation from God*, otherwise known as *death*."

I let that hang for a moment before I elaborated. Sally looked indignant. She didn't like it when I reiterated concepts we had already gone over thoroughly. She considered herself an expert. But Judith was engaged, and Walter and Cole grew more invested in the lesson. Cathy-Anne, on the other hand, looked queasy.

"The moment Adam and Eve disobeyed God, they had to face the consequences of their actions. The greatest consequence was being separated from God. Another consequence was that they lost their immortality. Meaning that eventually they died a physical death. So, yes, we're talking about physical death, but we're also talking about spiritual death. To commit sin is to forfeit the possibility of spending eternity with God in heaven. Now, God's promise to *us* is that we will be graced with the opportunity to spend our eternal afterlives with him in heaven so long as we ask the Lord to save us, and so long as we believe that Christ died on the cross as a sacrifice to absolve our sins, *and* so long as we *believe in the resurrection.* Amanda Dover, while she certainly suffered a mortal death, did not sustain a spiritual death. She has life everlasting now in heaven."

"Are you sure about that?" Sally challenged. "Your mother doesn't seem to think so."

"Amanda Dover was attending this church, as you all have heard. She was saved," I maintained.

"Pastor Gracie said that Satan got his hands on Dead Amanda Dover," she argued.

"Please stop referring to her as *Dead Amanda Dover.*" I scowled. "Only God the Father, and his Son, and Amanda herself, know whether or not she believed in Christ and was therefore granted eternal life with the Father."

"What about Dead Jewel Payson?" Cathy-Anne asked worriedly, and Judith wasted no time flipping through the Gospel of Luke in a desperate search for answers.

"She wasn't a *member* here," Sally groaned. "She wasn't *saved.*"

"Are *you*?" I sternly countered. "Are any of you? Have you asked yourselves? Have you searched your own hearts?"

The kids quieted, becoming thoughtful and introspective. Even Sally piped down and a little color rose in her cheeks.

"I expect an answer," I told them. "Instead of speculating on the salvation of people you don't know, why don't we go around the table and share with one another our own experiences of Christ. Sally, let's start with you. When did you ask the Lord to save you and why do you trust that he has?"

I didn't like having to be so firm with them. They were teenagers after all, some of them barely thirteen. But if they were old enough to judge the Christian faith of a dead woman, then they were old enough to assess their own beliefs.

As Sally got off to a rocky start, describing the day her aunt passed away and how the ordeal shook her to her core and ultimately led her to trust in the Lord, I couldn't help but think about Arthur Kowalski.

The harrowing truth of the matter was that I hadn't been able to get him off my mind since the execution. Talk about the salvation of a person I didn't know. On the one hand, I wholeheartedly believed that Arthur had been saved by the Lord. He had cried out to Jesus as he had been dragged off to the death chamber. He had asked for forgiveness. He had asked to be saved. Christ wasn't complicated. He didn't look for reasons to *exclude* people from salvation. Quite the opposite, in fact. He was a generous God who constantly searched for any opportunity to uplift a sinner into his holy fold. But I had no way of truly knowing if Arthur had believed in Christ wholeheartedly in his final moments.

And for this reason, I couldn't be sure that I had succeeded in my mission.

I wanted to embrace the victory. I wanted to pat myself on the back, and I had definitely accepted my father's praise and my mother's celebratory, homemade pie—the prison initiative had only just begun and Mom had decided our new family tradition would be to indulge in strawberry rhubarb pie every time I successfully converted an inmate to the Christian faith—but the memory of Arthur writhing in agony on that gurney had spoiled the celebration.

His execution had been utterly horrific.

I had to ask myself how many more executions could I stomach? All of them? How long would I really hold up? Indefinitely? I doubted that.

A mere week from today, Clifford Oppal would face the death penalty. He was the next inmate on Death Row who was scheduled to be executed. Ministering to him thus far had been futile. He was deaf, dumb, and blind, a classic case of a sinner who refused to be saved. Whenever I mentioned Christ and highlighted the Lord's desire to cleanse Clifford of his horrendous crimes, he had argued that dead little boys were beautiful.

Clifford was impossible.

To my recollection, Christ had never attempted to minister to sinners as depraved as Clifford Oppal. If the Messiah hadn't bothered, then why should I?

This wasn't to say that Clifford was a lost cause. But it was to say that I was starting to question whether or not my goal, which was really my parents' goal, was realistic. Just what exactly in God's name did I think I was doing at Vaughn? Whenever Clifford went off on a graphic tangent, I stopped him. But I was never fast enough. A bitter taste had been accumulating in my mouth. I felt filthy.

I could foresee that no amount of Mother's strawberry rhubarb pie would be able to get the horrible taste off my tongue. Did I really want Clifford to enter heaven? I taught kids, for God's sake. The fact that I was living in two different worlds was starting to drive me crazy.

I wanted to save all of the inmates on Death Row. I truly did. I wanted women like Amanda Dover and Jewel Payson to repent and return to the flock, too. I wanted Crystal Swan to turn from her sinful ways—after meeting her at the prison, I had done some digging and had learned that her so-called line of work was identical to the two murdered dancers...

But was I kidding myself?

Was my never-ending mission destined to fail?

I already knew the answer to that perplexing question.

I was a sinner like all the rest. But I was worse, because I was masquerading as a saint while my faith decayed from the inside out.

Interrupting Cathy-Anne, whose testimony had brought her to tears—her father had forced her to behead a chicken last year and unlike Abraham who didn't have to go through with sacrificing his own son, God had *not* intervened in Cathy-Anne's trauma—I told my students:

"It looks like we've run out of time." They immediately jumped up from the table, leaving their bibles where they lay. I called out after them, "You may find your parents in the vestibule, but please do not run! Be respectful of the elderly! Sally, hang on!"

She returned from skipping off with her friends, folded her arms, and frowned at me.

"The other kids look up to you," I said, complimenting her so that she would be receptive to what I had to say next. "Do you think it would be possible to leave your news reports about Amanda Dover and Jewel Payson at the door, and only bring your *Christian* thoughts into the church?"

"No," she informed me, sticking her nose in the air. "There's a serial killer on the loose. Channel 7's Missy Chance says so, and we should all be very, *very* alarmed."

"I would really appreciate your cooperation," I told her, hoping to God it didn't sound like I was pleading. It had, so I changed the subject. "Do you know why Seth wasn't here with us this morning?"

"I have it on good authority that Seth's long, lost biological father is the killer."

"Of course, you do."

She caught me rolling my eyes.

"Don't you watch the news, Pastor Asa? If you did, you would've seen Seth on TV this morning. When Missy Chance was covering the second Woodland Beach murder, Seth was right there in the background!"

"He was?"

Now it was her turn to roll her eyes. "You really should make an effort to keep yourself informed. How else do you expect to relate to people? Everyone is terrified and everyone wants to know what God is planning to do about all of this."

When I reached the vestibule, having excused Sally, I discovered precisely how right she was.

The entire congregation was disturbed. Parishioners were huddled in their respective groups, swapping tidbits about the second dead woman whose body had been found in the grassy dunes. Some churchgoers were clustered around the coffeemaker, trying to make sense of the gruesome details, while others filtered into the sanctuary, passing rumors back and forth, comparing notes, and separating fact from gossip.

I overheard Suzanne whisper to Bethany, "…just like our Cherry."

"Why would the killer try to hide the second body in the dunes when he had left the first one on the beach for the public to see?" wondered Mary-Catherine. Her entourage of co-workers nodded in puzzled agreement from where they all stood in the rear of the sanctuary.

"Pastor Gracie says we've already prayed, and that we must be patient for God to expose the killer, but if you ask me, we haven't prayed enough."

"I'm all for the power of prayer, and Lord knows that where two or more Christians are gathered, the Holy Spirit is there with them, but I've lived in the world long enough to know that God the Father doesn't stop bad things from happening."

"Why were her closest friends referring to her as *Original* Jewel? Is that street slang?"

"I think it's a cocaine term."

"Oh, it's not a cocaine term, Suzanne!"

"I heard *Angel Dust* is a cocaine term, and I find that offensive. Angels are the Lord's messengers, you know."

The ladies of our modest congregation weren't the only ones theorizing why a second stripper had been found dead on the beach. The men from Dad's bible study had their own ideas.

"Shame about Jewel Payson," one of the men said.

"I heard she was in Playboy last year, not that I look at that type of stuff," said another.

"Oh, yeah, I heard she was quite the model, but I don't look at dirty magazines anymore."

"I don't either, but Lord, she had a pair of jugs on her."

"Not that I've ever been to Mermaids, but I heard she was quite the dancer."

"I heard that, too, not that I've ever been."

"Too bad," said the first man, shaking his head.

"What a waste."

"What a waste, indeed… The things I would've done to her, you know, before I came to Christ…"

"My cousin banged her—"

"Jesus, Curt!"

"What?"

I rushed up the aisle, passing parishioners, and joined my tremendous father at the lectern. He was organizing his sermon notes, oblivious to the dark conversations amid the congregation.

"Dad! I really think you're going to have to address what's been happening down on the beach!" I insisted. Of course, my bloodhound mother overheard me. As she excused herself from chatting with a pair of elderly churchgoers, I told Dad, "Everyone's talking about the dead women! We can't gloss over this crisis! You have to address it—"

"I've got it covered," my mother interjected, hissing at me as though I, and not the murdered strippers, was the problem. "I revised his sermon this morning."

"You did?"

"Calm down!" she ordered. "You're making everyone nervous!"

"*I'm* making everyone nervous?"

"Shoo!"

My mother hadn't shooed me since I was twelve years old.

I made my way down into the front pew and took a seat. My father flipped on the lectern microphone and gained the congregation's attention with the opening call to worship, while I held myself together, praying fervently and inwardly.

Once again, I asked the Lord to save my soul.

THE EXECUTIONER

OF ALL THE KINDS of trouble Seth could've gotten himself into…

We were seated in the living room with the police. Seth and I were on the couch. One uniformed officer was sitting on my recliner. The other officer was standing. A coffeepot and two steaming mugs were resting on the coffee table, but the officers hadn't touched them.

Two cruisers were parked outside. Their flashing lights cut through the windows, coloring the living room. I could hear detectives hollering at one another from the sandy dunes behind my house. The sounds of walkie-talkie chatter, footfall stomping through the sand, and vehicles crawling past my house made this situation all too real.

The body had been found less than twenty yards from my seaside cottage. My nephew had discovered it. This did not look good.

Seth was hunched forward. His defenses were up. White-faced and shaken, he kept trying to explain himself to the cops, but he wasn't answering their questions in a straightforward manner.

Speaking on his behalf, I told the officers, "If he says his friend Thomas showed him the body, then shouldn't you try talking to Thomas about all this?"

One of the officers said, "I assure you, Mr. Nash, that's precisely what we would like to do, but we need a last name—"

"I told you, I don't know his last name!" said Seth.

"Don't be disrespectful!" I barked.

Seth screwed his face up and hardened into an obstinate ball, his defensive walls flying up even higher.

"If you don't know Thomas's last name," said the other officer who was seated on the recliner and taking detailed notes, "then you'll need to give us an accurate description of the guy so that we can get an APB out."

This wasn't how I was planning on spending my Sunday morning. I was hungover, and I should have been reveling in flashbacks of Crystal and the many nights we had spent together. But instead, I was trapped in a waking nightmare that had placed my nephew at the center of a double-homicide investigation.

"A white male who's approximately thirty years old doesn't exactly narrow it down," one of the officers reminded me.

If I had known that Thomas wasn't Seth's age...

I would've forbidden him to hang out with the guy.

Or, would I?

Ah, hell, who knew what I would've done? The fact of the matter was that I had no control over what Seth did. Seth had been getting into all kinds of trouble since school had let out last June, and I hadn't been able to do a damn thing about it.

"Does Thomas have any distinguishing marks? Tattoos?"

Seth shook his head, but I got the impression he was being stubborn.

"Tell them what Thomas looks like," I pushed, but Seth pressed his mouth into a hard line, refusing.

"Hair color? Hair length? Eye color?" the officer went on.

"Describe your friend already!" I barked.

"He didn't do it!" cried Seth.

"You don't know that!" I yelled, losing my temper. Christ, the police were this-close to suspecting *me*, for God's sake. I had ties to Mermaids thanks to Crystal. If this got any messier, I would have to leave Delaware. "You better answer their questions, boy, or you won't see the light of day until September when you go back to school!"

He frowned, twisted his face up something fierce, and huffed and puffed, but then he cooperated. "He looks like a surfer. He has a dark tan. I guess his eyes are brown—"

"You *guess*?" I challenged so that the officers wouldn't have to.

"His eyes *are* brown! His hair is dark-brown, kind of shoulder length, but he didn't do it!"

"Do you know who did?" the officer who was seated on the recliner asked him.

"No," said Seth in a small voice.

"Then you don't know he *didn't* do it." I told the boy.

The standing officer went on, "Height?"

"Taller than me."

I offered, "Seth is five-six," and the seated officer made note of the specifications.

"Walk me through the timeline and use as many dates as possible," said the officer who had been standing. "When did you meet Thomas? What activities did you do with him, and when did you do those activities? Maybe we can piece together where he works, the friends he has, his routine, and track him down."

Seth sighed, exasperated with the constant barrage of questions. "I think we met three weeks ago—"

"Before or after Amanda Dover was killed?"

"After," he said, then he glared at me. "Thomas didn't kill Amanda Dover."

"Go on," said the officer, prompting Seth to focus.

"I met him on the beach. Well, technically he was walking on the sea when I first saw him."

The officers exchanged a funny look. I was about ready to smack Seth. I knew the boy had been developing a habit of embellishing, twisting the truth, and *lying*, but this was no time to be clever.

The standing officer asked for clarification, "What do you mean he was *walking on the sea?*"

"What do you mean, what do I mean? That's what he was doing. He was standing way out on the sea and then he walked towards me, *on the water*, and he introduced himself to me on the beach."

"Oh, for God's sake, Seth!" I blurted out. I laughed and started explaining to the officers, "I've got him enrolled in a bunch of programs over at the church. He's a confused child. He lost his mother when he was only an infant and I've done the best I can." Turning back to Seth, I warned, "Thomas didn't *walk on the sea.*" Defending my nephew, I pleaded with the cops, "Seth obviously looks up to the guy. Of course, he's going to think his new friend walks on water."

The police were willing to move on, thank God. They rattled off more questions with the aim of piecing together a solid timeline, but Seth kept providing weird, unbelievable answers. Thomas could walk on water. He could read Seth's mind. He could appear and vanish like a ghost. It was ludicrous.

Apparently, forcing the boy to spend so much time at Lighthouse Ministries had messed his head up. I had half a mind to march into the church and have a good, long talk with the pastors about what they'd done to my nephew. But the fact of the matter was that I had no intention of setting foot in the place. Hell, considering what I had been up to with Crystal, I would probably go up in flames if I dared to cross the threshold.

As I listened to Seth defend Thomas and cough up tall tales about how he had been spending his time with the guy, my mind suddenly turned an even darker corner.

Seth had been looking less and less like his mother—my deceased sister, Abby—and more and more like a stranger. His expressions, his attitude, and even his posture were indications that he was growing up to resemble his father. Had Seth gotten his bad habits from his father, too? Abby never would've pulled this kind of garbage. Did Seth have bad blood running through his veins?

"Look!" he cried out as if he had been pushed too far. "Just because Thomas brought me to Dead Jewel Payson doesn't mean he killed her! He didn't do it! He didn't kill any of them! I was the one who found Dead Amanda Dover at sunrise! I hadn't even met Thomas yet! You see? He's innocent!"

"*You* found Amanda Dover's body?" one of the officers asked, stunned.

"Yes, so if you suspect anyone, it should be *me*!"

"Don't be a jackass, Seth! You didn't do it!" I said, appalled. What the hell was he thinking? Pleading with the cops, I insisted, "He didn't do it. He's just a teenage boy."

The cops didn't believe me.

And for a disturbing moment, I didn't believe myself, either.

Could Seth have killed two women?

THE STRIPPER

PAYING FOR A PINT of beer at a bar was not an expense I could afford in my current state of unemployment, but I didn't see myself getting through this meeting without one.

I had convinced the girls—and *Lars*, of all people—to meet me at Foster's, an Irish pub located on the promenade.

We were seated outside at one of the large tables that had an excellent view of the gazebo where Lars' Queen cover band was setting up their equipment and getting ready to play a set.

Dusk gathered across the sky, but the temperature was no less sticky than it had been at the height of the afternoon.

We didn't have much time. I was the only exotic dancer who had walked out of Mermaids, effectively quitting in response to Jimbo's brand-new *all nude* policy. Miracle, Destiny, Amber, and New Jewel only had about half an hour to spare with me at Foster's before they would have to head over to the club. Lars had a bit more time before his Swedish bandmates would expect him to join them at the gazebo and start performing Euro-pop renditions of popular rock songs.

We were all thinking the same thing. Original Jewel had been murdered just like Cherry. What the hell was going on?

I was recovering from shock and it was twofold. I couldn't believe Original Jewel had been killed and I also couldn't believe, knowing what the girls now knew, that all of them were still working at Mermaids. The murderer was connected to the club. It was blatantly evident. Even news reporter Missy Chance could see that. Two of our own had been killed because they were strippers. It was irrefutable at this point.

"Pepper spray will get the job done," Amber informed us, as she slapped a compact canister of Mace on the table.

"You can't dance with that in your hand," I argued.

"No one's getting attacked at the *club*," Destiny reminded me, as she produced her own weapon—a switchblade. It looked dangerous, and the way she flipped it open, knives swishing like a butterfly, I knew it would only be a matter of time before she lost a thumb. "If anyone ambushes me on my way to my car, they'll be in for it."

"I bought a gun," New Jewel said, giving her purse an affectionate pat. "What? Cherry and Original Jewel weren't *shot*. They were *overpowered*. No one's going to mess with a woman who brings a gun to a fist fight."

Lars nervously gulped his beer. He looked a sad mix of worried and exhausted. When the girls had first sat down, they had accused Lars of murdering Cherry and Original Jewel, but I had defended him. I had gotten to know him over the past week, and he wasn't a killer. He was a trust fund kid who had loved Cherry. Eventually, the girls had believed me, but the accusations had left Lars on edge.

Admittedly, we were all on edge, thinking the same thing. Which one of us would be next?

"You guys are crazy not to walk out," I told them.

"*You're* crazy to have *walked out*," Amber countered. "I'm making *bank*."

"You're kidding," I said.

The other girls nodded, emphatically agreeing with Amber. There were dollar signs in their eyes.

New Jewel said, "The club has been packed."

"Seriously, Crystal," said Miracle, "the money is great. Jimbo might be completely insane most of the time, but he struck gold with his fully nude idea. People really are coming in from all over. Even the tips I get when I'm on stage are rocking my world."

"But all those customers are going to make it easier for the killer to hide in plain sight," I reasoned. "Whoever works there will be in danger."

"You shouldn't have quit," Destiny told me.

"What? I shouldn't have *quit*?" I questioned them. "Yes, I should have, and you should, too."

"Sorry, Crystal, but there's no way I'm leaving Mermaids now," Amber agreed as if her safety was beside the point.

In fact, none of the girls seemed scared for her life. Each had convinced herself that she would be able to protect herself if she encountered the killer. The opportunity to make a ton of money had blinded them to the dangers at hand.

It was maddening.

I leaned in and tried to be as discreet as possible so that the other customers wouldn't hear me. "What if you're attacked in the private rooms? How are you going to defend yourself if you're naked?"

Destiny crossed her arms and reminded me, "No one has gotten attacked in the private rooms. I don't know why Cherry was out on Woodland Beach that night, and I don't know why Original Jewel would've gone out there after what happened to Cherry, but Missy Chance has been saying that both of them were killed on the beach, *not* at the club. I don't appreciate you trying to scare us out of working at Mermaids."

"I don't, either," Amber agreed.

"You can't get mad at me for caring," I said, standing my ground. "By continuing to dance at the club, you're putting yourselves in harm's way. It isn't smart."

"You think we don't know about the danger *you've* been putting *yourself* in?" Amber hissed.

"What's that supposed to mean?"

"You think we haven't noticed your little *strategy* of leaving the club *less than a minute* after the prison guard?"

She knew about that?

"No wonder you quit. I bet he pays you nicely for whatever it is that you do with him outside of the club." She snorted a laugh and shook her head. "And you think *we're* the ones who aren't being smart?"

"He's not the killer," I snapped.

"He's an executioner!" Amber yelled. "He literally kills people!"

"You think I don't know that?!"

"Ladies!" Miracle shouted. Customers at the nearby tables were staring. "Bottom line, the fact of the matter is that we're all going to do what we're going to do for cash. Plain and simple. As long as no one gets lured out onto the beach at night, no one's going to be in harm's way."

Exasperated and mortified, I guzzled the rest of my beer and immediately looked around for our waitress.

"Oh, that's good," New Jewel said, criticizing me. "Get tanked."

"Shut up, New Jewel," I grumbled. "You don't know my life."

As I tried to get our waitress's attention and order a refill, Destiny reminded all of us that neither Cherry nor Original Jewel had slept with the killer prior to their murders. This wasn't exactly groundbreaking news. Missy Chance had repeatedly mentioned that detail during her Channel 7 reports. What *was* news—and news to *me*—was what Amber said next:

"The medical examiner is still trying to determine if the cause of death was drowning. Both of the bodies showed signs of strangulation, but new information has surfaced that both the girls had saltwater in their lungs."

"How do you know that?" I asked, impressed.

"If you really must know," she cautiously responded, "Channel 7's primetime news anchor, Andy Ailey, has been seeing me at the club."

"He has?!" I blurted out. "The guy who broadcasts from the studio?!"

"Shh," she said, as she looked around. Speaking in hushed tones, she told us, "He's been coming into Mermaids ever since Original Jewel turned up dead. He thinks I'm too stupid to know who he is, as if I don't watch the news." She rolled her eyes at that. "He's working undercover, trying to be a big shot investigative journalist. But I've gotten more information out of him than he's gotten out of me."

Intrigued, everyone leaned in, including Lars, whose bandmates had been calling for him from the gazebo. He ignored them, as Amber divulged everything that she had learned from Channel 7's Andy Ailey in exchange for shaking her tatas and flashing her promised land.

LATER THAT NIGHT, I careened into my bedroom, my arms full of office supplies.

I had caught a 70% off sale at W.B. Mason's, a local store that was going out of business. I had scored one giant bulletin board, a ton of notecards, multi-colored highlighters, pushpins, rainbow Post-its, a handful of black Sharpies, and *red string*—I had been watching enough Magnum P.I. to know *exactly* how to track an investigation on a bulletin board, and red string was a must!

I dumped everything I had bought onto my bed and got to work.

While Miracle, Destiny, Amber, and New Jewel were dancing at Mermaids across town, I began piecing together two timelines on the bulletin board, one for Cherry and the other for Original Jewel. Each timeline represented the night one of the girls was killed. I used a notecard to record every detail I had learned over the weeks, including what Amber had disclosed at Foster's earlier. I organized the entire board using a color-coded system.

According to what Channel 7's Andy Ailey had let slip to Amber, even though Original Jewel had been found on Woodland Beach the morning of August 7th, she had actually been killed a week earlier, on July 31st.

After checking her day planner during the meeting at Foster's, Destiny had confirmed that Original Jewel had been at the club the night of July 31st. Destiny had also been on the schedule that night, which was how she knew Original Jewel had been there. Despite my skepticism, she insisted she was certain. Destiny had marked July 31st on her calendar with a little pink flower, recording the first day of her menstrual cycle. Below the flower, she had made note of the fact that she had asked Original Jewel for a tampon that night, even though I had told her a million times to always pack plenty of tampons in her stripper bag! *This meant that* Original Jewel had *definitely* danced that night at Mermaids.

I documented all of this on my bulletin board, color coding everything—July 31st, Mermaids, Destiny tampon, 2 am club closed, and murdered 5 am. I added a question mark after the notecard that said *murdered 5 am*.

Then I built a timeline for Cherry.

When I stepped back and reviewed Cherry's final hours, the timeline looked remarkably similar to Original Jewel's.

Cherry's final night alive included—Aug 6th, Mermaids, 2 am club closed, and murdered at 5 am, with a question mark.

The night Cherry was killed, New Jewel hadn't been on the schedule. Miracle and Destiny, who had danced that night, left earlier than Amber. Amber had been able to remember that when she had left the club, Cherry was still there with Jimbo, Timbo, and Original Jewel, but this had been after closing. Meaning that all the customers had already left the club by the time Cherry and Original Jewel had been wrapping things up with Jimbo and Timbo.

Interestingly, the night Original Jewel was killed, I had been working along with Miracle, Destiny, and Amber, but I had left before Original Jewel. Apparently, Original Jewel had stayed longer that night to complain to Jimbo about New Jewel, but that was nothing new.

Unless I was reading too deeply into things, it was starting to look like Jimbo and Timbo might have been the last people to see Original Jewel alive. And they might also have been the last people to see Cherry alive.

I didn't like how disturbed I became, staring at Jimbo and Timbo's names on my bulletin board.

Could the cousins have killed one girl then the next?

Even though I didn't like it, I kept going, using Post-its to fill in what I knew about both girls.

My mind started racing. There was too much information bouncing around my brain.

Then another detail surged to the forefront of my mind.

When I had stopped by Cherry's apartment weeks ago, Mr. and Mrs. Dover had said that Cherry had been *going to church*. Lars had mentioned the same thing to me when I had first spoken to him in his dilapidated beach house.

Both the Dovers and Lars had characterized Cherry as a woman who was fighting to overcome inner darkness. She had been trying to turn her life around, and she was killed before she had a chance to really change.

I hadn't thought much about the church angle until New Jewel had told me something curious during our meeting at Foster's. She had said that while the battle of the Jewels had been in full swing, Original Jewel had lashed out at her in a peculiar manner.

"I stopped drinking!" Original Jewel had said. *"I'm in the program now!"*

According to New Jewel, Original Jewel had said this to prove that she was holier than New Jewel, who had developed quite a drinking problem.

I took a moment to ponder that. Cherry had been trying to improve herself, and so had Original Jewel.

Original Jewel was in *the program...* Alcoholics Anonymous?

Didn't AA encourage its members to trust in a *higher power?*

I mulled that over as I sat on the edge of my bed amidst scattered notecards and strewn highlighters. Staring at the bulletin board, the note cards I had mapped out, and the red string I had used to connect one element to the next, I tried to wrap my mind around the big picture.

Cherry had started going to church, and Original Jewel had started going to AA meetings to kick her alcohol addiction, an aspect of which involved trusting in a higher power.

Where had Original Jewel been attending AA meetings?

THE QUESTION OF where Original Jewel had been going for her AA meetings wasn't the only one on my mind when I woke up the following morning with Post-it notes stuck to my face and a highlighter wedged in my armpit.

How in the hell was I going to keep myself afloat financially when I had quit my job?

My cabinets were bare. My refrigerator was empty except for a drop of half 'n half and old eggs that didn't look edible. And my bank account was dangerously low.

I made coffee, convinced I could sustain myself on caffeine and pure adrenaline. It was delusional, but I was determined to keep going. I would run on fumes if I had to.

After consuming enough coffee to make my hands shake and my heart race, I threw on a bikini, a baggy tee-shirt that fell off one shoulder and refused to cover my stomach, and my trusty denim skirt.

With a pair of wedge heels on my feet and my purse slung over my shoulder, I headed out to Woodland Beach, looking shabby but feeling sharp.

The beach was desolate. There wasn't a soul in sight, which was to be expected after Original Jewel's murder.

The police had long since cleared out of the area, having taken their crime scene tape with them, but I was able to find the stretch of beach grass where Original Jewel's body had been found. The grass was matted down.

I glanced around the seascape. The tide was low, the skies overcast.

Muggy weather.

The air smelled stormy.

What had attracted both Cherry and Original Jewel out here? Had the killer enticed them? Or had each girl been forced against her will?

I started walking down the beach with my heels dangling from my hand. The sand felt cold and damp between my toes as I neared the shore.

Staring out across the water, I couldn't tell where the sea ended and the sky began.

I turned around and scanned the beach.

Robert's seaside cottage was a nugget in the distance.

Seeing his house made me wonder about my future. Made me wonder about what I was doing. Why had I bolted from Mermaids that night without a second thought? Why was I acting as though I was made of money when I barely had a dime to my name? I shouldn't have been so hasty, quitting the club. The girls were doing really well there. What had I been thinking?

I had no job, no prospects, I was no better off than I had been the day I'd flunked out of community college.

I was right back where I had started and it made me want to scream.

For some naïve reason, I wanted to believe that the executioner who lived in that little seaside cottage beyond the dunes might be my ticket out.

I wondered if my mother had thought the same thing about Arthur Kowalski at first.

Arthur had alleviated my mom's financial burdens. He had helped put food on the table, and he had given me clothes. For a while, Mom and I hadn't known that Arthur had been using stolen money to meet our needs. Until we caught on to his schemes, we had lived—*barely, but happily*—as our own dysfunctional family.

It had been good enough for me. It had been real. It had been nice.

It had almost been normal.

Did I want to have something real with Robert?

And if I got it, would I wake up one morning and realize I was living my mother's life?

Thinking about it made my head hurt.

I was about to turn back towards the sea when a boy caught my eye—Robert's nephew.

He was walking across the dunes from the back of Robert's seaside cottage, carrying a boogie board under his lanky arm.

He spotted me and froze.

He was too far away from me to see his facial expression. But considering our last encounter, I doubted he was happy to find me on the beach.

Apparently, I was wrong.

He started jogging towards me with a sense of urgency.

"Crystal!"

How did he know my name? I hadn't introduced myself the morning he had called me a heathen, and it was safe to assume Robert hadn't told him about me. Why would he?

He was really coming at me, charging down the beach.

I didn't quite know what to do, but standing my ground felt like the only option. I didn't like how he had spoken to me at the house. Telling me I was going straight to hell.

Maybe I did want a life with Robert.

Maybe showing the boy that I wasn't going anywhere was the smartest thing to do.

Breathless, he reached me and said, "I'm Seth."

"Hi," I responded, wary of him.

The twinkle in his light eyes, the overzealous smile forming across his young face, struck me as peculiar. Why would he be happy to see me?

"Should you be out here all by yourself?" I asked him. "You heard about what's been happening, haven't you?"

"I could say the same to you," he said, looking suddenly deranged. His smile wasn't sitting on his face right. "*Teenage boys* haven't been turning up dead."

His implication was clear. He didn't have to add, *Women like you are.*

"I can take care of myself," I assured him.

"What are you doing out here?"

"I knew both of the victims," I told him. "I wanted to see the place for myself."

"I found the bodies, you know," he informed me.

Female intuition told me to keep my distance from him and my guard up. "You *found* them?"

"Want to go for a swim?"

"What?" I asked, thrown.

"You're wearing a bathing suit," he noticed. "Have you ever boogie boarded?"

"I don't feel like going in the water."

"Let's go for a swim," he said, advancing on me.

Before I could get away, he captured my wrist and began yanking me into the surf.

"What are you doing?"

Alarmed, I tried to jerk free, but he was too strong.

"We have to go in the water now!" he told me, as he dragged me out farther, the incoming waves slapping against my legs.

"Thomas!" he called out.

Overpowering me, he jerked me hard and I stumbled forward into the water. Saltwater splashed up and stung my eyes. Adrenaline shot through my veins and I couldn't see straight.

The next thing I knew, we spilled together into the sea. I belly flopped. The boogie board slipped out of the boy's grip and bonked me in the side of the head, disorienting me. Panic surged through my gut. Had he just hit me in the head?

In the confusion of it all, I didn't press my mouth shut and an incoming wave smacked straight down my throat. Water filled my lungs, and, terrified

I was choking, I began coughing and flailing desperately.

No air was getting in, I couldn't breathe!

He popped up from the surf, laughing and swishing his way towards the boogie board that had gotten away.

As I fought to suck oxygen into my lungs, struggled to get my bearings, and stand, he retrieved his boogie board and circled back to grab me.

A moment later, he was on me, wrestling me into the surf.

"Thomas! I have her!" he called out.

I couldn't scream without inhaling more water and I couldn't get him off of me.

"Thomas! She's ready for you!" He kept calling for someone named Thomas, but I was too badly panicked to comprehend why.

"Stop!" I managed to yell.

That's when I understood he was laughing, *playing*.

This didn't feel like playing.

It felt dark. He didn't know his own strength, and for a flashing moment, I thought he might accidentally drown me.

Through cackling laughter, he sang out how he shouldn't have spoken to me the way he had, and how he would like to be friends.

I'd had enough. Just as he yanked me deeper into the sea, I freed my fist and punched him square in the nose.

Stunned, he held his nose.

We were both out of breath and fighting for air.

"Damn, you're bleeding."

I had given him a bloody nose.

He touched his lip, glanced at the blood on his fingers, and said, "I just want to save you."

What the hell was that supposed to mean?

We stood facing one another, as waves of warm sea water smacked into us sideways, knocking us towards the shore every time we were hit in the shoulders.

He reached for my wrist again, but I jerked away before he could take hold.

I began making my way to the shore, swishing and sloshing through the strong surf.

"Crystal!" he called out after me.

When I reached the beach, my legs gave out.

"You need to be saved!" he said, fighting the surf to chase after me.

Where was my purse? In the sea? Damnit!

When he joined me on the shore, I yelled, "Stay back!"

He seemed confused about why I was so mad.

"What the hell is wrong with you?"

"I just want to be friends," he said innocently.

Was he mentally ill?

"I'm worried about you," he went on.

His nose was gushing. Blood was streaked down his mouth and chin. His bare chest had red smears.

"Worry about yourself," I told him. "I think I broke your nose."

"I've never felt better."

I didn't have time for this. I scanned the shore for my purse, the contents of which were bobbing in the water. My lipstick rolled out to sea. Cash was floating on the surface of the water. Soaked tampons pushed across the sand with an incoming wave. My heels were nowhere in sight.

As I grabbed my water-logged purse and began collecting what I could, muttering curses under my breath and barking at the boy to keep back, he followed my every move and pleaded with me.

"We can be friends! I'll introduce you to Thomas! I want to save you!"

"Save me? As if!" I muttered, furious.

He offered me a soggy tampon he had found.

I snatched it from him. "You almost drowned me!"

"I thought you should meet Thomas."

"Kid, I don't know you!"

"He's out there," he insisted, pointing at the sea.

"Listen, kid, there's no one 'out there,' okay? That's the ocean. Human beings like you and me are supposed to stay on dry land, period."

He began insisting all over again that he needed to *save me.*

It gave me pause.

I studied him as he continued ranting.

"You have to stick with me. Thomas said so. I can protect you. We can get you saved. I think you'll make it."

Get me saved?

Cherry and Original Jewel rushed to the forefront of my mind.

She was going to church!

I'm in the program now!

"Save me, how?" I questioned. "Are you a Jesus-freak or something?"

He shrugged, offered me a worried, little smile. "Or something."

He glanced around the beach and scanned the sea. "I thought my friend, Thomas would show up if I got you out into the water. I didn't mean to scare you. I just want to be your friend."

Connecting the scattered dots, I asked him, "Are you saying something bad will happen to me if I'm not saved?"

"I'm not saying anything," he corrected me. "That's just what Thomas told me."

"That I need to be saved or else something bad will happen to me?"

"And you need to start going to church," he added.

Thomas sounded like a real nut job. "Which church?" I asked.

"The only one in town. Lighthouse Ministries. Do you want to come?" he asked, perking up.

I didn't answer. I continued to study him, and as he began looking around again, hopeful that his friend would turn up—*I really thought he would come if I got you in the water, Thomas is the best!*—I got the distinct impression that Seth might be a very disturbed, young boy…

…but I also got the distinct impression that he knew exactly who had killed my friends.

Would I find the killer at Lighthouse Ministries?

※

THUNDER CRACKED overhead and lightning splintered across the stormy sky as I followed the boy into the seaside cottage he shared with his uncle, having accepted his invitation to lunch.

I was damp, sandy, and salty. Seaweed was tangled in my hair. I felt chilled to the bone. A few of my fingers had turned white, and my teeth chattered.

The boy, on the other hand, seemed immune to the sudden cold.

He waved me into the dimly lit living room where Robert was sitting in a recliner, drinking a beer, and watching sports on TV. He was barefoot in jeans, his sleeves were rolled up, and he was extremely surprised to see me entering the house behind his nephew.

Robert couldn't jump up fast enough.

He gaped. Didn't believe it. His eyes must be playing tricks on him was what his expression seemed to say, as his nephew bounded into the kitchen—chipper—and announced:

"Crystal's here for lunch! Where's the salami?" Seth was already rummaging through the fridge. "You like mustard, right?"

Dumbfounded, Robert looked on, as I found my voice and responded. "Um, yeah, I like mustard."

"Mayonnaise?"

"Sure," I said, absently replying as Robert and I stared at one another.

Astonished, he looked me up and down, taking in the ratty sight of me, as his nephew skipped and slid around the kitchen, slapping sandwiches together as though nothing about the situation was out of the ordinary.

I opened my mouth, prepared to give an explanation, though I wasn't sure *how* I would explain why I was dripping wet in his house on a Saturday afternoon, but Robert blew past me and stampeded into the kitchen.

"I told you not to leave the house without my permission, Seth!" he scolded the boy in a tone I had never heard him use before. "You went out anyway?"

"Crystal was on the beach," he said, totally thrilled about it.

His brow furrowed, and he cut his gaze to me.

Advancing on me, he hissed, "Does he know about us?"

"He's not stupid," I whispered.

Robert cursed under his breath.

"He saw me leaving the other morning," I confessed.

"Did you tell him why you were here?"

Offended, I scoffed, "Oh yeah, when he caught me, the first thing I did was tell him his uncle has been paying me to—"

"Alright," he snapped to shut me up, not that his nephew could hear us.

Seth was bopping around the kitchen, spreading mustard over sliced deli meats that he had slathered with mayonnaise and talking to himself as if he was two people—*I can't believe you weren't out there, but I'm glad you're here now! Crystal is here, did you see? We're friends!*

"Look," I began, speaking in a hushed volume and praying Robert would understand, "another girl from the club was killed so I went out to the beach, thinking…" I sounded like a lunatic. "I don't know what I was thinking. That I would find clues? I didn't go out there expecting to run into your nephew, and I certainly wasn't trying to come here—"

"Lettuce and tomato, Crystal?" the boy called out from the kitchen.

Robert told him, "She can't stay."

My heart sank, but I tried not to show it. Seth scooted out from the kitchen, sliding into view and looking as disappointed as I felt.

"You can't?" he asked me.

Robert said, "She was just being polite, but she has to go."

As Robert took hold of my arm and began escorting me to the door, I said, "I'm starving and I love sandwiches. Lettuce and tomato, please!"

Seth beamed a toothy grin, and while Robert shot me a warning glare, Seth returned to the kitchen where he continued talking to himself and putting our sandwiches together.

"What are you doing?" hissed Robert, but he didn't give me a chance to respond. "He's clearly unstable. He found both of the bodies. We've been in and out of the police station all week. The last thing he can handle right now is learning about you and me, and our unexplainable relationship—"

"He's already aware of our relationship," I hissed right back, "and he already told me he found both bodies. I think the murders have something to do with the church."

"What?"

"Lunch is served!" Seth announced, entering the living room with a tray full of humongous sandwiches.

"Give us a minute," his uncle told him as he pulled me into the kitchen that Seth had made a mess of.

Paying us no mind, the boy set the tray down on the coffee table and cozied up on the couch.

In the kitchen, Robert said, "The police have been dropping in unannounced. It's not a good idea for you to be here."

"Why is that?" I challenged.

"Why is that?!" he balked, stunned that I didn't get it. "Because a dead woman was found in my backyard. Because only strippers from Mermaids have been turning up murdered. If the cops find me socializing with a stripper here, they're going to jump to their own conclusions."

"I'm not a stripper anymore."

That got his attention.

"I quit," I informed him. "I don't work at Mermaids. I walked out. Jimbo wouldn't take me back even if I begged, so if you're worried about—"

"I *am* worried," he maintained.

"Well, so am I!" A sting of tears welled up in my eyes and my voice turned raw. I couldn't stand my emotions, but I couldn't get rid of them unless I got them out. "I don't have any money. I don't know what to say, I *am* hungry, alright? I'm literally *hungry*," I admitted.

He softened, pulled me in, and held me.

Desperate to compose myself, I urged him back and wiped the tears from my cheeks. "I feel like I'm losing my mind. Your nephew scared me half to death out there," I rambled, making zero sense. "I just wanted to see you, and I'm sure you're right. I'm sure he's unstable. But so am I at this point, and when he invited me to church—this is going to sound crazy, but—" I couldn't find the right words. My logic was my own, and I knew that the connections I was starting to form would only make sense to me. I was convinced someone from Lighthouse Ministries, perhaps a member who also frequented Mermaids, perhaps *Thomas*, might be behind the murders. "I just want to have a sandwich. Maybe dry off a little. Then I'll go."

Rain started pounding on the roof and slapping against the windows in sheets, the storm outside swelling. Thunder cracked directly over the house and a cool breeze cut through the open kitchen windows, rattling the chimes.

"What I've been doing at Mermaids," I went on, trying and failing to make more sense than I had a moment ago. "I walked out because I can't do it anymore. I don't want to do it. I need to change my life." I searched Robert's eyes and dared to ask him, "After what you did at Vaughn to Kowalski…don't you want a new life, too?"

A pained look came over him and he curled me in tight.

Spreading my fingers, palms pressed against his chest, I wanted to tell him that I could do *this*. I could be with him. I wanted to be with only him. Every night.

But instead, I breathed, "Take me to church?"

THE MISSIONARY

MINISTERING TO Clifford Oppal had infected me. The man was diseased, I was sure of it, and his sickness was contagious. Every time I left the prison, having listened to his depraved ramblings about beautiful, dead, little boys, I felt biblically unclean and had to quarantine myself in the church rectory for at least three hours before I became once again fit for human company. But even after I had scrubbed the rot from my mind, clutching a wooden cross and praying fervently, and emerged from the basement, I could never tell my parents about the hellish wasteland that was the battlefield where I fought to save Oppal's soul, and lost every time.

The man was unrepentant.

I used scripture to combat his perverted comments. I preached loudly over his deviant anecdotes, invoking the power of Christ to silence Oppal, but the man was nostalgic for his past sins.

Every time I went to the prison, the devil trampled all over me.

My efforts to convert Oppal resembled exorcisms. Failed exorcisms to be exact. But I once got the demented man to confess how he had obtained formaldehyde and the other chemicals he had used to preserve the corpses of the seven boys he had killed. His explanation had been warped, but the warden appreciated the information, which he passed on to the police, who relayed the details to the victims' families.

The truth always mattered to the families, no matter how late it came.

But for me, this was hardly a silver lining.

I grew exhausted in the days leading up to Oppal's execution. I was constantly feverish. My blood felt as thick as sludge in my veins.

The Christmas photo of Kimberly, young Crystal Swan, and Arthur Kowalski kept me motivated, however. Gazing at the once-happy family reminded me that there were inmates on Death Row who wanted to be saved, and who deserved the opportunity to repent.

I knew I shouldn't have kept the photo. Arthur had asked me to give it to Crystal along with his other possessions, but I hadn't been able to part with it. I needed the reminder. I had led a man to Christ. I had made my parents proud. I had succeeded at a single mission, and the Kingdom of God was one step closer to Earth because of it. That meant something.

Clifford Oppal be damned.

Wishing for Oppal's damnation wasn't a godly prayer, but I couldn't help how I felt, as I clamored down the fellowship hall stairs, following my Sunday School students.

The vestibule was congested with parishioners. Some were clustered around the coffeemaker, taking turns filling their cups, while others chatted about how the Lord had gotten them through another difficult week.

Talk of murdered strippers underscored their otherwise cheerful conversations, which was to be expected. The killings had been dominating the news. You couldn't find a single channel that wasn't broadcasting gruesome details about strangulation, lividity, and what salt water exposure did to decomposition.

Andy Ailey's news broadcasts on Channel 7 had become unsavory. I didn't know how, but he had obtained undercover footage of the strip club. Apparently, the strip club was to blame for the murders, which made perfect sense to my mother and most of the congregation.

The Channel 7 production team had done a sloppy job of censoring nipples and bums during their broadcasts of Mermaids, but I suspected the higher ups at the station had allowed it on purpose to boost ratings.

Woodland Beach's very own beloved news reporter, Missy Chance, had been covering the murders. Her reporting had gone into depth concerning the political tension between the county and the club, which had caused the club owner, a man named Jimbo, to rebrand Mermaids as the only gentlemen's club in Delaware that featured fully nude exotic dancers.

The entire news story was a bad influence on our congregation. It had corrupted our parishioners, and I saw the effects firsthand. Not only were our members obsessed with the crimes, but their children were, as well. Some of the kids were beginning to ask extremely troublesome questions. Sally, in particular, seemed weirdly impressed with how much money strippers earned during an average shift. Where she had obtained that kind of information was beyond my comprehension. Walter and Cole had encouraged little Cathy-Anne to flash them her private parts. And, hopeful to gain their friendship, the girl had, which made Judith jealous enough to do the same. Thank God, my mother hadn't caught them. Unfortunately, I had, and I didn't exactly know what to do with them. I had lined the children up, quoted Ephesians 6, and prayed that the Holy Spirit would forgive them.

I kept a watchful eye on the kids now, as they darted, laughing and tagging one another, through a group of gossipy church ladies.

When Sally skipped by, however, I gently took hold of her arm and asked, "Have you seen Seth?"

"You mean on the news?"

"Very funny. He wasn't in Sunday School again this morning. That makes two Sundays he's been absent, and he hasn't been to Youth Group all week. You seem to always have the inside track."

The compliment worked. She straightened her spine, proud, and informed me, "I heard the police have been questioning him because he's close friends with their prime suspect."

My stomach tightened. "The police have a suspect?"

"They do," she told me, matter-of-factly. "Some surfer guy. Seth told the police he thinks the surfer is thirty years old, but if you ask me, he's probably Seth's long, lost biological father. Either way, he sounds like a real weirdo."

"Huh," I murmured, releasing her.

Seth was an odd one. I didn't like him missing church, but I was relieved to hear that the police had a prime suspect. I took a moment to pray they would arrest the guy. That way, all of Woodland Beach might be able to move on.

My father waddled over to me, defying the laws of physics with his every step. It really was a miracle that he was still alive, especially considering that Mom's new strawberry rhubarb pie tradition wasn't exactly low calorie. I supposed it was lucky for Dad that I had only converted one Death Row inmate to the Christian faith so far.

"How're you holding up, son?"

I knew what he was referring to. I was due at the prison later that night for Clifford Oppal's execution. I should have been dreading it with every fiber of my being, but I honestly felt relieved. In less than twelve hours, I would never again have to endure Oppal's depraved company.

"I'm holding up well enough, thanks to the Lord," I said. "I would never get through this otherwise."

"Amen to that," he praised. "Thanks be to God our Father."

"Amen."

Just then, I did a double-take at what I saw walking into the vestibule of our humble church.

For a split second, I had trouble placing the three people who had entered, but my mother's warm, Christian greeting helped jog my memory.

"Mr. Nash!" my mother exclaimed as she rushed over to the executioner, the stripper, and the boy. "What a pleasant surprise! Hello, Seth. And who is this fine lady you've brought with you this morning?"

My mother flicked her judgmental eyes down the length of Crystal, whose outfit would have been more appropriate at a bar than in a church.

As my father made his way over to shake Robert's hand and introduce himself to Crystal, Robert touched eyes with me and our gazes locked.

Clifford Oppal had been sentenced to hang in the gallows, and come midnight, we would both be there to watch.

For the time being, however, Robert was going to pretend he wasn't a killer…

He wasn't the only one pretending.

DEATH ROW INMATE 601
Prinkerton, William

On March 28, 1975, the mutilated body of eleven-year-old Elizabeth Dandridge was found tied to a black walnut tree situated along the National Historic Trail that runs from Pennsylvania to Delaware. Elizabeth Dandridge, who was handicapped with Cerebral Palsy, had been burned and dismembered. The assault she had endured appeared to be Satanic in nature—a pentagram had been carved into the ground and red candles had been placed at her feet. The time of death indicated that the victim was killed on Good Friday and investigators believed the crime was committed as part of some kind of ritual sacrifice.

Precisely two days prior to the offense, William Prinkerton, a street musician, broke free of police custody as he was being hauled into the Wilmington precinct on charges of loitering. His escape route, it was later confirmed during the criminal investigation, cut through the Dandridge's backyard the very night that the little disabled girl had gone missing.

A case against Prinkerton was built, postulating that Prinkerton had kidnapped the child to use as a hostage in case the police found him. The case also postulated that soon after taking the girl, Prinkerton decided to sacrifice her to Lucifer in exchange for musical talent.

The killing of Elizabeth Dandridge was tried as a capital murder case due to the fact that the crime involved the following aggravating factors:

- *The murder was committed by a person in, or who has escaped from, the custody of a law enforcement officer or place of confinement.*
- *The victim was particularly vulnerable due to a severe intellectual, mental, or physical disability.*
- *The victim was a child younger than 14 years old.*
- *The murder was committed against a person who was held or otherwise detained as a shield or hostage.*

Prinkerton was found guilty after conviction by a court of law and has therefore been sentenced to be executed by lethal injection at the James T. Vaughn Correctional Center in Smyrna, DE.

Addendums:

On May 7, 1977, in an attempt to overturn his sentence, Prinkerton filed a standard appeal for a stay of conviction with the court, citing issues from the trial that needed to be rectified such as the prosecution's speculation that the perpetrator was right-handed, an experienced hiker familiar with the National Historic Trail, and a Satanist, none of which characterized Prinkerton.

In November 1979, after oral arguments for and against the appeal were presented to Delaware's panel of judges, Prinkerton's appeal was denied without prejudice.

He filed a second appeal on January 30, 1981 with the intermediate courts when a new development surfaced, casting a long shadow of doubt over the verdict—another girl had turned up mutilated and murdered along the National Historic Trail while Prinkerton had been imprisoned.

The second appeal was denied on October 18, 1983, again without prejudice.

Desperate to reverse his death sentence, Prinkerton filed a Federal habeas corpus, petitioning the United States District Court for a review of all evidence and trial proceedings, this time listing juror misconduct, tampered evidence, and coerced witness testimony among the State's wrongdoing. This precipitated a hearing, and new findings were then presented to the United States Court of Appeals on June 7, 1984.

Finally, the appeal was brought to the United States Supreme Court where it has been sitting, unreviewed, since April 22, 1985.

As of August 14, 1986, Prinkerton's death sentence and date of execution remains in effect pursuant to State law due to Prinkerton having exhausted every legal option available in Delaware, though his appeal is still pending with the United States Supreme Court.

Execution to commence: August 27, 1986

THE MISSIONARY

"AS IT IS WRITTEN in 1 John 18, *'Dear children, this is the last hour; and as you have heard that the antichrist is coming, even now many antichrists have come. This is how we know it is the last hour.'*"

"Amen, Pastor Asa!" William Prinkerton sang out with clear eyes and a full heart from within his cell, or so I imagined. "Save me, Lord!"

Sitting on my stool in front of Willy's locked steel door, I went on, "*'But you have an anointing from the Holy One, and all of you know the truth…'*"

Willy blew into his harmonica to underscore the verses I had read from the scriptures, and all of Death Row was filled with Willy's blues harmony.

"*'As for you, see that what you have heard from the beginning remains in you. If it does, you also will remain in the Son and in the Father. And this is what he promised us—eternal life.'*"

"Lord, save me from damnation! Let the truth rain down upon Delaware! Let your righteousness be my shield!" he cried out.

Willy was scheduled to be executed in less than two weeks, but unlike Clifford Oppal who had clung to his sins until the bitter end, Willy had called the Lord into his heart. The Holy Spirit was with him now. All of heaven was waiting for Willy with open arms on the other side…

…but he wasn't ready to go.

He had salvation, but he wanted freedom and exoneration.

And that was the hardest part, because I knew he wasn't going to be freed.

Willy sucked air in and out of his harmonica, breathing twangy chords.

"I pray for my soul, Lord! I pray for the governor! I pray that the truth shall set me free just like Christ has promised with his holy word!"

As Willy played and prayed, I kept reading, "*'See what great love the Father has lavished on us, that we should be called children of God! And that is what we are!'*"

"I'm a child of God, Lord!"

"*'The reason the world does not know us is that it did not know him.'*"

"Whosoever believes, Lord, they shall be saved, and I believe, Lord!"

"*'…we know that when Christ appears, we shall be like him, for we shall see him as he is. All who have this hope in him purify themselves, just as he is pure…'*"

"Purify me, Lord!" Willy cried. He pressed his harmonica to his mouth and began playing a heart-rending melody in a minor key.

After weeks spent ministering to Clifford Oppal in vain, I couldn't have asked for a greater reward than this.

Ministering to William Prinkerton was an even better reward than the Lord had blessed me with last night when I had watched that lunatic, Oppal, hang in the gallows.

Well, the reward hadn't been watching the man die. Rather, I had felt reassured, and receiving the Lord's reassurance was a reward I had needed.

Reassurance that heaven was reserved for the truly repentant.

Reassurance that the devil's own would be kept out.

And reassurance that the work I was doing here at the prison was serving a higher purpose than I could have ever imagined.

William Prinkerton was a joy to minister to.

But he wanted me to pray for his exoneration and release.

I couldn't do that.

"Lord!" he cried out in a howling lament as I pressed deeper into 1 John 3:11-16.

'We should love one another…This is how we know what love is: Christ laid down his life for us…'

"Open the governor's eyes! Bless his heart! Change his mind, Father God, change the man's mind and compel him to exonerate me!"

Almost immediately upon sitting down with Willy, I had come to understand that he had maintained his innocence from day one. Ever since his conviction, Willy had been fighting to overturn the ruling. He had filed appeal after appeal, but each one had been dismissed, albeit dismissed without prejudice. Willy had persisted, kept filing appeals, and his petition had slowly but gradually moved up the legal ladder to the highest court in the land where it was currently awaiting review.

I feared his case was collecting dust somewhere in the annals of Washington. Probably in some forgotten corner of a mailroom. I imagined the thick envelope was sitting, unopened and unread.

Willy had done his research over the years, and because of it, he had addressed his final appeal to Thurgood Marshall, the only African-American justice who had been serving on the Supreme Court. Willy thought Marshall was the most likely to be favorable towards him. The strategy had one caveat. Marshall had to actually open, read, and review the appeal. If Marshall never took the time to pour over the petitions, briefs, and letters that Willy had consolidated and sent to him, then all hope would be lost.

Willy had every reason to be hopeful, or so he had told me. His latest appeal to Thurgood Marshall contained new findings that proved Willy hadn't committed the crime.

Willy had even obtained a dying declaration from Tabetha Dandridge, the murdered girl's mother, which stated her biggest regret in life had been agreeing with the police when they told her that she must have seen Willy lurking in her backyard the night her daughter Elizabeth had been kidnapped.

Though Willy had waited patiently, a response from Marshall never came, so Willy had handwritten a letter to the governor of Delaware pleading for a temporary stay of execution. In his letter, Willy had argued that a temporary stay would create enough time to give Justice Marshall a chance to examine the information Willy had compiled in his latest appeal.

As of yet, however, Willy had not gotten a response from Marshall nor had he gotten a response from the governor, and my gut was telling me he never would.

"*'Grace, mercy and peace from God the Father and from Christ, the Father's Son, will be with us in truth and love'*," I declared, having skipped ahead to 2 John 1:3.

"I beseech you, Lord, for a miracle!" Willy exclaimed, sounding terrified. He wasn't ready to die. "I implore you, Christ my Savior! Let the governor read my letter! Let his heart be softened and his mind changed, Lord!"

Inspired, I flipped farther ahead in my bible and read from the Book of Revelation, "*'Look, he is coming with the clouds! And every eye will see him, even those who pierced him, and all people on earth will mourn because of him! So shall it be!'*"

"Shut up!" Gary Olson yelled from inside his cell. The former pig farmer was scheduled to be put to death a week after Willy, and as the date approached, he had grown intolerant of any reminders. "Ain't no lord coming to save you, Prinkerton! Best that you pray the executioner won't put you down as sloppy as he did to old Kowalski! That's all you can ask for! We're gonna die, man, every last one of us in here! Don't make it worse by begging! I can't stand hearing it! I can't stomach it!"

The musical note Willy had been blowing through his harmonica faltered and then cut out.

I fell silent as well, and a deafening stillness spread throughout Death Row.

No one stirred. The air felt heavy, as the inmates quietly acknowledged their fate. No one made it out of Death Row, except in a body bag.

The cells that Arthur Kowalski and Clifford Oppal had once occupied were evidence of that.

Pulling my stool as close as I could get to the open slot of Willy's steel door, I searched my soul for the right words to say.

"Pray for me, Pastor Asa?" he asked, sounding downtrodden and small, through the slot. "Pray that justice will prevail? Pray that the governor hears my pleas?"

"Willy, I can't."

It killed me, but I couldn't lie to him.

There was silence on the other side of the steel door.

Anger followed, and Willy howled, "Lord, save me!"

"The Lord wants you to join him in heaven, Willy. It's time for you to accept God's will and be brave."

I DROVE BACK TO Lighthouse Ministries. The memory of Willy Prinkerton's dashed hopes reverberated deep within the marrow of my bones, as I listened to my favorite Christian radio station, trying not to feel horrible.

There was no justice in this world, I reminded myself, as I turned up the volume so that the soothing Christian tune playing through the speakers could wash over me, but the song ended.

The radio announcer launched into a news update about the recent Woodland Beach murders. The primary suspect was a surfer named Thomas who had been evading police for weeks now. Anyone with information about Thomas was asked to contact the Woodland Beach police station, but I had heard enough.

I hit the dial and the station cut out. In the past month, I had choked down more death, dying, and killing than most people dealt with in a lifetime. I couldn't listen to it any more, not during my scenic drive home. Nightmares of Arthur Kowalski's horrendous execution had been plaguing my dreams. The sight of Clifford Oppal dropping as the floor gave way beneath him in the gallows had remained burned in my brain, adding to other morbid images that I would have to live with for the rest of my life. I didn't need to hear disturbing details about dead strippers, which would only cause me to conjure even darker visions in my mind, and keep me tossing and turning restlessly all night.

If anything, I wanted to lie down in the rectory and fall into a dreamless state of rest, but when I arrived at the church in the late afternoon, having parked my car and entered the vestibule with my bible in hand, I realized that sneaking off into the basement wasn't in the cards.

Dad was talking with a few men in front of the coffeemaker, and deep in the sanctuary, Mom was seated with Crystal Swan in the pew closest to the pulpit.

"Son, you remember Emmet DeGraves," said my father, waving me into their conversation when all I wanted to do was slip past everyone, unnoticed.

Offering what I hoped wouldn't come across as a disinterested smile, I joined them and shook Emmet DeGraves' hand. I gave Charles Riley, the other man next to my father, a friendly nod.

I was familiar with both men, though I had never formally met them.

It was no secret that DeGraves and Riley had been reluctant to become members of Lighthouse Ministries. They had a reputation around town and it had nothing to do with the automotive repair shop they ran. DeGraves and Riley liked to booze it up afterhours. Sometimes that led them to drift in and out of Alcoholics Anonymous across town, which was where Dad had found them. Dad was in the habit of swinging by the AA meetings once a month to invite the newly sober to our Sunday services.

DeGraves and Riley were hardly sober, and their motivation for showing up to AA meetings was hardly innocent. For them, Alcoholics Anonymous was just another place to pick up vulnerable women when Mermaids had sucked their wallets dry.

That being said, I had full faith that my father would help them see the light. Knowing Dad, I was certain that before long, DeGraves and Riley would accept Christ as their personal Lord and Savior, attend church every Sunday, and even tithe when the collection plate came around. Heck, my father might even convince them to get baptized in the bay before autumn hit.

If anyone could lead DeGraves and Riley to Christ, it was Pastor Joseph Asbury.

Which meant that I wasn't needed at the moment.

"Emmet DeGraves and Charles Riley are interested in joining our men's bible study," Dad went on, but I felt too depleted to contribute.

"Charles' daughter might like to enroll in some of our Christian youth programs for the rest of the summer."

"Wonderful," I said, feigning interest. As I went on to tell them about Children's Sunday School and our Kids for Christ program, Emmet's attention wandered and he began leering at Crystal Swan from across the church. Crystal was still seated in the pews, talking with my mother. A weird grin came over Emmet's face as he stared at Crystal.

I didn't like it, and I lost my train of thought, which caused me to start rambling.

Dad interjected, picking up where I left off and elaborating on the mission of our humble church.

I was distracted. Were Charles and Emmet taking turns getting an eyeful of Crystal?

"You look a bit tired, Son," my dad commented once Emmet and Charles had exited the vestibule and driven off in a pickup truck.

Helping myself to a cup of coffee, I reminded him, "I was at the prison until nearly three in the morning last night."

"That late?"

"Things don't always start on time," I said with a shrug. "I only got a few hours sleep before I had to turn around and drive back to the prison all over again to minister to Prinkerton."

Dad passed me the box of sugar, treating me the way he would like to be treated. Had my father been exhausted, he would need a lot of sugar in his coffee.

I politely declined, and he said, "The bible tells us that whatever we sow here on earth, we will reap tenfold in heaven."

Tenfold didn't sound like enough, but I replied, "Amen."

After taking a sip of coffee, however, I felt something inside me shift, or perhaps snap. I couldn't keep lying to him.

"It's wearing on me. Wearing on me, bad," I said. "I don't think I'm going to last very much longer ministering at the prison."

A severe look came over my father and his eyes darkened.

"Christ has made you strong, Asa. He has perfected you. There's nothing you can't accomplish."

For a split second, I didn't recognize my father.

Did he care about me?

"I can't take it, Dad," I went on. "Watching Kowalski die. Watching Oppal hang. I can't get the images out of my mind—"

"Toughen up," he warned.

"I have been toughening up," I snapped. "But I'm losing the light, Dad. I can feel myself changing. That prison has been changing me for the worse from the start. The second I set foot in the prison, something evil got ahold of me, and I can feel it trying to take over—"

"Asa!" he barked, startling me. Piping hot coffee spilled down the side of my cup, burning my hand. "You have the Holy Spirit inside you and nothing else—"

"But Dad—"

"I won't hear this! You're strong! You are an agent of the Lord! Do you understand me? There is nothing you cannot endure, because God's holy hand is guiding you! Think of the Apostle Paul! Think of the years Paul spent suffering! The torture he withstood! What did Paul do? He listened to God! He wrote scripture! He produced the majority of the New Testament for Christ's sake, and I mean that, Asa! He *literally* wrote the bible *for Christ's sake!* All you have to do is minister to a few inmates and then eat your mother's pie!"

"But—"

"Grow up!"

I didn't like how he was looking at me, like he was ready to disown me.

Red-faced and quaking, my tremendous father fought to compose himself. He shook his head. He frowned and winced and frowned again. Then he informed me:

"What you need, Son, is a good Christian wife."

What?

I had never felt less connected to my father and it was all my fault. I shouldn't have been honest with him. Shouldn't have shown him the chink in my armor. My shortcomings reflected badly on my dad, on our church, and on Christ. There was no room for weakness in our world. We were Asburys.

"You know best," I lied to get back into my father's good graces.

Softening, he explained, "Son, you're nearly in your mid-thirties. You think I don't remember what that's like? The hormones? The urges? The *frustration?* You're out there in the world every day, fighting for the Lord and encountering all these puffy-haired, big boobed women who listen to Cyndi Lauper and like gymnastics—"

What in the hell was he talking about?

"Of course, you feel like you aren't going to last very long, but it isn't because you aren't strong enough to make it out there despite what you see at the prison and in the streets. It's because you're coming home every night to sleep in a damp basement instead of in the arms of a warm woman. You need a wife, Son. In marriage, there is no such thing as sin between the sheets."

As Dad continued explaining how all would be right in my world once I was married, I turned my attention to Crystal and observed her through the open sanctuary doors.

She hadn't moved from the pew where she had been talking with my mother.

Maybe my father was right. Maybe I did need a good Christian woman in my life. Maybe curling up with a loving wife every night would make all the difference in the world. But years ago, I had tried. I had been head over heels in love. Dad knew that. He knew that I had floated through seminary school on Cloud 9. And then one day, when I'd stopped by her parents' house to surprise her with chocolates and flowers, secretly planning to propose to her on the beach, I caught her with another man.

Dad knew all of this and he also knew that I had never recovered.

I wasn't interested in meeting anyone, not that Dad and I had ever talked about it.

After my heart had been broken, all my father did was pat me on the shoulder and remind me that just because I wanted something, didn't mean that receiving it was in God's plan. Dad had acted like all I'd done was skin my knee.

A knee could heal.

My trust in women never had.

I nodded towards the sanctuary and asked, "What's that about?"

"Ms. Crystal Swan?" he said. "She came to church yesterday with Mr. Robert Nash."

I knew that.

"After the service, Crystal filled out a Connection Card and checked the Christian Counseling box," he added.

"She did?"

"Praise God," he said.

I couldn't take my eyes off Crystal.

She was gorgeous.

I didn't trust her.

THE STRIPPER

I FELT WATCHED, glanced over my shoulder, and briefly touched eyes with Pastor Asa Asbury. He looked haggard from where he was standing in the church vestibule next to his father. He was holding a cup of coffee in one hand and a small, leather-bound bible in the other. He acknowledged me, tipping his head, but I returned my attention to his mother who was sitting next to me in the first pew of the sanctuary.

I had told her the broad strokes of my life story, the PG-version, because she had asked for them. Explained how I had grown up in a trailer park with my mother. Had never known my father. Had moved into a Section-8 rowhouse when I was twelve, found my mother dead half a year later, and had been sucked into the foster care system as a result. Fast-forward a bit, and dropping out of community college had come next. I had met Robert Nash some years later.

I didn't have to mention Mermaids or that Robert had been my best customer at the club. Pastor Gracie seemed to know that I was a stripper, or that I used to be a week ago. I supposed it was obvious from the way I dressed and carried myself.

What she didn't know, however, was my real motive for having checked the Christian Counseling box on her church's Connection Card yesterday during the Sunday service. I had slid the card, fully filled out, onto the tithing plate when it had come around. Robert had shot me a funny look. I had returned a little smile. As far as he knew, I had asked to come to church because I wanted to turn my life around. My plan was to give Pastor Gracie the same impression. It wasn't anyone's business that the real reason I had come to Lighthouse Ministries was to investigate Cherry and Original Jewel's murders. Both girls' involvement in this very church had gotten them killed, I suspected, and I wanted to uncover why.

When Pastor Gracie had called me, inviting me in to speak with her about the Methodist faith and the various programs offered at Lighthouse Ministries, I had jumped at the chance to sit down with her.

She was judging me, though. I could feel it.

Had Cherry and Original Jewel sat down with Pastor Gracie in this very manner? Had the woman judged them, too? Had Pastor Gracie smirked at the girls in the same way that she was looking at me now with severe judgment plastered all over her heavily made-up face?

As our conversation continued, she offered me another backhanded compliment, "It's a *miracle* you're here, you know. You attended only one service, and here you are, learning about our Christian programs. Your interest in Christian Counseling is miraculous."

"Are other people reluctant to join your church?" I asked.

The question didn't seem to please her. "No one is *reluctant* to join this church, my dear, thanks to Pastor Joe's powerful sermons."

"Then why is it a miracle that I'm interested in joining?"

"Because of your personal history and because of your, shall we say, line of work," she answered bluntly. "You're living proof, my dear, that the Lord can correct anyone's mistakes."

I wondered if she realized how insulting she was being, but I remained polite and said, "I see."

"Your attendance at church is a *miracle*," she reiterated. "The Lord has even used you to inspire Mr. Nash to return to us. We are just so *happy* to have you both, and *you* did that. *You* brought Robert back to Lighthouse Ministries. Can you see how the Lord is working through you at this very moment?"

I was skeptical. God wasn't working through me, as far as I could tell. Robert had been the one to bring me to church, not the other way around. She started laying the praise on a little thick, perhaps to compensate for having insulted me earlier. Or maybe it wasn't praise. Maybe she was trying to manipulate me into agreeing with whatever she said. Something felt off.

"You might not be able to comprehend it," she went on, mixing insults with compliments. "But I can see it, and all I can say is, Hallelujah! Pretty soon, you'll be quoting scripture and spreading the gospel!"

Trying to slow her down, I said, "I don't know about that—"

"Of course, you will!" she exclaimed, barreling full steam ahead. "And you will share your testimony with the entire congregation, too!" she informed me, pointing to the lectern where her husband preached all of his sermons. "You'll stand at the pulpit and warn our members not to make the same sinful mistakes as you!"

"I'm not sure I want to tell everyone about the skeletons in my closet."

She chuckled, but I wasn't sure if she was laughing at her own enthusiasm, or at me.

"I want to be clear with you," I said, trying once again to pump the brakes. "I'm definitely interested in learning about the church, but I haven't made any decisions yet—"

"Yes, yes, of course, of course." She turned her attention to the glossy pamphlets in her hand. "I almost forgot. These are our programs!" Opening the first pamphlet, she asked, "Are you familiar with the *Methodist* denomination?"

Was I familiar with denominations?

I had spent the majority of my adult years wrapped around a pole…

"No?" she accurately guessed. "That's perfectly understandable."

She scooted closer so that we could both look at the first pamphlet, which featured a joyful married couple hugging their sunny-looking children. The family was backlit by the glowing light of Christ.

"I can tell you everything you need to know about our denomination and it'll take two seconds. Ready?"

Skeptical, I said, "Okay."

"Our denomination is the *right* one."

That was quite a claim. My eyebrows shot up to my hairline, but Pastor Gracie didn't so much as blink, her conviction was that strong.

"The *Methodist* denomination is the right one?" I questioned.

"Plain and simple," she confirmed.

"So… the other denominations are—"

"The other denominations are incorrect."

"I see."

"No, you don't," she informed me, as a knowing smile spread across her face. "But you will."

"Can't wait."

"Look no further than Lighthouse Ministries," she concluded. "We are the right church."

"I have absolutely no plans of looking at any other church," I promised, telling her the truth. Cherry and Original Jewel had ties to this church. Investigating any other congregation would have been pointless. Of course, I didn't tell Pastor Gracie any of that.

"Now, as you can see," she went on, sharing the glossy pamphlet with me, "we offer several bible study classes for women. You can attend in the mornings or the evenings, or both. We like to offer as much variety as possible to accommodate the needs of our members. You already know about our Sunday service, but we have an adult Sunday school class the hour prior, as well. Lighthouse Ministries is also affiliated with the Alcoholics and Narcotics Anonymous programs that are held over at the YMCA—"

"Really?" I was genuinely interested, but not for the reason that Pastor Gracie assumed.

A pained, empathetic look came over her. "Crack?"

"What?"

She sucked in a deep, fortifying breath. "The power of Christ can get you off crack, dear."

"I'm not on crack."

She seemed surprised. "Ganja?"

"I don't think people call it that anymore—"

"Well, whatever you're on, we'll get you off of it in no time."

"I'm not on drugs—"

She gave me a maternal pat, and I realized I wasn't going to win this one.

"I only have five minutes before I have to go upstairs for the next women's bible study," she explained.

"Are there any co-ed bible study groups?" I asked, curious if Cherry or Original Jewel had attended one. The killer could've met them there. Pastor Gracie scowled so I quickly lied, "For Robert and me. We would like to go together."

She wasn't buying it. "My dear, I'm giving you the benefit of the doubt. I've chosen to trust you, because I trust the Lord. But I will not tolerate hanky-panky in my church."

"I'm not here for hanky-panky—"

"We offer separate bible studies for each gender so that no one falls prey to temptation."

"I wasn't planning on tempting anyone—"

"And yet, you're dressed like a floozy in a house of worship," she rudely pointed out.

I thought I looked nice.

"Let us pray." She grasped hold of my hands, closed her eyes, and bowed her head. "Heavenly Father, we thank you for the miracle of compelling this young woman to come to church. I pray to you, Lord, that you continue to guide Kristen—"

"Crystal—"

"—in her walk with Christ. Open her eyes, Lord, and soften her heart. Show her the error of her ways and force her to understand that giving up her sinful lifestyle will uplift her into your holy graces."

I glared at her.

"Lord, I ask you to transform this woman. Wash away her sins with the power of the Holy Spirit, and compel her to cover herself up when she comes to church, for her body was meant to be a temple of God, and—"

"Okay, thank you," I said, freeing my hands as I sprang to my feet. I had heard enough. "Thanks for the pamphlets."

I couldn't get out of there fast enough.

She called after me, "You have my number! I'll see you this Sunday?"

ROBERT PLACED a Frankie Lymon record on his turntable, lowered the needle, and an upbeat doo-wop song filled the seaside cottage.

Seth had tucked himself into his bedroom, leaving Robert and me in the living room where we sipped whiskey sours and enjoyed the snappy music.

Robert, Seth, and I had eaten pasta primavera with grilled chicken for dinner, which I had cooked with Seth's help. Seth had slid around the kitchen in his socks, handing me ingredients whenever I had asked. All the while, Robert had gotten some paperwork done, making the most of the twilight hours before the food was ready.

I didn't expect Robert to help in the kitchen. He had fulfilled his end of the bargain by supplying me with as much money as I needed to buy groceries.

I had no other way of feeding myself, and our almost nightly meals had been, for the most part, extremely sweet—Seth going on and on, telling wild tales of summertime fun, Robert eyeing him from across the small table, everything about his disposition a silent warning that the boy ought to get his head out of the clouds. I had looked on and wondered if we were almost a family.

I felt strangely endeared to them.

But getting to know Robert was difficult. The man was a brick wall. He rarely opened up. His domestic side was rigid. He never altered his routine, but he made room for me within it.

He always woke minutes before his alarm went off and hopped in the shower, leaving me to wake up to the ear-piercing bleat of his alarm. I would roll over, smack the thing, and try to fall back asleep. But as soon as Robert returned from his shower, he would nudge me until I climbed out of bed.

He drank a single, black coffee for breakfast, and he never let me linger. I had to be out the door when he was. If he wanted me in the evening, I would wait outside in my car with fresh groceries on the passenger's seat until he showed up at half past six.

Seth and I developed a system for making dinner, and I discovered that I liked spending time with the boy. But I wasn't necessarily getting to know him. He was just as closed off as his uncle. And when both of them were seated at the dinner table, neither seemed willing to open up. There was no intimacy between them. They treated each other like strangers, or at least that was how it seemed whenever I was around.

Was I pushing them apart? I couldn't tell, but I hoped not.

Complicating matters was Thomas.

Thomas remained the prime suspect who police believed was responsible for murdering Amanda Dover and Jewel Payson. Investigators had even issued a State-wide manhunt to track him down. You couldn't watch TV or listen to the radio without hearing about him. And you couldn't spend time at Robert's seaside cottage without hearing Seth go on and on about Thomas' innocence. Seth considered Thomas his closest friend. He continued to insist that Thomas couldn't have killed those women. The police were hunting the wrong man. Every time Seth defended Thomas, Robert became furious. He didn't want the boy to spend any time with the prime suspect.

Nearly a week had passed since I had last set foot in Lighthouse Ministries. I needed to go back. I was convinced that I would find the killer there, and like the police, I suspected Thomas.

Seth had to know more about Thomas than he was letting on. He was covering for the criminal. He might even be in cahoots with Thomas. Robert refused to consider that angle, but I could tell he was guarding his suspicions of the boy.

As for myself, so long as I lived, I would never forget the stormy day Seth tried to yank me out into the sea, calling for Thomas as if the man would appear out of nowhere and strangle me to death in four feet of water.

"How long have you been going to Lighthouse Ministries?" I casually asked Robert one evening after dinner.

We were seated next to one another on the couch in the living room, but he seemed a million miles away. He hadn't looked at me since dinner. The muted TV had his full attention when he wasn't fiddling with the record player or stirring his drink.

I had come to accept that he was a closed-off person, but he clammed up even more in response to what I thought had been a neutral question.

"I don't really go."

"You did the other day. Thanks for bringing me, by the way."

"They were kind to Abby when she moved home," he said as if that would be the end of it.

He almost never mentioned his dead sister, but I had picked up the gist of what had happened. Abby had returned to Woodland Beach, pregnant. She had died in childbirth. Robert had raised Seth because of it.

"I donate regularly," he added with a shrug. "Seth goes to their Kids for Christ program. That's the extent of it." Finally, he held my gaze. "I think we both know I'm not the churchgoing type."

I wasn't either, but he was kind enough not to point that out.

He hadn't questioned my interest in the church, and he hadn't stopped paying me every time I came over. We had struck a good balance between good and evil, and I didn't want to jeopardize that, but I was too curious to hold my tongue.

"Has Seth ever mentioned seeing Thomas at the church?"

Instead of answering, he stared at me for a very long moment and I had no idea why. I couldn't read his expression or guess what he was thinking.

"What?" I asked when he still hadn't said anything.

"You'll be fine as long as you stay away from Mermaids."

"How do you know that?"

"You think a serial killer is frequenting Lighthouse Ministries?" he questioned.

"I don't know what to think."

"Stay out of Mermaids."

"I am," I snapped, taking a tone with him. "Are you?"

"You think that's your business?"

"Isn't it?" I asked, getting worked up.

"Calm down, I haven't gone there since… all of *this*… happened." He was referring to the odd relationship we had formed in which Robert massively overpaid me to cook his meals, launder his dress shirts, and sleep over. "What *is* this, by the way?"

"What do you mean?" I asked.

"You know what I mean."

"I don't know what this is," I answered honestly. I felt attacked, but I didn't want to fight. "You're the only reason I *don't* have to work at the club, and I would like to keep it that way. Isn't that what you want?"

"I want you to stay away from Mermaids," he agreed, but he sounded severe, almost threatening.

We locked eyes.

"Alright," I agreed.

"And if you start going to church, you better mean it. I've made a lot of errors in my life, but the one thing I've gotten right is that if I'm unfit for church, I don't go there."

"Are you saying I'm unfit for church?"

"I'm saying, don't mock God. He'll know, and you won't like the punishment."

What was that supposed to mean?

"Crystal?"

"Fine," I said.

"Don't set foot in that church unless you mean it," he said again, repeating the warning.

"No problem!" I blurted out, offended.

As if Robert would ever know my true motivations for going to Lighthouse Ministries…

As if God would know…

Yeah, right.

I was going to find out who had killed my friends and I wasn't about to let Robert, God, or anyone stop me.

If Robert could be closed off, so could I.

LARS LOOKED AS ridiculous as I felt. We weren't so much dressed for church as *costumed* for it.

We had found everything we needed at the local GoodWill for under thirty bucks. Though I wasn't entirely comfortable spending money on a church lady costume that I doubted I would wear twice, the outfit was a necessary expense. If I wanted to get close to the parishioners and try to find Thomas, I was going to have to look the part and blend in with the other attendees of Pastor Gracie's Friday afternoon women's bible study.

The skirt suit I had bought was two sizes too big and itched something fierce as soon as I put it on, but it was worth it. I had even found a vintage pillbox hat, a pair of embroidered lace gloves, and kitten-heel pumps that were more rigid than Pastor Gracie herself.

Lars was my secret weapon.

The plan was to infiltrate both the women's and men's bible study groups, which I needed Lars for since Lighthouse Ministries kept the sexes segregated. Once Lars and I had established trust in our respective bible study groups, we could then poke around, and see if anyone knew anything about the mysterious murders of Cherry and Original Jewel.

Lars had been all for it until he saw the costume I had pieced together for him.

"Crystal, there's no way."

Convincing him to wear a seersucker suit wasn't easy. But once he got used to it, he let me style his hair in such a way that no one at the church would ever guess he usually slicked it up in a mohawk.

"You look great!"

"I don't believe you."

Lars and I had also made a secret pact to ask people about Thomas. Maybe Thomas was going by a different name. We wouldn't know unless we went deep undercover and asked the right people the right questions. We figured, the longer we stuck around, the better our chances would be to discover who Thomas was, where he was, and what he had done to the dead strippers.

Lars and I were in it for the long haul.

Our biggest priority was to find out who had killed Cherry and Original Jewel.

My second biggest priority was to make sure Robert didn't find out what I was really up to.

The stakes could not have been higher.

No sooner than we entered the church vestibule, Pastor Gracie did a bit of a double-take from where she stood. She was conversing with a cluster of elderly church ladies, but broke free of them and exclaimed, "I almost didn't recognize you!"

All eyes were on Lars and me. We had even stolen Pastor Joe's attention along with all the blue-collar types that were gathered around him.

Swallowing my pride, I approached her, ushering Lars along, and said, "It's so nice to see you, Pastor Gracie. Hello, Pastor Joe! This is my friend, Lars Svensson."

"How do you do?" sang Lars as if he were auditioning for a high school musical. He shook one pastor's hand then the next, greeting them with a cheerful attitude. I thought he might click his heels together and start tap dancing, he was so chipper. "Lovely afternoon to worship the Lord!"

Delighted, Pastor Joe lit up in agreement. "Indeed!"

"I understand the men's bible study is focusing on the Book of Hosea?" Lars asked, using the information I had provided him with.

As Pastor Joe got him up to speed while introducing him to the other members of the men's group, Pastor Gracie shepherded me towards her group of church ladies.

"I'm Crystal," I announced before she could butcher my name. "*Crystal* Swan. Nice to meet you," I said, shaking one lady's hand then the next until I had met everyone. "*Crystal* Swan. Pleasure to meet you. *Crystal*. Hi, nice to meet you. *Crystal* like the fancy glass, yes. So good to be here. Hello, I'm *Crystal*."

Once I had been introduced to Ms. Bethany, Ms. Suzanne, and Ms. Mary-Catherine who was surrounded by her Christian co-workers, the names of which I couldn't keep straight because they were all variations of *Catherine*—Cathy, Kitty, Cath, Katherine with a K, Catherine with a C, and Kathleen, with one out-of-sorts Sue-Ellen in the mix—Pastor Gracie told the ladies, "Crystal recently came to Christ. She is such an inspiration. We all have a lot to learn from her about the power of forgiveness. You see, Crystal harbors no ill will towards the man who murdered her mother. Crystal has let go of all anger. Her wounds have been completely healed. She is a new creation in Christ, and has no need to dredge up the past."

That was news to me. Brazen, offensive news. I had told the pastor about what had happened to my mother, but right now it sounded like she was *telling everyone* that I was fine.

Why would I be fine?

Pastor Gracie wasn't interested in *counseling* me. In the span of a minute, she had dismissed me and every bad thing that had ever happened to me. It was bizarre.

As the women fawned over me, offering me praise and congratulations for having such a strong, forgiving heart, I felt painfully awkward.

Putting me even more on the spot, Pastor Gracie encouraged me to tell my story.

Did she expect me to go along with her fabrication?

"I'm sorry, I didn't think I would be talking about this," I stammered, feeling embarrassed and hot.

Speaking on my behalf, not that I had asked her to, Pastor Gracie went on, piling one embellishment on top of the next.

"Crystal is ready to do the Lord's work. We talked about the area of ministry she would like to go into."

I was baffled. We hadn't talked about any of that. But again, I got the distinct impression that the pastor was *telling* me, in her own way, what I ought to think, be, and do.

"Perhaps this Sunday she'll share her wonderful testimony with the congregation," she added.

It gave me serious pause, but I managed to squeeze out, "We'll see…"

I glanced over at Lars who was being smothered by Pastor Joe in the same manner. Uncomfortable,

Lars widened his eyes at me as if to suggest we should abort the mission, but I shook my head at him. We couldn't turn back now!

One of the other men caught my eye and leered at me, but Pastor Joe said, "Emmet, come along," and he followed after them as the entire men's group exited the vestibule, heading upstairs for the fellowship hall.

Emmet… Emmet… why did he strike me as vaguely familiar?

"We've been studying the Book of Acts," said Kathy or Cath or Kathleen—I couldn't keep them straight. She urged me into the sanctuary where Pastor Gracie was leading the ladies up the aisle. "If you would like to sit next to me, we can share my bible. I have the New King James version, the large print edition. I have an extra pair of reading glasses, if you'd like to borrow them, but please don't forget to return them. People are always forgetting to return my reading glasses…"

Throughout the next hour, in addition to breaking down the hidden meaning behind the first four chapters of the Book of Acts, Pastor Gracie gave me a whole new life story, one that was chock-full of Christ even though, in reality, Christ had never made an appearance during my upbringing, nor had he been present during my adult years. She completely erased the childhood I had spent in a trailer park. Every time she lifted her nose from her bible, she related the verses she had read to my miraculous life journey, not that I'd had one. Thanks to Pastor Gracie, as far as the other women knew, my mother had never been a hooker and I hadn't ended up just like her. Rather, Pastor Gracie had characterized my mother as a hardworking lover of the Lord. If that hadn't been bad enough, she had also recharacterized my relationship with Robert, leading everyone to believe that he and I would soon be married.

She had placed me at the center of the bible study for reasons I couldn't understand. It was as though she didn't want the church ladies to know about my real past. But instead of letting my private business be my own and trusting me not to divulge my ties to the strip club, she had decided to reinvent me.

I felt like a nail that was being hammered farther and farther down into a plank of wood until it was reduced to a dot of metal. I wasn't different from any of the other women, according to Pastor Gracie. I was no longer unique and troubled and angry. Pastor Gracie had obliterated me. She had even mistakenly referred to me as *Kristen* again, and she was so confident about it that the other ladies started calling me *Kristen* as well, convinced that if Pastor Gracie thought my name was Kristen and I didn't, then I was probably the one who was mistaken.

"Pastor Gracie?" I said, getting her attention once the bible study had let out. "My name is actually *Crystal.*"

"Oh! Darn it! Did I flub your name again? I'm so sorry about that! Shoot!"

"It's okay," I said, even though it wasn't. "But, um, could I talk to you?"

"Certainly!"

She waved goodbye to the other ladies as they made their way out of the vestibule and into the sunny afternoon. I glanced through the doors that led to the fellowship hall, hoping I would see Lars leaving the men's bible study group, but he was still trapped up there. I could hear Pastor Joe's thunderous voice carrying down through the floorboards.

"It's just that—"

"Yes, dear?"

"I couldn't help but notice, you seemed to *tell* everyone *who I am* every chance you got, but what you were saying about me wasn't accurate."

"Such as?"

Was she serious? *Such as everything,* I wanted to say.

"Such as, well, you led everyone to believe I had a Christian upbringing—"

"Oh, that," she balked as if I was overreacting. "That's nothing. Once you walk with the Lord long enough, you'll realize he was with you all along."

"Even still, it made me uncomfortable. I would appreciate it if you stuck to the facts, or you could simply not say anything about me. I mean, I was sitting right there the whole time. If I wanted to open up about myself, I would have."

"I'm aware of that, dear, but you see, I didn't want you to." Her tone had an edge.

I was taken aback.

She offered me a tight smile. It wasn't genuine.

Then she informed me, "I know you used to be a stripper and I very sincerely hope you've given up that type of employment, I really do. You'll have to forgive me, but considering everything that's happened on Woodland Beach; considering what happened to those poor girls—and I know you used to work with them—I think it would be best if the parishioners of this church don't find out about your prior line of work. Wouldn't you agree?"

"I didn't come here to broadcast my personal business," I assured her.

I was about to say more when she chirped, "Good."

"Okay…"

She wasted no time escorting me to the door. "You have a blessed day, now!"

I stumbled out the door mainly because she pushed me. "I *will* have a blessed day!"

"Toodle loo!"

I had learned nothing about Thomas's whereabouts, nothing about Cherry and Original Jewel's murders, and nothing about whether or not Thomas had really killed them. I was pissed. I felt insulted, and I was melting under my church lady costume, it was so hot out. I could've screamed or punched the door or charged up to the fellowship hall and demanded answers from the men. The killer was somewhere inside that church—he had to be!—but I knew that being impatient and forceful wouldn't help.

Sweltering, I jerked my blazer off, grateful I had been smart enough to wear a bikini underneath, and flung one of my kitten-heel pumps off my foot then the other and watched them soar into the street where the second heel struck Seth in the head.

"Ow!"

He had been peddling his bicycle but the blow caused him to lose control, wobble, and spill across the sidewalk.

"What the heck?"

"Sorry!"

As he picked himself up, dusted himself off, and began assessing his bike to see if the fall had done any damage, I jogged towards him in my bare feet, holding my inside-out blazer in my fist.

No one knew Thomas better than Seth Nash.

When he hopped onto his bicycle and took off again, I called out:

"Hey, wait up!"

THE BOY

CRYSTAL APOLOGIZED, as she examined my forehead where her pointy heel had bonked me.

After determining I would live, she offered to make it up to me with ice cream.

I gladly accepted, and she collected her flung shoes from the middle of the road, brought me to her car, and found a nest of tangled bungee cords in the trunk, which we used to strap my bicycle to the roof.

Driving over to Woodland Beach felt like a dream.

I cranked my window down. Hot wind punched through the car, whipping Crystal's blonde hair in her face. She didn't take her eyes off the road. She concentrated on downshifting and upshifting as we rounded one bend then the next, following the curving bay as the road made its winding way towards the ocean.

She hadn't initiated conversation, which was nothing new.

For the most part, Crystal was awkward around me. Guarded. She rarely made eye contact at the house, choosing rather to study me when she thought I wasn't looking, her way of figuring me out, perhaps. Not that I could begin to guess what she was figuring out. I had gone from openly despising her to trying with all my might to be her friend. I often assisted her in the kitchen whenever she cooked dinner. She remained consistently suspicious of my help, however. I had even gotten in the habit of handing her detergent, fabric softener, and dryer sheets whenever she did the laundry, and if she was vacuuming, I moved furniture so she wouldn't have to. She probably thought I was lying in wait to attack her again, but I wasn't.

Thomas had told me to love her, and that's what I was trying to do.

To my surprise, I had actually grown to like her quite a bit. I liked her huge, sad eyes and how she never complained. I liked the anger that would rise up in her cheeks whenever the temperature in the living room felt too hot, and most of all, I liked how she had inserted herself into our lives. She had made our house a home, and I couldn't help but compare her to my deceased mother. I wondered if my mom would have been anything like Crystal.

Would my mother gasp at the sounds of pocket change rattling around in the dryer and throw the door open the moment it occurred to her that she might have accidentally washed cash as well? Crystal did that all the time. Had she lived, would my mother grumble curse words under her breath whenever she chased a fat fly around the kitchen with a rolled electric bill in her fist, swatting and missing and swatting again until she squashed the thing? Would she, like Crystal, smell of flowers and salty skin—sunkissed and feminine—whenever she glided from one room to the next in search of a misplaced earring?

Sometimes I caught myself staring at Crystal. She was the closest thing to a mother I had ever had.

I didn't want Thomas to be right about her fate. I didn't want her to turn up murdered. I couldn't bear the thought of losing her, but I didn't know how to love her in a way that would guarantee she would live to see the summer turn to autumn. I didn't know how to love Crystal in the way that Thomas loved me. Thomas was magical, mystical, and spiritual, and I was just a boy.

"Close your eyes," she said, having parked in the very back of the public lot near the promenade. "I have to change out of this polyester skirt before I go insane."

She had driven barefoot in her bikini top, but her starched skirt, which sat high on her waist and hung down past her knees, was the main reason she was glistening with sweat.

I did as I was told and pinched my eyes closed, as she pushed her seat all the way back, rummaged through a bag, and began changing.

"You go to the church a lot?" she asked.

"Every day, sometimes twice a day."

"Yeah? What do you think of those people? Keep your eyes closed!"

"I thought you were done—"

"I'll tell you when I'm done!"

"I didn't see anything," I promised and squeezed my eyes shut so hard they hurt. "The people at church are nice."

She stopped moving around in the driver's seat, and if I had to guess, I would say she was staring at me in disbelief.

I leveled with her. "Uncle Robert thinks I need constant adult supervision. The church is my own personal prison." I shrugged. "But it's not like I *live* there."

"I don't know about those people... I don't know about Pastor Gracie... She's got those women wrapped around her finger."

"She's strict," I agreed. "She once smacked me with a ruler."

Crystal considered the information and asked, "Did you deserve it?"

"Probably," I admitted.

"Keep your eyes closed."

"I am!" I complained, as I blindly felt around my door for the manual hand crank to open my window some more. "Pastor Asa is the one who runs all of the kids' programs," I explained, rolling my window down until I could drape my arm out of the car. "Pastor Gracie only sometimes fills in, thank God. She's brutal, but her son is alright. He wants us to like him. That's the difference."

"You like Pastor Asa?"

"I like him enough. I mean, he answers my questions, which is more than Pastor Gracie does, but I don't always like his answers."

"Questions about...?"

"The bible. God. Whether or not my mom is in heaven. Whether or not Uncle Robert is going to hell—"

"You ask him stuff like that?

"Sometimes."

"You can open your eyes now."

We climbed out and started for the beachy promenade.

Walking side by side, Crystal towered over me in her heels. Her bangles jingled on her wrist. Her tank top flapped in the warm wind.

I stole glances at her and felt a curious rush of tenderness swell in my chest that I didn't quite understand.

"Pastors Joe and Gracie…" I went on, thoughtfully. "It's hard to explain… they don't like it when you ask questions. They *say* it's good to ask questions, but you can tell they don't like it. Like one time, I asked Pastor Gracie about a story in the bible where God told an army to kill everyone and everything in an enemy town. The soldiers didn't want to kill the women and children so they only killed the men. I asked Pastor Gracie, did the soldiers sin because they didn't murder *everyone*?"

"What did she say?"

"She told me that Christ changed everything."

"Meaning, there's no point in even asking?" she said, correctly guessing Pastor Gracie's attitude at the time.

"See what I mean? I got in trouble, too. She treated me like a criminal for the rest of the winter after that."

"Like you're a kid trying to get away with murder…"

She looked at me differently and I didn't say anything, as we came to the promenade where restaurants, bars, and shops arced around the gazebo, not far from the arcade. Tourists milled about, taking family photos and making memories. Teens on skateboards used the gazebo steps to pop tricks. A little girl with cotton candy passed us, and I briefly wondered where she had gotten it, then the girl's father scooped her up into his arms before she could get lost in the crowd.

Crystal and I neared the ice cream stand, and she asked me what I wanted, as she found cash in her purse.

Moments later, we were walking down the fishing pier, the busy promenade falling away behind us. I couldn't lick my melting vanilla cone fast enough. We reached the end. The atmosphere was so clear, I could see New Jersey in the distance where my mother had once lived.

Crystal looked beautiful nibbling her chocolate cone—beautiful, and as if she needed me. She had never asked me so many questions. My uncle probably wouldn't have been able to answer her questions. He hadn't been to church for as long as I had known him, except for last Sunday when Crystal had expressed interest. He hadn't acted very happy to be there, and I doubted that if Crystal had wanted to know more about Christ, he would have taken the time to tell her the gospel.

"Seth, does your friend Thomas ever go to Lighthouse Ministries?"

I screwed my face up.

Why was she asking me about Thomas?

Suddenly suspicious, I felt my guard fly up. I knew that all of Delaware thought Thomas had killed Dead Amanda Dover and Dead Jewel Payson, but I hadn't known Crystal thought that as well.

Why would she want to risk spoiling our time together? The sun was shining. Our conversation about the church had been good. We were having ice cream. Why ruin all that?

"Does he?" she pushed.

"I've never seen him there—"

"When did you see him last?"

Was this a joke? How many times had I told Uncle Robert that Thomas hadn't done it? How many times had Crystal been sitting right there when I had presented a perfectly logical case in defense of Thomas from the sea?

I lost my appetite. Vanilla ice cream dripped down my fingers.

"Seth?"

"I see him all the time," I blurted out, irritated.

"Do you understand that the police are looking for him?" she berated me. "If you know where Thomas is, you have to say something."

I couldn't even look at her.

"You're just a kid and you're probably blameless, but when you pulled me out into the water that day, you were calling for Thomas."

I caught the implication. "I wasn't trying to hurt you."

"You said you were trying to save me. You're confused. Did Thomas put you up to that? Did you pull Amanda Dover and Jewel Payson into the sea, as well?"

"No," I told her, feeling betrayed.

I threw my soggy cone and watched it plunk into the water far below.

"Where is Thomas, Seth?"

"You want to know where he is?"

"Yes."

"He's out there!" I said, pointing to the horizon line where the ocean blended into the sky. "He comes from the sea and he returns there! He walks on water! He's God! You won't find him in the church, because he's out there in the sea!"

She stopped pushing. Alarmed, her pretty face went slack. She looked scared for me and also scared *of* me. There was pity in her eyes, but caution as well.

Very carefully, she asked, "Seth, do you think that Thomas is Jesus?"

There was no point in answering. She didn't believe me.

She sighed, pulled me in, and hugged me, holding me close and protectively and maybe even motheringly.

I had never felt anything like it before. No one at church hugged me. Uncle Robert certainly hadn't. Ever. Other than the occasional pat on the shoulder from Pastor Asa, I wasn't sure I had ever received affection from anyone.

I could've stayed on that fishing pier, hugging Crystal forever.

"We don't have parents," she told me as if we were two peas in a pod. "We don't have fathers or mothers. We've been damaged from the start. We haven't gotten what we need, and there's no point in complaining to anyone because no one gets it. This is what we're left with. Madness."

She stroked my hair and swayed me. I closed my eyes and felt the walls give way.

"I'm not going anywhere, Seth."

I wanted so badly to believe her.

❄

I CARRIED THE feeling of Crystal holding me long after she had let go.

The rotating fan on my desk blew warm, briny air across my bedroom. Night had fallen. I was stretched out, lying on my bed with my bible open to the Gospel of Luke. My bible study workbook was resting in front of me on the covers. I tapped my pencil against the workbook, stumped.

I hadn't made much of a dent in the section that Pastor Asa had assigned, and something told me Thomas wasn't going to let me listen to Dire Straits until I had.

He was my best friend, for sure, but he was also determined to be a good influence on me, which was his only flaw.

He said that my essay answers were important. Pastor Asa and the kids at church would benefit from my perspective, Thomas often told me, but I seriously begged to differ.

At the moment, Thomas was lounging on my chair where a stack of comics usually sat hidden under a mountain of sandy tee shirts.

Thomas had become gradually luminous since I had met him. It was getting to the point where I didn't actually have to turn on the lights when he was around. His hair wasn't brown anymore, but looked like liquid gold. His skin had turned bronzy and glowed. Though he still wore swim trunks, a tee-shirt, and sandals, the material seemed to have absorbed his radiance.

Crystal was out in the living room with Uncle Robert listening to some old doo-wop record, but I couldn't hear them chatting because Thomas had waved his hand earlier, and like magic, my bedroom had become soundproof so I could concentrate.

I could hardly concentrate.

I longed to sit next to Crystal in the living room. I longed to listen to her soft voice until I dozed off. Longed to pretend that she was my mom and that we were a family and that nothing else mattered.

I doubted Uncle Robert would allow me to enjoy her company, though. He hadn't seemed too pleased when he had come home from the prison to find Crystal already in the house. I had let her in. Why should she have to wait outside if I was home? Uncle Robert had the weirdest rules.

I tapped my pencil against my workbook, annoyed with the first question. "The Gospel of Luke presents what cornerstone theology?"

Thomas knew everything so I glanced at him, hoping he would answer the workbook question and save me the trouble.

"Are you asking me?" he said.

"Are you willing to tell me?"

He frowned.

I frowned.

"I'll come back to that one," I said after failing to get my friend to take the bait. "The next questions are fill-in-the-blanks," I went on, as I tapped my pencil harder against the workbook. "*Today in the town of David a Savior has been born to you; he is the Messiah, the Lord. This will be a sign to you, a* blank *and a* blank'..." I murmured as I flipped through the New Testament, looking for the verse, "Where is it…? Where is it…?"

I glanced at Thomas.

He had mercy on me and said, "A baby and a manger. Chapter two… verse twelve…"

"Found it!" I jotted the entire verse down and moved on to the next question. "*'Every year the Lord's parents went to Jerusalem for the Festival of the'* blank."

"The Passover," he supplied.

I quickly noted the answer. "*'While they were still talking about this, the Lord himself stood among them and said to them, 'Peace be with you.' They were* blank *and* blank, *thinking they saw a ghost.'*"

"Shocked and terrified."

"Huh, my translation says *'startled and frightened'*."

"They were definitely shocked and terrified when they saw me after the resurrection," he maintained.

"*Shocked* and *terrified,* it is!" I exclaimed, penciling in Thomas's exact wording. Lifting my nose out of the workbook, I asked, "They didn't recognize you?"

"Many didn't."

"After all the time they had spent with you?"

"I didn't look the same to them. They doubted, and it clouded their vision." He held my gaze for a long moment then asked, "Did you know who I was when I found you?"

Shaking my head, I told him, "Not immediately."

"But now you believe."

"Well, now it's obvious!"

He smiled brightly.

I returned a grin, but all of a sudden, my spirits drooped.

"The police are looking for you, Thomas. What if they find you? What if they arrest you and you're convicted of killing those women? No one will recognize you. No one will understand who you really are—you said it yourself. My uncle will be the one who executes you."

Unconcerned, he shrugged and said, "They can't crucify me twice."

"No," I agreed. "They use lethal injection now."

THE EXECUTIONER

WHEN I HAD STORMED into Warden Cromwell's office and demanded proper medical training before the next execution, the last person I expected him to procure was Senior CO Silas Digby from Missouri, but here we were, stuck in the seventh ring of hell all over again.

This time, in addition to his pamphlets, Digby had come armed with a how-to demonstration on VHS and—far more disturbing—an actual cadaver. The human cadaver was packed in ice but leaking all over my office. Digby assured me the body itself wasn't liquifying due to decomposition. The liquid was only melting ice, he said. However, the stink it gave off told a different story.

We watched the VHS tape through to its useless conclusion, after which I knew nothing more about locating and successfully penetrating the femoral artery than I had the night of Kowalski's execution. What I *had* learned, however, was that if you couldn't see or feel a bulging vein, you were pretty much destined to fail. The nurse on the video had performed an IV insertion on three patients—a woman, a man, and lastly a child—and every time, she didn't make a move until their vein had popped up, blue and ropey, from their skin.

The patients on the video had not been men who were facing their own executions. They hadn't been terror-stricken. They hadn't been anticipating the agony and shame that came with being put to death. In fact, they hadn't been patients at all. They were bright-eyed, bushy-tailed actors who had probably been paid handsomely for their appearance in the medical video, thinking they were well on their way to stardom.

If I had learned anything over the years working on Death Row, it was that the prison cells alone could cause an inmate's balls to shrivel up into his abdomen. Blood ran cold on the Block. Vessels constricted. If I wanted an inmate's vein to bulge in the death chamber, everything about the situation would fight against me, and I would probably lose. Even if I cranked the heat up to 100℉, there would be no guarantee that the inmate's femoral artery would emerge from deep within his elbow.

I wanted to smack the smug look right off Cromwell's face, as he glanced from the television monitor to me and then to Digby, grinning like an idiot.

"Very informative," said Cromwell, praising the video.

Had he been paying attention? Digby's video hadn't been informative at all. But apparently, I was the only one who had been annoyed by the bad camera angles and the fast-talking nurse.

"What's next, CO Digby?" asked the warden.

Digby planted his shaky hands on the table and hoisted himself to his feet, looking like a man closer to death than Prinkerton who was slated to die come Sunday. There was a black syringe case the size of a paperback book on the table, which he unzipped. Inside, syringe needles were lined in a neat row. A plastic bag full of latex gloves was nearby and after pulling a pair on, he told Cromwell and me, "What is next is that we practice on the cadaver."

That was when the tutorial got really grim.

Digby unzipped the body bag and a revolting stench hit me like a punch to the nose. Cromwell covered his mouth, gagging, and leapt away from the cadaver, but my office wasn't big enough to escape the smell.

If anything was going to get me through this, it would be my determination to give Prinkerton as smooth and humane an execution as I possibly could.

William Prinkerton hadn't done it. He hadn't killed that little disabled girl. He hadn't deserved to get locked up a decade ago, and he certainly didn't deserve to die. Whenever I heard Willy's heartfelt prayers emanating through Death Row, I felt sick to my stomach, and even now my heart burned at the savage injustice he was facing.

But I had no power, no control. There was nothing I could do other than make his execution quick, and make sure he didn't suffer a second longer than he had to.

With that in mind, I suppressed my emotions, gritted my teeth, and pulled on a pair of latex gloves. Until I was consistently able to insert a needle into the femoral artery, I was not going to let myself leave this room.

"Let's go, Digby," I barked.

The stench had pushed the old man to the far side of my office. Cromwell slipped out and I heard him heaving in the corridor.

When Digby hadn't moved, I suggested, "You take the left arm and I'll follow your lead with the right."

Digby bolted for the door, making his escape after the warden. I heard him mutter, "Jumping Jehoshaphat, I'm a month from retirement!" before he disappeared.

Alone, dizzy with nausea, my eyes stung and began tearing up, the revolting odor was so thick in the air.

I uncapped the first syringe needle and began poking the cold, inner elbow of the thawing cadaver, feeling around for a vein I could puncture and also feeling that getting hired at the Vaughn Correctional Center was the worst thing that had ever happened to me outside of my sister Abby's death.

I knew right then and there that I was not going to come back from this...

...but I was already too far gone.

HOURS LATER, Digby returned with two men wearing hazmat suits to haul the cadaver away. By then, I was slumped in my office chair, staring into space, wishing that the whiskey I had found in my desk would hit my bloodstream already and calm me down. I had guzzled every last drop but it hadn't helped.

If Digby was offering me any words of encouragement, I didn't hear him. Didn't lift my gaze or acknowledge him in any way, shape, or form, and the next thing I knew I was alone again with the door closed.

I had struggled and gagged. Sweat had broken out across my forehead and my chest, drenching my uniform. For all my efforts, I didn't have a clue whether or not I had punctured the right vein even once.

I was going to have to execute Prinkerton. There would be no getting out of it. But for God's sake, I didn't want to *kill* him. It was my job to take his life, but I didn't want to *murder* him. There was a difference and the fine line separating the two included skill, training, preparedness, and confidence, all of which I lacked.

I really wasn't sure how much longer I could keep living this life.

Crystal had been helping immensely. She had been reviving me. She recalibrated my spirit whenever I got home. She wasn't a wife and she wasn't a girlfriend and in a lot of ways she was bleeding me dry financially, but having her gave me a taste of normalcy—the kind of domestic, humdrum, blissfully boring sort of routine that made me happy.

I was starting to think I loved her. There was something weirdly miraculous about having a woman in my bed night after night. Long ago, I had accepted the probability that having someone significant in my life wasn't going to happen.

My logic was due in part to raising Seth. He had been a handful from the start, and I had never been especially good with him. Changing diapers and warming baby formula on the stove hadn't come naturally. But resigning myself to a solitary life was also due in large part to my own choices. Abby's death had been a tragedy that I had never fully moved on from. It had destroyed me.

Was Crystal significant?

All I knew was that she didn't seem to mind that I was broken. She was a collection of shattered pieces herself. Together, our jagged edges fit, hers sparkling and mine rough and as dark as stone.

I didn't know if I could fully let myself love her—didn't know if I could openly show her the true feelings that had been churning inside me—because I knew that if I did and if she was taken from me like Abby, I would lose my humanity and become the essence of pure, unbridled, and irreversible godlessness.

From deep within Death Row, Prinkerton began wailing.

"Lord, save me from death!"

Listening to his desperate pleas made my soul ache.

"I beseech you, Lord! Bless me with freedom and salvation!"

My stomach tightened.

"Deliver me from evil, Christ my Lord, and deliver me from the hands of men! Don't let them kill me, Lord! You are the highest authority, my God! Please don't let them take my life!"

I couldn't stomach listening to him, but the door was already closed. There was nothing more I could do to muffle his cries. It was the hope in his voice that made it excruciating. He truly believed the Lord would intervene.

"Pray for me, Pastor!"

Pastor Asa's response was too low for me to hear, but I could guess what he was saying.

The young missionary had recently been moved by Willy's faith. Instead of focusing his prayers solely on the inmate's *eternal* salvation, Pastor Asa had started praying for Willy's release, too. All week, they had been fervently appealing to God Almighty, asking the Lord to compel the governor to issue Willy a stay of execution. Shouting until their throats went raw and their voices turned hoarse, their prayers had been unrelenting.

CO Lyle McKay had retaliated whenever their earnest cries filled Death Row. Hotheaded, he had banged his baton against Willy's steel door and threatened Pastor Asa with bodily harm, but McKay's aggression couldn't stop them. The two had persisted, convinced that Christ was on their side.

I wasn't convinced that Christ was on anyone's side.

Across Death Row, Pastor Asa and Willy's prayers went quiet, and a few moments later, I heard footsteps approaching my closed office door. A knock came next.

"Mr. Nash?"

"Come in!"

Pastor Asa was timid about entering even after I had invited him in with a wave.

"I wondered if I might have a word?"

I had assumed as much.

He neared my desk, walking around the folding table where a dead cadaver had lain an hour ago. He didn't sit down, but rather wrung his hands together nervously.

"I would like to make a case for William Prinkerton—"

"Asa, my hands are tied—"

"If there's some form I could fill out on his behalf—"

"If there was a form, *I* would fill it out, believe me—"

"There has to be something that can be done about this. He's appealed time and again, and his latest petition is currently with a Supreme Court Judge. Surely that means something. Surely there's a way to at least delay his execution date until the courts issue a final determination."

"There isn't."

He straightened his spine and looked me square in the eye. "Surely, as a Christian, you cannot execute this man."

I sprang to my feet. "You think it's up to me?"

"I have very strong convictions that—"

"You can take your convictions back to your church! They don't belong here! Here we do what we're told, and if you think I have any say in the matter, you've got another thing coming! I could get hit by a bus tomorrow and Cromwell would just replace me with another CO come execution day, so don't you dare make this about Christianity and assume I have a choice. The legal system has tied my hands behind my back, and if you don't like it, maybe you should try being a lawyer instead of a preacher!"

His expression hardened and he said darkly, "I'm going to pray for you."

It wasn't until he had left my office that I realized Pastor Asa had threatened me.

THE STRIPPER

WHILE THE POLICE were on the hunt for Seth's imaginary friend, Thomas, I met with Lars at my apartment.

Since I had seen him last at the church, Lars had fully embraced his Christian persona. He had quit the band, bought a bible, and had dumped his Euro-pop wardrobe off at GoodWill. He was dressed in a three-piece suit and sitting on the edge of my bed.

Lars had been going on and on about Pastor Joseph Asbury, who he was in complete awe of.

Apparently, Pastor Joe had been helping Lars emotionally recover from, and spiritually reconcile, what had happened to Cherry. He was no longer devastated, but seemed strangely at peace with her murder.

"God works in mysterious ways, and I'm now able to see that thanks to Pastor Joe," he went on, as I patiently waited for Lars to finish his long-winded point and focus on the clues I had tacked to my bulletin board. "I can't tell you how supportive he is. His capacity for empathy is tremendous. I no longer feel alone. He cries when I cry. He gets angry when I get angry. But when I feel lost, he offers words of wisdom that really do soothe me."

I was extremely surprised to hear that, given my experiences with Pastor Gracie, but that was neither here nor there. Lars and I had gone into the church for a specific reason and I was eager to learn the information he had gathered as a result of attending the men's bible study.

"Listen to this," he said, returning his attention to his open bible and diving in. "Christ said, *'Let not your hearts be troubled. Believe in God; believe also in me. In my Father's house are many rooms. If it were not so, would I have told you that I go to prepare a place for you? And if I go and prepare a place for you, I will come again and will take you to myself, that where I am you may also be.'* That's the Lord speaking in John 14, verses 1 through 3."

Clearly, our mission had backfired—terribly.

"Cherry had reconnected with the church," he reminded me, his wide eyes filling with tears. "Before she was killed, she had restored her faith. She's in heaven now. You see? Christ prepared a room for her in his Father's house. I think the Lord decorated the room he prepared for Cherry with the paisley curtains and pink pillows she always liked. Pastor Joe helped me understand this. Isn't it beautiful? Wait, there's more…"

Before he could read the next verse, I stopped him. "What did you find out about Cherry's actual *involvement* in the church? Was she interacting with anyone questionable?"

Standing in front of my bulletin board, I was poised and ready to document his leads. I had four uncapped pens and highlighters in my hands and a stack of notecards under my arm. I had even pre-stuck a slew of colored Post-its to my forearm for easy access.

Lars closed his bible and gave it an affectionate pat. "Lots of really good stuff in there."

"Lars?"

My patience was wearing out, but I waited as he wiped a tear from his eye, bowed his head, folded his hands together—*oh, no*—and said, "Let us pray—"

"Lars!" I snapped.

"Fine, Crystal!" he snapped right back.

I huffed, he puffed, then he finally got on with it.

"This is what I learned. Cherry had been floating in and out of the Sunday services at Lighthouse Ministries. She was enrolled in Christian Counseling, and my understanding is that she only made it to a few counseling sessions with Pastor Gracie before she ended up canceling altogether in a voicemail message. No one at the church thought much of it. That kind of thing happens all the time. Jewel Payson, on the other hand, never set foot in Lighthouse Ministries, but she did meet Pastor Gracie after an AA meeting at the YMCA."

"I knew it. They recruit alcoholics, don't they—the pastors?"

"I'm not sure *recruit* is the right term, but yes," he allowed. "They're good people, the pastors—"

"We don't know that," I reminded him.

"Oh, Crystal, come on. Joe and Gracie are good people," he argued.

"What else?" I asked to keep my eyes from rolling up into my skull.

"There's only one person at the church who I suspect at this point. A new member named Emmet DeGraves."

"DeGraves," I repeated as I wrote the man's name on one of my color-coded notecards. I fit the notecard onto my bulletin board and said, "Does DeGraves connect to Cherry or Jewel?"

"Both of them."

I locked eyes with Lars. "Both of them?"

"He's been going to the same AA meetings. He could've easily met Jewel Payson there."

"And he's been going to the church, obviously?" I added as I struggled to open a container of push-pins. I needed to jot down all of these clues and tack them to my bulletin board.

"Yes, he's been going to church, *and* he's a regular at *Mermaids*," he said.

I was so astonished to hear about the *Mermaids* connection that I accidentally jerked open the push-pins container, causing hundreds of tiny, metal tacks to rain down over Lars.

He weathered the storm, unperturbed thanks to Christ, then informed me, "I overheard Emmett talking with another man named Charles Riley about going to the strip club. They didn't know I was eavesdropping, but I caught their entire conversation. During one of the bathroom breaks, they made plans to drop by Mermaids tonight. If you ask me, Charles Riley is ready for the Lord. Emmet is the one who strikes me as evil. He hasn't been attending church earnestly, in my opinion."

I pinned red string to the Emmet DeGraves notecard I had made and attached the other end of the string to the first notecard on Cherry's timeline. With another piece of red string, I did the same for Jewel's timeline, connecting her murder to DeGraves. All the while, I made a mental note to question DeGraves myself, not that I knew how I would pull that off.

"Emmett DeGraves…" I said, wracking my brain. "If he's a Mermaids regular, I would've seen him. What does he look like?"

"He's a little taller than me, maybe six-feet tall. He looks like a working-class man." Nearly everyone who went to Mermaids looked like a working-class man. "He's muscular, and has an almost stocky build," he went on, listing other physical characteristics. Lastly, he told me, "Emmet kind of looks like a rusty bucket."

I knew exactly who he was talking about. Bizarrely, it was the *rusty bucket* description that instantly brought Emmet DeGraves to mind. But I didn't remember him from the club. He was the man who had been staring at me from the church vestibule when I had first sat down with Pastor Gracie in the sanctuary to discuss the possibility of starting Christian counseling. That day, I had felt watched. I had glanced over my shoulder and had found Emmett leering at me.

"Crystal?"

"I've seen him," I said, having slipped into deep, troubling thought.

I knew what I would have to do if I wanted to catch Emmett DeGraves before he killed again…

I would have to go to Mermaids and beg for my old job back.

OUTSIDE MERMAIDS, Jimbo's sidewalk sign was flashing *LIVE! NUDE! GIRLS!* in neon print. A cop car was parked along the curb as always. And the humid sea air smelled just the same as I had remembered. But if I thought nothing had changed since the last time I had set foot in the club, I quickly discovered how wrong I was the moment I got inside.

The place was packed.

Clearly, the appeal of watching *LIVE! NUDE! GIRLS!* dance on stage had attracted paying customers from all over, and not one of them minded that they couldn't order an alcoholic drink.

As I squeezed my way out of the anteroom and into the club, I noticed one of the police officers. He was seated at the edge of the stage and tossing bills at Destiny's fully-naked pole dance. I wondered if he had ditched his partner, who was outside in their parked cruiser, or if they were taking turns.

I scanned the floor for Emmett DeGraves. Customers bumped into my giant stripper bag as they passed, knocking me around. The strobing lights and mirrored disco ball glimmering across the lounge were mesmerizing. There were too many men and I didn't recognize most of the exotic dancers. Jimbo must have gone on a hiring spree when business had started booming.

If I wanted to get changed into my stripper outfit and really start investigating, I was going to have to bite the bullet and face Jimbo, but he was nowhere in sight.

His cousin, Timbo, however, was standing at his usual post behind the long bar counter where customers were seated, not because they wanted drinks but because all the other spots in the lounge were occupied. Strippers oozed over them as the men stuffed cash into the sides of their G-strings.

I pressed through the thick crowd, weaving my way towards the bar.

Timbo was instantly delighted to see me.

"Crystal?" he shouted over the loud music.

Donna Summer's *She Works Hard for the Money* was playing. Not my favorite tune. A little cheesy for a strip club, but the song was better than anything Bruce Springsteen had released in the past year. Finally, Timbo had taken my musical advice.

"Tell me you're back!"

"I'm back!" I exclaimed as I leapt across the bar counter and gave him a great big hug. He felt as damp as ever. His bold Hawaiian shirt was soggy to the touch. I teased, "Did you miss me?"

"I missed you like hell, Crystal!"

Damn, I missed this place, too. I missed the booming music and the glittery lighting. The smell of cigarette smoke brought back fond memories. Even the stupid-looking mermaid mural on the wall had me tearing up.

Suddenly, I realized I was home.

"You're going to have to talk to Jimbo!" he told me once I had slid back to my side of the counter. "We hired five new dancers, but he would be crazy not to put you on stage!"

"Where is he?" I asked, scanning the crowded lounge again.

"He wasn't in the front? Must be in his office!"

"Thanks, Timbo!"

As I started off, he called out, "What song should I cue up for you?"

I felt tingly just thinking about it. "*Da Ya Think I'm Sexy!*" I decided. "I've been craving Ron Stewart for weeks now!"

"Classic!"

Having learned nothing from my time in church, I grooved my way through the club, soaking up the energy as I lugged my giant stripper bag along. Feeling the music, I swayed and bopped and grinded against one customer then the next even though I was still in my street clothes.

"Crystal?"

"Amber!"

I pushed towards her and gave her a quick hug before I realized she was lap-dancing all over Channel 7's renowned news anchor, Andy Ailey.

"I knew you would come back!" she said as a new song started booming through the club. "Girl, you need to get in on this cash flow! I'm telling you, Jimbo turned this place around!"

"I can see that!" Thoroughly impressed, I drank in the sight of her. "Your nails look amazing!"

She fluttered her fingers in front of my face and bragged, "Destiny quit that dumb salon, but they've been giving us group rates anyway! Mani-pedis for twenty a pop so long as you pay cash. You just have to name-drop 'Mermaids'!"

"Cool!"

"Jimbo's in his office," she said, reading my mind.

Channel 7's Andy Ailey grinned up at Amber so she asked him, "Ready for a private room, baby?"

"I'll see you later!" I said, leaving her to coax the broadcaster out of his chair and into one of the expensive private rooms.

I reached the velvet curtain in the very back of the club and slipped into the dimly lit hallway. The ladies' dressing room was to my left. Jimbo's office was farther down. I came to the open doorway and knocked.

Seated on the business-side of his desk, buried in cash and credit card receipts, Jimbo did a bit of a double-take when he saw me filling the doorway.

He wasn't surprised to see me, but he didn't look happy.

Setting the calculator he had been using aside, he leaned back and showed no signs of emotion.

For a worried moment, I thought he was going to tell me to go to hell.

But he didn't.

"Come in, shut the door."

"I have to hand it to you, Jimbo. You really turned things around. I hear the girls are happy."

"They *are* happy," he confirmed in a tone of voice so neutral that for a split second I questioned if I had ever known him. Folding his arms, he stated, "They trusted me. They stuck with me. They were loyal, and it paid off."

"I should've trusted you and stuck with you," I admitted, groveling because that was what he wanted to hear. "I shouldn't have left. I can barely afford to put gas in my car."

"Oh? What have you been doing with yourself?"

The correct answer that Jimbo was looking for had nothing to do with low-key prostitution, so I lied. "Working in the stockroom at the Dollar Store."

"What a shame," he said as he stood and rounded out from behind his desk to get a better look at me. "My mermaid, who in their right mind would hide you in a warehouse?"

"Some jerk."

"Do you want your job back?"

"If you'll have me."

"Let's take a look at you."

The thick scent of his cologne washed over me, as he took my face in his large hands and began examining me like a horse breeder would a thoroughbred to assess if she had what it would take to win the blue ribbon.

"Your skin looks clear," he noted. "You'll need to put on dramatic makeup. Did you notice I changed the lights?"

"Yes, the club looks great."

"Do you have red lipstick? Everything must pop."

"Yes, I can redo my makeup in the dressing room," I assured him.

Taking a slow lap around me, he remarked, "You've put on a few pounds. It suits you."

"Thanks," I said as he came to face me once again.

He narrowed his gaze, deciding whether or not to take me back.

My heart was in my throat. He didn't *need* me to dance. He probably had too many dancers as it was. He could easily send me home. But I couldn't let him do that. I had to be here. I could feel in my gut, with every shred of my female intuition, that I would encounter Emmett DeGraves out there in the lounge if I waited long enough. Earlier today, Lars had overheard DeGraves and Riley discuss their plans to come to the club. Lars had told me as much. Tonight was the night. Leaving Mermaids would not be an option.

"Jimbo?"

Dropping the act, he threw his arms open and exclaimed, "Welcome home!"

"Yay!"

I had never felt so relieved in my life. I jumped into his arms, wrapped my legs around his thick, gorilla waist, and smothered him in kisses—*Thank you! Thank you! You won't regret this!*

Laughing, he spun me around and then set me down. "You have fifteen minutes, then I want you on stage!"

I was about to fly out of his office when Jimbo said:

"Crystal!"

I twirled on my heel, smiling.

He reminded me, "*Fully* nude."

A lump instantly formed in my throat, but I swallowed it back down.

"Fully nude," I agreed, hating how unsure of myself I sounded. I swallowed again and said, "Got it." My voice was like wind over reeds.

Timbo had a double shot of vodka disguised as a bottle of Evian water waiting for me at the side of the stage by the time I emerged from the ladies' dressing room, having dolled myself up and thrown on a pair of stiletto heels and a string bikini.

Ron Stewart's classic rock song kicked into high gear.

That was my cue.

I swigged as much vodka as I could stomach and told myself to scan the crowd for Emmett DeGraves as soon as I got up there.

Timbo pressed the microphone to his mouth and announced through the PA system, "Gentlemen! You're in for a real treat! Our very own, very sexy Crystal has returned to Mermaids! Isn't she a sight for sore eyes!"

I hustled up onto the stage, skipped down the runway, and took strong hold of the dance pole, feeling sparkly and alive.

Flying, I twirled around the pole, which got the crowd going.

Men tossed bills on the stage, as I kept moving and dancing and back-bending. I twirled and followed the motion with a tight pirouette before oozing down to my knees and peeling my bikini top off.

Cash rained down on me, as I danced and worked up the nerve to strip out of the rest of my outfit.

Timbo's voice came through the PA system again, but this time, he sounded like a fast-talking auctioneer.

"If you can handle all six-feet of this gorgeous bombshell, Crystal will be available for private room dances immediately following her set! Nothing gets her going like cold, hard, cash, fellas! Private rooms start at only two hundred bucks, that's quite a steal, boys, for a gorgeous woman like Crystal! There's no telling the fun you will have with her in private! And we mean that literally! *We won't tell!*"

What?!

Even the cop perched at the front of the stage was hooting and hollering at the prospect of having me all to himself for twenty minutes in a private room.

"Fully nude! Only at Mermaids! Come hungry, leave *satisfied!*" Timbo said as if it was the new club slogan. "Show 'em the goods, Crystal!"

Holy mother of God...

Horrified—*what in the world?*—I was so appalled at what Timbo had implied that I'd forgotten to take my bikini bottom off.

Fortifying myself. Determined to find DeGraves out there in the crowd, I pulled the strings at the sides of my bikini bottom and let the thing fall to the stage.

I totally numbed out after that.

I danced, but I felt very far away.

I twirled around the pole, but I couldn't hear the music, couldn't focus, couldn't see straight.

I didn't notice when the song changed. The rest of my set was a blur.

Finally, Timbo used the PA system to urge me to gather my clothes and cash.

When I finally hopped down, I was bewildered, buck-naked, and trembling. A man smiled at me and said something about a private room, but I was too foggy to comprehend him. It was like I was outside of my body.

"Back off!" I yelled.

"I'm so sorry," he muttered under his breath, wildly confused by my attitude. He disappeared into the crowd after apologizing again.

I scrambled to put my bikini back on, and it was only after I had covered up that I was able to think straight.

"You okay?" Miracle asked, having pushed towards me from out of nowhere.

"Why wouldn't I be?" I snapped.

"Bite my head off, why don't you?" she shot back and I deserved it.

I would've apologized, but she was already walking away. When she passed Destiny, who was approaching me with the same concern, Miracle told her, "Don't bother, she'll just snap at you," and the two veered off together.

I tucked myself into the ladies' dressing room with the bottle of vodka Timbo had given me, and it was a very long time before I felt like myself.

Eventually, Jimbo found me. "Crystal, are you kidding me?"

I was seated at one of the vanity mirrors.

"Customers are lined up around the block to get a private room with you! What are you doing in here? You're drinking?!"

He snatched the empty vodka bottle out of my fist and threw it in the trash bin.

"Let's go! On your feet, girl! I've got you booked for the rest of the night!"

Jimbo helped me up. My equilibrium was a bit off, but it wasn't like I would twist an ankle if I had to dance.

"You're going to make a thousand-dollars tonight if you can keep it together."

"Do you know Emmett DeGraves?" I asked. "He comes here sometimes."

"He's on your list—"

"DeGraves is here?"

"Yes," he said. "He's on your list of customers who signed up for a private room, but you can't see anyone until you sober up! Company policy!"

I was nowhere near sober by the time I headed into a private room and danced for the first two customers on my list.

Then came DeGraves.

As I held the velvet curtain aside and welcomed Emmet DeGraves into the private room I had been occupying, he leered at me.

I felt my gut clench. The hairs on the back of my neck stood on end. I tried not to look nervous, but I did not want to be trapped in a room with this man. He was dangerous. I could feel it in my bones.

"Have a seat," I said.

As he squeezed past me and got comfortable on the red vinyl bench, he asked, "Is it true that what happens in the private rooms stays in the private rooms?"

I shut the velvet curtains, turned on my heel, and told him:

"No."

He frowned. "Is that why you aren't naked?"

I glared at him.

Suddenly, his entire demeanor changed. His dark eyes widened and a guilty look washed over him.

He ran his hand down his rusty bucket face and groaned, "What am I doing here? Riley told me not to come."

He ran all ten fingers through his thick hair, shook his head, and couldn't hold my gaze, he was so ashamed of himself.

"I shouldn't be here," he said as if the thought had just occurred to him. "You shouldn't be here either," he added. "I shouldn't be here with you and you shouldn't be here with me."

At first, I didn't know what to say.

"I have a weakness, Crystal," he confessed. "It's boobs! But I want to turn my life around. You want to turn your life around, too, right? That's why you were at Lighthouse Ministries that day? Are you working here tonight because you're hard up for money?"

All of a sudden, I had no idea why I was working here tonight. "Yeah."

"Even after what happened to those girls?" he asked, as he took out his wallet. "You must be in a tough spot if you came to Mermaids after everything that's happened."

If he was a serial killer, I really wasn't getting that vibe from him.

"Here," he said, getting up from the bench and offering me everything he had. "It's almost three hundred. I hope it helps."

"You're leaving?"

"I would hate for any of this to get back to the pastors..."

"I won't say a word."

"I want to turn my life around. I'm going to start going to church for real. Christian women have boobs, too," he realized and it seemed to give him a lot to look forward to. "I've had enough of this life. I'm going to give it up. I hope you do the same."

I PULLED INTO Robert's driveway in the dead of night. More cash than I had ever made in one shift was spilling out of the top of my giant stripper bag, which rested on the passenger's seat beside me.

As I climbed out of my car, I was met with a warm, brackish breeze and a feeling of regret.

I hadn't called the house earlier that night to let Robert and Seth know I wouldn't be coming over to make dinner. Instead, I had become so preoccupied with the idea of going to Mermaids, that I'd actually gone. Obsessed with the hope that I would find Emmet DeGraves there and trick him into confessing to the murders of Amanda Dover and Jewel Payson, I had completely lost track of time. I had also gotten severely sidetracked at the club, which had resulted in the pile of cash beside me.

Mermaids wasn't my home.

This was.

I wanted to sneak into Robert's adorable seaside cottage. I wanted to tiptoe into his bedroom and curl up next to him. I wanted to make him coffee in the morning and cook eggs for Seth. I wanted to drop Seth off at his Kids for Christ program, spend the day tidying up around the living room, pick him up again from the church, and take the boy out for ice cream. I wanted to go grocery shopping and joke around with Seth while I made an extravagant dinner. I wanted to dote on Robert, and I wanted it so badly that my heart hurt just thinking about it. Listening to doo-wop and sipping whiskey sours with Robert had become my heaven.

I wanted to love and be loved…

…but when I neared the front door of the house and saw the hardened look on Robert's face as he met me under the portico light, I knew in an instant I wasn't going to get what I wanted, not now, and maybe not ever.

"Can I come in?"

"Where have you been?"

He was asking, but he already knew. My heavy eye makeup and false lashes, the cigarette stink on my skin and the perfume clinging to my hair, had given it away.

"I've been waiting up for you all night," he hissed.

"It's late. Can we talk about this in the morning?"

"We can talk about it now. Where were you?"

He was a brick wall.

"I think you know where I was."

"At the club?" he asked.

When I wouldn't admit it, he barked, "Were you at Mermaids?"

"You want me to say it? Fine. Yes, I was at Mermaids. Can I come in now?"

"No."

Disbelief crashed over me. "Are you serious?"

"What were you doing there?"

I couldn't believe he was going to make me say it. "What do you think I was doing there?"

Taking me by the arm, he ushered me away from the house, not that it would prevent his nephew from hearing our argument.

"Do you have any idea how much money I've been giving you?" he yelled. "I pay your rent. I feed you. I've given you more than enough to get your hair done and do whatever the hell else you spend my money on—"

"Hold on a second," I tried to interrupt, but he wasn't finished.

"—and you went to the club?"

"I did, but I didn't go to make money!"

He glanced over at my car and saw the overflowing bag of cash on the passenger's seat. "No?"

"I was trying to figure out what happened to Cherry and Original Jewel—"

"You're lying! You've been using me from the start! Bleeding me dry!"

"I have *not* been using you!"

"Sneaking off to Mermaids every chance you get—"

"I haven't once gone to Mermaids other than tonight, and the only reason I went there was because of a lead—"

"I think I'm in love with you!"

My mind went blank, and I struggled for a moment to think straight. "You think you're in love with me?"

"You can't go to that club, Crystal!"

"You're in love with me?"

"I can't let myself love someone who wants to take her clothes off for other men just to make a buck!"

"Stop yelling at me!"

"I didn't expect to feel this way about you!" he went on ranting, furious with me and himself and his emotions, all of which were beyond his control. "I didn't ask for this! I didn't see this coming! I've got a job that's killing me and a boy I don't know how to raise! My hands are full! I can't be in love with a stripper who's asking to get murdered every time she sets foot in that club! I can't do it, Crystal! I won't do it!"

"I think I love you, too—"

"It's not enough," he said, shaking his head. "You can't go there anymore."

"I won't. I promise."

I reached for him, but he stopped me.

"Robert," I said, trying and failing to connect with him. "Did you hear me? I just said that I love you, too. Can we go inside?"

"I would like you to leave."

"What?" I asked, thrown.

"When you asked me to take you to church, I thought you meant it. I thought you wanted to change."

"I do want to change."

"Then change!"

"I will!"

"Until you do—"

"Don't send me away, Robert."

"It would be best if you left," he maintained.

I couldn't believe it. "I'll go to church—"

"Don't mock it—"

"I'm not mocking it, Robert, I want this to work. It's been working. I can make church work. I can make everything work."

"I'm going to have to see that."

"Okay, I'll show you," I agreed.

I felt overjoyed—*he loved me!*—but he still wasn't willing to let me inside. He wasn't willing to hold me and kiss me. He didn't trust me.

"I'll see you on Sunday," he said before he turned and started for the house.

I watched him return to the front door and disappear inside. Two windows over, Seth was staring at me with his nose pressed to the glass. I waved, but he didn't wave back.

"CRYSTAL, IT'S SO wonderful to see you this afternoon. You've come to the right place," said Pastor Grace Asbury.

"Thanks," I said even though I felt like a fraud.

I was once again dressed to play the part of a pious church lady. Wearing a blouse and a starched skirt that made my skin itch, I had shown up at Lighthouse Ministries in a desperate attempt to save my relationship with Robert. I could not lose him, that's all I knew. If I did, my life would careen towards disaster.

Fear had motivated me to sit down with Pastor Gracie for my first official Christian Counseling session. We were seated in her small office, which was adjacent to the fellowship hall on the second floor of the church. A standing fan whirred on the windowsill and blew hot air into the already stuffy room.

"I'm not sure what I expect to get out of this," I told her, which was honest.

In fact, my expectations were pretty low. I knew what I *wanted* to get out of Christian Counseling, but it had more to do with making things work with Robert than anything else. I certainly wasn't here for spiritual reasons. If anything, I was baffled by Lars' genuine interest in Christianity, and I couldn't quite comprehend that Emmet DeGraves had also seemed authentically convinced that this religion could turn his life around.

"You can expect to get the truth with a capital T," she informed me. "You can expect to get a new outlook on life that will help you live correctly, and you can also expect to receive the free gift of salvation, if you ask for it."

Skepticism was written all over my face, but I needed to play along. I wasn't here to become a Christian. I was here so that Pastor Gracie would have something positive to report to Robert if she happened to speak with him. Robert wanted me to take church seriously, and I wanted Robert to take me seriously.

"Why don't you start by telling me about what you're struggling with specifically?" she suggested. When I hesitated to respond, she said, "Don't worry, dear. You can tell me anything. I have experience counseling all kinds of troubled women."

"Like what kinds of troubled women?"

"Oh, all kinds," she promised, but didn't offer any examples. "Women just like you."

Cherry and Original Jewel came to mind.

"If your life was perfect, you probably wouldn't be here," she reasoned, "so why don't we see how the Lord can help you make sense of what's happened to you in the past?"

I didn't think it would be a smart move to open up about myself.

"I'm really disturbed that two women were killed on Woodland Beach," I told her, and we were both surprised by my honesty.

"A lot of parishioners at this church were disturbed by the murders," she said to let me know that I wasn't alone. "The murders have forced our congregation to take a good, hard look at their lives, and to contemplate the fact that any of them could die at any moment. All we can do is avoid sin and be grateful for our salvation, not that you're saved yet, dear. And we must also forgive the killer, because in the grand scheme of things, we simply don't know God's plan for us."

That didn't sound right. "Are you saying that the murders were part of God's plan?"

"Nobody knows," she said, "which means that nobody can judge."

"Those women didn't deserve to be killed."

"You don't know that," she said as if she knew something I didn't.

Pastor Gracie didn't know anything about Cherry and Original Jewel. She didn't know about their difficult lives. Heck, I didn't even know about their difficult lives. All I knew was that none of the strippers at Mermaids had achieved their dreams, and it wasn't because we were lazy. None of us had turned out the way we had hoped. Pastor Gracie couldn't possibly comprehend why some of us kept getting forced down a dark road no matter how hard we tried to be normal.

"I'm sorry, I don't think you're right about that," I argued.

"Those girls were killed because they were sinners," she told me definitively.

I couldn't have been more offended if she had spat in my face.

I was offended on behalf of my dead friends, and I was offended on behalf of myself. Pastor Gracie knew that I was no different than Cherry and Original Jewel. Was she calling me a sinner? Was she saying that I deserved to be killed, too?

"Sinners don't deserve to be murdered," I maintained.

"Try telling that to the God of the bible."

This woman was insufferable.

She offered me a tight, compromising smile. "As soon as a sinner repents, gives up their sin, and seeks the Lord's salvation, then they will be saved from God's wrath. Do you see how easy it is? That's why I can't feel sorry for women who are killed because they refuse to give up their sin."

Tears welled up in my eyes and my chest felt suddenly hot. I hated this woman, but I hated her because part of me thought she might be right.

"Don't cry, dear. What I'm saying is good news. I'm telling you that the Lord is merciful. He's waiting with open arms to forgive sinners."

I blinked until my vision cleared.

"If only my mother had known that," I said in a small, sarcastic voice, "she might still be alive today."

"There, there." She gave my shoulder a little pat. "Think about the Lord's great mercy."

"What mercy?"

"The mercy he showed to Arthur Kowalski. My son ministered to Arthur on Death Row. He shared the good news of Christ's salvation with Arthur, and Arthur was saved as a result. Do you see how powerful the gospel is?"

"If what you're saying is true, then God is to blame for all of this."

She scowled, displeased with my attitude. "I'm afraid you're missing the point."

"God should have made sure that Cherry and Original Jewel and my mother knew about salvation, if that could've kept them alive. He should've made sure they were saved."

"He's making sure that *you* are saved," she pointed out. "Can't you see what he's doing for you right now? He's making sure that your life will be spared. Don't be so foolish as to turn down the free gift of salvation that he's offering to you."

I wondered if she had any idea how bad she was at Christian Counseling.

"Let's focus on everything that God has done for you," she suggested when I hadn't responded. "Well? What has the Lord done for you?"

My answer didn't come right away, but when it did, there wasn't a shred of doubt in my mind that I was right. "He crippled me."

"*God* crippled you?" she questioned.

"Yeah, he did," I said, convinced. "I didn't ask to be raised in a whore house. Sorry to be crass, but there's no other way to describe the trailer park I was brought up in. I didn't ask to be exposed to what my mother exposed me to. I didn't ask for Arthur to come into our lives and get my hopes up, and I didn't ask for him to kill my mother. I didn't ask for any of that."

"Crystal, I don't think you understood the original question. The question was, what has God done *for* you? Meaning, what blessings has he given you?"

"Are you kidding me?"

She did me the courtesy of having a long think on that. "Holding the Lord responsible for Arthur Kowalski's *actions* is a mistake, and you can't hold the Lord responsible for your mother's actions, either."

"God didn't intervene. I'm holding God responsible for his actions, or lack thereof."

She studied me for a long moment then said, "Didn't he intervene, though?"

"Did God *intervene* and save me from my terrible upbringing that ended up destroying my chances of being happy and normal? No, he didn't."

"Yes, he did."

I screwed my face up. "What are you talking about? No, he didn't."

"Yes," she maintained. "As a little girl, you did not ask to be raised in that kind of environment, correct? Well, the Lord intervened. He removed your mother from your life, and he also removed Arthur from your life."

I laughed at that. "But things got *worse* as a result!"

"You're referring to the foster care system you were placed in after your mother's death?"

I wasn't sure how she knew, but that was exactly what I had referred to and I told her as much.

"Listen, Crystal, in order for Christian Counseling to be productive, we should focus on the choices that you make *today*. You are responsible for your own actions. Salvation starts with repentance."

"I wouldn't be the adult I am today if it hadn't been for those two, and if it hadn't been for the years of bad foster homes I was stuck in, and if it hadn't been for the never-ending hellscape of monsters I had to deal with."

"I would really like to see you come to terms with your past, Crystal, and it might be a hard pill to swallow, but the only way you're going to come through this is if you learn how to forgive."

Her smug son had suggested the same crap when he had cornered me at Arthur's execution.

"It doesn't have to happen overnight," she allowed. "Have you considered that you might have to forgive God?" When I didn't respond—in fact, I *hadn't* considered that—she went on, "Forgiveness doesn't mean that you condone what was done."

"Obviously," I said dryly. "You know what pisses me off? We were happy. The three of us. Arthur, my mom, and me."

I felt the dam inside of me burst and thirty years' worth of resentment came pouring out.

"We were a family and Mom was pregnant and Arthur was thrilled and we loved that house. It didn't matter that it was tiny and drafty or that the walls were paper thin or that the oven smelled like a dead mouse whenever we used it. I loved my mother for trying to make our lives better, and I loved Arthur, even when he came home with stolen goods and unbelievable lies. He once brought a brand-new VCR home. He told us he had won it at work for being an outstanding employee. I so badly wanted to believe him. All he wanted was for Mom and me to look at him like he was a winner. He wanted us to be proud of him. He wanted us to jump for joy at his victories. So, I did. I jumped for joy as often as I could. But Mom wouldn't. She refused."

I pressed my fingertips against my eyelids to stop the tears from spilling down my cheeks.

"Arthur and I had wanted the same thing—to be a happy family. We had wanted it so badly that we started pretending, but Mom wouldn't pretend, and Arthur couldn't stand it. If she could have just let him be who he wanted to be, without calling him out on his lies, and if she could have just jumped for joy, too, and if she could have simply pretended like we were pretending, Arthur wouldn't have killed her—"

"Crystal, I understand all that—"

"I don't think you do, and I don't appreciate you treating me like I'm at fault because I'm not forgiving—"

"I didn't mean to make you feel that way—"

"As if I owe Arthur forgiveness! I don't appreciate your son telling me how sorry Arthur is, as if I don't know that; as if I'm not sorry a million times over; as if I need a complete stranger to tell me what to think and feel—"

"Asa means well, but I'll admit he can come across a bit *clumsy*—"

"—as if your son knows Arthur better than I do, or did, or whatever," I raged on. "I don't appreciate how judgmental you people are—"

"I'm going to stop you right there," she asserted.

But I wasn't finished. "You're telling me not to judge murderers, but you judge victims. You're a hypocrite!"

"You don't know anything about me!"

"I haven't read the bible, but I doubt you're representing *Christ*—"

"Crystal," she warned. "I can see you're upset and I can see you don't want to be told what to do so I'm not going to do that. I *am* going to say, however, that I *do* represent Christ, and I represent him *perfectly*, so you better believe me when I say, you need Christ!"

"I need Christ like I need a hole in the head!"

"You watch your mouth!"

"What's he going to do for me?" I demanded. "How's he going to help me? He doesn't save anyone from anything. Not really. He lets little girls get raised in horrible environments, lets them turn into strippers, lets them get murdered years later. All the while he looks on? He watches? And he judges me? Every low-life thing I've ever done is the direct result of all the low-life things that were done to me, you know!"

"You're focused on being saved from the wrong thing."

"Hardly!"

"You should be thinking about eternal damnation. You should be begging to be saved from *that*. But some people can't see the big picture. Some people can't handle being saved. It takes determination not to sin after you've been saved. That's why some people should only be saved on their deathbeds. That's why I tell myself, baptize the sinner only when you're certain they won't have the opportunity to sin again."

THE MISSIONARY

MY MOTHER'S ARGUMENT with Crystal Swan had been growing louder from the office. My entire class was distracted. We were gathered around one of the tables in the neighboring room—the fellowship hall—with our bibles open. Nothing but three inches of uninsulated drywall and an old bookshelf separated us from what was starting to sound like a volatile fight.

Seth had volunteered to read his essay answers from his Kids for Christ workbook, but he stopped abruptly when my mother yelled at Crystal on the other side of the wall:

"Don't you dare cut your nose off to spite your own face!"

"I don't have to take this!" Crystal fired back.

"Maybe not from me!" my mother agreed, her voice turning shrill as she retaliated. "But one day soon you will have to stand before God and explain yourself, and I can promise you, he'll issue you the same warning!"

The sounds of Crystal storming out of the office came next.

When Crystal threw my mother's office door open and slammed it shut, Sally and Judith startled at the noise. The clatter of Crystal charging down the stairs and racing out of the church followed, and then an eerie quiet spread throughout Lighthouse Ministries.

Walter and Cole looked at Seth, and so did I.

Everyone seated around the table was anticipating Seth's explanation for why Crystal had challenged my mother so vehemently. We were all aware that the boy had a close relationship with Crystal. For nearly a month, she had regularly dropped him off and picked him up from the church. It was no secret that she had become something of a guardian to him, though I couldn't recall her dropping him off this morning.

Seth glanced from one kid to the next around the table until his attention landed on me. "What?"

Sally answered, "Your new mom flipped out at Pastor Gracie," as if Seth could've possibly missed the explosion.

"She's not my new mom."

"Do you think Seth's new mom is possessed by the devil?" she earnestly wondered. "Sinners who refuse to repent often are—"

"Sally," I warned.

"Pastor Asa," she objected. "I have it on good authority that Crystal works at Mermaids as an exotic dancer!"

Judith shrank in her chair and asked, "Exotic dancers aren't demon possessed, are they Pastor Asa?"

"Yes, they are," Sally insisted. "It's common knowledge!"

"Just because someone's occupation is morally questionable," I told all my students, "doesn't automatically mean that they're being influenced by Satan."

"Actually, that's exactly what it means," argued Sally. She was giving me the stink eye. "Really, Pastor

Asa, sometimes I wonder if you've ever even read the bible."

"Are you talking about 'Mermaids' the *strip club*?" asked our newest addition, Gretchen Riley. Intrigued, she turned to Sally. "The strip club where Channel 7's Missy Chance has been investigating undercover?"

"The very same one," Sally told her.

As an introspective eleven-year-old, Gretchen loved Dolly Parton and worried her father was an alcoholic. She had been peeking in and out of her shell all week.

Gretchen cautiously offered, "My dad says Missy Chance is asking for it." She stared up at me with her giant eyes and blinked. "What does he mean when he says that, Pastor Asa?"

Once again answering on my behalf, not that I had asked her to, Sally said, "It means your father needs to lay off the sauce."

"Sally!" I barked.

"They're all asking for it!" she insisted. "Even Seth's new mom is asking for it!"

"Crystal isn't asking for it!" Seth protested.

"Asking for what?" Gretchen demanded, thoroughly frustrated.

"To get killed!" said Sally.

It disturbed me to know that Sally was right.

Anyone who continued to strip at Mermaids, in full knowledge that the murder victims had been targeted because they worked there, was asking for it. Crystal included.

Though Crystal might have temporarily abstained from dancing at the now-infamous all-nude strip club, she had recently returned. This was according to Emmet DeGraves.

Emmett had made a full, heartfelt confession to my father about the fact that he had suffered from a moment of weakness and gone back to the club. That was where he had discovered Crystal. In fact, Crystal had been the reason he had decided, right then and there, to repent. Emmet had promised my father his strip club days were behind him. As far as I could tell, the man's earnest vow to never again go back to Mermaids had been genuine. Gretchen's dad, Charles Riley, had also turned a corner, though he still needed to get his drinking under control.

In all honesty, when Crystal had knocked on my mother's office door a half hour ago for Christian Counseling, I had sincerely hoped that she had shown up for the right reasons.

Now, I didn't know what to think, and unfortunately, I didn't trust that Crystal had turned the same corner as Emmet and Charles and the other members of our humble congregation.

Or was I wrong about her?

Had Crystal legitimately repented? Was that why she had come to Lighthouse Ministries today? Had my mother's abrasive version of Christianity caused Crystal to run from the building screaming?

Or had the blue-eyed beauty swung into my mother's office with ulterior motives and nefarious intentions?

And if she had, should I be concerned? Should I keep a watchful eye over my shoulder? Did I need to worry about staying one move ahead of her at all times?

I didn't want to have to think about it. I had enough garbage churning around my head. Willy Prinkerton's execution was coming up. Whenever I thought about the injustice of an innocent man being put to death, my bowels loosened.

Competing for mental real estate in my mind were thoughts of hanky-panky, and these thoughts were constant thanks to my father's bizarre advice about finding a good Christian woman.

Oh, the ideas that had formed since then…

Complicating matters was the relentless heat. It had been unnaturally hot in the rectory of the church where I slept, and I was starting to suspect that mold had begun to grow in my brain. My thinking had turned wooly; my mood, troubled; my sense of self, *perverse*. Praying and worrying and masturbating in the rectory had congealed into a sort of spiritual diarrhea that sloshed around my skull and stunk up my soul. I felt utterly foul, and despite the fact that I was almost constantly under my parents' noses, neither of them had gotten a whiff of how vile my thoughts had truly become.

My students' incessant speculation about dead strippers was giving me a migraine.

"Silence!" I shouted over them and they all piped down, slouching in their seats. "God has granted every single human being free will! Christ has afforded those of us who accept him as our savior to be completely absolved of our sins! Our past, present, and future sins! The moral of the story is that you must accept the Lord as your personal savior! It's the only get-out-of-jail-free card there is to play, and only a damned fool would refuse it!

"Now! Seth! Read your answers for the class, and Sally, you better keep your mouth shut, or so help me God, I will shut it for you, and the Lord will not hold me responsible for the pain that befalls you as a result, because I am saved and forgiven of all sin, no matter what I do!"

Sally glared at me, flipped her crimped hair aside, and said, "Gee, Pastor Asa, that sounds like something a serial killer would say."

❄

NIGHTTIME. The air was muggy. Hot. My skin felt slick with sweat.

I drove with the windows open through the darkened streets of Woodland Beach. My blood flooded with adrenaline—acidic and scalding my veins. I was wound up tightly, slicing along a razor's edge of untenable stress. I couldn't handle it.

Bile stung the back of my throat. My stomach turned sour. I was practically vibrating with raw fear. I felt threatened by what Sally had said, but I also felt alive. Wild and pure. Ready.

"All of my sins have been washed away by the blood of Christ—past, present, and future sins," I reminded myself.

It wasn't a lie. I *had* been washed clean. It was right there in the bible. I had told my students the truth. I'd enlightened them.

I gripped the steering wheel tighter and excitement rocketed through my chest when I saw the familiar neon glow of those pink, orange, and red flashing lights.

Mermaids was just around the corner…

I removed my foot from the accelerator, squeezed the brakes, and slowly drove by, eyeing the strip club that sat on the corner. Its big, voluptuous mermaid sign was all lit up like the burning gates of hell.

A police cruiser was parked curbside, out front, but there didn't appear to be any cops sitting inside it.

Huh.

There were, however, a number of men smoking near the entrance, joking around, and passing what looked like a bottle of alcohol between them.

I crawled past the club and began circling the block.

My heart rate kicked up as I rolled by the rear parking area to see if Crystal's sedan was there. I would recognize her car anywhere. I had memorized the license plate number.

"Forgive me, Father," I breathed, "for I know exactly what I'm about to do."

I didn't see her vehicle, so I kept driving through the narrow lot until I came to a side street.

Percolating under my arousal was rage.

My dad hadn't been wrong when he had suggested that I ought to find a God-fearing woman to settle down with.

But I had already found her years ago. I had already fallen hard, and I'd already lost her.

I wished I had married her. I could have had two or three children by now. I would have had a beautiful family. I would have my own congregation at my own church. Carrying on the strong Asbury name had always been my greatest aspiration.

I had wanted to be a husband and a father.

But that wasn't how my life had turned out.

The love of my life had cheated on me. She had rejected me. And she had left me heartbroken on the shore of Woodland Beach.

I didn't want to be here, cruising around the block like a predator and fantasizing about strippers.

I didn't want to revel in the delusion that somewhere inside Mermaids I would find my future wife.

But the idea had become my happy place. It made me sick. It also turned me on and kept me coming back.

I had been downward spiraling for a very long time.

I came around another corner, slowed to a crawl, and gradually pulled up behind the vacant police cruiser that was parked in front of the club.

Muffled music boomed across the sidewalk. The colored lights of Mermaids' flashing sign—*LIVE! NUDE! GIRLS!*—triggered something animalistic inside me.

But before I could climb out of my car, a woman leaned in through the open passenger's side window. She grinned at me, fluttered her thick eyelashes, and cooed, "You looking for a date tonight, sweetheart?"

She was gorgeous.

"I am."

"I'll spare you the trouble of going inside," she said with a wink. She flicked her gaze over her shoulder at the club. "It's crowded like you wouldn't believe. There's a two-hour wait to get into a private room, not to mention there are a couple of cops in the mix, which could be a problem, if you know what I mean."

I might have been raised in the church, but it was impossible to miss the implication. I knew exactly what she meant and I liked hearing it.

"Get in."

"It's a hundred," she told me.

"That won't be a problem," I said. "Get in the car."

Once she had, I pulled out into the street.

"I'm Amber."

"It's nice to meet you, Amber."

"So," she said, smiling as she glanced around the clean interior of my spacious station wagon. "Where are you taking me?"

THE EXECUTIONER

PRINKERTON'S DAY had arrived.

I hadn't gone to church that morning even though I had told Crystal I would see her there. Cromwell had rearranged everyone's shifts in the 24-hour death watch leading up to the execution and when I'd learned I would have to be present at the prison throughout the entire 24-hour period, I hadn't fought the warden one bit.

I wasn't ready to see Crystal and I wasn't sure when I would be. She had stirred inside of me all kinds of emotions I had never thought I would have to face. Love and fear, mostly, but also jealousy and a whole host of other intolerable feelings I wasn't prepared to deal with. The characteristics of my own fragility were not something I felt like examining, and if that meant never seeing Crystal Swan again…

Well, I wasn't about to make a decision in that regard just yet.

At the moment, I was concentrating on nothing but getting through the next hour. Giving Prinkerton as humane an execution as I could was all I was going to allow myself to care about.

I had been waking up at dawn for days now and using the time to practice puncturing my own femoral artery at home. I had smuggled Digby's hypodermic syringe needles out of the prison, certain that if I could find my own vein, I would be able to find the inmate's when the time came. In the privacy of my own bedroom, I had succeeded. While performing under the gun, however, I wasn't certain things would go as smoothly, but I had reason to hope they would.

Cromwell had been in a state. He had been buried under a mountain of paperwork. This was due to all of the legal appeals that Prinkerton had filed over the years in his attempts to overturn the ruling. Hundreds of forms had to be collated and filed with Delaware State, as well as with the Feds, which had frustrated Cromwell so badly that at one point, he had called the governor directly to ask for a stay of execution on the inmate's behalf, not that he gave a damn about Prinkerton or justice. Cromwell had called the governor for no other reason than to alleviate himself from having to dot every "I" and cross every "T" administratively.

That being said, the call had gotten my hopes up. I had even prayed for Cromwell to successfully secure a stay, not that I had God's ear. I was a joke in that department.

But leaving a voicemail message with the governor was as far as Cromwell had gotten, unfortunately. He had tried to follow up with a fax, but his cranky machine had disconnected during the dial-up phase, which had caused him to stomp around his office like a petulant child. Ultimately, his efforts had been completely ineffective.

The clock struck midnight.

I was standing post in the death chamber, alone.

The window blinds were down, but I'd been told that the viewing gallery was full of Prinkerton's supporters, as well as a couple of journalists who had latched on to the story. Pastor Asa was out there, too, and this time I was glad for that.

Prinkerton needed him. The pastor had come to the prison every chance he'd gotten; had spent every spare minute he had praying with Willy. It had been a great comfort to the inmate, and to me as well. Asa was alright by me.

Prinkerton's cries billowed through all of Death Row, growing louder and more panicked as he neared the death chamber, escorted by CO McKay and two others.

Then the heavy door buzzed open and I felt my blood run cold as I watched the innocent man get dragged into the death chamber and strapped down onto the gurney.

"Lord, save me!"

"Try to remain calm," I advised.

"I ain't supposed to be here! This ain't right! I don't want to die!"

As McKay sneered from the sidelines, I told Willy, "Take a few deep breaths. I need you to keep your arm very still, Willy. Please."

He began sucking air through his clenched teeth so hard that I thought he might hyperventilate, but he managed to keep his arm still for me.

I tied the tourniquet around his upper arm as tightly as I could, and with a gloved finger I began feeling his inner elbow for a popping vein. I found it.

Letting out a shaky breath, I set the tip of the syringe needle against his dark skin. When I had practiced at home, my veins had turned thick and blue, but Prinkerton's skin was too brown for me to get a strong visual. Feeling the ropey femoral artery under my finger would have to be my guide.

Prinkerton began lamenting, "I am a child of God and the truth shall set me free." Over and over again, he sang those words, as sweat beaded up across both of our foreheads. "I am a child of God and the truth shall set me free, Lord!"

McKay wasn't having it. "Shut your mouth, Willy!"

I charged at McKay and shoved him into the wall, the needle still in my hand. The IV line yanked. "Let him sing!"

"Christ, Robert—"

"He has rights, McKay! He can sing if he wants to, and he'll address the gallery with his last words after that!"

The other COs looked on. Warden Cromwell wasn't there to separate McKay and me, and the COs were unsure about whether or not they should break us up.

Releasing McKay, I returned to Prinkerton, felt for his thick vein all over again, and pressed the needle to his skin.

"Once I get the IV in," I explained because in Digby's video I had learned that articulating every step of the execution to the inmate would help to keep him calm, "I'll prop the gurney up, open the blinds, and you'll be able to say your peace to the spectators in the viewing gallery."

Prinkerton locked eyes with me. "I forgive you."

I could've told him not to do that, not to offer me what I didn't deserve, but I thanked him instead.

I pushed the needle deeper but his vein slid sideways and a hot flash of frustration burned through my chest.

"I am a child of God…" Willy went on singing, his eyes pinched shut, his skin turning cold, but his faith increasing.

I tried a second time, but his femoral artery wouldn't hold still for me. It slid this way and that.

It was Kowalski all over again.

Furious, I took a lap, paced away from the gurney then came back again, examined the tip of the needle and searched for his vein that was shrinking by the second.

One of the correctional officers asked, "You good, boss?"

"You've got someplace to be, Jefferson?" I snapped, hotly irritated.

Again, I punctured Willy's skin, and again his stubborn vein dodged the needle.

Damnit!

I wiped sweat from my brow, forced some air into my lungs, and tried again.

"Save me from this injustice, Lord!" Willy cried out and his arm moved on the gurney.

God, help me send this man to you, I mentally prayed. *Without pain, in full mercy, God, help me.*

Whether it was a valid prayer or not, the needle clipped in just right. I could feel it pop through the arterial wall and correctly settle in place. A spurt of blood shot into the syringe, indicating I had succeeded.

I let out a rocky breath and taped the IV in place.

"Lord, help me!" Willy begged.

I found the lever beneath the gurney, released the lock, and lifted Willy, bringing the gurney into a vertical position so that he could address the gallery as soon as I opened the blinds.

"Save me, Lord!"

I neared the wall where the electric console was located beside the viewing gallery window.

"Please, God!"

Pushing the button to open the blinds, I felt bone-splitting compassion for Willy.

The blinds began retracting upwards.

"McKay, the microphone," I instructed, and the CO moved behind the black curtain and turned the mics on so that everyone in the viewing gallery would be able to hear the inmate's last words.

A moment later, everyone who was seated in the viewing gallery could see Willy within the death chamber.

McKay gave me the nod, indicating that the inmate could speak. I told Willy, "It's time for your last words, Prinkerton. Say what you need to say."

Willy took his time. His dark eyes welled up with tears, and he began addressing his supporters and Pastor Asa. As he spoke, journalists and news reporters pressed their pens to their notepads and recorded every word.

"I've made mistakes in my life," he admitted. "I've sinned, but Lord knows I didn't do it. I didn't kill that little girl." Pleading with every single person who was sitting on the other side of the window, he asked, "Pray for me? Pray for me? Pray for me!" He began howling. "Pray for me! Pastor Asa, pray for me!"

Moving swiftly towards him, I said, "Willy—"
"PRAY FOR ME!!!"

"Cut the microphone!" I told McKay as I turned on my heel for the death machine behind the black curtain. I ordered the other COs, "Lower the gurney."

"DON'T LET THEM KILL ME, GOD!!!"

I rounded behind the black curtain, entering the executioner's alcove. I neared the death machine and stared down at the glowing buttons. A bead of sweat rolled down my face, slid off the tip of my nose, and plopped onto the machine.

My hand was shaking as I delicately rested my fingertips on the first set of buttons, working up the nerve.

I let out a stuttering breath, feeling sick. I didn't want to do what had to be done.

But before I could press the buttons to initiate the lethal protocol, Warden Cromwell burst into the room.

"Stop!"

The COs at the gurney froze. I darted out from behind the curtain. All eyes were on Cromwell who was waving a piece of paper in his hand.

"He's pardoned! Prinkerton has been pardoned! The governor issued a stay of conviction!"

From the front row of the viewing gallery, Pastor Asa shot out of his seat and pressed his hands to the glass, astonished. Willy couldn't believe it. Shock washed over him. I was gripped in a state of disbelief, myself.

McKay understood that Willy had been freed from the prison. He cursed under his breath.

"Get him off of there!" Cromwell ordered and I wasted no time pulling the needle from Willy's vein, as the other COs began unstrapping him as fast as they could. "The State of Delaware no longer finds him guilty of the crimes!"

Willy looked dumbfounded.

Then the news hit him. He brightened. His eyes widened, and when he completely understood what Cromwell had said and the magnitude of what it meant, he sang out:

"HALLELUJAH!!!"

Hallelujah wasn't a big enough word.

NEVER IN MY LIFE had I witnessed a bona fide miracle. I had never seen prayer work. I'd never seen a man make a case to God that resulted in the Almighty granting him what he had asked.

I felt moved.

It was going to take a day or two to get William Prinkerton's paperwork processed before we would be able to release him from the prison. In the meantime, we moved him back into his cell, which got the attention of every last inmate on Death Row. No one had ever returned from the gallows once the COs had marched them out. Kowalski certainly hadn't come back from the death chamber alive and well. The fact that McKay and I were escorting an inmate down the corridor was shocking.

"Who's there?" Gary Olson wanted to know.

"Willy?" another Death Row inmate asked.

Prinkerton exclaimed, "Jesus saved me! Thank the Lord!"

CO McKay looked about ready to punch a wall as we tucked Willy into his steel cell and locked the door. All the while, the other inmates hollered at us, asking for the pastor—*I'm scheduled next, I need Pastor Asa! I'm ready for the Lord! I didn't do it, either! When's the pastor coming back? Willy, which prayers worked the best, do you think? Which ones did the trick? Tell us!*

McKay chucked his baton hard as all hell against Gary Olson's steel door, furious at the defeat, and I barked, "Walk it off, Lyle!"

"This is crap!" he muttered.

"Walk it off!"

McKay tore through Death Row, punched the door release, and as it unlocked with a loud buzz, he barreled out like a sore loser.

"I need a pen and paper to write a letter to the governor!" said Samuel 'Dirty Sam' Braun upon hearing *specifically* how Willy had been pardoned.

"When's Pastor Asa coming back?"

"Lord, save me like you saved Prinkerton!"

I shouted down the length of Death Row, "Lights out, fellas! No talking!"

I had been running on zero sleep for over twenty-four hours. Whatever paperwork Cromwell might have left for me in my office could wait. It wasn't that I needed to pass out. I felt exhilarated and wide awake. The Vaughn Correctional Center might have always felt like a godless wasteland, but tonight the Holy Spirit had shown up to free Willy. I didn't want to squander the feeling that had come over me at the prison.

Leaving the cell block and making my way to my car, I crossed the parking lot where silver moonlight illuminated every vehicle.

"Son of a bitch!" I heard McKay grunt.

The distinct sound of a human fist connecting with a man's jaw came next, and I turned to find CO McKay angled over Pastor Asa, throwing one punch after another, as the pastor cowered on the pavement with both hands protectively covering his head.

"It's your fault!" McKay yelled as he kicked Asa in the ribs over and over again. "You think this is funny? You think this is a game?"

I ran over as fast as I could.

As I tried to jerk McKay off the man, he elbowed me in the neck, spun around, and got a mean punch in before I decked him with one fast blow to his cheek.

He stumbled sideways, shook the sense back into his head, and came at me, shoving me and taking a swing, but I dodged his balled fist, hurled another right hook that connected with his jaw, and sent him flying into a parked van.

When he hit the pavement, I yelled, "Stay down!"

Pastor Asa had gotten the snot kicked out of him, but he worked his way to his feet, holding his ribs and blotting his split lip with his finger, as McKay cursed up a storm.

"I'm writing you up, McKay! I can tell you right now, don't bother coming in for the rest of the week! You're suspended without pay until further notice!"

"To hell with you!"

Ignoring McKay who was fighting to catch his breath, I returned to Asa.

Asa was keeled over and unable to stand up straight, his ribs hurt him so badly.

"You okay?" I asked. "Any broken bones?"

"I don't think so."

I shouted at McKay over my shoulder, "Get out of here!"

McKay stood his ground.

I took another run at him and cocked my fist back, threatening to throw a mean punch.

McKay shuffled backwards defensively, but he didn't have any fight left in him. He cursed, lowered his fists, and stomped off towards his car.

As McKay drove through the prison compound, curved along the long road that led through Smyrna, and disappeared into the night, I clapped my hand over the pastor's arm and, filled with admiration, said:

"Let me buy you a drink."

"THAT WAS A miracle, right? I mean, you're the expert. You would know."

We were seated at the long bar counter in Foster's, the only bar in Woodland Beach that stayed open until 2:00 am. The bruises were really coming in across the pastor's face and his lip was fat, but that didn't stop him from gulping the draft beer I had bought him. I was less interested in my pint than I was in hearing his take on what had happened back there in the death chamber.

"A miracle, yes," he confirmed.

He didn't look as excited as I felt, but as a man of the cloth, maybe he had seen more miracles than I was aware of.

I felt electric with awe. "I still can't believe it. Now I *know* the Lord is listening. I never knew that before. I always figured there was a great distance between man and God, but now I know there isn't. He can hear us."

As the deepest layers of my soul woke up, I examined the miracle more closely:

"I was thinking, Pastor, I couldn't find his femoral artery at first—the vein where the IV needs to be inserted. For weeks, it was like nothing I effing did—excuse my swearing, Pastor, sorry about that—"

He shrugged. "I'm used to it."

"Nothing I did to practice finding that vein was working, so I have to ask you, do you think that was part of God's plan? Do you think the Lord orchestrated that? Do you think the Lord *prevented* me from being able to properly find the vein? Because I was thinking about how Cromwell barged into that room right in the nick of time. If I had found Prinkerton's femoral artery on my first try, then Cromwell would've been too late. Do you see what I'm saying?"

Pastor Asa squinted at me with bleary eyes and had no enthusiasm when he answered, "The Lord works in mysterious ways."

"Yeah, okay, but it seems like the Lord worked in a very logical, straightforward way."

"True," he allowed before taking another gulp of his beer.

"I mean, from where I'm standing," I went on, in total amazement of the miracle at hand—the miracle I'd been *a part of*—and explained, "it's like God used me as an instrument to ensure a man's prayers were answered."

"That's God's M.O.," he agreed before reaching the bottom of his pint. He shook his glass at the bartender and the guy refilled it right away. "I often think about you, Robert. About how you've stayed away from church all these years, unwilling to set foot inside. My parents might have their opinions about your line of work, but it's not for anyone else to say whether or not being an executioner is a sin. Killing, in and of itself, isn't a sin. God told the Hebrews to kill people all the time in the bible, and you know what? It would have been a sin for them not to."

"Well, I can't say God *wants* me to do what I've been doing, but I've got to tell you, after what I just saw back there… I've known for a long time now that I need to get out of that prison, but now I really understand that I need Christ. Man, what the Lord did for Prinkerton, my God! Can you believe it?"

He leveled his eyes on me, unmoved. Perhaps he was irritated at my astonishment or because I couldn't stop gushing or because I kept questioning if he could believe it, himself.

"Of course, *you* can believe it," I realized. "You of all people know exactly what God is capable of. I'm just blown away."

"I can see that," he said dryly.

"I think I'm ready for the church," I decided. "I'm ready to get my act together, dive into Christianity head first, and finally start living spiritually."

"Wonderful."

If I was going to clean up my act, then I needed to clean up my relationship with Crystal.

"Maybe I shouldn't tell you this," I began, "but I might need help with the girl I'm seeing."

"With Crystal?"

"You see," I said, lowering my voice and leaning in, "the issue is wrapped up in how we met. It's probably no secret that she used to dance over at Mermaids, but the thing is, our relationship..."

I wasn't sure how to come out with it. I hadn't confided in anyone about Crystal and making confessions didn't come naturally.

"Yes?"

I leaned in even closer and whispered, "I've been paying her."

"You've been paying her?"

My voice was a decibel above breathing, "You know, to stay the night." When he didn't quite get it, I mouthed the words, "For hanky-panky."

I let that wash over him, straightened up, and talked in a normal tone.

"I didn't really think it through. I had gotten to know her, you know? So it felt like I was just helping her out a bit more, you know financially. Plus, with those women turning up dead, I didn't want her at the club, so that helped me justify, you know, what we were doing together."

"And this is still going on?"

"Well, now I want to start something real with her. I don't want cash to change hands, you know? I want to take care of her like a man would a woman. Have something real. But see, I caught her."

"Caught her doing…?"

"I think she's been going to Mermaids. I'm afraid that she's still living that life, and I think I need your help. How can I do this thing right?"

Asa drew in a deep, thoughtful breath, quietly considering the situation.

But instead of offering a helpful solution, he questioned me, "You don't think that her time at the church has been priming her heart for the Lord?"

I laughed, letting out a good hearty chuckle and, man, a good laugh was just what I needed. "The only reason Crystal has been going to Lighthouse Ministries is because she's gotten it into her head that the killer has been hiding out there."

A dark glimmer clouded over his otherwise friendly eyes as he questioned, "*That's* been her reason for attending, has it?"

"She's *convinced.*"

"Quiet down, everyone!" said the bartender, as he turned the volume up on a Channel 7 news report that was playing on the TV.

Wearing a pink bikini and holding a foam microphone under her mouth, Channel 7's Missy Chance filled the screen as she reported—*LIVE!*—from outside Mermaids.

"I'm standing outside the infamous strip club, Mermaids, where the late Amanda Dover and Jewel Payson had once danced."

Missy pressed her fingers to her right ear, holding her earpiece in place and concentrating.

"I'm just now getting word that yet another *dancer, Amber Everhart, has been found dead on Woodland Beach."*

Pastor Asa stiffened on his barstool, his pint hovering just below his swollen mouth, while patrons at Foster's gasped and the bartender murmured, "Why can't they catch this guy?"

"Amber Everhart was last seen right here outside of this very club before getting into a vehicle," Missy Chance went on, speaking at a fast clip. *"An eye witness told police that Everhart went into a station wagon, but they did not see the driver. This could be the killer, folks. Police believe that the driver is the man they have been referring to as* Thomas. *They urge residents to contact the local Woodland Beach precinct if you have any information. You should now be seeing the crime-stoppers hotline at the bottom of your screens. Again, if you have* any *information that could help police, do not hesitate to call the number. I've said it before and I'll never stop saying it until Thomas is caught. We have a serial killer in Kent County. This is Missy Chance reporting* LIVE! *from Mermaids! Back to you, Andy!"*

The bartender turned down the volume as a commercial for Folgers coffee came on. You could've heard a pin drop, it was so quiet. Patrons stared at the TV in abject horror, having lost their appetite for alcohol.

Worried, I said, "I have to keep Crystal out of that club."

Pastor Asa set his beer on the bar and told me, "Yes, you do."

DEATH ROW INMATE 756
Olson, Gary

On June 7, 1981, a routine food & safety inspection at Porkies Slaughterhouse in Smyrna, Delaware, uncovered what appeared to be a large ball of human hair. The inspector alerted the FDA about the contamination issue, which precipitated a USDA quality control assessment. This quality control assessment confirmed contamination and further discovered that the source of contamination included additional human remains.

Forensic investigators identified the human remains, which also consisted of skull and bone fragments, and a deeper investigation linked those remains to members of the Dovi crime family, who had gone missing.

Prior to their disappearance, these members of the Dovi crime family had agreed to testify against their Chicago rivals, the Bandido crime family, in a criminal case wherein the Bandidos had been charged with laundering money through Porkies.

Authorities believed that pig farmer Gary Olson was responsible for mixing the missing mob members with the meat, because Olson had access to Porkies Slaughterhouse and was a Bandido by blood.

When arrested, Olson spoke in riddles, which sounded like nonsensical conspiracy theories according to investigators. Included in Olson's mad ramblings was the statement to "never eat pork during Pentecost," a reference to the Old Testament in which God condemned the eating of pigs. Far from coherent, Olson's bizarre proclamations confused investigators even after biblical theologians were consulted.

The D.A.'s office called Olson's religiously-based statements "nothing more than a poor attempt to demonstrate insanity." After a psychological evaluation, Olson was deemed mentally fit to stand trial.

The criminal offenses were tried as a capital murder case due to the fact that the crimes involved the following aggravating factor(s):

- *The murder was committed against a person who was a witness to a crime and who was killed for the purpose of preventing the witness's appearance or testimony in any grand jury, criminal or civil proceeding involving such crime, or in retaliation for the witness's appearance or testimony in any grand jury, criminal or civil proceeding involving such crime.*

Olson was found guilty after conviction by a court of law and has therefore been sentenced to be executed by lethal injection at the James T. Vaughn Correctional Center in Smyrna, DE.

Execution to commence: August 31, 1986

THE STRIPPER

AFTER THE FIASCO with Pastor Gracie at the church, I saw no alternative to dancing at Mermaids full-time.

I didn't know for sure whether or not Pastor Gracie had told Robert about our blowout at Lighthouse Ministries, but I assumed she had, which meant that patching things up with Robert was not going to happen.

Bottom line—Robert wasn't talking to me, and I needed money.

Yes, I had gotten ahead financially thanks to the last time I'd worked at Mermaids, but the cash I had made that night wasn't going to stretch very far. Returning to the club sooner or later was inevitable, and as dangerous as the situation was, I couldn't avoid the place just because another stripper had been killed.

This wasn't to say that I wasn't devastated by Amber's murder.

I was.

I loved Amber!

Last night, I had stared at my TV in rapt horror as Channel 7's Missy Chance had reported *LIVE!* from outside Mermaids. As I'd watched the broadcast, my jaw had dropped, my knees had given way, and I had collapsed onto the side of my bed, overcome with a feeling of heart-sinking dread so severe that it took my breath away and scrambled my brain.

I couldn't believe that another friend of mine had been murdered. I couldn't believe that the police didn't know they were chasing the figment of a teenage boy's imagination—they were completely unaware that their prime suspect wasn't real! And I couldn't believe that every lead I had followed with the hopes of discovering the killer's identity had been a dead end.

For God's sake, who was behind the murders of Cherry, Original Jewel, and Amber?

No one knew, and it was maddening!

Worst of all, I really couldn't believe that I was headed back to Mermaids.

And yet…

There I was, lugging my giant stripper bag and walking across the rear parking lot, having parked my car behind the club. I was all dolled up and wearing next to nothing, the heat was so oppressive.

As I turned the corner, coming onto the main drag, I collided with a man.

"Ooph!" I said, startled. Clutching my chest and laughing, I blurted out, "Sorry!"

When I looked up and recognized the man I had bumped into, I had a mild heart attack.

Oh, my God!

"Pastor Asa?"

Seeing Pastor Asa among the shameless characters that were known to loiter around Mermaids was jarring to say the least. Even more jarring was the sight of the bruises on his face. It looked like someone had put him through the ringer.

"I'm so sorry!" he exclaimed, as the flashing neon sign behind him screamed *LIVE! NUDE! GIRLS!* and illuminated a nearby cluster of patrons. The men were smoking cigarettes and using a foul sense of humor that I had learned to tune out years ago. "I would have grabbed you in the parking lot behind the club, but I couldn't find a spot."

The hairs on the back of my neck pricked up.

He added, "I was hoping to speak with you…"

At the strip club?

The way he was looking at me—leering—immediately made me uncomfortable. Both of his hands were in his pockets. My female intuition kicked in and alarm bells started going off left and right.

"Why were you hoping to speak with me, and why *here*, of all places?"

"I would like to tell you, but first, let's go to my car—"

"*Why* are you here?" I questioned. "Why do you want to talk to me?"

"I parked a few blocks over," he said as if I might be up for taking a walk.

The nearby cluster of men stomped on their cigarette butts and entered the strip club, leaving me with Pastor Asa on the hot sidewalk. I didn't trust the guy. Had he followed me here? And if he had, from where? Did he know where I lived?

He pushed, "I would really like to speak with you privately… in my car—"

"I'm late as it is," I told him, declining as I tried to get around him.

Letting out a little embarrassed chuckle, he stepped in front of me and said, "You look scared."

"I really have to get inside—"

"I'm here to talk to you on Robert's behalf," he told me and I stopped trying to get around him.

In the blink of an eye, he had my attention.

Robert had sent him?

My interest was fully piqued.

"What are you talking about?" I asked.

"Let's just say, last night he confided in me. I know about your *relationship*. About the hanky-panky."

"He told you about that?"

"Only because he wants my help. Could we talk privately? My car is just two blocks away."

"No one's around to hear us," I pointed out, which was true. The sidewalk had cleared. Music from the club cut across the street in muffled booms. "What did Robert say to you?"

"I'd be a lot more comfortable if you would come with me. It'll only take five minutes."

"You're catching me off guard here, and like I said, I don't want to be late for my shift," I wavered, debating whether or not I should hear him out.

"Just two blocks," he coaxed.

I really wanted to know what Robert might have said to him...

"I don't know..." I debated.

"Come on, please? People know who I am, not that I'm some kind of Christian big shot, but I feel paranoid just standing here. If word got back to my parents that I was seen hanging out on the sidewalk in front of Mermaids, it could ruin the church's reputation."

"If you're worried about that, then you shouldn't have come here," I said bluntly, as I again tried to walk around him to get to the entrance of the club.

"Crystal, wait."

I didn't wait. I didn't even glance over my shoulder at him. I took hold of the handle and pulled the glass entrance door open.

"Robert wants to be with you."

I spun around. "What?"

I felt a glimmer of hope. I let the door go and locked eyes with Pastor Asa.

"He really does want to be with you," he went on. "The way he lights up when he talks about you—Robert loves you."

Still? He loved me? Really?

"He doesn't want to see me," I said, overwhelmed with emotion and hoping to God I was wrong. Of course, I wanted Robert to want me. But I couldn't ignore how he had treated me when I had last seen him at his house. He had given me an ultimatum not to dance, and I had failed. What was I supposed to do? My hands were tied.

"He does want to see you," Pastor Asa promised. "But not if you go in there."

"*'In there'* is where he met me."

"I understand that. But Robert is growing. Don't let him outgrow you."

"What does he expect me to do? I was at his house the other night. I told him I would walk away from all this," I explained, gesturing at the flashing *LIVE! NUDE! GIRLS!* sign behind me. "He sent me away. If you know about our relationship, then you know I need money. What am I supposed to do? Not work until I win him over? I can't afford to do that. Do you see what a financial Catch-22 that would be?"

He cut his eyes over his shoulder like a man who didn't want to be seen talking with me in public.

"How can you come here after what's been happening to those women?" he challenged.

"I'm sticking with my girls until they catch the guy—"

"Robert doesn't want you to put yourself in harm's way. You'll be in danger if you continue to work here, Crystal—"

"I'm aware, trust me," I snapped as I began drifting backwards for the entrance. "I need to go—"

He wasn't going to let me.

He caught my wrist, taking a rough hold of me with his strong hand.

Was he crazy?

I felt adrenaline rush across my skin, and a sharp wave of panic shot through me.

He released me before I had time to freak out. Then he insisted, "I don't want to see you jeopardize what could become a solid Christian relationship. Robert wants to seriously start attending church. He talked about retiring from the prison. Christ is refining him and it's beautiful, and Robert wants you right there by his side."

I wanted that, too. But I sensed Pastor Asa was dangerous.

"Meaning what?" I complained, feeling seriously torn. "No offense, but I didn't last long with your mother. The whole reason I showed up the other day for Christian Counseling was because Robert wants me to give the church a shot, and I was willing to try, but Pastor Gracie is a nightmare, and quite frankly, you're not much better."

"I'm sorry for that," he said. "I know how my mother can be, and I sincerely apologize for how off-putting I may have come across when I introduced myself to you at Kowalski's execution last month. Every day, I tell myself to be more like my father and less like my mother, but since both of them raised me, I have to stay hypervigilant if I want to inspire rather than horrify. I'm a work in progress, but I'm here with the best of intentions. I'm here as Robert's advocate. I'm here to be of service."

I found him convincing, but I was also afraid of him.

Or was I overreacting?

Maybe Pastor Asa had innocently grabbed my wrist a moment ago?

If I didn't so badly want things to work out with Robert, I wouldn't have asked, "What are you proposing?"

The light behind Pastor Asa's eyes twinkled and he said, "Robert needs to see a good faith effort on your part and he needs to know that you aren't working in the club."

"I can stop working here," I compromised, knowing full-well that I would definitely be dancing tonight. "But what kind of 'good faith effort' are you talking about?"

"We could meet for Christian Counseling, you and I."

"Yeah, right," I laughed sarcastically. "Your mother would love that. If I've learned anything from your mom, it's that the opposite sexes can't be alone together."

"We can meet outside of the church so that no one knows, except for Robert, of course. We can keep things private otherwise."

"I don't know," I hesitated, backpedaling.

"Robert wants to be able to love you freely, but he has his limits. I'm sure I don't have to tell you that you can't dance forever." When I didn't immediately combat him, he added, "He wants a wife."

"He said that?"

"Yes."

"He said he wants me to be his wife?" I questioned, feeling suddenly optimistic.

"He doesn't want anyone else," he said as if it was a guarantee. I believed him, wholeheartedly. "He wants you, Crystal."

I couldn't stop smiling. "Okay, let's do Christian Counseling," I agreed. "But right now I have to go."

"Please, Crystal, come with me. I don't want to have to tell him that you went back in there."

I was tempted. I could've left with Pastor Asa. I could've thrown caution to the wind, abandoned my promise to Jimbo, and done whatever it would take, right here and now, to ensure I would have a future with Robert Nash.

But something screaming from the pit of my stomach told me not to disappear into the night with Pastor Asa, so I said, "If you don't want to tell Robert that I went into the club tonight, then don't tell him."

THE CLUB WAS bustling and alive. Pushing my way through the crowd wasn't easy, but I made my way into the ladies' dressing room before Jimbo started making any announcements.

The girls looked long-faced and shaken. Extremely on edge with Amber's murder on their minds. Their dramatic makeup couldn't hide how disturbed they felt at what had become of their fellow exotic dancer, Amber Everhart.

"I'm keeping my switchblade in my money-bag," Destiny decided.

"Do you think she was drugged?" Miracle speculated. "Maybe someone offered her a drink and it was spiked with something, and that's how she ended up in that station wagon."

A new girl named Honey said, "I bet you anything it's the private room situation. There's been a really long wait. What if Amber went outside with a customer, you know, so that she wouldn't lose him during the wait, and things got out of hand?"

Jimbo shouted, "Girls!"

I was quickly changing into my bikini top and G-string in the corner, but gave him as much of my attention as I could spare.

"Did anyone see the station wagon?" asked New Jewel.

"That's what I was wondering," Miracle chimed in. "Someone must have seen the driver."

Jimbo used an even louder voice, shouting over the strippers. Failing that, he wedged two fingers into his mouth and whistled, startling everyone.

"Thank you," he said when the girls quieted down. He placed his large hand over his hairy chest where his purple Hawaiian shirt should have been. It was so hot in there that Jimbo had unbuttoned his shirt clear down the front. "Amber will be deeply missed. Deeply. She was a fantastic, gymnastic stripper and I'm sure we will all miss her personality and flexibility. But, as I'm sure many of you noticed, Amber had lost patience."

"I knew it," Honey murmured as she shook her head.

"Amber wasn't willing to wait for the private rooms," he went on. "She often left the club without telling me. We all know that she was getting into cars. I couldn't stop her. Of course, I *tried* to stop her, but I've been preoccupied with keeping our VIPs happy, which as you know, involves running around all night and trying to procure cocaine. Amber was doing her own thing and breaking the rules. I couldn't protect her.

"If you break the rules and leave the club, I can't help you," he warned us. "Please understand, I love all of you. I don't want anything bad to happen to you. But you cannot do what Amber did. I want to hear you say it."

Hesitant and thoroughly confused, we all glanced at one another then responded in overlapping, incongruent mumbles—*Don't want anything bad to happen; Cannot do what Amber did; Jimbo loves all of us.*

Jimbo winced and we gave up.

"The fact of the matter is that I don't know who's behind the murders, but I *do know* who has been behind the Kent County campaign to get Mermaids shut down!"

"You do?" I asked.

"The spineless weasels thought I'd never find out! But I did! And now, my mermaids, we finally know who we're fighting!"

"Who?" asked Destiny from the back of the dressing room.

Jimbo told us, "Some Methodist church called *Lighthouse Ministries.*"

One of the new girls screwed her face up. "A church?"

"Those bastards aren't going to know what hit them!"

OF ALL THE places that Pastor Asa could have suggested for our first Christian Counseling meeting, I thought the shore of Woodland Beach was in very poor taste.

I kept my opinion to myself, however. The only thing that mattered was that Pastor Asa was going to help me fix my relationship with Robert by first helping me fix myself.

While I thought meeting on the same stretch of Woodland Beach where Amber Everhart had washed up—strangled, drowned, and dead—was creepy to say the least, the location certainly guaranteed privacy. Pastor Asa had been correct in that regard. The residents were once again avoiding the beach, which meant that there was no one around to see us.

In general, the pastor was beyond paranoid. He did not want *anyone* to see us together. Period.

When I reached the desolate beach, there wasn't a soul in sight.

I took off my heels and started walking barefoot across the warm sand towards the water. My heels dangled from my fingers. Occasionally, a gust of wind tore through, but the air was otherwise briny and mild.

Dusk gathered across the wide sky, as I neared the water's edge. The sea looked as smooth as glass yet shimmered with the light from the setting sun at my back.

Suddenly sensing that I wasn't alone, a very bad premonition slammed through me.

I felt watched, and the next thing I knew, a cold hand took hold of my arm from behind.

"Ah!" I exclaimed, jittery and whipping around.

"It's just me!" said Pastor Asa. "I'm so sorry!"

"You have to stop doing that!" My heart was galloping up my throat and it took more than a moment before it settled back down into my chest. "You scared me!"

"I was calling your name and jogging after you, but you must not have heard me with the wind in your ears."

He had brought a beach blanket, which was draped over his arm, and in his other hand, he held a picnic basket.

"Thanks for meeting me here," he said, as a weird smile spread across his bruised face.

"It was a creepy suggestion. You know that, right?"

"I apologize, but I couldn't risk meeting you at a populated spot, and thanks to the murder of Amber Everhart—"

"You knew no one would be here," I supplied, feeling even more creeped out.

"I wouldn't want anyone from church to see us together," he repeated for the millionth time.

"Fine. I'm here. What now?"

"Now, we get comfortable."

Pastor Asa set the picnic basket he had brought with him on the sand and shook out his blanket. The wind gave him some trouble as he tried to place the blanket down onto the hard, damp sand.

For a split second, as I watched him struggle with the corners of the blanket, I wondered if he thought this was a date.

"Have a seat," he said once the thing was finally secure. He removed his loafers, sat down, and found his bible in the picnic basket.

I obviously couldn't refuse the invitation, even though my gut was telling me to get the hell out of there.

I settled down, facing the sea, and reminded myself that without Pastor Asa, I wouldn't have a prayer of being with Robert.

"I'm here because I care about Robert," I stated.

I didn't want him to misunderstand my motives now that we were seated beside one another in what felt like a bizarrely romantic setting with the shimmering sea before us and twilight closing in.

"Plus, you're right. I can't dance forever."

I let that hang. Pastor Asa didn't take his eyes off me.

"I've also noticed," I went on, giving credit where credit was due, "some people get a lot out of the church, though I have no idea why."

"Oh?"

"Like my friend Lars Svensson and another guy, Emmett DeGraves."

"Oh yes, Lars and Emmett. They *have* become members."

"I just want to do whatever Robert wants me to do to make this work," I said.

"Robert will be very glad to hear that." Pastor Asa flipped open the picnic basket lid and produced a container of what appeared to be sliced pie.

"My mother started this tradition," he explained. "Every time I convert someone to Christianity, she makes a strawberry rhubarb pie."

"I haven't converted," I dryly pointed out.

"Oh, this wasn't baked because of you. I've had a lot of success at the prison recently. *A lot.* The inmates cannot convert fast enough, praise God. Care for a slice?"

"I'll pick at it."

He popped the top off the container and set the pie between us. Next, he found two plastic spoons in the picnic basket and offered me one.

I poked the pie and scooped up a bite, but only stared at the piece. "Is it true that Lighthouse Ministries has been trying to get the club shut down?"

Uncomfortable, he stiffened and couldn't quite look me in the eye. "That's my mother's crusade."

"Why am I not surprised?"

"You sound a *little* surprised," he pointed out.

"How does she have time to antagonize the strip club? Isn't she running a congregation?" I shook my head.

"Listen, I know what she's like. I know what people think of her. I don't disagree with people who can't stand her. She's awful."

He went on to open up about his mother and what being raised in the church had been like for him. Listening, it occurred to me that he might have been abused, not as badly as myself and not in the same ways, but he was describing growing up in what sounded like a heavily sheltered cult, one which hadn't allowed him to express himself, engage with anyone who wasn't Christian, or reveal to his parents who he really was.

The way he was leveling with me in terms of how he really felt, caused me to reconsider the assumptions I had made about him. Maybe he wasn't creepy. Maybe he was weird because of how Pastors Joe and Gracie had raised him. I felt endeared towards him. I, too, was weird thanks to the sordid types who had ruined my childhood.

I soon got the impression that, like myself, Asa was living a life that wasn't designed to work for him for very long. His life had less to do with the

Lord—his words, not mine—and more to do with obeying his parents' strict interpretations of the bible.

As we talked, nighttime gradually closed in, and before long, twinkling stars pierced the black sky, forming countless constellations.

"Crystal, no matter what you think of my parents or our church—no matter what *I* think of them—and no matter what their shortcomings are, or mine for that matter, I have to tell you that accepting the Lord as your savior is the answer."

I really didn't know about that.

He admitted, "I realize how I sound, and I know what you're probably thinking because of it, but it's the truth. If you walk with the Lord, everything else in your life will fall into place, including your relationship with Robert."

"Sorry, but I doubt that."

"If you don't believe in the Lord, what do you believe in?"

I couldn't say, because I wasn't sure.

THE EXECUTIONER

THE EXECUTION OF Gary Olson, former pig farmer and convicted killer, went off without a hitch.

I was able to pierce Olson's femoral artery on the first try, which I took as further evidence that the Lord had, without a doubt, used me as his divine instrument to save Willy Prinkerton's life the prior Sunday.

The day after Olson's execution, I drove to Lighthouse Ministries, eager to attend the men's bible study led by Pastor Joseph Asbury.

I had picked up a brand-new bible for the occasion and had tried to tackle reading the Book of Hosea, since that was the focus of the men's group. Apparently, they had been working their way through that section of the Old Testament all summer.

Truth be told, I hadn't been able to get through more than a few pages. I gleaned that God had told a prophet to marry a prostitute, which had brought Crystal to mind, and I gave up after that.

I figured the pastor would get me up to speed soon enough. I would rather listen to Pastor Joe explain it, anyway.

I presented myself with a good-natured attitude when I entered the church and joined the other men in the fellowship hall on the second floor.

As I pulled up a chair, Pastor Joe offered me a warm welcome.

"Great to have you with us today, Robert."

Shaking his hand, I said, "Glad I could be here. I don't know how regularly I'll be able to come, but I usually have a few Monday afternoons off each month."

"If you don't know everyone," he said as he began to introduce me to the other Christians around the table, "meet Lars Svensson, Emmett DeGraves, and Charles Riley, who you might've seen at our Sunday services."

I acknowledged each of them with a firm handshake if the man was seated close enough. Otherwise, I nodded and told myself not to feel awkward.

Emmet DeGraves and Charles Riley returned their attention to a large Wanted poster that the men had been passing back and forth.

I had seen the Wanted posters around town. The police had hired a sketch artist to render a facial composite of the killer based on Seth's fanciful descriptions of Thomas.

"Am I crazy," Emmet asked, as he tilted his head and studied the Wanted poster, "or does this guy look exactly like the Messiah?"

He wasn't wrong.

The Wanted poster featured a serene-looking man with large, soulful eyes and long, flowing, shoulder-length hair. The sketch artist had penciled a shadowy beard on the suspect's face, and a halo emanated from the crown of his head.

Charles Riley agreed. "That's Christ, right there. No doubt about it."

Lars leaned in and commented, "Finally, the Lord is *wanted* in Woodland Beach."

"A miracle," Emmet agreed.

"Praise God," added Pastor Joe.

"Hey, Robert," said Charles. "Didn't your son see the killer?"

"He's my nephew, actually," I answered, annoyed.

I didn't know whether or not Thomas was responsible for the murders, but I knew that Seth had been messing with the cops when he had told them what his friend looked like. Investigators had taken Seth seriously, and the result was that the Woodland Beach police had put an APB out for Jesus Christ. The incompetence was phenomenal.

"I really can't say if my nephew saw the killer," I added. "He's a confused boy."

"He did the right thing by helping the police," Emmet said, offering me a reassuring smile as all the men around the table agreed that Thomas looked strikingly similar to the Son of God.

Pastor Joe said, "As Christians, we will naturally see the Lord everywhere we look—in clouds, in pine cones, in dish soap bubbles—"

"Like Italian nuns who see the Virgin Mary in water stains and buttered toast," Lars chimed in. He was sitting awfully close to the pastor. How Lars wasn't melting under his polyester, three-piece suit was a mystery.

"I hope they catch the bastard," Emmett muttered under his breath and the other men vented with equal disgust. "I can't believe all the cops have to go on is a station wagon. No one saw the license plate number? No one saw the driver? Hell, Channel 7's Missy Chance and Andy Ailey were at the club that night and neither of them saw anything? All summer, cops have been parked in front of Mermaids, and the one time it mattered most they weren't sitting in their police cruiser when the killer pulled up right behind it?"

"All we can do, gentlemen, is pray," said Pastor Joe.

"Yes, Pastor," Lars agreed, folding his hands and bowing his head.

As Pastor Joe began praying, I clasped my hands together, closed my eyes, and begged myself to keep an open mind.

I said "Amen" with everyone else when Pastor Joe had concluded the prayer.

Then, we all opened our bibles and turned to Hosea 10:1.

Going around the table, we took turns reading.

I tried my best to pay attention, but the allegories, metaphors, and symbolism in the bible were way over my head, or so I thought.

All of a sudden, I felt a sense of connection to the content. I identified with Hosea, who had been commanded to marry a harlot. God had hardly commanded me to pay Crystal for hanky-panky, but there were enough similarities between Hosea and myself that I became more and more engaged in the bible study as the hour passed.

"He's not a broken man," I determined, once Pastor Joe had asked the first discussion question. "This Hosea guy doesn't seem broken."

"Please, go on," he encouraged.

Crystal came to mind and I felt betrayed all over again. How could she have gone back to dancing at Mermaids after everything I had done for her?

"Hosea isn't broken," I repeated. Trying as hard as I could to make sense, I went on, "Or maybe Hosea never loved the prostitute he married. All I know is that when a man has been broken by life, he won't be able to survive betrayal. Hosea's wife should have given up her prostitution the moment she married him. But she didn't. She betrayed Hosea in that sense, and all I'm saying is that Hosea either didn't love her or he wasn't a broken man to begin with, because he kept on keeping on no matter what as if he was fine."

I couldn't articulate myself so I began shaking my head instead.

Gently, Pastor Joe pointed out, "Hosea didn't fall apart every time his wife snuck off to return to prostitution, because God made him strong. Does that mean that Hosea wasn't a broken man to begin with? The text doesn't say. Hosea might have been a disaster before he connected with God. You see, God asked Hosea to marry a woman who would betray him over and over again. Those repeated betrayals are an allegory for how the Israelites betrayed God by worshiping idols. That being said, God didn't want Hosea to suffer. So, wouldn't God strengthen Hosea to ensure that Hosea would be able to obey his command?"

I didn't have an answer, but it got me thinking. "Why didn't his wife give up her old lifestyle?"

A sympathetic look came over Pastor Joe, and he placed his hand on my shoulder.

"We're not talking about Hosea, are we?" he asked.

It was too much to bear. I felt the flood gates open up. I wanted to pull away, but these men understood me. Pastor Joe really *got* me even though he didn't even know me. This was not something I could walk away from.

I let it out—the hard emotions—as I opened up about everything that had broken me over the years, starting with the death of my late sister Abby.

I told them how Abby had been the most important person in the world to me. I shared with them how I had always looked out for her and had protected her in high school. I had beaten up boys who thought they could talk trash about her. A few years later, I had fought Abby tooth and nail when she declared that she was going to move to New Jersey.

As I went on, explaining the heartache of losing her to the other side of the bay and then losing her for good when she had given birth to my nephew, there wasn't a dry eye around the table.

"I've never been a father to that boy," I said, putting words to my biggest regret. "I can't even hug him, and I know he's messed up because of it. The guilt I'm carrying around is crushing me. I'm broken. I can't handle much else. I can't fall in love with a woman who's destined to betray me like Hosea's wife betrayed him every chance she got. Awe, damnit."

I cursed. I couldn't fight the waves of emotions that were rising up my throat.

"Am I a fool to expect a woman like that to change for me?" I didn't know how else to phrase it. All I knew was that Crystal and I couldn't be together unless she gave up the club and changed. I needed a guarantee that I wouldn't get hurt, and yet, I knew there were no guarantees in life. "Am I a fool to hope that I can change, too?"

Pastor Joe reminded me, "It's never foolish to have faith, Robert."

As I looked around the table, all the men were nodding in agreement, their eyes round and honest.

After the bible study, we made our way out of the fellowship hall, coming into the church vestibule. Some men walked out into the sweltering afternoon heat while others grabbed coffee to-go at the coffeemaker.

I decided to grab a cup of coffee, myself. As I did, I noticed Pastor Asa was joining his father beside the exit door. As Pastor Joe thanked each Christian as they left the church with their bibles in hand, Pastor Asa locked eyes with me and then quickly asked his dad to excuse him for a moment.

"Robert, hi," he said after meeting me at the coffeemaker. We stepped aside so that other men could grab cups of coffee. "What did you think of Dad's bible study?"

"I want to see Crystal."

"Oh?"

"The bible study made me realize that I've been a jackass towards her. Now, I definitely don't want Crystal working in that club. But I can't act like I don't want to see her until she changes. I want to see her. She's a work-in-progress, but so am I."

"Oh, oh my…"

"What?"

"Well, I was able to speak with Crystal and it was very, *very* productive," he promised.

I was all ears.

"She was receptive," he continued, "but as we got to talking and really started digging into her issues, she told me that she doesn't want to see you."

"Oh."

"Crystal feels it would be best if she takes some time to work on herself without having the added pressures of being in a relationship."

My heart sank. "I see."

"This isn't a bad thing, Robert," he quickly assured me. "It's a very good thing. She's willing to work on herself, and she's open to my spiritual guidance."

I felt obligated to agree. "Sure, that's good."

"She really needs time and space *away* from you."

"Got it."

"I'm going to work on her, Robert. I know you two will be something special one day—one day soon!" he said. "Just give her time."

"She doesn't want to see me at all?" I questioned.

"Not at all."

THE BOY

DEAD AMANDA DOVER! Dead Jewel Payson! And now, Dead Amber Everhart?

I was furious, and wolfing down cotton candy wasn't helping!

I knew *exactly* who Thomas was, and as far as I was concerned, he was just as culpable as the killer!

Why hadn't he stopped any of this?

He was all-knowing and all-powerful, the highest authority on earth and in heaven, and he had allowed another atrocity?

I wasn't intrigued by murder anymore. I was sickened by it!

Why had Thomas led me to the body of Dead Jewel Payson that day? Why had he walked me up those dunes and shown me that another woman had been killed? Why had he told me that Crystal would be the next to die unless I did something?

It was all up to me?

If I didn't love her hard enough or fast enough or soon enough, would she be killed like the others?

Time was running out! I knew it! I could feel it! And yet my best friend wasn't helping me?!

I stuffed cotton candy into my face as I stomped along the promenade, furious.

Thomas knew what Crystal meant to me. Would he *really* let her die? What a jerk!

From out of nowhere, Thomas appeared beside me and said, "You're mad at me, but I don't deserve it."

He was a ghostly, glowing apparition I hadn't meant to conjure.

"Go away."

"I can hear you blaming me and I have a right to face my accuser."

"You're not allowed to invade my brain!"

"*Allowed* isn't a concept that applies to me."

My face twisted up into a knot, he had me so flustered. "Semantics!"

People nearby were beginning to stare at me.

I turned on my heel and cut through the crowd, but I couldn't lose him. My flip-flops smacked against my feet, as I squeezed towards the gazebo. Anything to get away from Thomas. But as I wove my infuriated way through tourists, Thomas kept after me, following closely when all I wanted to do was breathe.

"Leave me alone!" I yelled over my shoulder at him.

"That's spiritually impossible. Seth, would you stop and talk to me, face-to-face?"

"No!" I snapped.

"Please?"

I didn't want to have it out with him in public, but I knew Thomas well enough to know he wasn't going to drop it.

I spun around, ready to give him a piece of my mind!

But two police officers were standing on the promenade where Thomas should have been.

The police officers didn't hesitate to ask me if I had recently taken any hallucinogenic drugs.

"What?" I said, feeling irritated and out of sorts. "No, I haven't taken any drugs!"

"Then who were you talking to?" one of the cops asked.

I couldn't tell them the truth—that I had been arguing with their prime suspect—so I grumbled, "No one."

They glanced at one another, and then the shorter one said, "Seth, we're going to have to ask you a few questions about Amber Everhart."

"I don't know anything about Amber Everhart," I told them.

I was sick of having to answer their questions. I had already cooperated more times than I could count! They had questioned me with Uncle Robert in our stifling living room after Dead Amanda Dover. They had questioned me on the beach after Dead Jewel Payson. They had questioned me again and again, asking the same questions as if I would give them better answers each time. What more did they want? I didn't know anything about Dead Amber Everhart. I hadn't found her on the beach.

"I already talked to you about the other women and I really don't know anything about the latest victim!"

"Great," said the first officer as he took hold of my upper arm and began hauling me towards the parking lot where his police cruiser was idling. "You can tell us all about it at the station."

"But I don't know anything!" I protested.

"We'll see about that," said the taller cop as he shoved me from behind.

"Excuse me!" a woman shouted.

I would recognize that voice anywhere.

It was Crystal!

Again, Crystal called out, "Excuse me!"

As the cops dragged me along, I glanced over my shoulder, and sure enough, Crystal had locked her huge blue eyes on me. She pressed through the crowd and shouted at the cops, "Hey, you can't take him!"

She dove in front of the officers and prevented them from shoving me into the back of their idling police cruiser.

Angry and out of breath, she told them, "You can't take him! He's a minor! You can't talk to him without his guardian present! You know the rules!"

"Ma'am, please step aside," they warned, but she wouldn't move.

She pulled me towards her and as she held me protectively, she asserted, "You can't take him."

The police didn't have a leg to stand on, but that didn't stop them from thinking they could trick her.

"You're welcome to accompany him," one of them suggested.

"I'm not his guardian," she snapped. "If you want to talk to him, you'll have to get permission from his Uncle first."

"Maybe we should haul *you* in for questioning," the shorter one threatened as he looked her up and down, getting an eyeful of her tiny dress.

"You'd like that, wouldn't you?"

She steered me away from the cruiser, and as we made our way back through the promenade, she told me, "Don't give those jerks a second thought. They're just trying to scare you. They should be ashamed of themselves for thinking they can get away with breaking the law. No one can make you talk. You remember that, okay?"

"Okay."

Overcome with emotion—I had missed her, there was a giant hole in our house where Crystal used to be!—I threw my arms around her and hugged her with all my might.

But my emotions quickly turned into rage. I felt my eyes sting and the next thing I knew, tears were blurring my vision.

She was to blame! I didn't want to be worried about her! I didn't want to live my life in a constant state of terror that Crystal would be murdered next on Woodland Beach!

I lost control of myself and shoved her.

Stunned, she returned the sentiment and shoved me as hard as she could.

I stumbled backwards and spilled across the promenade, which made the right kind of tears spill down my cheeks.

"Ow!"

"Well, what did you shove me for?!"

She helped me to my feet and pulled me in for another hug. "There, there," she breathed as she gently stroked my hair. "I know you miss me and blame me. I miss you, too."

"I'm not crying because I miss you—"

"Yes, you are."

"I'm crying because you shoved me," I insisted, unable to resist her warm embrace.

"I hardly shoved you—"

"I'm crying because, because," I stuttered, overcome with emotions that I couldn't control. "Because you're asking for it!"

She urged me back and searched my face. "Asking for what?"

"Asking to get killed!" I blurted out. "Everyone says so!"

She challenged me, "*Everyone,* as in, *the church kids you hate?*"

"So what if I hate them! They're right! You should be at home! Come back home to us!"

She sighed, remorseful. "Your uncle doesn't want me there."

"But *I* want you there!"

"I want that, too, Seth, but it's complicated."

"No, it's not!"

"Come here," she said, pulling me in again.

I didn't fight her. I soaked up her hugs instead.

She went on to explain, "Things got a bit messed up between Robert and me, but I'm trying to un-mess them up."

"You can't do what you've been doing," I told her. "You'll get killed."

I had wrapped myself around her like a barnacle, so tightly that she had to pry me off.

"Let me give you a ride home."

I didn't want a ride home. I wanted a mother!

But I couldn't refuse the crumbs she was offering me. I was starving and I gobbled them up.

When we arrived at the seaside cottage, my uncle's car was parked in the driveway, so Crystal pulled onto the shoulder of the road to drop me off.

I opened my door, but I didn't climb out. "Come in for dinner?"

"You're breaking my heart," she said.

I believed her, and it gave me hope that I might be able to convince her to come back home.

"We've been having ramen and SpaghettiOs," I moaned so she would pity us. "*Crunchy* ramen and *cold* SpaghettiOs."

"Not at the same time, I hope."

"Please come in?"

"I'm going to close my eyes, Seth, and when I open them, you're going to be in the house."

I let out a heavy sigh, knowing that I had no choice but to do what she said.

She closed her eyes, and I finally climbed out, closed the car door, and made my way into the house, but I wasn't happy about it.

Once I was inside, I dragged my feet, moaning and groaning, all the way into my bedroom where I slammed the door closed and spilled across my bed.

My uncle gave my bedroom door a little knock and when I didn't get up to let him in, he spoke through the door, asking me if I wanted to do a bunch of activities that didn't make sense like going for a walk, getting some food, and reading the bible together.

Had he been drinking?

Probably.

Alcohol would explain his sudden urge to bond.

"I want to be alone!"

"For how long?"

I groaned loud enough for him to get the message. He shuffled away from the door.

I hadn't even gotten a single moment of peace when Thomas materialized on my armchair from out of nowhere.

"You again," I grumbled. I couldn't deal with him.

I buried my face in the pillows, but he insisted on bothering me.

"I don't like seeing you like this," he said.

"How dare you!" I lifted my face and glared at him. "You don't like seeing me like this? You're the reason I'm like this!"

"I'd like to hear you out," he offered, but it sounded like a compromise.

I wasn't willing to compromise! A compromise of any sort would be too little, too late!

Infuriated, I sprang to my feet on the bed, pointed my finger down at him, and harnessed every shred of personal power that I possessed.

"I command you to save Crystal! By the power vested in me, I command you!"

"She has to want that, Seth—"

"I COMMAND YOU!"

He looked peaceful and unshaken, which I hardly appreciated.

Raising both of my hands to the sky—or ceiling, rather—I cried out to the heavens, "God, save Crystal!"

Thomas had given me his full attention, but I felt mocked.

I pointed my finger down at him again and proclaimed, "You *will* save Crystal! You will save her eternal soul, and you will save her from bodily harm, or so help me God—"

Both of his eyebrows shot up to his hairline and I *knew* I was treading on very thin ice, but I loved Crystal too much to back down now.

"Or so help me God," I continued, "I will never talk to you again!"

"That would make me very sad, Seth."

"You will save Crystal! I command you!" I shouted before declaring, "Or else I will report you to the *authorities*!"

That got the kind of reaction I was looking for.

Thomas jumped out of his chair. "Judas!"

I gasped. "You're calling *me* Judas?!"

"You would turn me in for crimes I didn't commit?"

"By not stopping the murders, you're as guilty as the killer!"

"Don't you dare *Judas* me!" he warned.

I threatened, "I will Judas you like a *verb* if you don't save Crystal!"

He gasped, but I kept going.

"You might as well stab me in the back if you're going to stand there and refuse to save her!"

"She has to want to be saved, Seth!"

I felt like I was going to explode.

I had to get away from him.

I jumped off my bed, threw my bedroom door open, and slammed it shut as soon as I had slid into the hallway, but Thomas was already on the other side of the door, which scared the bejesus out of me!

"Ah!"

I threw my door open and dove back into my room, but again, he was already there!

I couldn't get on the right side of the door!

Leaping back and forth, I opened and slammed and opened the door again, unable to dodge the Messiah, who appeared wherever I went.

From the living room, my uncle looked on and watched the commotion, not that he could see Thomas.

Uncle Robert pinched the bridge of his nose, let out a long sigh, and said, "I need a drink."

THE STRIPPER

"THIS IS MISSY Chance, reporting LIVE! from outside Mermaids! For all our Channel 7 viewers at home, let me start off by saying, Woodland Beach has achieved a monumental victory! The infamous strip club, Mermaids, has been officially shut down! As you can see behind me—Chucky, can you get a wide angle of the club?—Behind me, you can see cousins Jimbo and Timbo Guerra, the co-owners of Mermaids, are loading up a moving truck. Early this morning, co-owners Jimbo and Timbo Guerra were served an official Marshals Eviction, ordering them to shut down their questionable establishment in light of the recent murder of Amber Everhart. The Marshals Eviction Notice, which is right here—Chucky, can you get a close-up of the notice?—cites suspicion of criminal activity, as its legal grounds for eviction. The notice does not *state the pending criminal charges that the club is suspected of, but I'm told that prostitution is on the list. —Chucky, am I back in the shot?—If you ask me, Andy, this has been a long time coming and should've been put into effect months ago. If it had, who knows how many lives could have been saved? Perhaps all three victims would be alive today. Let me also say that closing Mermaids for good was a team effort, and could not have been accomplished without the persistence of Pastor Grace Asbury from Lighthouse Ministries!"*

"You think this is over?"

"Oh, look, it's Jimbo Guerra!—Chucky, get a close up!—Mr. Jimbo Guerra, I'm Missy Chance with Channel 7 News! Do you have a comment for our viewers at home?"

"Yeah, I have a comment—"

"Chucky, get a close-up!"

"My comment is for Pastor Grace Asbury and everyone at Lighthouse Ministries—"

"Sir, please don't take my microphone—"

"I've got one thing to say to you people—"

"Sir, please give me my microphone—"

"You think you can mess with me?!"

"Sir—"

"I'M COMING FOR YOU!"

"Release my microphone! Geez! There you have it, folks! I'm Missy Chance reporting LIVE! from outside Mermaids. Back to Andy in the studio!"

I HAD WATCHED Missy Chance's news broadcast late last night, but nothing could've prepared me for Jimbo's retaliation against the church.

I arrived early at Lighthouse Ministries for the Sunday service and took a seat in one of the pews in the back.

Familiar faces entered the vestibule and filled the sanctuary. Elderly church ladies who were dressed in their Sunday-best claimed the front rows, while working-class men fisting cups of coffee joked around and settled in the back.

Pastors Gracie and Joe stood under the archway and greeted the parishioners as they entered, offering warm welcomes, kind blessings, and other companionable Christian greetings.

Lars found me and handed me a cup of coffee. He looked dapper as always. I slid over, making room for him to sit beside me, and asked him if he had heard the news about Mermaids.

He had.

Instead of sharing his opinion with me, however, he told me that I looked nice.

I had dressed more like myself today, but had been mindful not to reveal too much skin. I didn't want to be disrespectful, but I also couldn't go on pretending that pillbox hats and polyester skirts were my style. Pastor Asa had helped me come to accept that about myself. I wasn't going to pretend anymore, and he had approved of my newfound commitment to act honestly even if it resulted in a sideways glare or two from his mother. He said that the people at Lighthouse Ministries would benefit from seeing actual diversity in their congregation. The face of modern-day Christianity didn't have to resemble a 1940s Norman Rockwell illustration. It could look like me.

Our Christian counseling sessions had been going well. They were still a secret, but we now met daily on Woodland Beach at dusk. Pastor Asa always brought his blanket and a picnic basket. He always offered me pie and bite-sized advice that wasn't too hard to swallow. Whenever I told him I felt ready to talk to Robert, however, Pastor Asa discouraged the idea. He would often explain that I wasn't spiritually ready to be in a relationship and that Robert would only turn me away if I tried to talk to him before I had matured in my Christian faith. As a consolation, Pastor Asa would then place another slice of pie on my plate, which I often ate right up, not that either were very easy to digest.

At the moment, Pastor Asa was standing at the front of the sanctuary near the pulpit. We touched eyes briefly, and I could tell that he knew what I was thinking. Robert and Seth were sitting across the aisle from me and I so badly wanted to smile their way. Pastor Asa's sympathetic eyes urged me not to, however. I didn't want to blow it with Robert so I kept my attention straight ahead, as Pastors Gracie and Joe made their way down the aisle, stood behind the lectern, and addressed the congregation.

Pastor Joe was barely able to wish the parishioners a blessed *good morning* when a sudden commotion in the vestibule stole his attention.

His jaw dropped, and Pastor Gracie let out a furious-sounding gasp, as a sea of newcomers flooded into the sanctuary.

I glanced over my shoulder to see what was going on.

Oh. My. God.

I sensed more than saw Tom Selleck, the star of Magnum P.I., standing at the back of the church...

Then my brain started working again.

Jimbo?

Hawaiian shirts. Dark aviator sunglasses. Chest hair and pinky rings.

Every stripper that had ever worked at Mermaids with the exception of me and the dead ones were standing behind Jimbo and Timbo at the back of the sanctuary.

Jimbo flashed a thousand watt smile and said, "Time to get our Jesus on!"

Pastor Gracie flew into a squawking tizzy. Horrified, she pushed her husband to say something and take control, but Pastor Joe was befuddled.

"What do you think you're doing?" she squawked at Jimbo, as the girls winked and whispered to nearby parishioners, *Hey, baby.*

"What can I say, Pastor Gracie," said Jimbo, "you've helped me see the light!"

Jimbo stuck his thick fingers into his mouth and whistled loudly, startling the entire congregation, which prompted his cousin to move into phase two of their organized infiltration.

Timbo ushered the girls into the pews, this way and that, spreading them throughout the sanctuary like an intelligent virus designed to infect every cell it came in contact with.

Wearing stiletto heels and mini-skirts that barely covered their bums, the girls were showing skin. *A lot* of skin, which became abundantly obvious as they oozed down the pews, squeezing past parishioners. They were showing the kind of skin you would ordinarily find in a strip club on *Saturday night.*

"Tell them this is a house of God!" Pastor Gracie hissed at her husband.

Bewildered, Pastor Joe replied, "I believe they know where they are. Perhaps this is the Lord's doing?"

"I never!" she seethed—vexed—as she glared at her husband, her face all screwed up with astonishment.

I tried not to giggle, but it was impossible. When I laughed, Robert glanced my way, smiled, and shook his head at the comedy of it all.

Unlike the church ladies, who were appalled at the strippers, the men in the congregation grinned as if a recent prayer of theirs had just been answered. They moved heaven and earth to make room for the girls. They invited the strippers to sit right next to them, and introduced themselves, all the while, they praised the Lord, certain now more than ever that God was real.

"Welcome, newcomers," said Pastor Joe.

"They aren't welcome!" Pastor Gracie blurted out, as she heaved her obese husband aside and stole the lectern. "You aren't welcome here!"

Holding his ground, Jimbo peeled his aviator sunglasses from his eyes, drank in the sight of his girls peppered in among the parishioners, and said:

"I see some sinners in this congregation who I think my girls are gonna get along with just fine!"

The look of outrage that came over Pastor Gracie's face was priceless.

THE FIRST WEEK of September felt like an Indian summer. Temperatures flared, but the tourists had left town, leaving all of Woodland Beach quiet and eerily empty.

Jimbo, Timbo, and the Mermaids strippers persisted, attending every Sunday service and bible study they could, which I didn't mind. Their presence at Lighthouse Ministries took the focus off me. I was no longer the new girl. Pastor Gracie had a bigger, ongoing disruption to contend with that had made my previous confrontation with her seem like a walk in the park by comparison.

The strange mix of characters at the church resulted in clashing cultures that cracked me up. It also resulted in Robert and I locking eyes across the aisle during the Sunday services. There seemed to be no limit on the lengths Jimbo would go to desecrate Pastor Gracie's otherwise holy assemblies. Evidently, exotic dancers could gyrate to *any* song, and the worship team was told not to play hymnal music at the start of the service because of it.

No matter how connected I felt to Robert on Sundays whenever we briefly touched eyes from across the pews, he otherwise kept his distance from me. It seemed that now all we had between us was Pastor Asa, who I hoped would soon give Robert the green light to approach me, but it hadn't happened yet.

With Mermaids closed and Robert keeping his distance, I had more than enough time on my hands to panic about my finances and investigate the serial killer, who had been successfully dodging the police at every turn.

Lars was no longer helping me investigate at the church. He had told me that he didn't need a constant reminder that the love of his life had been murdered. I couldn't blame him for that, but I also couldn't move on.

I had to find out who had killed my friends.

My bulletin board was packed tightly with notecards, colored Post-its, and red string.

I convinced Channel 7's Missy Chance to meet with me a few times, which gave me even more information. The information seemed promising but hadn't led to anything concrete, *yet*.

This was what Missy Chance had divulged—a wallet-sized photograph had been found near Amber Everhart's body on Woodland Beach. Police believed that the killer had accidentally dropped it while fleeing the scene. The photograph featured a little girl who the police had identified as Amber at thirteen-years old. Next to young Amber in the photo was a woman who, according to Missy, was Amber's late mother.

What this told me was that Amber had opened up to her killer. She had shown him the photograph, perhaps because the photo had captured a happy moment from her past. It also told me that the killer might have felt a large enough connection to his victim that he had wanted to keep a memento of her life. A trophy of sorts.

Had the killer kept trophies to remind him of Cherry and Original Jewel, as well? I believed he would have, but I didn't have the resources to investigate that avenue. As far as I could tell, neither did the cops.

I had stopped in the police station a handful of times to ask the lead detective on the case if there were any new clues, even though he clearly despised me.

All the lead detective had been able to tell me was that there was an A.P.B. out for an early model station wagon with wood panel siding and a busted tail light—the killer's vehicle. He told me that two checkpoints had been set up in town, and every station wagon fitting the description would be pulled over and the drivers would be questioned. There was also an ongoing A.P.B. out for Thomas, along with hundreds of Wanted posters, which were plastered all over Woodland Beach.

But of course, I knew the cops were chasing a mirage. Thomas couldn't be caught. He wasn't real. He existed in Seth's imagination and wasn't responsible for murdering three women.

At least the lead detective never threatened to arrest me like the police officers had on the day when I'd rescued Seth on the promenade. But then again, it wasn't like I was doing anything illegal anymore. Since I had stopped seeing Robert, my life had become squeaky clean.

For all my trips to the station house, however, I hadn't learned anything beyond what Missy Chance had divulged about Amber's photograph.

I had begun to feel a constant, maddening sense of turmoil. It worsened the longer I studied my bulletin board.

Why wasn't the killer's name jumping out at me?

My stomach growled so I gave up on racking my brain in favor of getting something to eat, but when I reached the kitchen, there came a knock at my apartment door.

I wasn't expecting anyone.

I opened the door and found Robert's nephew standing in the corridor.

"Seth?"

He was out of breath and upset. I pulled him inside, closed the door, and tried to understand what he was saying, but he was talking too fast.

"Slow down, what's going on?" I asked, never minding how he knew where I lived, as I welcomed him to the couch and sat him down. "Is everything okay?"

"No, everything's not okay! Where have you been?"

"What do you mean?"

"I always see you in the afternoons! I leave Kids for Christ at the same time you arrive for bible study! But I haven't seen you all week and I thought you were dead!"

"I'm not dead," I assured him, stupidly pointing out the obvious.

"How was I supposed to know that? I've been watching the news, afraid Missy Chance is going to say your name! You can't do that! You can't disappear!"

"I didn't disappear," I promised as I pulled him into my arms. "I'm fine. You don't have to worry."

"I can't live like this!"

"You don't have to worry about me, Seth—"

"Yes, I do!"

Emotions erupted and he couldn't string two words together, he was sobbing so hard against my shoulder. I rocked him and he soon calmed, sat up, and wiped his cheeks.

"I need to know you're saved," he stuttered as the last of his hiccupping cries came out.

It was clear what he was referring to, and this time, I was willing to appease him.

"If it means that much to you..." I offered.

"Really?"

"I don't want you to be upset."

"You want to be saved? You're willing?"

I honestly couldn't say I really believed in all that—saying a few vows and trusting I was eternally redeemed as a result. I couldn't even say I was fully convinced that the bible was anything more than a collection of perverse and strangely paranormal stories about family members betraying and murdering one another while God looked on and occasionally wiped them all out. And I really couldn't say I wanted to wholeheartedly join the ranks of Lighthouse Ministries' congregation, home of some of the cruelest women I had ever encountered. But I wasn't going to let Seth suffer like this.

So, I said, "Yes, I'm willing."

"Really?" Tears of joy streamed down his cheeks and his entire demeanor brightened.

"What do I do? How do we do it? Should we go to the church or something?"

"Crystal," he said in a serious tone of voice. He took both of my hands in his and a determined look came over him. "I will save you."

"Good, thank you."

"We can do it right here."

"Oh?"

"Yup."

"That's good news," I said, hoping all this would cheer him up.

It already had.

"Okay," he began. He took a deep breath, looked me square in the eye as we sat facing one another on my couch, and asked, "Crystal, do you accept Christ as your Lord and Savior?"

After a hesitant beat, I said, "I'm supposed to answer now?"

"Say, *I do.*"

In wholehearted respect of how important this was to Seth, I straightened my spine, used a clear voice, and repeated after him, "I do."

He stared at me, perhaps watching for some kind of spiritual phenomenon to take place within my soul, as I glanced around, looked at him, and waited for the big finale.

"So…?" I asked.

Throwing his hands in the air, he exclaimed, "You're saved!"

"That's it?"

"That's it!" he said, beaming with joy. He dove into my arms, nestled against me, and with a sigh of immense relief, he breathed, "You're finally saved!"

It was singlehandedly the most anticlimactic moment of my entire life.

"Do you feel better?" I asked him.

"I feel *a lot* better."

DAYS LATER, I opened all the windows in my apartment to get a cross breeze going. I'd been cleaning late into the afternoon, scrubbing the kitchen counters and sweeping the floors, and had worked up an unbearable sweat.

After placing a standing fan on the windowsill, I straightened the bedsheets, tucked my chair into my desk, and tried to figure out why Arthur Kowalski had been on my mind all day.

Maybe it was because I'd had too much downtime recently. Filling out employment applications at places like the Dollar Store and Walgreens hardly took up the bulk of my day. Or maybe it was because cleaning tended to remind me of how Arthur liked to crank up Sinatra whenever he had to use a little elbow grease to scrub a dirty pot. I couldn't be sure why he kept coming to mind, but I was starting to feel the urge to open his box, the one Pastor Asa had given me the day of Arthur's execution.

It was right where I'd shoved it months ago. On my hands and knees, I pulled it out from under my bed, sat cross-legged on the floor, and felt a surge of regret as I flipped the cardboard flaps aside and peered down into the box.

There wasn't much inside. Arthur's birth certificate and other paperwork relevant to his sentence were inside. A journal, its every page filled with Arthur's jagged handwriting. I set the journal aside and found the letter I had once sent him. It was preserved in its torn envelope, its postage faded. The pages were soft and rumpled as if Arthur had folded and unfolded the letter a thousand times over.

All these months, I never thought I would have the strength to read it, but I couldn't stop myself from doing that now.

As I did; as I poured over what my younger self had so badly wanted to believe—that I'd forgiven Arthur, that I was happy attending my brand-new community college classes, that I was going to graduate in two years with a business administration degree and hopefully run a fancy corporation one day, that the years in foster care had been just fine, that *I* was just fine, that I wanted Arthur to know that I harbored no ill will against him—I realized how much I had truly loved him.

None of those things that I'd told him in the letter had been true, and I was far from fine back then. But I had wanted Arthur to be free from hating himself for what he'd done so that I could be free from hating myself for knowing that I would never forgive him.

I had desperately needed permission to allow myself to feel the brutal, scalding pain of what he had caused me. I had wholeheartedly wanted to accept that I would never be able to move on from that pain. All I had wanted was to be able to coexist with emotions that I knew I would never be able to heal.

But as I sat there on the floor, absorbing every sentence I had written to Arthur, I also felt—overwhelmingly so—that somewhere along the line, at a place and time I might never be able to pinpoint, though I sensed it could have happened recently, I had released him.

There was no blame in my heart. The anger that had once felt like broken glass in my lungs wasn't there. I couldn't feel the churning rage that usually soured my stomach and turned my thoughts violent. There was a warm feeling in my spirit where crippling hatred used to be, and for a startling moment, I didn't recognize myself because of it.

All those years ago, when I had written the letter to Arthur, I had also enclosed a Christmas photo.

The Christmas photo had captured one of the best memories I had ever made with Arthur.

I could remember that in the photo, Arthur's arms were wrapped around my mom and me, my mom was smiling like a beauty queen, and we all looked happy.

I had wanted to mail Arthur the photograph to remind him of what we had once been—a family.

But looking in the envelope now, I couldn't find the photograph.

Growing annoyed, I searched through the contents of the box and rummaged through Arthur's journal and loose papers, but the photo wasn't there.

Arthur couldn't have brought it into the death chamber with him…

Why wasn't the photo I had mailed to him all those years ago among his possessions in the box that Pastor Asa had given me?

THE EXECUTIONER

I LEFT THE PRISON early after assuring Cromwell that I would have a finalized version of Samuel Braun's Inmate Report by the time I returned tomorrow. I had a typewriter at home I could use to update the report.

I had been trying to make an effort with Seth. Connecting with the boy wasn't easy, but I found that being home more often helped. I had gotten in the habit of asking him about himself and trying to show him I cared, as if it wasn't already too late.

Maybe it was.

On the way home, I stopped at a sporting goods store and picked up a baseball and a pair of leather baseball gloves. Tossing a ball around seemed like a good place to start.

Seth had been talking to me less and less, and talking to some imaginary friend more and more. He was too old for that, but at this point, I was willing to take responsibility for what had become of the boy. I knew I hadn't raised him properly, if I had raised him at all. He was odd and I was to blame.

"Seth?" I called out when I got in the door.

Rock music was booming through the house from his bedroom, but he turned the volume down and responded. "I'm doing my bible study homework, Uncle Robert!"

As I moved through the house, grabbing a beer and setting the shopping bag on the coffee table, I told him, "Come out when you're finished! I've got a surprise!"

"Is it Crystal?"

I wished it was.

"No! Just come out to the living room when you're done!"

In the meantime, I got down to business with my report.

After placing my typewriter on a TV tray and getting situated on my recliner, I started typing up a conviction summary for Samuel "Dirty Sam" Braun. The summary included the crimes that Braun had been charged with, the jury's verdict at the time of the trial, and Braun's execution date.

Cromwell hadn't had much criticism of my administrative work over the years. All he wanted was for my reports to be concise and filed on time. I was cutting it awfully close with this one, however, but Cromwell understood that if he gave me a hard time about anything, I would up and quit. He was smart enough not to push it. My fuse had become very short as of late and everyone at Vaughn knew it.

I was itching to retire from the prison and put every last memory I had made there over the years behind me.

Drinking my beer, I leaned back and read through what I had added to the report. It looked good. No typos. The execution date at the bottom was correct. Braun was scheduled to be executed tomorrow.

I didn't want to think about it.

Since becoming the sole executioner in 1976, I had killed a total of twelve men, and four of them had been executed during the past year alone. Those executions had been scheduled, one after the next, practically every weekend. The frequency of executions I had performed had taken a toll on my psyche.

I couldn't say that attending church had been helping matters, other than to reinforce the fact that I needed to stop working at Vaughn. I really couldn't call myself a Christian, while at the same time, I regularly put one man to death after the next. It was getting harder for me to sleep at night. A burning, all-consuming sadness kept me up—wide-eyed and miserable.

In those tortured moments during the dead of night, Crystal often came to mind. I had no one to thank but myself for our estrangement. I had treated her like garbage the night she had shown up at my house, smelling of cigarettes and looking beautiful but guilty. I had no choice now but to trust Pastor Asa would put Crystal and me on the right romantic path when he deemed that both of us were ready.

Seth emerged from his bedroom and shuffled into the living room, sliding around in his socks.

"Are you here for your surprise?" I teased.

He regarded me with a cool mix of intrigue and skepticism.

"Think fast!" I tossed the plastic bag full of sporting goods at him.

Brightening, he tried with all his might to catch it, but his athletic effort was all over the place, and the bag plopped to the floor.

"We'll work on that."

He picked up the bag and peeked inside. "Baseball stuff?"

"Put your shoes on, and we can toss the ball around on the beach."

"Can I wear my flip-flops?"

"You can wear your flip-flops if you want to trip all over yourself and sprain your toe," I barked. "Put some sneakers on! You need to be able to run!"

Seth wasted no time throwing on his sneakers and lacing them up tightly. We used the back door of the house to get to the beach. Once we crossed the dunes, we started across the loose sand, and when we reached the shore where the sand was flat and hard, I took one of the baseball gloves from the plastic bag and handed him the other.

I told Seth to put some distance between us even though I had brought him out there to do the opposite.

"Get your baseball glove on your hand!" I shouted, as the hot afternoon sun dipped behind the house, causing long, golden shadows to form on the beach. "Give your glove a few punches to loosen it up!"

The leather glove was as stiff as a board covering his hand, but ready or not, I served him a nice, easy ball.

The baseball plonked into his glove, but Seth couldn't clutch it properly, so the thing bounced right out and rolled across the sand.

"That's okay! We might have to break the glove in before it'll work for you! Toss it back!"

I gave him a few pointers, and he threw the baseball in a high arc. I caught the ball, and soon we settled into a decent rhythm, throwing and catching the ball back and forth between us.

Seth was clumsy but also spirited. He added a little skip every time he tossed the ball, which wasn't helping his aim, but I cut him some slack. He developed a clever tactic for capturing the ball which involved slapping his glove against his chest.

After a while, when he threw the ball back, I pocketed it and crossed the damp sand, took his baseball glove off his hand, and began bending the stiff thing this way and that.

"Tell you what we're going to do tonight," I explained as I worked some flexibility into his glove. "We're going to get some canola oil and big rubber bands. We'll oil up this baseball glove and keep it folded with the rubber bands."

"What will that do?" he asked, interested.

"It'll soften the leather so that you'll be able to catch the ball."

"Cool."

As I continued working his baseball glove open and shut like a book, I finally found the words to say to him that I had been hunting for all week. Or maybe I had been hunting for the right words to say to Seth his entire life.

"Did I ever tell you about your mother Abby?"

He looked up at me, and though I could tell he was excited to hear about his mother, he also looked guarded. It told me that the way I'd treated him over the years had taught him never to ask about his mother.

"I should talk about her more," I admitted. "When she was your age—mind you I was a few years older than Abby—we used to come out here and play catch."

"You did?"

"She liked to act all big and tough, like she was one of the boys… Your mother was a wonderful person, Seth, and I miss her every day. I'm sorry you never got to know her. She would be proud of you."

He asked me about Abby. He had a million questions. He wanted to know about the kind of kid she had been, and he wanted to know why she had gone to New Jersey after she'd left the seaside cottage. I answered as honestly as I could, and when emotions rose up and I couldn't talk about one area of his mother's life or another, I was at least able to tell him why.

When we returned to the house, we started cooking dinner on the stove. I wasn't the greatest chef, but I had picked up a thing or two observing Crystal all summer. At the very least, I had decided that there would be no more ramen and SpaghettiOs in this house from now on.

We sat down at the Formica table and dug into our plates of pasta and meatballs with a mountainous side of green peas.

As if it had been on his mind all day, Seth said, "I miss Crystal."

"So do I."

That seemed to surprise him.

"I think you should talk to her," he told me.

"She doesn't want me to talk to her."

He perked up. "Yes, she does."

MY COLLARED, PRISON uniform felt like it was choking me, as I pulled my car into the church parking lot the following morning. Seth was riding in the passenger's seat with his oiled baseball glove on his hand.

"You're not going to bring that glove into the church," I told him, as I squeezed the brakes and angled my car into one of the parking spots near the entrance.

Straining and grunting and sweating, Seth closed the baseball glove with one hand, bringing the leather thumb to the glove's webbed fingers.

"Alright, don't hurt yourself," I said.

"It's almost flexible enough, see? I can't stop now."

"Fine, you can bring the glove into church," I grumbled, and he shot me a toothy grin.

"Don't distract anyone with it," I warned.

I glanced at the rearview mirror and did a bit of a double-take.

Crystal's clunky sedan swung into the church parking lot and puttered into a vacant spot at the rear where a line of trees kept the pavement shady.

As she climbed out of her sedan, a gentle breeze lifted her long skirt, and for a moment, she looked like a blooming flower. She slung her purse over her shoulder and gave her blonde, feathered hair a shake before shutting her car door.

Seth turned to see what had distracted me.

As Crystal started for the walkway that led to the entrance of the church, Seth began calling her name through his open window, and he wouldn't stop even after I told him to pipe down.

She saw him and smiled.

But when she saw me climb out of my car with Seth, her sunny mood clouded over. She slowed her step, as if she was unsure whether or not she should say hi, or keep going.

To my delight, she asked me, "Are you coming in for the service?"

"No, I have to go to the prison."

"Oh."

I couldn't tell if I was detecting genuine disappointment in her tone, or polite indifference, but I took a risk and said, "You look nice."

A little smile rose in her cheeks and I thought she might say something, but Seth bounced over to her, waving his huge glove in the air and ruining the moment.

"Nice, where did you get that?" she asked the boy, referring to the baseball glove.

"From Uncle Robert!" He took her by the arm and suggested, "You can sit next to me today."

"Seth, give us a minute," I said.

He released Crystal, but lingered, unwilling to go into the church without her.

"Go on!" I pushed.

When he finally started off, Crystal drifted towards me until she reached my car.

Speaking over the hood and wishing my vehicle wasn't between us, I asked, "How have you been doing?"

"I've been good," she said, but I could tell she was holding back.

Seth distracted me before I could respond to her. He was peering around the corner of the church, staring at us and eavesdropping. I shook my head at him.

"Is Crystal coming?" he shouted.

"Seth, go inside!" I barked.

She glanced over her shoulder and called out to him, "Save me a seat," which did the trick. Seth disappeared around the side of the church, this time, for good.

"He misses you," I told her. "He says so all the time."

"I miss him, too," she said, softening. "I should get inside before the service starts—"

"I want to give you your space if that's what you want."

Her brow furrowed. "That's not what I want."

"No?"

"No," she said.

I could not suppress the smile that was coming over me.

I mentioned how I would be at the prison until late tonight, not that she was interested in that information.

Or, on second thought, maybe she was.

"I have a Christian Counseling meeting with Pastor Asa this evening," she said, and unless I was reading too far into things, it sounded like she was trying to make plans with me. "Things have been going well with him. We've actually been meeting in your backyard, more or less, on the beach."

"I'll be home around 1:00 am after an execution."

"Are you inviting me over?"

"Yeah," I said, feeling a little nervous that she might turn me down.

She didn't.

She smiled at me, and I realized this was my second chance.

"I can come a little after one in the morning," she offered. "Or, if it's alright with you, I could come by earlier and make dinner for Seth, maybe tidy up a bit——"

"You don't have to clean my house, Crystal."

A wall of tears rose up in her huge blue eyes. "I can't stand that you thought I was using you. I have to do *something* to show I care."

"I had jumped to conclusions that night," I explained, "which was wrong of me."

"I'm probably to blame for that."

"Come by tonight. You can come as early as you want for Seth," I suggested.

"Yeah?"

"Yeah, he would love that."

She blinked the tears from her eyes and sniffled, composing herself. "I'll come straight after I meet with Pastor Asa. I'll tell Seth."

"I'll see you tonight then," I told her, thrilled.

Then a funny look came over her and her pretty face was filled with darkness.

"What?" I asked.

"It's Asa..." She shook her head as if she couldn't quite figure out what she thought of the pastor. "He's going to tell me not to see you tonight... I know it. He wants to help me, but I'm not sure he wants to help *us*. You and me."

"If there's one thing I trust about Pastor Asa," I assured her, "it's that he's been doing everything he can for us. He's a man of God."

"Right," she said, but I could tell she wasn't sure whether or not she agreed. "I guess he means well."

As I left the church and drove to Smyrna, I couldn't get the image of Crystal's worried face out of my head. There was something about Pastor Asa that wasn't sitting right with her. She was apprehensive about him, and the more I thought about her apprehension, the more my gut instincts kicked in.

Was Pastor Asa dangerous?

Looking back, I should have listened to my gut.

THE STRIPPER

WOODLAND BEACH at sunset had never looked so heavenly. Sparkling waves rolled in, lapping the shore. The sky was painted shades of shell-pink and lavender, a marbleized sunset touching blue waters in the distance. Even the wind-swept sand stretching in both directions as far as the eye could see looked celestial.

I stood with my bare feet in the sea, strappy high heels in hand, as I savored the magnitude of how incredible I felt.

Everything I had ever hoped for was falling perfectly into place.

I couldn't wait to see Robert. I couldn't wait to stroll up this very beach after Christian Counseling when darkness would gather across Delaware. I turned around. There, tucked behind the dunes, was Robert's adorable seaside cottage. Seth was somewhere inside of it now. I couldn't wait to cook dinner with him and watch him slide around the kitchen in his socks as he gathered ingredients.

I felt elated. Waves rushed, warm and foamy, around my ankles, but I felt as though my feet weren't touching the ground.

I was finally going to get what I wanted, and it was coming with so much more than I could have ever hoped for!

I never thought I could be a wife or a step-mother or have a family, but the moment Robert had climbed out of his car and held my gaze earlier today at the church, I knew—*I could feel it!*—that he needed all the same things I did. He wanted what I wanted, and he was going to give me everything he could.

I loved him so deeply that I couldn't distinguish where I stopped and where he began. I loved him, not *despite* his flaws, but *because* of them, and when I thought of Seth, I felt a kind of tickled fondness so heartwarming that it made me want to scoop him up in my arms and never let him go. Just thinking about the boy made me giddy with a feeling of pure delight.

I couldn't wait to tell Pastor Asa about how much he had helped me, and I couldn't wait to thank him for how far I'd come. I had won Robert back, and that was all because of Asa.

"Crystal?"

Pastor Asa was crossing the sand in his loafers. Wearing a pressed button-down shirt, his khakis rolled up to his knees, he held a bouquet of flowers in one hand and a red box of chocolates in the other, but neither gave me as much pause as the glint of infatuation in his eyes.

As he neared me, a flash of courage sparkled across his face and I instantly knew that our secret meetings over the weeks had led him to believe there was mutual attraction between us, even though from my end nothing could've been further from the truth.

I tried not to let it show, and I tried not to wince, openly feeling sorry for him, but when he offered me the flowers and chocolates, I couldn't conceal how uncomfortable I felt.

"These are for you. You look beautiful. I hope you weren't waiting long."

"Pastor Asa—"

"Please, take them," he said as he urged me to accept his gifts.

I was embarrassed that he had brought me flowers and chocolates, and I couldn't quite look at him as I took them in my hands.

"I don't know what to say—"

"Crystal, I believe we've really gotten to know one another," he began as if diving into a prepared speech.

"Pastor Asa, please," I interrupted, trying to stop him.

But he wouldn't let me.

"I have something to say to you," he insisted, pinching his eyes closed for a moment before he forced the words out. "I've seen you transform, Crystal. I've watched you become a lovely Christian woman and it has endeared me to you tremendously."

When he locked eyes with me next, I feared where he might be heading with all this. He was too intense, coming too close, and gazing too deeply into my eyes.

I felt invaded.

"I'd always dreamed of meeting someone like you—someone who would be receptive to my ministry and who would allow me to counsel her. A woman who would bloom in response to my spiritual watering. As deeply as I had wished for this, I never truly thought she would come into my life. Why would I deserve such a blessing? But she has come into my life! Praise God! She's you."

"That's really very sweet, Asa, but, oh—!" I breathed, dazed at the unexpected sight of the pastor pulling a little, black jewelry box from his pocket, opening it, and presenting a diamond engagement ring.

I snapped out of my shock the moment he began lowering down onto one knee.

Clumsily, I dropped the flowers and chocolates, desperate to free my hands and pull him up.

"No," I said without a shred of grace. "I'm so sorry, Pastor Asa—"

"*Asa*. Please call me *Asa*—"

"You can't do this. I'm so sorry. Oh, God, I'm so sorry if I led you on. I can't marry you. Please don't look at me like that. Forgive me, oh, I've made a mess of things, haven't I?"

Dejected, Pastor Asa struggled to scrape his broken heart off the damp shore and fit the bloody thing back into his chest cavity.

I felt horrible watching him pull himself together, lift his chin, and recover.

He feigned a smile, but he was far from okay.

"Pastor Asa, *Asa*," I quickly corrected myself. "If it wasn't for Robert and me…" I began, trying to soften the blow by suggesting that I would be thrilled at his marriage proposal if it wasn't for my pre-existing relationship with the executioner. "Robert and I have gotten back together."

His hurt expression twisted, turning incredulous. "*Robert?*" he questioned. "You aren't ready for Robert. Crystal, you and I have a real shot at making it, because of my commitment to the Lord, but

Robert…? You can't be with Robert. He's no more ready than you are."

"I'm not stripping anymore," I reminded him, suddenly feeling the need for his approval. "I've been going to church—"

"You've been going through the *motions*," he allowed.

"That's not true. I've been going for the right reasons," I said, taking issue with his assumption. "In fact, I should've told you this earlier, but I'm saved. I've been saved."

He stared at me for a very long moment as the sky cooled off, darkening. Dusk closed in.

"You might think that, but we haven't gotten you there yet—"

"I did the whole getting saved thing with Seth Nash, and I appreciate your concern, but I'm not going to wait any longer to be with Robert. I was looking forward to thanking you for your help and all you've done for us, but we're ready to be together now."

Sinking into what appeared to be disturbed, layered thought, Asa furrowed his brow and glared at me through his eyebrows.

"I wouldn't want to discontinue our counseling," I offered.

"Were you baptized?" he asked.

"Baptized?"

"I'm sure Seth's heart was in the right place, but he's just a boy and he doesn't understand the vows that a new Christian must make in order to receive salvation from Christ."

"Oh," I said. I hadn't known.

Pastor Asa stared at me, devastated but also sly as if captured by a warring mix of emotions he thought he could control. He collected himself, and, lifting every bone in his body, he said, "I want what's best for you and despite having made a fool of myself a moment ago—"

"You didn't make a fool of yourself," I assured him.

"You're too kind. I want to help you, Crystal, and I want you to be happy. If Robert will make you happy, then I'd like to support your relationship, but I don't know how to do that in good conscience if I allow you to go on unbaptized."

"Okay," I agreed, feeling eager. "When Seth insisted that I be saved, I asked him if we needed to go to Lighthouse Ministries and he said we didn't, but I should've known better."

"We can do it right here. I can baptize you in the sea."

"We can?"

He lit up with compassion and knowingly asked, "You're planning on seeing him tonight?"

"I am."

"Then, let's get you baptized," he said as he took my high heels from my grasp and let them fall to the sand.

As he worked his loafers off, I asked, "Now?"

"God is always with us, Crystal, and there's no time like the present."

He offered me his hand and we waded out into the cool waters of the sea.

When we were in up to our waists, the brackish waters ebbing and flowing around our chests as smooth waves swelled by, he held both of my hands and a glittering starburst of happiness shot through me. I could not stop smiling.

"I'm glad to see you're so enthusiastic," he commented darkly. "I'm going to ask you the sacred questions. Just answer with an open heart."

"Okay!"

"Crystal, do you believe that Christ is your Savior and Lord? If so, say, *I do*."

"I do!"

"Do you have the assurance that your sins are forgiven through faith in Christ? If so, say, *I do*."

"I do!"

"Last question, will you by this act of baptism testify to the world that you are a Christian? If so, say, *I will*."

"I will!" I proclaimed, feeling elated as waves splashed past us and the twinkling night sky shimmered overhead.

Pastor Asa turned me and I pinched my nose, preparing to be dunked backwards in his arms.

He declared, "In the name of the Father and the Son and the Holy Spirit—"

Under the water I went.

Salty bubbles swirled around my head and the pastor's voice became muffled above the surface.

Here I was!

Being baptized!

Being made new in Christ!

Being fortified with the spirit of God so that I would have a fighting chance in this world! A fighting chance at being Robert's partner and a loving guardian to Seth!

I felt pure and holy and filled with joy!

But when I tried to lift back up and raise my head out of the water, the pastor held me down.

I needed to remain a moment longer in the sea so that the Lord could fully wash away my sins…

That's what this was, right?

Pastor Asa was holding me down for dramatic effect?

I needed air.

Using more force, I tried to lift my head out of the water.

He wouldn't let me.

Oh God!

Trying not to panic, I pushed both of my hands against Asa's stomach.

Maybe he was caught up in the moment and didn't realize I couldn't hold my breath forever…

Suddenly, the wallet-sized photo of Amber Everhart with her late mother surged to mind. Police had found it on the beach. It was critical evidence. It was currently being tested for fingerprints.

The missing Christmas photo of Arthur, my mother, and me…

It should've been in Kowalski's box, but it wasn't.

The only other person who had touched that box was Pastor Asa…

I felt his huge hand clamp around the top of my head, and he pushed me down into the water even further.

It was then that I understood what he was doing.

Killing me, like he had killed all the others.

Clawing at his arms, kicking though my legs moved through the water in what felt like slow motion, I began to fight.

But I needed air. My lungs burned. I got a hard kick in, but he wouldn't release me.

No! No! No!

Mind-splitting terror ripped through me. I could feel myself weakening—*I needed air!*—and then, despite mentally screaming at myself not to, I inhaled.

Desperate to breathe, my lungs filled with salt water and the cutting agony that came next felt like a thousand knives slicing through my chest.

I went limp after that and started slipping away.

Darkness closed in.

Then...

A bright light pierced through me.

I could feel the light, not only its warmth, but the calm that sparkled over me because of it.

Suspended between this world and the next, I felt at peace.

Then, the light grew blindingly bright, so bright that I almost couldn't bear it.

A moment later, the bright, unapproachable light miraculously transformed into Seth's imaginary friend, Thomas.

I didn't know how I knew that—that the spiritual presence before me was Thomas.

I just knew.

"Crystal," he said, his voice like the sound of rushing waters. "It's not your time yet, but when it is, decades from now, I will come for you."

The next thing I knew, I had returned to my body.

My limbs felt limp. I had no strength. I could barely crack my eyes open. But I knew I was being dragged out of the surf.

Pastor Asa had me by my ankles. He was jerking me up the shore.

Winded, he let go of my limp body.

Without warning, I coughed seawater out of my lungs, gasped for air, and then coughed out more water.

Pastor Asa cursed.

I strained to open my eyes just as Asa cocked his fist upwards into the air.

I had very little fight in me, but when I saw his balled fist rocketing down towards my face, I scrambled away and his punch connected with hard sand instead of my head.

"Help," I tried to scream, but only a strangled-sounding wheeze came out. "Help me."

Crawling across sand, my vision bleary, I saw the boy charging down the beach.

"Get off of her!" Seth yelled.

A hard blow struck the back of my head, but I refused to collapse.

Seth tackled Asa before the pastor could strike me again.

Red and blue lights began flashing in the distance…

Were police cruisers barreling over the dunes?

I hacked up more salt water, straining and gasping for air, as horrendous pain cracked through my skull.

I managed to roll onto my side, and when I did, I saw the pastor beating the boy.

"Stop!" I shrieked, my voice hoarse.

I had no clue where my strength came from, but I sprang up, tripping and spilling towards Asa, and threw myself onto his back.

Together—Seth tangled beneath the killer and me on top—we fought like crazy, kicking and screaming and scratching and punching, until the police arrived.

As the cops apprehended Pastor Asa Asbury, Seth and I clung to one another, crouching, sandy, and soaking wet.

Alive but barely.

Holding onto the boy, I knew Seth wasn't the only one who had saved my life.

DEATH ROW INMATE 836
Asbury, Asa

On July 8, 1986, the drowned, strangled body of Amanda Dover was found on the shore of Woodland Beach, DE, the first of three murders to take place in a string of killings that terrorized the small, seaside town. Following Dover, Jewel Payson was found dead, having been killed in an identical manner on August 7, 1986. The killing of Amber Everhart on August 27, 1986, followed. All three women had been working at a gentlemen's club called Mermaids.

Investigators had little to go on, but developed a criminal profile based on a man called "Thomas," the physical description of whom was provided to police by a thirteen-year-old boy. When questioned, the boy stated that "Thomas" had led him to the body of Jewel Payson. "Thomas" soon became the prime suspect, and the police issued a statewide manhunt in an effort to track him down.

On the night of September 14, 1986, the Woodland Beach police received an urgent call to their crime-stoppers hotline. The caller identified himself as "Thomas," which got their immediate attention, but what he told them next confounded everything that the police had thought they knew up until that point. Claiming to be the "Son of God," Thomas informed them that another Mermaids stripper named Crystal Swan was in the throes of being murdered on Woodland Beach. Convinced they were dealing with a real whacko, police rushed to the location, hoping to intervene before "Thomas" could kill again.

Asa Asbury was arrested for the attempted murder of Crystal Swan. Upon his arrest, Asbury insisted that he was not "Thomas" and that he didn't know the guy. Though Asbury looked nothing like the description that the boy had provided, he did confess to all three murders, explaining that "the best time to baptize a sinner is when you're certain they won't have a chance to sin again," a perverted axiom that he said he had learned from his mother. This salvation strategy required that death must immediately follow baptism, according to Asbury.

To this day, investigators still do not know who "Thomas" is or how he connected to the crimes. While mystified, police agree that if "the Son of God" hadn't called into the Woodland Beach crime-stoppers hotline that night, Crystal Swan would not have survived.

The murders of Amanda Dover, Jewel Payson, and Amber Everhart, and the attempted murder of Crystal Swan were tried as a death penalty case due to the fact that the crimes involved the following aggravating factors:

- *The defendant's course of conduct resulted in the deaths of 2 or more persons where the deaths are a probable consequence of the defendant's conduct.*

Execution to commence: June 29, 1992

CRYSTAL

WHEN ASA ASBURY'S execution date came in the early summer of 1992, I didn't go.

As the sole surviving victim, I had received a letter from the county notifying me of Pastor Asa's execution date. The letter had also noted that the pastor had opted to die by lethal injection.

His sentence would be carried out at midnight tonight.

I had already seen the State put one man to death. I didn't need to see another.

I had come to Woodland Beach instead.

The breeze was stiff yet warm, the night dark, serene. I often couldn't believe how so many stars could fit in one sky when there seemed to be so little room. Tonight, I felt like the moon was shining just for me, but I also felt sad.

Pastor Asa really had helped me as a result of our secret Christian Counseling meetings, and in a way, I had liked him…

…but I had been wrong about him and naive to trust him.

In the years since that scary night on this very shore, I had often thought about how I'd almost been met with the same fate as my mother.

Throughout my life, I had tried so hard to become nothing like her, but when it came down to it, I had turned out exactly the same. I had lived darkly, trading hanky-panky for money. Like my mother, I had trusted a man that I shouldn't have and he had attacked me. But unlike Kimberly Swan, I hadn't died that night.

Today, my life no longer resembled my mother's.

Why hadn't Pastor Asa been able to kill me all those years ago?

Oftentimes, I felt like I had no idea why.

But then sometimes, on quiet nights like this one, it was possible for me to grasp the reason why I had been able to survive the attempted murder. The pent-up rage that I had been nursing since childhood had come out of me that night, but it wasn't the reason I had fought like hell, and it hadn't been the source of my strength.

The power that had enabled me to take the first reviving breath while clawing my way across the sand hadn't come from me, as much as I would've liked to take credit.

God had been in control.

Robert joined me on the shore. He wrapped his arms around me and before he even asked, I told him I was fine.

Checking his wristwatch, he said, "In the next five minutes, they'll put him down."

I nodded, as memories of Pastor Asa washed over me.

Robert had retired from the Vaughn Correctional Center a month after the attack. He had wanted to quit the very next day, but doing so would have jeopardized his pension, so instead he had dropped a letter of resignation off with Warden Cromwell. In the resignation letter, Robert had made clear that he would not perform another execution, period. The warden hadn't argued. Everyone had heard that the pastor who had been ministering to the inmates on Death Row had turned out to be the Woodland Beach serial killer. The only CO who hadn't been shocked by the news was Lyle McKay. The rest of the COs had been stunned, but not as much as Robert and myself.

To this day, Robert was still shocked, deep down. To this day, part of me was as well, but I had come to accept how complicated, cruel, and perplexing the world could be. Pastor Asa had done a lot for Robert and me. I might never understand how the same man could also kill so many women. I might never understand why he had done what he did.

"I feel like going for a swim," I said.

"You sure?"

I stripped out of my sundress and started for the lapping water in a modest two-piece that showed enough and covered the rest. I dipped a toe in, then waded out to my ankles. Soon cool, salty water splashed against my calves, as I pushed farther and farther into the surf.

As Robert kept a watchful eye on me from the beach, I floated up from my tiptoes, soft waves rising to my chin, and I began swimming.

I needed to be all by myself—just me and the sea—when the moment came. The moment when the State would execute the man who had killed Cherry, Original Jewel, and Amber; the same man who had helped me restore enough perspective to realize that I didn't have to be perfect to be loved; the same man who I had considered my friend until the night he tried to kill me.

Before Robert and I had gotten married, I ended up going back to community college and finally earned a degree in business administration. I had been working as the manager of a local bank for the last few years. What could I say? I loved the feel of cash between my fingers.

I was still close with Lars Svensson.

Jimbo and Timbo's retaliation against Lighthouse Ministries had resulted in the unexpected. Christianity had accidentally taken root in their hearts, and they soon bought the church from Pastors Gracie and Joe, who had packed up their things and moved out to Smyrna, too ashamed of their son's crimes to face the congregation.

Last I had heard, Pastors Gracie and Joe were in the habit of visiting Asa every chance they got, ministering to him in the visitors' center while clinging to the once-strong Asbury name as a family.

As far as I knew, Emmett DeGraves and Charles Riley were still members of Lighthouse Ministries, and Miracle, Destiny, New Jewel, and most of the other girls frequented the Sunday services, as did a lot of Seth's old childhood friends, but the place had completely transformed under Jimbo's reign. It was a hip church now, full of color and lights, Hawaiian shirts and pinky rings, mustaches and clapping hands, sequined dresses and little dances to go with every rock 'n roll worship song…

But I had never gone back.

I had my own relationship with God.

So long as I lived, I would never forget my near-death experience. I knew what had happened to me that night.

I knew who had prevented death from taking my soul.

I knew what was real.

When I swam back to the shore, Seth was standing next to Robert, who was holding a giant towel open for me. I ran into it—*Brrr!*—and he snuggled me up tight, kissed me, and told me I was nuts to have taken a dip. Seth concurred.

Robert whispered in my ear, "It's done."

A relieved kind of sorrow filled me.

When I glanced at Seth, I could see that feelings had surfaced in him, as well.

"I've been praying for Asa," he said. "I forgive him."

Hardly a boy anymore, Seth was even taller than Robert now. Nineteen years old and looking forward to his sophomore year in college, he was a young man. A *good* man. Sensitive, he had a way with words. He had even told me on a number of occasions that he was going to turn everything that had happened to us into a book. I hoped so. Someone had to make sense of what we had lived through during the summer of 1986.

It had taken me a really long time to understand who I was. I used to think that I was a stripper, as if the word defined me—THE STRIPPER. But I wasn't. I had never been. All along, I had been so much more than that.

Robert wasn't THE EXECUTIONER anymore. That title had ended when he had stopped working at Vaughn.

And Seth was no longer THE BOY, if he'd ever been one in the first place. To me, Seth had always been larger than life, far too grand to have been a mere boy.

"Let's get warmed up inside," Robert suggested and we started up the beach for our little seaside cottage.

When I realized Seth was lingering at the shore, I told Robert to go on ahead, Seth and I would catch up in a minute.

I neared Seth, who was staring out at black waters. Scanning the darkness. Searching.

"I keep thinking I'll see him out there," he said.

Seth had not seen Thomas since the morning after Pastor Asa had attacked me. That morning, Seth had stood on the shore of Woodland Beach and watched Thomas return to the sea. He had told me this years later.

He hadn't seen Thomas since.

"He was real," said Seth.

"I know."

THE END

ALSO BY MIRA GIBSON

Thomas from the Sea

Who Killed Leeanne?

The Kensington Killers: The Complete Series
Lunatic (The Kensington Killers, Book One)
Crank (The Kensington Killers, Book Two)
Maniac (The Kensington Killers, Book Three)

The New Hampshire Mysteries: The Complete Series
Daddy Soda (A New Hampshire Mystery, Book One)
Rock Spider (A New Hampshire Mystery, Book Two)
Tar Heart (A New Hampshire Mystery, Book Three)

ABOUT THE AUTHOR

I write mystery novels, detective novels, sleuth mysteries, and psychological literary fiction! You can find me most days working on my computer in the sunshine of beautiful Long Beach, NY where I dream up small town characters and write dark mysteries that are filled with unsuspecting tenderness.

Find me on Facebook! **/MiraGibsonAuthor**

Visit MysteryRoyalty.com to learn more.